Sarah Bilston is British but lives in Connecticut. She is an academic and teaches at Trinity College, Hartford. She is married with three children. Her previous novel, *Bed Rest*, is also published by Sphere.

Praise for *Bed Rest*

'A very clear-sighted novel about how tough it is for women to juggle career, marriage and childbirth – I laughed out loud and I couldn't put it down' Marian Keyes

'Prescribe yourself some of the same, so that you can bask in the humour, poignancy and warmth of this gorgeous novel' Elizabeth Noble

'Even if you've never been pregnant you'll be as instantly hooked on this addictive novel as I was. While most of us dream of days on end in bed with nothing to do but eat and watch television, Q shows us the true nature of being a caged animal' Plum Sykes, author of *Bergdorf Blondes*

'Every woman out there juggling with career, marriage and childbirth will love every rib-tickling minute of this story' ****** *Peterborough Evening Telegraph*

'You'll laugh out loud at this novel' *Bella*

'Very witty' *Closer*

'Quinn soon discovers that her vantage point from the sofa is the perfect spot from which to watch the lives of those around her unravel' *First*

'Wit, humour and self-realisation come in equal measures in this first book from Sarah Bilston' *She*

'A light and witty read' *Woman's Way*

'At times laced with delicious humour, at others pathos' *Book Mark Online*

Also by Sarah Bilston

Bed Rest

Sleepless Nights

Sarah Bilston

SPHERE

First published in Great Britain in 2008 by Sphere

A CIP catalogue record for this book is
available from the British Library.

ISBN 978-0-7515-3834-2

Typeset in Sabon by M Rules
Printed and bound in Great Britain by
Clays Ltd, St Ives plc

Papers used by Sphere are natural, renewable and recyclable
products made from wood grown in sustainable forests and certified
in accordance with the rules of the Forest Stewardship Council.

Mixed Sources
Product group from well-managed
forests and other controlled sources
www.fsc.org Cert no. SGS-COC-004081
© 1996 Forest Stewardship Council

Sphere
An imprint of
Little, Brown Book Group
100 Victoria Embankment
London EC4Y 0DY

An Hachette Livre UK Company
www.hachettelivre.co.uk

www.littlebrown.co.uk

For Rosa and Karl

Acknowledgements

A number of friends have given me advice or information on issues confronting lawyers and the practicalities of the lawyer's existence: special thanks to Sharon Volckhausen, John Buretta and Sarah Stevens-Cox. Thanks to Margaret Mary O'Rourke for providing me with such a vivid and arresting portrait of a small-town lawyer's life, and to Richard Falkenrath for putting us in touch. For advice on family law, warm thanks to my mother-in-law Inga Markovits. And finally thanks, as always, to my husband Daniel Markovits, for his always engaging, always thought-provoking observations on the ethical issues of lawyerly life.

*We held hands once and were beautiful. But what
   followed?
Sleepless nights, oh, sleepless nights.*

Jamaica Kincaid, 'At Last'

1. Q

New York

The party was in a massive Brooklyn brownstone. I stood on the sidewalk, staring up at the rearing expanse of red-brown brick, on a hot evening in late June. Above the door, a string of protuberant gargoyles grinned and glowered at the street and at the Gorgons bulging over the casement cornices. A hot oily breeze stirred fronds of trailing ivy in two giant, swollen urns beside the door. Little piles of itchy grit swirled in the air, down the long flight of steps and into my eyes. An old man enjoying the evening grinned as he passed, and touched his hat. 'Waitin' don't make it any easier, you know,' he said softly, chuckling.

I rearranged my acre-wide blue dress across my belly, shapeless as a burst balloon, and began to mount the deep stone steps. As I lifted each leg I could feel the sharp pull in my scar, a hot numbed mouth pressed awkwardly closed. At the top of the stoop I smoothed my red hair, rearranged my cotton over-shirt across my chest, and hit the buzzer.

Inside I could hear voices and laughter, and the deep pound of a bass. There was a pause, a shout suddenly close by ('Don't worry, I'll get it!'), and the door flew open; a pale, glamorous woman of forty appeared, dressed in a microscopic shirt dress, with long dark hair flowing glossily over one shoulder. 'Quinn, how nice,' she said, fractionally rearranging her posture (more

1

upright), her smile (less vivid), and her hair (less sensuous). 'People call you Q, yes? You're taking time off, of course; good idea. Come in.' She ushered me into the rich, air-conditioned coolness. 'There are a few other associates here already, so make yourself comfortable.'

Caroline is the youngest woman ever to be partnered at my law firm, Schuster & Marks. She has had a string of lovers in the five years I've known her but no husband, and she swears she doesn't want one 'until I've lost my looks. The only reason to get married is so you can fuck when you're too old to get it any other way. Right?' She lavishes the six-figure sum she earns at Schuster on herself – whenever she's away from work long enough to spend it, obviously, which is not often. She thinks she's a role model for me and the rest of Schuster's female associates.

She pushed open the door into her long, high-ceilinged sitting room, then immediately walked off, bony arms swinging by her side. I could see the points of each sharp elbow, little pink eyes glaring back at me. It was not even eight o'clock, but already the place was alive. Groups were settled on each of the three grey sofas ranged around the marble fireplace, and others were collected in little comfortable heaps on the polished parquet. There were at least ten people in the kitchen area, spilling off bar stools or leaning across the granite counter tops while a man stirred something steaming and blackberry-coloured in a copper vat on the stove. A few more were smoking out on the balcony overlooking the slim strip of garden. Everybody seemed to be laughing. Everybody was extraordinarily well dressed.

'Q! My God, I can't believe it's you!' It was Fay, another of the partners from the firm, a diminutive over-achiever from somewhere in the Midwest. 'Christ, how did you manage to get away?' She laughed uproariously, slipping her arm around the waist of a young blonde woman, who giggled nervously. 'Can

I get you a drink? Caroline had vodka imported from Russia specially for the party. It's over there . . .' and she gestured to a white table on which stood twenty unlabelled bottles beside several towers of stacked shot glasses. 'After the first six you don't notice the shit-awful taste any more. Karen, why don't you get her—'

I shook my head, and reached out to stop the slim, doe-eyed girl. 'Thanks, Fay, and Karen, that's really kind of you, but I can't. Drink, that is. I'm – I'm nursing,' I explained, *sotto voce*.

Fay blinked at me. 'I thought you were on maternity leave,' she said, slowly.

'Not nursing in a hospital! I mean I'm *breastfeeding*,' I explained, laughing, looking down at my body, feeling a little start of shock at my own extraordinarily unfamiliar shape. 'You know, feeding my baby *from here*.' Since Samuel was born, my nipples, new brown moons, have taken to poking through my clothes to see what's up. My shirt, I realized suddenly, had fallen aside.

The waves of conversation filling the room crashed into staggering silence; about thirty pairs of fascinated eyes swivelled to my vast, swollen chest and my brightly alert nipples – which became immediately, predictably, overexcited from all the attention. Milk: I felt it, warm and dark and spreading through my dress, and hastily readjusted my shirt – too late; a man six feet away turned palpably green, and there was an audible snicker from somewhere in the kitchen. Fay made a gurgling noise that was half a cough, and started backing way. 'Right. I see. How – stupid of me. Of course. I think' (touching her moist brow with the back of her hand) 'there's water over there, or juice, or whatever it is that – that nursing – er – people drink. Enjoy the party.' She almost ran off towards the steps leading down into the garden, dragging the confused-looking blonde, eyes wide as saucers, behind her. Invisibility had never seemed so appealing.

But – I looked down at my mother's body – I'd never been so far from achieving it.

I fixed my gaze on a vast modern art canvas on the opposite wall, a block of shining black slashed with hell reds and oranges, and tried very hard to look as though I was appreciating its aesthetic complexity. Covertly, desperately, I examined the rest of the party-goers. Bland faces with sharp, glittering eyes moved like other-worldly shadows around the room. I didn't recognize most of the people (Caroline's friends from other firms, most likely), although nearest the fireplace sat Michael, a Schuster partner, now deep in conversation with Marta, an associate hired a few years after me. Sitting beside her was a cohort of mine named Julie. Very slim, very self-confident, we'd never quite managed to be friends.

Tom, why did I ever let you talk me into this . . . Taking a deep breath, I lumbered over to the little circle and positioned myself awkwardly on its periphery.

'It was a triumph, Michael,' Marta was saying, her bobbed hair nodding as she leaned breathily in towards him. She was still in her suit. 'When the chief financial officer took the stand my heart just *sank*. You could see how confident he was. But then you presented him with those receipts—'

Michael shrugged. 'It helped that the prosecutor was an absolute idiot, obviously.'

Julie took a swig at her vodka glass. 'Don't sell yourself short, Michael, your cross-examination was masterly. Once you'd shown the jury the CFO's hands could be dirty I knew we were – oh, hi!'

Seeing my shadow fall over her hands, Julie looked up, surprised, then managed a smile: 'Q, wow. I can't believe it's you.' Michael stood up and shook my hand formally, then sat down again; Marta nodded politely, and murmured something indistinct.

Julie, however, patted a small space beside her. 'It's really nice to see you. You've been away for – what, four months? It seems even longer. So much has happened; I take it you heard we won the Litchfield case? You could hardly have missed it, of course, it's been all over the *Times*, together with smiling photos of that smug CEO. I hear he's just bought a new house in the Hamptons . . .'

Observing the six-inch spot of sofa dubiously, I took a perch on the sofa's plush arm instead, and congratulated them on a brilliant trial – not, in fact, that I knew most of the details, since I'd barely had time to open a paper since my son was born. Marta and Michael, still heady with success, immediately picked up the thread of their conversation again ('I didn't think juror three was going to make it'); unexpectedly, however, Julie smiled at me with a flicker of real warmth. 'It's great that you made it here. Your husband's babysitting tonight? Must be *such* a relief. Every mother needs time off. Well, that's what my mom always said. Mind you, she was an alcoholic, so what did she know?' She laughed mirthlessly. 'Let me get you a drink, Q, I'm guessing you need one.'

'Thanks, I'll have a vodka,' I answered, giving up. The stuff tasted like iced meths, but there are times when even iced meths has its appeal. I took a sip that I felt in my eyeballs.

'So tell me: what have you been doing with yourself all this time?' Julie clearly expected a list.

Giving birth to live young . . . 'I was on bed rest for three months at the end of the pregnancy,' I explained.

'Oh yeah – I think I heard that. Crazy. One time I broke my leg skiing in Denver, I couldn't move it for a whole week, couldn't get into work, almost went off my head. I can't imagine doing three whole months. And it's not clear it even works, right? *I* would have told the doctors to stick it, but that's just me. I'm like that. Not,' she went on, seriously, 'that *I'll* be getting pregnant

5

any time soon. Christ, no! Ed was talking the other night about starting a family, I said "Unless you can find a surrogate mother, forget it. I'm not turning *this* body into a baby-making machine!"'

She began to laugh, then stopped herself with comical abruptness. 'I don't mean – Well, I'm sure in *your* case – I mean, it must be so great to have this – er – I mean, babies love you unconditionally, right? I can see that must be – nice . . .' She trailed off awkwardly. I wondered where to start.

Several of the other elegant willowy women in the room had come up behind me, I noticed suddenly, and were peering at me now with curious eyes. 'I heard you just had a baby,' one of them remarked abruptly; I nodded, and turned around to face her.

'Yes. I have a little boy called Samuel, he's five weeks,' I explained. The woman raised her eyebrows.

'Wow. How grown-up!' Everybody laughed. 'I can hardly look after myself,' she went on, grinning, accepting the joke. '*Seriously*. I can't even imagine looking after a kid.'

'I can't believe it myself, sometimes,' I admitted. 'I hear Samuel cry and it can take me a moment to realize he's my responsibility.'

'You're somebody's mother,' the young woman went on enthusiastically. 'It seems so amazing. Someone my age is actually a mother . . .'

Six or seven women had collected around us now, and the atmosphere had subtly changed. People began asking me questions, and actually listening to the answers. Noticing the little crowd, Caroline surged over and cut in. 'What are we talking about?' she enquired with a little confident hip-shimmy as she assumed a position at the epicentre of the group.

'We were discussing motherhood,' I replied evenly. A cloud passed over her brow.

'Really.' One eyebrow palpably twitched; her eyes sought out

Michael's, but he was plunged back in conversation with a young associate about the trial. 'Different people make different choices,' she went on after a moment, blandly. 'For some of us, of course, the thought of being covered in someone else's *shit* is too awful for words. But maybe we'll turn into clichés and regret our barren wombs when the clock stops ticking, mmm?' She laughed loudly; Julie and the other willowy women laughed too, although perhaps a little less easily.

'Now then,' Caroline went on sweetly, '*what* are we all doing for the rest of the summer?'

Immediately, the tone of the discussion changed again, as everyone began the struggle to outdo everyone else with ever-more elegant, exclusive social fixtures. Such was the excitement and energy generated in the group that other people were soon sucked in; a handsome, very young associate mentioned surfing with an X-games gold-medallist friend in Puerto Escondido but was quickly trumped by an invitation to a Kennedy wedding. Caroline described her weekend helicoptering around the Azores, then struggled to maintain her composure when Michael flaunted the giant yacht he was chartering around Hawaii for two thousand dollars a day.

Clearly irritated, looking for someone to scratch, Caroline turned at last to me. 'You'll be looking after your baby the whole summer, I suppose?' she said, oh-so-politely, narrowed eyes like blue shards of glass; there was a little movement in the group, as if everybody was thinking, Well, I might not be going to Hyannis next month but at least I'm doing better than *that*. 'I seem to remember your husband Tom was into white-water kayaking and paragliding. I suppose all that is in the past now . . . ?'

'Actually, no, we'll be staying in Paul Dupont's house this summer,' I said abruptly, before I could think properly, and was rewarded by an audible gasp of astonishment.

'Paul Dupont?' ejaculated Julie beside me. 'The superstar

7

partner at Prince & Cohen? You're not serious! I didn't know you even *knew* him.'

Caroline's expression was all the impetus I needed to keep going. For a moment, she looked quite old. 'Oh yes, he and Tom are good friends from Paul's days at Crimpson Thwaite,' I explained airily. 'My husband's firm, you know. Paul offered us his house for the summer, and we've decided to accept.' I crossed my fingers behind my back.

'I'd forgotten he was at Crimpson until Prince head-hunted him,' remarked one of the quiet senior partners, a quiet man named Alvin, who had just joined the group. 'Paul Dupont is a brilliant lawyer, and a man of excellent taste.'

'And didn't he date – well, you know,' squeaked one of the youngest, most willowy girls, who looked to me like a summer associate. She was teetering giddily on six-inch heels, her shirt split open almost to the waist. 'I saw him at the Four Seasons last week when Caroline took us out for lunch, I recognized him from that piece in *GQ*. He's, like, I mean – well, he's totally *hot* . . .' The other women, who were all clearly thinking the same thing, rolled their eyes and tutted at her schoolgirl effusiveness; Caroline murmured something disdainful to Julie about 'chicks on heat'. The squeaky girl looked mortified.

I smiled kindly at her. 'He's very nice, actually; surprisingly down-to-earth. And his house is quite beautiful,' I went on, in my most English accent, because I couldn't resist it. 'Tom and I are very excited to spend time there this summer, with Samuel. I don't know how many days Tom'll be able to take off from Crimpson, of course, but when he does come up to Connecticut we're hoping to do some serious sailing. Paul has a large dock.'

'And he's friends with that dot-com billionaire, Adjile Olawe, right?' whispered another young summer associate, with a nervous side-glance at Caroline. 'I heard they were neighbours. He's supposed to be a real recluse, but people say he has a mansion built on the rocks . . .'

I smiled expansively as I picked up my purse. It was obviously time to leave; everybody's eyes were glued upon me. 'Yes, that's quite right,' I affirmed, leaning forwards to kiss my hostess's cold white cheek. 'We're planning to visit him as well, as a matter of fact, while we're up there. I saw some photographs of Adjile's place in that piece in the *Times* last year about "Defining Architecture of the Millennium" but I haven't been there myself yet. Anyway. Thanks for a wonderful party, Caroline. I doubt I'll see you for a while, because we'll be at Paul's, but do enjoy your . . . whatever it is you're doing this summer, won't you?'

I walked out past the wall of faces through the hall, and swung open the huge front door. The summer air met me in a warm wave of fine, dusty pollen; I grinned at nothing in particular, and took a deep, happy breath as I set off down the stoop. The street was quieter now; a lone Volvo was nosing its way into a parking place as I passed beneath the leering globe gargoyles, then off along the root-cracked sidewalk to the subway. The unbroken line of brownstones reared above me like a massive, indifferent army. But inside the houses I heard the unmistakable, eternally familiar sound of families settling in for the night: children playing their last games before bedtime; mothers shouting up and down the stairs; fathers whispering a tender 'I missed you'.

I quickened my step. I couldn't wait to get home.

2. Jeanie

London

I probably shouldn't have picked up the bowl. It was the only one I had without a crack so big the milk flows out of it faster than you can spoon the cereal into your mouth. But it was the first thing that came to my hand.

'Take that, you bastard.'

Dave ducked. It hit the wall. No more cereal for me.

'And that.' This time it was a mug. I think my mother gave it to me. No loss there. It had itsy-bitsy sprigs of lavender on the outside and a terrible indelible tea-stain on the inside.

'If you'll just listen to me—'

'And that—' An egg-cup. My flatmate's. Turns out this is surprisingly painful if it hits the right spot. Dave yowled.

'You loon!' he yelled, dancing about clutching his groin when he was finally able to draw breath. 'I – didn't – touch – her!'

'No, but you were thinking about it,' I shouted, aiming a toasting fork at his foot. He skipped out of the way.

'I wasn't!'

'You were.' I was running out of things to throw.

'I *wasn't*!'

'You were staring at her cleavage the whole time. I *saw* you crane to get a better look! And I think you dropped your napkin deliberately so you could get a better look at her chubby legs under the table.' I found a teaspoon in the sink.

'I didn't,' he replied, catching the teaspoon neatly in his hand and putting it down on the table.

'You did,' I said, making for the teaspoon again.

Dave grabbed my hand deliberately as I entered his orbit and twisted it firmly behind my back. 'Stop it, stop it, *stop it*, Jeanie. You've gone bonkers. OK, I'll admit it. *If* you stop throwing things. I did – sort of – maybe a little bit – look at some bits. Of her. It was hard not to. C'mon, Jeanie, they were so – available . . . owwwww . . .' (as I wrenched myself free and thumped his shoulder). 'No, wait,' and somehow his arms were around my arms again, and I was held fast. 'I looked. I didn't touch. I'm not going to touch. Ever. I *promise*.'

I twisted around to look up into his earnest, stubbly face. He's not exactly handsome, my boyfriend, but he does have nice grey eyes, and his features – well, you wouldn't say chiselled, I suppose, but I've never really known what that means anyway. 'I'm going to be away from London for *months*, Dave. How do I know you're not going to chase after Ellen the moment my plane leaves the ground? You're going to see her every time you go to visit your mum. I can see it now, you'll be spiritually drawn to the woman who is tending your ailing mother, you won't be able to help yourself, and then she'll bend over to change a bedpan and you'll catch a glimpse of her pink suspenders and—'

'Jeanie, I won't. I promise. She isn't – I mean, it isn't going to happen. Really. Have I ever been unfaithful to you? No. Right. And anyway whose decision was it to go halfway round the world for months on end? Seems to me if anyone should be doing the plate-hurling round here, it's me, love.'

I heard the little choke in his voice. I stopped struggling and stood still, allowing my head to subside on his chest. There was something in his argument.

'All I did was get a little look at . . . well, what was on offer. You name a man who wouldn't have done the same,' he said, reaching out to stroke my hair, my face, my throat. 'But it doesn't mean I'll lay a finger on her. I might look, but I'll never touch. I'll be waiting here for you to come back. While you're with your sister and the baby in New York, I'll be here, same old Dave, just like always. Come on, Jeanie . . .' he whispered into my ear, his hands moving down to my breasts, pulling my body roughly into the contours of his, 'why don't you show me a bit of what *you* have on offer, eh? Then I'll never think of Ellen again, I promise you . . .'

The truth is, I thought to myself, a couple of hours later, working my way through my dinner (six sizzling rashers of bacon and a large glass of wine), I feel guilty about Dave. He's got a perfect right to be upset with me at the moment. We've been together for a whole year, now I'm going away for four months to America to help Q, leaving him here all by himself to cope with his mum's Alzheimer's, his dad's depression, his job struggles. It's a lot to ask of a boyfriend, no question about it. Why shouldn't he have a little goggle at Ellen now and again? I'm getting to live in the States; he's getting an eyeful of Ellen's plump thighs. In a sense, it's a fair exchange.

My flatmate Una crashed in about eleven, which is early for her, accompanied by a very tall man called Holly or Solly or something. She let him feel her up while I explained earnestly why half the kitchen was in pieces on the floor. 'To be quite honest, I don't give a shit,' she said at last, after a cursory examination of the shattered bits, helping herself to a slug of wine straight from my bottle and a rasher of dripping bacon from the grill pan. 'Smash the whole place up if you want. And as for Dave, I think you should just dump him,' she added, somewhat irrelevantly, I felt. 'Don't content yourself with maiming the bastard. Kick him out.' The unknown man's right hand was now inside her top, and for a moment or two our conversation was halted by the fact that his tongue was sloshing around in her mouth. I waited patiently for her to come up for air.

'That's just because you don't like Dave,' I said, when the unknown man paused for a gulp of beer from his bottle. 'Because he doesn't have the hots for you, most likely. I'm not going to dump him for *that*.'

'Don't be silly,' Una replied irritably, investigating the fridge. 'I don't like him because he lectures me about recycling yoghurt pots. Because he's *boring*. Because he thinks he's better than me. Like that sister of yours. You should dump him and find yourself an American rock star, that's what I think. Or a tortured actor. Or alternatively one of those enormously sexy, ve-ry hot' (this slowly and meaningfully) 'ver-y *fuckable* basketball players . . .' At this point, the unknown man of great tallness half laughed, half moaned, grabbed her from behind and started dragging her down the corridor and into the bedroom. I deduced from this that we had reached the end of our conversation. Gales of giggling and some screaming ensued, plus a lot of furniture rearranging. I shoved my fingers deep in my ears as the noise crescendoed, discovered that that didn't help, then grabbed my bag and jacket and swung out of the door, down the steep stairs, and into the summer darkness.

On the whole, I decided as I paced the pavement beside the long row of tall Victorian terraced houses peering loftily down at me, I regret the decision to move in with Una a year ago. I answered an advertisement in *Loot* when I was accepted on to my Master's in Social Work at Kingsbury College, London: 'Fun chick needed for spacious two-bedroom.' I was a fun chick; I needed a spacious two-bedroom. Tick! What could go wrong? What went wrong was that Una's idea of 'fun' is incompatible with even part-time, half-hearted studying. Every time I open a book, or (heaven forfend) switch on my aged computer to do anything other than surf porn sites, she grumps furiously that I'm 'bringing her down'. She is technically enrolled on a fashion course in south London, but is enraged if her teachers so much as ask her to come in for a seminar ('Who the fuck do these people think they are?'). I have actually resorted to working in a library. She is failing everything, and doesn't give a damn; I'm just about scraping through, and I wish I was doing better.

Now, twelve months on, the course is finished, the last piece of coursework's submitted, and when I get back from America I'm going to move. I don't know where yet. I don't even know how I'm going to afford to live anywhere else (the place is heavily subsidized by my flatmate's surprisingly wealthy, almost invisible father). And I can only hope I've done enough to get the degree, and that I'll be able to find a job.

I sat down on a long wooden bench, erected in loving memory of some much-beloved grandma, and got out my mobile phone to ring my middle sister. The brick buildings radiated back the day's warmth, but there was a cool night breeze prickling my skin. I waited three rings; there was a click, and the line opened up into my sister's elegant white Pimlico villa. I could hear the discreet methodical ticking of the heirloom grandfather clock in the hallway. 'What?' She sounded half asleep. 'Oh, Jeanie, it's you . . .'

'Listen,' I breathed, 'I had to tell you. I just *had* to. You've been right all along. I see it all now. Really. I've got to change . . .'

3. Q

My sister Alison – the one squeezed uncomfortably between Jeanie and me – is one of the most elegant people you'll ever hope to meet. She's tall, but not too tall; slim but not bony; and her wardrobe spans every shade from beige to taupe. She has flawless mid-length nails, glossy mid-length hair, and inexorably mid-length hemlines. She married a minor aristocrat straight out of college, which surprised none of us. If my mother didn't have a plausibly precise story of pregnancy and giving birth, Jeanie and I would assume a mischievous cuckoo placed her in our family of big-boned women. Just to show us up.

'My darling, I'm just phoning to see how dear Samuel is doing,' Alison announced superbly this morning, 'and how you are coping with motherhood,' as an apparent afterthought. I saw her agenda immediately.

'Samuel is doing extremely well, and I've taken to motherhood like a duck to water.' (Pace a little too quick, but in other ways quite good.)

Pause. 'Well, I'm very happy to hear that,' she replied crossly. 'If there are any problems, dear, I hope you know you can always pick up the telephone and ask my advice. After all, I *do* have two children of my own, I'm a very experienced mother.'

Alison was indeed the first in our family to procreate, and she'll never let any of us forget it. Serena and Geoffrey are the kind of children you long to see covered in paint and mud tumbling backwards through a hedge. As it stands, whenever they are presented to guests, their hair seems glued to their little white foreheads, their matching outfits are pressed, and their socks cling grimly to knees that seem unnaturally red. I don't think I've ever seen them with so much as a bruise, and I've certainly never heard either of them raise a voice – in Alison's presence, that is. It's a different story when Mummy's out of the way. I took the kids to the Natural History Museum once and I swear I saw the animatronic Tyrannosaurus flinch before Geoffrey's vociferous onslaught ('I's goin' to eat it, I's goin' to *kill* it, lemme at it, Auntie Q!').

'Thanks for the offer, Alison, but really, motherhood isn't *rocket science*!' I laughed uproariously, and felt the barrier at the other end of the line come satisfactorily ringing down.

'I see,' she muttered, sounding distinctly mortified.

'But if I *do* have any little problems, Alison, I'll be sure to ask you, never fear,' I added earnestly. 'After all, I know Geoffrey and Serena have given you plenty of practice. Now, I must go, Tom and I need to start packing for our Connecticut trip. Did I mention it? Just a few weeks in Paul Dupont's house . . . the one from *GQ* . . .'

In fact, Tom and I were in the process of tidying up our two-bedroom apartment after a visit from my husband's terrible parents, Peter and Lucille, before I finally brought myself to admit my conversation with Caroline. For three days I had been biding my time, looking for a good moment to indicate the pressing need to move – temporarily of course! – out of the city to Connecticut. When snobbish, superior Peter and Lucille announced their intention to visit, I saw my opportunity. Time, first, to lay the groundwork. 'It will be so delightful to see them!' I said brightly to my husband, and from the moment Peter and Lucille walked in until the second the door banged closed behind them, I was a model of restraint, tolerance and respect. I affected great interest in Peter's research papers on cardiac surgical procedures and joined in energetically with Lucille's perpetual whines about 'those careerist women's libbers'. 'Motherhood has improved her,' I heard Peter concede to his wife as they walked off down the corridor.

This is not to say it was easy to maintain my perfect daughter-in-law image. Peter and Lucille came ostensibly to spend time with the baby and 'help out', but actually to reinforce the idea that they did everything *right* and we do everything *wrong*. 'The baby sleeps in a bassinet,' Lucille asked, eyebrows disappearing into her expensive blond hairline, 'not a crib? It's so tiny! I'd be worried about suffocation myself . . .' And later: 'Do you think it's *wise* to use these disposable diapers? Have you thought about chemical – er – *infloration*?' Last was the production of a small box of rice cereal from her bag of 'useful things for babies' (none of which were remotely useful for a five-week-old. She clearly viewed Samuel's lack of interest in the spinning top contraption she produced as evidence of dangerous developmental delay). 'Give him two teaspoons of rice cereal for breakfast, lunch and dinner, and he will sleep through the night,' she asserted confidently, opening the box and preparing a bowl of the stuff with cows' milk straight from the fridge. '*Guaranteed*. It's a little trick my mother taught me,' she added, smiling beatifically. (She only conceded defeat when he'd smeared half the bowl over her face with a single well-placed kick and thrown up the rest of it into her lap. It was almost worth it, I decided, watching puked cereal slowly seeping through the crotch of her beige trousers, for that.)

As we restored order to the place (Peter is one of those people who seem to imagine that tiny elves pick up towels off the floor), I casually introduced the idea of a month-long vacation away. My tone was as insouciant as I could possibly manage. But for

all that, my husband looked at me as if the illusion of a transformed Q was, for him at least, beginning abruptly to fade. 'All
through your pregnancy you accused me of not spending enough
time at home,' he said wrathfully, standing in the kitchen with a
dishcloth in his hand and a painfully aggrieved expression on his
face. '"What will happen when the baby comes?" you said.
"You need to be a better father," you said. "You need to watch
your son grow up," you said. Now the baby's here, I've cut back
on my night hours at Crimpson and, lo and behold! Q wants to
fly out the door with Samuel and leave me behind . . .'

I squawked self-defensively, sweeping the innards of the
newspaper into a box (Peter's strategy is to disembowel the
Times, section by section, throwing everything he doesn't want
on the floor). 'It's not that, darling, it's just that I haven't been
anywhere in a year except here and the hospital, the pregnancy
was so hard, and now the weather's turned hot it seems a
shame to pass up the opportunity of a house by the sea—'

'You seem confident that it *is* an opportunity,' Tom cut in
acerbically, 'but I should perhaps point out that Paul hasn't
offered us his house in a year.'

This, I had to admit, as I attacked Lucille's lipstick-stained
teacups, was a problem. Last summer Paul was warmly insistent that we should go and stay in his summer place, but at the
time we were both working too hard; since my pregnancy,
we've hardly seen him at all (Tom was in his office almost
around the clock in order to try to make partner at his firm,
while I was confined to my bed).

'Perhaps you could ask him . . .' I tried not to wheedle.

'Q,' Tom snapped, 'I don't understand you—'

There was a muffled yelp from our son, who was sleeping on
the sofa, and we both turned hastily to look at him. His mouth
was agape, drool spilling gently on to the cushions; he was a
little red around the eyes still from a bout of furious crying that

afternoon. He is beautiful; and he is (everyone agrees, from bejewelled old ladies in the street to the plump cashier at the bank) the spitting image of his father. He has a shock of fine dark hair, black eyes that are turning to green, and hamster cheeks. He is warm and floppy in my arms, a little frog with bandy legs and spread-out toes, and somehow the look of too many fingers on his reddened crumpled hands. Sensing his own wrist near his face, he opened his mouth, cracked his eyes ajar, and began furiously sucking. Slowly, his eyelids turned heavy, then drooped, as his tiny body relaxed again in sleep.

My husband and I caught each other's eyes, and smiled.

'Listen, Tom,' I went on, walking over and putting my arms around him, 'the truth is, I was thinking: what if you *came too*? What if you said to yourself, Forget it, they're not going to partner me – Crimpson made that clear before Samuel was born, you know they did – so I'm going to use up all my holiday entitlement and go away for a month with my wife?'

My chest thumping now, I stared at the bit of my husband's shoulder in front of my face. It was a very nice bit of shoulder, as it happened, broad and firm, and covered in starched white cotton. I pleated a bit of it in between my fingers, and waited, hoping.

Tom craned down to look into my face. 'You want me to commit suicide at Crimpson?' He sounded incredulous.

'I know how it sounds,' I admitted. 'I know what the partners will say. I know what they'll *think*. But what do we have to lose, really? They can't actually fire you for this – you haven't taken a holiday in years – and what they say about you doesn't really matter any more. You're just biding your time there now, waiting to find a new job.'

'There's my professional reputation,' Tom retorted, immediately. 'I need to get another position, unless you imagine I'm going to take up apple-picking for a living.'

19

'People know you in town, Tom, and it's not as if you don't have friends and long-term associates in other firms,' I said reasonably. 'Paul himself, for example. He might be willing to put in a word for you at Prince, or another Wall Street firm for that matter. You don't need to impress Crimpson any more. In fact, I think you should view their decision not to promote you as sort of liberating.'

Tom, pulling away, went and sat on the window seat and looked out into the evening. The sun was spreading its last colours across the millions of windows outside our own, a sea of orange fire engulfing the island of Manhattan. Samuel sneezed in his sleep.

'You can do what you want now, Tom,' I said gently, coming to stand in front of him. 'Darling, *we* can do what we want. We can—'

'You were playing me last night,' Tom interjected, shaking his head at me, but I could see that the corners of his mouth were twitching. 'I see it all now. Trying to get on my good side. I *thought* it was too good to be true. "You're so expert at mothering, Lucille, can you show me that burping position again?" "Peter, tell me more about minimally invasive coronary-bypass procedures." Very subtle.'

I sat beside him. 'I want a holiday with you,' I explained, taking his hand. 'The last year has been . . . well. You know. Now I want to forget firms, and jobs, and careers. I want to take Samuel in the sea. I want to walk out of the house into warm sand. I want to lie on the beach with you. And Jeanie—'

'You know *she's* going to want wall-to-wall cocktails and parties and stretch limousines when she gets here, that's why she's coming out to New York.'

'Leave Jeanie to me, I can persuade her. And she's not really like that, you know,' I murmured reproachfully. Samuel stirred again, and opened his mouth in a cat's yawn; this time, after a second or two, he whimpered and opened his sleep-darkened eyes. I glanced at the clock; it was time for a feed. I picked him up and curved him into the crook of my arm, lifted my T-shirt and spilled myself into his tiny, insistent mouth. We listened to his gentle suck-swallow, suck-swallow as the window square blackened and the stars appeared to prick out the sky.

'OK,' Tom said slowly, at last. 'I'll phone Paul tomorrow.'

4. Jeanie

I Love New York (Madonna). *I Feel Safe in New York* (AC/DC).
Summer in the City (The Lovin' Spoonful). *Skylines and Turnstiles*
(My Chemical Romance).

My i-Pod is brimming with New York-themed music. I spent
two days downloading songs and even the occasional album to
get myself in the mood, although I haven't got around to organ-
izing it all yet. So at the moment Frank Sinatra is acting as a
warm-up for Busta Rhymes, Paul Simon for Snoop Dogg,
which is a little bit disorientating.

I absolutely love flying; I don't know why anyone finds
it scary. I love the adrenalin rush as the jet speeds down the
runway. I love the little dinky dinners in square white boxes. I love
sipping gin and tonics at eleven in the morning while watching
movies of scenically catastrophic destruction. Not that flying is
without its downsides, of course: I don't like tucking my knees
into my belly button (a necessary feat if someone belonging to
the human race is to fit into an economy-class seat), and I don't
enjoy being told off by gaunt ladies with ugly hats. But there's
always the pleasure of needling the ugly ladies through mild acts
of rebellion, e.g. reading a magazine four-and-a-half seconds
after being asked to desist. *And* the relief of leaving my problems
far, far behind me.

All The Critics Love U in New York (Prince). *City of Blinding Lights* (U2). *New York State of Mind* (Alicia Keys). *Big Apple Dreamin'* (Alice Cooper).

Somewhere back in Heathrow this morning, Dave was almost certainly yelling at the oil-soaked gaskets and widgets (or something) in the engine of 'Betty', his Morris Minor, as I soared overhead. I can see him now, fussing under the dented bonnet, rubbing his dirty hands distractedly on his greying T-shirt and frayed jeans, swearing furiously at Betty for her remarkable unwillingness to start whenever she's away from home. (Betty is consistent in nothing but this.) Eventually, after an hour or so, after much hammering and yanking and bashing, Betty will have spluttered apologetically back to life, and Dave will have hopped into the driver's seat and roared back down the North Circular Road into London. I hope he's all right. I hope he's managing without me. Perhaps Alison will drop by his flat sometimes, check how he's getting on. I can always rely on her.

Manhattan Skyline (A-Ha). *New York* (Ja Rule). *New York Fever* (The Toasters). *JFK to LAX* (Gang Starr). *I Run New York* (50 Cent).

I saw the skyline unfolding out of the dirty coach window with delight, the mad futuristic buildings thrusting through the yellow-grey haze. The city never looks quite real, somehow, more like a Hollywood production. (If you look carefully I'm sure you can see the ticky-tacky tape, holding it all together.) All the way into Manhattan I have been dreaming about the weeks and months I will spend getting to know the place properly. I will become the sort of person who can go back to England and begin sentences for the rest of her life with the phrase 'When I lived in New York'. The sort of person who'll throw phrases like 'uptown' and 'downtown' casually into conversation, and 'Broadway' and 'Central Park West'.

Dave will be fine without me, really.

Times Square (Marianne Faithfull). *To the Five Boroughs* (The Beastie Boys). *Welcome to Brooklyn* (Lil' Kim). *Central Park* (Pete Miser). *Manhattan Avenue* (Nellie McKay). *Cabbies on Crack* (The Ramones).

I'll be able to buy very cool clothes that nobody at home will have. I can take home magazines that nobody else will have read. I can buy not-very-expensive Christmas presents, write on the label 'a little something from New York', and get away with it. I can get myself a stunning haircut, then grouse about the fact that no one styles like that at home. (As long as I can afford the stylist, of course. What can you get for $40, I wonder?)

I hope Dave can hold out until I get back. His mother's Alzheimer's has been advancing so fast and his dad's moods have been getting blacker and blacker; sometimes I wonder how one family can take it all, the illness and the hurt and the loss. If the worst comes to the worst, I can always jump on an aeroplane and fly home again. I'm sure Q would understand.

Englishman in New York (Sting). *Lonely in New York* (Sophie Milman). *I Can't See New York* (Tori Amos). *Lightning Strikes (Not Once But Twice)* (The Clash).

*

'We need a change of scenery.'

'We need a break.'

Too bad, really; that's what I thought I was getting by coming out here. Now we're off to Connecticut. I don't even know where that is.

'The important thing is that I'm here to see *you*,' I said at last, coming to sit beside her, getting my priorities straight, dumping my Top Shop shoulder bag on the floor. My sister and I hugged each other. 'We haven't lived in the same house as each other in years, you know,' I added, 'and my visa says I can stay as much as six months. I'm so excited to meet Samuel, I wish he wasn't in bed already. Does he look anything like me?'

'A little,' Q offered, and then described her new son's manifold attractions while I sipped at my tea. Samuel is, I was given to understand, a paragon of a baby, the most beautiful, most advanced, most well-behaved child ever to be born – apart from the fact that he happens not to sleep at night and screams himself into a fit if she so much as steps outside the front door. Small flaws, clearly. I cooed in the right places, held his tiny babygros, and marvelled at the fact that my sister has a child of her very own.

'I've brought a list of newly opened clubs and boutiques,' I explained, when she finally lapsed into silence, producing a well-thumbed page torn from a *Time Out* special on New York. I saved it especially; every night, before bed, for the last month, I've been reading and rereading it, salivating at the thought that soon I – I! – will actually be beating the streets of New York City. 'And' (turning over the page) 'there's also a section on flea markets. Places where hip young designers flog their stuff. You know, the ones waiting for a lucky break. There'll be plenty of time, when we get back to the city, for us to work our way through them together, won't there, Q? It's so nice you're on maternity leave,' I went on enthusiastically, in answer to her short nod, 'we can really *do* things together this time!'

She was looking tired, I noticed suddenly – tired, and a bit lumpy. 'You need to get more rest,' I said solicitously, touching her tangled auburn hair. 'It's good I'm here, Q. I can really take care of you.' Her skin was almost grey; she's one of those people who is almost pretty when she's plump and sparkly-eyed, but quite plain otherwise.

She rested her head on my shoulder. 'That would be nice, Jeanie,' she said, heaving a big exhausted sigh, and then she rubbed her face slowly against my shirt, like a fond but knackered pony. 'It turns out it takes a while to get used to – all this.'

'I know, Alison said you'd be exhausted—' I began, but I swallowed the rest of the sentence when I saw her eyes flicker.

'Really?' my sister replied coldly, sitting up straight again. 'Thinks I can't manage, does she? Typical.'

'I wouldn't say that.'

'Well, I would,' Q returned flatly. 'You should have heard her on the phone the other day. "Motherhood doesn't come easily to everyone, Q. For *some of us* it's second nature, of course. But you mustn't feel it's a comment on your femininity if *you* find it hard . . ."' She mimicked Alison's voice in a scornful high falsetto. 'She's just longing for me to fail,' she went on sourly. 'She wants everyone to think she's the world's best mother and I'm just some careerist freak who can't even change a nappy. Well, I'll bloody well show her – and you, Jeanie,' – she turned to me owlishly – 'you can help me by staying "on message", OK? Whenever you talk to her, I mean. I deal with Alison on a strictly need-to-know basis, and she doesn't need to know *anything*. But look,' she went on, after a moment, putting her arm around my waist, 'let's forget Alison. I try to as often as possible. More importantly, did you finish your course? Your social work degree?'

'Of course,' I said, nettled. (Just how disorganized does she think I am?)

'So was it useful? What did you learn?' she enquired, sounding more like my mother than my mother.

'How to speak in words of nineteenth syllables,' I returned, irritably. That's the one skill I'm confident I picked up from my Master's course, actually. I used to have my friends in stitches at lunchtime, converting every event of the day into social-work speak: we don't catch the bus, we 'engage with a broad spectrum transportation network which facilitates the practice of time-keeping skills and coordinated cross-class collaboration'. Instead of cooking dinner we 'learn crucial choice-making in a domesticated setting, developing hand-eye co-ordination and temperature regulation skills, essential first-order disciplines for all health-care professionals'.

'It was fine,' I finished blandly, not feeling inspired to expand, 'really, fine.' She opened her mouth to start interrogating me (I recognise the signs) but fortunately at that moment Samuel started shouting in the other room. That child makes some noise! Thankfully, I took the opportunity to slip off for a long, hot shower, and some time to myself. Really, travelling is absolutely *exhausting*.

5. Q

'Don't suppose there will be any baby gear at Paul's house, will there,' Tom said doubtfully as we gazed around at the contents of the bedroom and the sitting room. My heart almost failed me at the thought of all the accoutrements that seem to have to accompany Samuel. Was this a good idea? If Tom hadn't talked Paul into offering us his house, and if I hadn't talked it up to Alison on the phone, I think we might have backed out at that point. 'Holidays in your own place can be so relaxing,' I heard Tom muttering disconsolately, eyeing the baby bath, the baby swing, the baby mobile the size of a family car, but who wants to be the kind of parents who get stuck at home, unable to move a step, because of their baby? Tom wrestled three vast suitcases out of the closet.

'I was planning on using the place myself this month,' Paul said when Tom phoned, deeply embarrassed, to ask 'for a favour . . .' But after a pause, he agreed. 'If you don't mind sharing with me for a night or two, perhaps a weekend when I come up to work on the boat, I guess it could work.' Tom actually views this as a plus ('We can catch a game, go fishing!'). 'But what are you doing about work?' was Paul's next, inevitable question, at which point my husband coughed uncomfortably.

'I'm thinking of taking some – um – holiday,' he said, and you'd have thought he was suggesting crack cocaine. Paul, however, received the information tolerantly.

'Great idea,' he agreed, 'you should spend some time with your new son.'

Tom relaxed visibly about the whole plan after that; it was as if Paul had given him permission. He marched into Crimpson the very next day and asked for two weeks off, impervious to all the needling looks and sharp comments as he prepared files and briefed his juniors about his cases.

We packed the rental car leaving just enough room for Jeanie to actually sit in – quite an achievement. Glancing back at our boot full of neatly stacked monochrome luggage, I felt strangely clean and pure. No junk, just necessities! We should live like this all the time.

After an energizing argument about the route, and after both of us had checked three times on the harness of Samuel's baby seat (too tight inspires fears of chest constriction, too loose incites images of fearsome car accidents), we threw ourselves into the Manhattan traffic heading out of town for the week-end, lurched over steaming potholes towards the press of the east-side highway, and dived amongst the cars heading towards the Triborough Bridge. At the toll, the air shimmered with the heat of a thousand idling engines. Samuel whimpered uncomfortably in his seat; Tom slammed an impatient hand against the wheel, cursed softly, then flicked compulsively through XM radio channels, while Jeanie and I meandered through a desultory conversation about our mother's yoga business back home in England.

But once the barrier finally rose to let us through, a new world opened up. 'I95 New Haven' announced a large green sign above the sweating, smoking asphalt. Picking up speed at last, we skirted the edges of a dozen small commuter cities, curved around the unprepossessing hotel fronts of Stamford, flew across Bridgeport's overpass, and then, as the scattered high-rises and implausible sheer face of New Haven's East Rock glimmered a tantalizing gold and bronze upon our left, sped beyond, around the underarm of the coast, into the deepest part of the state.

When we finally left the highway and struck out into the winding roads of interior Connecticut, we seemed to be in a different country altogether. The roads were narrow and the houses modest; a few clapboard farms, slightly dilapidated, sat in the midst of open, undulating fields, where cows half slept and nosed the grass and flicked flies along the banks of thickly rush-edged ponds. And then, quite suddenly, it got dark; we found ourselves racing down a narrow road edged high with pines and maples whose branches met above us. Down headed the road, further and further, sweeping around sharp corners set with low red Capes; until, at the very bottom, as the road traversed a neat triangle of carefully mown green grass, the sea appeared before us, orange and crimson and palest blue in the lights of the setting sun.

Sussex, the town where Paul's summer house lies, hugs a cove notched into the Connecticut coast. The house itself was – we knew from Paul's detailed instructions – located just outside the small centre, off a rough dusty path running perpendicular to the coastal road. Surrounded – almost encased – by trees, the white house gleamed in the semi-darkness like something out of a fairy tale as we bumped along the drive.

'Good size,' said Tom thoughtfully, looking up at it.

'Very charming,' Jeanie agreed.

The outside looked like a plain Quaker home, but the inside had, as we quickly discovered, recently received the loving attention of an expensive interior designer. The wooden floorboards had been evened out and stripped to a gleaming sand colour, and ocean-hued silk curtains tickled the floor in the breeze. Persian rugs and pillows were thrown next to pure white armchairs and sofas. A large modern canvas splattered with lines in declining shades of ochre stared down from the gloss-painted mantelpiece. The table and dining chairs were polished teak slabs, as were the kitchen cupboards. The dish-washer and washing machine sort of *hummed* as they worked. The oven alone was the size of a New York City apartment.

Upstairs were two enormous bedrooms with ensuite dressing rooms and vast, echoing bathrooms, equipped with claw-footed iron tubs and rain showers. Fawn-coloured glass tiles turned rich gold with a flick of the light-switch; amber-coloured towels as thick as a woman's arm lay neatly folded on silver rails (Paul employs a housekeeper to come in and clean once a week, and to set up the house for him and his guests). It was – we realized, as we ran from room to room, exclaiming at the size, the space, the coolness – like something out of a tourist magazine, *Martha Stewart Living* at the very least; a fantasy come to life, a dream of secluded quiet, a cloistered retreat equipped with swansdown and a dizzyingly expensive entertainment system.

Jeanie was deeply impressed. 'Blimey,' she said, staring wide-eyed at the expanse of opulent minimalism. 'How much d'you think all this stuff cost?' After we'd vacuumed down a quick pasta meal, thrown together from packets, she curled up on the sofa, tapping out emails to her friends in which she described the place in precise, intimate detail. Dave, she said, would be particularly intrigued; 'He just wouldn't believe it,' she said, looking up for a moment with a grin between gulps of chilled Chardonnay. 'All these rooms! The space! The huge bath-rooms! The weirdo art! Although' – her excited smile slipped down her face a bit – 'he might not approve.' She took another sip of wine, looking thoughtful. 'He's got very into the envir-onment these days, he'd probably sniff about the "carbon footprint" of the house.' She shook her head a little, then started tapping again. 'But I've *got* to tell him about the kitchen and the bathrooms, he'll be simply amazed . . .'

Tom and I, laughing, left her to it, and took ourselves upstairs to our room. A big downy quilt and floaty white pillows piled on top of an iron four-poster awaited us.

We had put Samuel to bed in his bassinet in our room before dinner; I picked him up now with cautious, gentle hands, nursed him while he slept, and levered myself into the cool sheets afterwards without making a sound. Tom, who had been anxiously watching the whole careful dance, produced a big thumbs-up gesture in the darkness; we settled down with matching sighs of relief. For ten minutes, Samuel slept the heavy, dreamless sleep of the innocent. I drifted off listening to his thin, even breaths. Then, a few moments after I'd lost consciousness, just as I was walking into a dreamland of warm black velvet and goose-down, I was woken by an ear-splitting shriek, a sound to tear body from soul. 'What the—'

Maybe it was because of the trip, maybe the change of surroundings, but the night that unfolded was nightmarish. Samuel was up at midnight, then again at 2 a.m., 3.30 a.m., 4 a.m., 5.15 a.m. and finally for good, chirruping hopefully, at 6 a.m. 'Can't you *do* anything?' Tom said raggedly, somewhere about 4 a.m., but by this point our son was acting as if feeding, cuddling and singing were all activities approximately akin to torture.

'Oh, right, I'll just switch the "off" button. Silly me, why didn't I think of that before?' I told my husband, and I think I even hit him at one point.

We fell down the stairs just as the first rays of sunshine were filtering through the window blinds in the kitchen, cheeks flushed, eyes hollowed. I had the oddest sensation of having lost the fluid around my cerebral cortex. 'Obviously, it was just a one-off,' Tom remarked in a ghastly voice, turning pancakes on the stove with shaking fingers as the room brightened to day. I nodded. (I think I heard my brain rattle.) 'Once he gets used to the place, it'll be different,' he went on, slapping a syrupy mess of half-cooked pancakes in front of me. 'We can work on getting him into a *routine* while we're here, Q,' he added, sitting down on the stool opposite me with the stiff jerky gait of a very old man. 'Then when we go back to work, at the end of our holiday, he'll be sleeping, reliably, throughout the night. We'll be *totally* in control by then.'

Outside, the pines stirred in the morning breeze, and the waves dragged shells in and out of the empty shore. Tom and I picked up our forks and set about our breakfast in silence; Samuel had gone back to sleep. The house was utterly quiet.

6. Jeanie

It's our third day here, and we've just got back from a walk around the town of Sussex. (Personally I'd call it a village, but that bit of Frenchery seems not to have made it across the Atlantic.) The centre is basically one long street that falls into water at the end; the main road turns into a footpath which becomes a boardwalk, and then the river. A few miles south the river opens out into the sea, and in my mind's eye the route continues – across the Atlantic, round Ireland's choppy bottom, to England. You can see signs of English heritage everywhere here, from the name of the town to the small village green, halfway along the street, to the shape of the houses (simple and square). But these New Englanders have brought their own twist, since everything – houses, barns, garages, shops – is made of wood. Walls, roofs, doors; you name it: wood, wood, wood, not a brick in sight. I can't help eyeing these wooden boxes and their wooden lids with an Englishwoman's inevitable bewilderment. 'They don't look safe to me,' I said suspiciously to Q, standing staring at one from the middle of the long narrow street. 'How come they don't rot or burn down? What happens when your neighbour lights up the barbecue?'

The place is nice enough, but perhaps not quite as beautiful as it once was; the paint on the houses is peeling, I noticed, the gardens chock-full of weeds, and the chimneys are tipping slightly to the side, like a woman who's taken to drink. The ships in the docks that fan out around the coastline seem to bring wrinkly-brown pleasure cruisers these days instead of roaring trade, and most of them stop for an hour or two at most, sampling microwaved French onion soup in small restaurants with names like Kat's Kozy Korner. Chain chemists and banks lurk down side streets in concrete bunkers marooned in asphalt. Q told me that Sussex is chiefly popular these days for its proximity to a very large 'outlet mall' (a place where you can wrestle comrades to the ground for a cheapie pair of Calvin Klein knickers, apparently). Tourists generally prefer the charms of places further along the coast (with more English names: Essex, Norwich, Old Lyme), towns that have a similar shape but more original buildings and more zealous old people committed to preserving them.

Paul, the man who owns this house, was apparently left it by an aged uncle, and I gather he more or less ignores the town, focusing instead on his expansive dock. He also owns a place in somewhere called 'the Hamptons'. I don't know what this is, or why it's plural, but Q and Tom discuss it with a slight air of consciousness, as if even mentioning the Hamptons in conversation gives you an 'in' to polite society. (I imagine an Edith Wharton novel, a place of tall white mansions reaching down to the sea, of conservatories filled with yellow roses lapped in eternal sunlight.)

We strolled down Sussex's long main street pushing Samuel, whose screams echoed up and down the narrow pavement. When he'd finally yelled himself into purple silence, we bumped the buggy up to a small coffee shop with cheery cotton curtains at the window, round wooden tables on a plain wood floor, and shelves piled high with model sailing boats, fully rigged, and drank our cups of coffee in welcome peace. Q kept touching Samuel to check he was breathing until Tom impatiently slapped her fingers away.

'Jeanie, how are things with Dave?' Q began, glowering across the table at Tom. 'We were – uh – sorry he couldn't come out with you, but it's great he let you come for such a nice long stay.' She dropped a brown knobbly cube of sugar into her mug and vigorously stirred it with a plastic twizzle stick, then surrepticiously touched Samuel's cheek when Tom wasn't looking.

'Yeah, good, thanks,' I replied. 'Thanks for asking. Dave's still having problems holding down a job, but it's hardly surprising, given how much time he spends with his mum. She barely knows where she is most days.'

'And he's got into the environment recently?'

'Mmm. It's his latest thing. It was his flatmate Badger who got him on to it—'

'*Badger?*'

'So-called because of the shock of white hair down the centre of his head.'

'I see. Makes perfect sense.'

'Well, yes. Quite. Although I think pierced tongues and tattooed knuckles are less characteristic of the English badger.'

Tom seemed to be watching a game of rounders played with helmets on the green outside the window.

'And Badger is an eco-warrior, is he?' Q went on a few moments later (she was now holding Samuel's hand under the table).

'Something like that. He's had a big effect on Dave. When I first met him he was a tabloid reader, *Sunday Sport*, *News of the World*, that sort of thing. Cigarette propped permanently over his ear. Favourite way to spend the weekend was down the pub. But over the past year he's been taking a lot more responsibility for his mum, and Badger's got him demonstrating against global warming and globalization. It's quite sweet really. I'm not sure he always knows quite what he's demonstrating against, but he does love a nice walk through Hyde Park with Badger on his shoulders.'

'Well, who wouldn't,' Q murmured neutrally. She's never been particularly fond of my boyfriends. 'And you still like him, do you? Is he – er – reliable, and trustworthy, and . . .'

'Faithful,' Tom supplied, still looking out of the window. I scowled at the back of his head.

'Of course,' I said crossly. 'All of those things. And more.'

'More?'

I expatiated further on Dave's manifold virtues. 'These last few months he's been giving his dad every penny he has to help get the best care for his mum,' I explained, 'even if it means he doesn't have enough to buy new shoes or pay his own bills. His sister's always telling me he's the best big brother in the world, and his dad depends on him. He would have been an amazing social worker, if he could've afforded to complete our course. He's really *strong*!' I banged my hand on the table for emphasis; the cold dregs of our coffee jumped and shuddered in their corrugated plastic pots.

'Impressive,' Q admitted. I smiled proudly.

'And he was happy for you to come out here for four months, was he?' Tom suddenly turned and looked me full in the face. 'I mean, it seems like a long separation,' he went on. 'I'm surprised he was OK with that. Dave, I mean. You too.'

I picked up my tepid coffee and dashed a gulp down my throat. 'I can't believe you're doing this' were Dave's actual words, as I recall, when I first outlined the plan. We were in our local at the time. He thumped his fist on the table until the beans-and-sausages shook and the barmaid appeared with a wary look in her eye. 'A crook of the finger and you're off! One day it's Alison, the next Q in America . . . And I don't understand why, Jeanie, because they don't really need you, but *I* need you. Your mother claims they need help with this baby, but as far as I can tell they've got plenty of money to get a nanny – a whole fleet of 'em if necessary. What happened to togetherness? What happened to *us*? How do you imagine we're going to have a relationship on two different continents?'

'Dave,' I began miserably, reaching across the rough, knotty pine table for his hand, 'see it from my perspective. This is my one opportunity to live abroad. My course will be finished, I won't have a job, it's the one time in my life I'll be free to travel. And it's my one chance to get to know Q's new baby . . .'

'It's your one chance to spend these four months with me,' he growled. 'We won't get this time back again, Jeanie. What's passed is passed. And you just expect me to sit around waiting for you, do you?' he continued suddenly, with a rasp that was almost a jeer in his voice. I felt my lip wobble. 'You think I'll just be hanging around for you, good old Dave, waiting like a patient dog for when you've finished your travels?'

'Well, I can't insist, but I was definitely *hoping* you would . . .' I replied. 'I mean, I'll understand if you don't want to, Dave, but I – I will be waiting for you—'

'And so will I, but the bloody difference is, I don't have a choice,' he said angrily, and stood up to order another couple of pints. He sniffed loudly as he went, rubbing his arm across his nose in a single, characteristic gesture. I watched him lope across the bar floor, navigating the yelling, laughing crowds, the heaped coats and duffel bags, the strewn bar stools, with practised ease. I love Dave, I thought to myself suddenly, I do love him, but I can't help wanting to see a bit more of the world than the inside of a London pub.

Q, I suddenly realized, was talking. 'I don't want you to worry about the cost of speaking with Dave; use our phone while you're here,' she offered. 'If Dave can't afford to ring you, just call him. We'll pay. It's the least we can do. Here's the thing, Jeanie,' she continued, leaning across the table, 'I know I was a bit negative about Dave when you first got together, but if he makes you happy, if he recognizes what he's got, then that's all that counts. I don't care that he doesn't have money—'

'Or a job,' contributed Tom, *sotto voce*; Q rolled her eyes.

'There are lots of ways of working, I understand that,' she said firmly, as if she'd made up her mind about something. 'Seriously, I do. Dave's work isn't the conventional sort, but it's extremely valuable. And saving the environment – I don't know what's more important than that these days.' She smiled in what I'm sure she hoped was an understanding way. 'Tom and I were talking about this. If Dave would like to come out and visit you once we get back to New York, we'll cover the cost of the flight. It'll be tight in the apartment, the five of us, but we can manage.'

'Thanks,' I said delightedly, imagining Dave's face. A trip to New York! 'That's really kind of you, I don't know what he'll say – it'll depend on his mother's health, obviously. Plus there's a Beluga whale press release to complete, a new project of Badger's,' I added importantly. And then, in response to a raised, delicately sceptical eyebrow from Tom, 'Well, not just Belugas, but all toothed whales; you have to think of the bigger picture, the full marine spectrum, obviously . . .'

'*Obviously*,' Tom echoed, and then he sharply twitched Samuel's blanket out of Q's hand with a muffled exclamation. He went back to watching the funny rounders game out of the window, while Q moved her hand millimetre by millimetre closer to Samuel's slumbering form.

7. Q

'Paul is coming to stay this weekend!' Tom announced delightedly, flicking his cellphone closed just after lunch, and I struggled to produce an expression of appropriate joy.

'Paul! Wow. That's so great,' I said enthusiastically. 'I'm pleased. In fact I'm *thrilled*! I can't wait. Paul. Way-hey!'

My husband stared. 'D'you have a crush on him or something?'

Truth is, I'm not making much sense any more, because I have the brain power of a flickering candle. After three nights of no sleep I am not actually a human being, I'm some sort of non-sentient lower organism. Something from the bottom of a pond, probably. Something without arms and legs that lies still and senses currents.

Samuel has given up sleeping and taken to crying instead. He's had three screaming fits so far today, each worse than the last. They come from what seems like nowhere: one moment he's staring into blank nothingness; the next his face folds in upon itself, his mouth puckers up, his skin turns a mottled, blotchy red, and he begins to yell.

The day itself didn't start out too badly. For the first half-hour or so after he woke up he was quiet – peaceful, even happy – snuggling into my shoulder, his round plump bottom tucked into my hand. In spite of my tiredness I tickled his toes, and laughed with him as he kicked and bounced, bounced and kicked, then reached hopefully towards my face with stubby, interested, exploring hands. But then, just as I settled down for breakfast, everything changed; gurgles became whimpers, which became, in a fraction of a second, in the lapse of a heart-beat, a scream. The pitch of his shriek seemed to settle just under my ears and then, drill-like, bored its way up into the deep inner lobes of my brain. Everything turned cavernous, orange; the world dwindled to one child, one head, one mouth, one scream.

'Tom,' I said hesitantly to my husband, remembering all this, 'd'you think Paul is going to want to spend a weekend with Samuel when he's like – er – the way he is?'

'Don't be ridiculous, Q,' my husband scoffed. 'All this screaming will be over by the weekend. *Obviously*. His crying jag is just a short-term thing. *Short term*. Blink of an eye, it'll be gone. Done. Over with.' (By which I realized that he too is losing the ability to construct grammatical sentences.)

I can only hope he's right, and that Samuel's behaviour will improve, because otherwise Paul will arrive here to find the three of us laid out cold. Either I'll kill us all, or Tom will, or Jeanie. The poor girl didn't sign on for this, and she is certainly not enjoying it. She rushed into the kitchen at eleven o'clock this morning to find me covered in sweat and shaking, Samuel writhing in my grasp like an armful of smoking serpents. 'What's going on?' she asked, confused, eyes still droopy, clutching her robe around her; Tom was out collecting bread for lunch (read: beating his head against a brick wall).

'I don't know,' I said, then repeated the words three times to make myself heard.

'Can I do anything?' she yelled uncertainly, shrinking away from me and the baby; I shook my head and shooed her out of the room. Alone with my son once more, I took a deep breath, a gulp of water, mentally shook myself, and tried a pacifier, but

Samuel beat me off as if what I was actually trying to do was torment him with tiny red-hot needles dipped in acid.

'Anyway,' Tom went on thoughtfully, peering down at Samuel, who was briefly asleep, 'it's probably louder than we think it is, right? The crying, I mean. He's our son, we're hyperconscious of him. I'm sure other people will sort of – er – tune him out . . .'

We had the opportunity to test this interesting theory out half an hour later, when the doorbell rang and a local fisherman's wife named Marie arrived with an order of sturgeon.

I went to answer the door, noticing the swirls of grey that now loomed on the very edges of my vision. The ground was pulling me into its force with a gentle tug upon the bottom of my eyebrows, my knees were stuffed with floaty puffs of cotton wool . . .

Marie's bright cheerful voice lifted me out of my stupor. 'Hi, you people, how're you settling in?' She is a familiar type of these parts, big-hipped with coiffed hair and large stately glasses; a connoisseur of celebrity gossip, yet utterly comfortable in a small town; a devoted reader of fashion magazines, while entirely unfashionable herself, and touchingly unconcerned by the fact. 'Ooof – that's some yell,' she observed, walking into the kitchen as Samuel opened his lungs.

Three minutes later, she actually had her fingers in her ears. 'Kid has volume!' she said, retreating to the door, having plopped the quivering damp package down on the table. 'Colic, huh? My eldest had it too. Gave us a crazy time.'

We stared at her. What?

'And the worst thing is,' she went on cheerfully, having achieved the comparative quiet of the front hall, 'there's nothing you can do. Just got to wait it out. Course, it seems never-ending at the time. I don't envy you . . .'

I stood with my hand clutching the door, waving her a faint

farewell as she heaved herself into her truck and swept out of the driveway. Colic? What is *that*? I vaguely remembered something about sweating colts in some James Herriot novel I read when I was ten . . .

I dragged myself into the bedroom and feverishly unearthed (from beneath Tom's tottering pile of gold-embossed thrillers) *After Birth: Surviving the First Year*, a book I slung into our suitcase when Tom was not looking. The cover was adorned with an image of peaceful, fulfilled maternity: a slumbering naked child slung over a serene woman's shoulder. No one was screaming.

After Birth had a whole section on 'Colic', I discovered, looking in the index, complete with subsections on 'Remedies', 'Possible Causes', and 'The Myths'. I was briefly euphoric; I haven't had much recourse to *After Birth* so far, but whenever I've used it it's had concrete, useable answers. What to do when the umbilical cord gets icky: keep clean, use alcohol wipes, don't worry. What to do with a scurfy head: use oil at bathtime, wash off, don't worry. A hundred other small but equally useful pieces of information bristle in its pages: use rectal thermometers for a really accurate reading; remember to keep blind cords away from your baby's crib; take your baby to the hospital if his fever tops 103. It's a how-to guide to motherhood, and it's never failed me so far.

Colic is a term 'for sustained infant crying', I learned in its pages. But there was something missing here, some crucial gap between word and meaning, since presumably all children with colic cry but not all children who cry have colic. What *is* it? According to Nurse Barbara Trimblethwaite, illustrious author of *After Birth* (over a million copies sold), no one really knows. However, she lights upon a comforting fact: colic is not 'serious', she claims (unless you call screaming for hours on end 'serious', of course) and gradually subsides by week twelve.

I slumped on to the floor, raking my hands through my lank dishevelled hair. Paul Dupont, one of New York's most dashing, brilliant, erudite men is coming here in three days' time, to find his house possessed by a monster. A six-week-old tiny pink banshee who could clear a stadium on Super Bowl night. Will he ask us to leave? Can we possibly put him off until week twelve, when the spectral possession will apparently pass from the body of my once-perfect child?

'No chance, Q.' This, sadly, was Tom's opinion. 'He's got to get a boat ready for a regatta down in Florida in a couple of weeks. Look, there's no point in worrying about this, we'll just have to explain what's going on,' (setting his shoulders manfully). 'Paul has handled the Supreme Court. Of course he can take the crying of a little newborn baby . . .

'You know, Q,' he continued in a whisper half an hour later, when we were both laid flat out on the floor, Samuel slumped out between us, 'I thought when we had a child – well, I thought he'd just sleep and play, and cry a bit when he was hungry, you know? But this colic thing, if that's what it is – I mean, he cries *for what seems like no reason at all*. Did you know that could even happen?'

I didn't, of course. I'm not quite sure what I expected mothering to be, but it wasn't this. It doesn't have to be perfect, I don't expect miracles. But could somebody please explain why it has to be like *this*?

8. Jeanie

The ghosts eat, but I'm not sure when; they eat in the middle of the night – in the middle of the morning – whenever Samuel happens to give them five minutes of peace. I make sandwiches and leave them in the fridge, and usually the next time I check they've disappeared.

'Alison,' I whispered into the phone this morning, *'it's not as much fun as I thought it would be.'*

Alison clicked her tongue at me. 'Darling, whoever said it would be fun? You're not there to have fun, you're there to help. So the baby cries a lot, does he?' She was obviously very interested. 'What's wrong, do you think? Is Tom helpful? Is Q coping?'

I had to describe Samuel's screeching fits while she clucked and muttered worriedly on the other end of the phone. 'It sounds like colic, you know. You should tell her to contact me, I can help,' she added confidently. 'I expect he's having gastro-intestinal troubles, perhaps caused by her milk composition, I think . . .' I switched off while she gabbled on.

But then she had to run off to collect her son from school. Feeling rather lonely, I turned to my computer for support, locating a stray wireless signal in the bathroom. I opened my inbox, where twelve new emails awaited. Seven were from Dave ('I LOVE YOU, YOU OLD BAG'); three were from my mother ('Just when *are* you coming home?'); one, strangely medieval, offered me the opportunity to 'improve my peniss lenght and enhance my ladys plesure'. One, from college, three days old, contained news that caused a profound darkening in my mood.

'Dear Jean Boothroyd,' it opened, and you know you have to worry when the writer drags in your last name at the beginning. 'We still have not received your' (big gap, text continues on next line) 'coursework for the independent study module (SW415)' (big gap, text continues three lines down) 'and we regret to inform you that you have not therefore fulfilled the requirements for the Master's Degree in Social Work and Social Policy. Yours sincerely, Ann Dougins (secretary to Professor Sibelius Mordaunt, Dept of SW&SP, Kingsbury College).'

This was something of a downer, since the day before I left England I submitted an application for a job in which I claimed – and I think this part really matters – that I am about to receive my Master's degree in Social Work. It was also quite bewildering, since I'd given a large bound copy of my final coursework (SW415) three days before that to the very same Ann Dougins, who is (I believe) cohabiting with Professor Sibelius Mordaunt and thus has ample opportunity to deliver said manuscript into his plumply wrinkled blue-white hands. In other words, the whole thing was a typical bureaucratic fuck-up of collegiate life, but one of those things that is nightmarishly hard to resolve when you are three-and-a-half-thousand miles away from London in a small American seaside town.

I finally got through to Professor Mordaunt, who did a very good job of acting as though he hadn't the faintest idea who I was (even though I've been sweating through his wretchedly tedious classes for months now). 'Jean? Jean?' he said fretfully (I'd clearly disturbed him in the midst of his mid-afternoon milky drink). 'Boothroyd?' he added, as though the name itself was an offence.

'Yes,' I explained patiently. 'Boothroyd. With a B. And a Y. And an – er – double O in the middle . . .' I discovered I was doing a simply horrible job of spelling my name, and stopped.

'And you've completed this coursework, you say?' he asked with evident suspicion. 'You've actually submitted it to Ann – to Miss Dougins?'

'Yes. Weeks ago. It's bound and everything,' I said, as if this was the important part. 'It's about the impact of short-term separations on families,' I explained, hurrying on into the meat of the subject, 'especially children aged between seven and twelve. Prison, family members serving as carers in other parts of the country, job relocations, that sort of thing. I worked with families in south London, placement in Brixton . . .'

'Wait a minute, yes, yes, I remember now . . .' Professor Mordaunt began slowly. 'But it's *Jean* Boothroyd, I think?' he shot at me suddenly, as if I'd been masquerading all this time as Cheryl or Amy or something.

'That's what I said,' I began, starting to lose a scrap of my patience, but he cut blithely through.

'I *did* read that,' he said happily. 'Yes, of *course* I did. It's all coming back to me now. I wondered why you *will* keep working on children, clearly not your greatest strength. You just don't have a real feel for family issues, do you?' he continued, without waiting for an answer (which was a good thing, on the whole, since I was temporarily bereft of the means of providing one). 'It was fine, not great, think I gave it a B–. Or maybe I felt generous and bumped you up to a B, I'm not sure. Not that it matters, really, eh? B, B–, all a bit of a fiction. Depends which way the wind's blowing, eh? Oh Lord, the thing must be around here somewhere, I wonder what happened. Yes, yes, I'll speak to Ann – Miss Dougins – and make sure the examination office is informed before graduation week that you've done everything you were supposed to, good-little-girl stuff, eh? If you haven't had the letter in a week or two let me know though, eh?'

I put the phone down and pounded some pillows for a bit, imagining Professor Mordaunt's puffy white face (and Ann Dougins's equally puffy, and probably equally white, buttocks) were in fact receiving my blows. First they lose the work drenched in my heart's blood. Then they tell me I can't graduate. And then, to cap it all, Professor I'll-sleep-with-anything-that-moves Mordaunt tells me I've no 'feel for family issues' *just* as I'm about to move into a life dealing with, well, family issues. I stared at a photocopy of the application I've just submitted for a job in Cumbria supporting the children of imprisoned parents. Oh dear.

Why don't I have a feel for family issues? What does that *mean*? Why did he wait till now to tell me about it? Do I have a feel for something *else*? Did I get a B or a B–? Oh fuck.

I phoned Alison back, to ask her what she thinks. She was home by this point; I could hear the kids yelling in the background. 'Darling, you can't let some professor make your mind up for you, you have to do that yourself,' she chided, and I explained disconsolately that after a full year of study, I still have no idea which area of my field interests me most. The course was quite long, and there were so many different subjects! 'Well, what does Q think?' Alison asked at last, quite sensibly, and I had to explain I haven't mentioned a word of this to our sister.

'They don't have time to talk to me *at all*, you know,' I said sadly. 'Not any more.'

9. Q

In three weeks' time, I will be going back to work.

When you go to work, no one sits on your shoulder and screams until your eardrum implodes. When you go to work, you get to come home in the evenings and have a few moments of quiet. When you go to work, you get to wear clothes that don't have milk, sick and poo on them. When you go to work, you have tea breaks, and you're allowed to eat lunch without a squirming ten-pound weight in your arms. When you go to work, even the most evil, obsessive, work-addicted partner recognizes that you have a right to four consecutive hours of rest at night.

Last night, in my three-and-a-half minutes of sleep, I had a dream in which I took on Caroline. It was a real humdinger, I'm telling you, sort of *Working Girl* meets *The Bionic Woman* meets *Crouching Tiger, Hidden Dragon*. Lots of impressive fight moves on my part and some pathetic gibbering on hers. 'What kind of a weakling are you?' I shouted, arms akimbo, laughing loudly with impeccable red lipstick and glossy hair blowing wild in the breeze. 'You *just* work? I can juggle a small child in one arm while wrestling a fresh-killed deer into the freezer with the other and looking up cases on Westlaw with a pencil stuck in my teeth.' To demonstrate my general superiority I turned cartwheels, produced ten-inch knife blades from my elbows, and finally punched her in the gut with my shoe-heels.

It ended with her begging me on her knees to return to Schuster 'with a raise'. Very satisfying.

However, the truth is, I don't know how I'm going to go back to the office in three weeks' time when I'm unable to lift a cup of tea to my lips without spilling the whole lot on the floor. I will have to be able to brush my teeth, walk in a straight line, and speak in full sentences at Schuster. These seem, at the moment, unimaginable feats.

Still, cornered by Tom, I phoned Samuel's new daycare centre to remind them that he will be starting soon, and arranged a preliminary visit to help him acclimatize to the place. Schuster is allowing me to go back part-time for the first month – a ludicrously humane decision for a Wall Street firm – so we can ease ourselves slowly into this new life.

That's the plan, anyway.

My mother-in-law is, of course, horrified at the thought of what she calls 'group child-care arrangements' ('You must check references, there was that case in Boston some years ago. Do they have a video link so you can check up from work?') and disgusted by my sordid careerism. She also made it quite clear to me, when she phoned to speak to 'my son Tom' today, that I am basely dragging him down.

I could hear the disapproval flowing down the line as soon as I answered the phone; I knew the speech that was forming in her mind as I sketched our days in Connecticut. 'My husband never had to change a single diaper,' Lucille would say, if she could. '*I* took care of the family so *he* could take care of his career. And what has he got now? A world-class reputation. What have I got? More Tiffany jewellery than my bony neck can possibly support, and the self-satisfaction of a woman who knows she's done everything that could possibly be expected of her.'

She restrained herself, however, and got straight to the point: 'I have good news.' (I've managed quite successfully in the past to hint that access to her grandson depends on a good relationship between the two of us. And a good relationship depends on her keeping her views about my domestic arrangements to herself.) 'Very good news. Tom will be delighted. A friend of his father's has a wonderful job opportunity, very solid income, excellent prospects. For when he leaves Crimpson, I mean. It would mean moving to DC, but—'

'Thanks, Lucille,' I cut in, brightly, 'thanks a lot, but Tom won't be interested. Not his sort of thing at all.'

Lucille tsked. 'I know you think you know everything about Tom, Q,' she returned icily, 'but I should perhaps mention that I've known him longer than you. And if I know anything about my son, it's that he needs *professional challenges*. This job of Peter's will get him in the eye of people in the current administration. It could open up real *political opportunities*! A future in the Capitol! I think you should support and encourage him, Quinn dear. I think—'

'Lucille, Tom doesn't have the remotest interest in a political career, as you well know, and frankly *I* think—' I began, but at that moment Tom himself appeared in the doorway. He looked over at me quizzically, then – when I mouthed 'Your mum' unwillingly at him – reached out and almost snatched the phone from my hand.

'Oh, hi, it's you,' he said, glaring; I flushed. He turned his back as he sat down and, as I let myself out of the room I could hear him embarking on conciliatory efforts. 'No, that's not what Q *meant*,' he assured her. 'What she meant to say, I'm sure, is . . .'

I sat and stewed downstairs, snuggling Samuel while moving plates pointlessly around the kitchen, until Tom reappeared. 'Q, Mom was just trying to help,' he began irritably. 'She's obviously concerned about me, which is reasonable under the circumstances.'

'Tom, she's not just worried, she's got fantasies of having a Senator son, and she wants me to be a quiet lady in pearls who stares adoringly up at you while you kiss babies,' I returned sourly. My exhausted brain seemed to be trying to sneak out of my ears. 'She thinks I emasculate you.'

'She's just from a different generation. She was a good mom and she's a good wife. I can't understand you sometimes,' he went on, back stiff and poker-straight. 'Let's face it, she's quite right that I need a – well, some kind of a career plan.'

'You should have heard her on the phone just now, Tom! I knew what she was thinking to herself, what she says to all her posh lady friends . . .'

Tom was looking at me with an unreadable expression on his face. 'Q, she told me what you talked about, and she's right. I need a new challenge. And I don't like changing diapers,' he added, abruptly. 'I'm bored. I don't like sitting around here all day. Samuel doesn't *do* anything yet, except cry and need changing. Whenever I bathe him I half drown him, and whenever I dress him I snap his fingers backwards or get the poor kid's skin stuck in those clippie things. It's a nightmare. I'd rather be at work, frankly.'

I gazed at him. 'Do you think I'm *enjoying* this? Do you think I'm having fun?'

'I don't know what you're feeling, to be honest,' he replied. 'You're a mystery. You don't seem particularly happy when you're with Samuel, no. But every time I suggest going out, or leaving him with Jeanie, you act like I've hit you. "I can't leave my son," you say, and "He'll cry without me." And sometimes: "He'll think we've abandoned him." Honestly, Q, if I hadn't seen the surgeon cut the umbilical cord, I'd think you two were still attached.'

'That's ridiculous!' I scoffed, but there was enough truth in it that I agreed, eventually, to go out with Tom for dinner tomor-

52

row night, before Paul arrives. Jeanie will babysit. It will be good for us; we've hardly had a moment to ourselves since Samuel was born – so silly, when we have Jeanie to look after him. But some deep, instinctual part of me worries that Jeanie will snap, that only a mother can withstand the terrible, tearing, tortured sound of his screams.

'That's ridiculous,' my sister asserted, her long, honest, pretty face genuinely horrified when at last I felt out this thought. 'I won't say it'll be easy, being alone with Samuel if he gets into one of his fits, but if things get too awful I'll put him in his bed, take a deep breath, and phone you. All right?'

And that, it seems, is the best we can do. 'Besides, Q, you're going to have to get used to it – leaving him, I mean,' Tom pointed out. 'After all, in just three weeks' time, you'll be leaving him with somebody else *all day*.'

I smiled brightly, nodded, and pushed his words into a corner in the back of a box in the very furthest recesses of my mind.

10. Jeanie

They've gone, at long last ('Are you sure . . . Do you think you can . . . What about if we . . .').

Paul Dupont will arrive in approximately five hours' time, between midnight and 2 a.m. Since there are only two rooms upstairs I've had to move my belongings out of the enormous double bedroom I've been sleeping in so far into a wardrobe off the living room stuffed with a jumble of greying mops, rags, and a Hoover. I remade the bed for him (with matching sheets) then folded out the green sofa and made it up for me, working very hard not to mind the loss of my lovely room. Samuel is on the floor beside me in his bassinet, blessedly asleep.

It's quiet as a church in here. A striking relief from the madness of the day. Q is winding everybody up at the moment, she radiates stress, it's crackling like electricity in the air. Thank goodness she's gone out. Think I'll pour myself a very large glass of wine. And have a nice, long, relaxing shower. It's *so* lovely to be alone for a change!

Oh my. I blame the glass of wine. Or no, maybe it was the order of things; I should have had the shower first and *then* the wine. As it was, with a heavy dose of Chardonnay thickening my brain, it seemed a perfectly good idea to leave my clothes off after the shower and stretch languorously along the sofa with magazines and a simple but rather fabulous meal of fresh fish, olives, bread and cheese.

I looked up at half past eight, conscious of a sudden chill, to find the front door open and a tall man staring wide-eyed at my utterly, entirely, inarguably naked *arse*. I did what I suspect any woman would do, yelped and started violently, at which point I unfortunately knocked my plate off the sofa-bed and on top of Samuel's bassinet. He began to scream as if his head had been bashed in, and I was in the unfortunate position of deciding whether to rush off the bed and pick him up, thereby giving the strange man an even better look at my naked body, or of rushing to cover myself with a sheet, which would have the unfortunate appearance of heartlessness and which might leave Samuel in a state of injury for longer than strictly necessary. My better self came to the surface and I hurled myself off the green sofa-bed, shouting, 'Look away, you git!' before scooping Samuel up; he – thank God – was entirely unmarked. However, he continued to scream with such passion and intensity that, in something of a panic, I frantically pulled his eyelids apart with my thumb and forefinger, trying to remember if his pupils should be *large* or *small* after a blow to the head.

At which point the very superior man staring, fascinated, at my bosom said, 'For Christ's sake, naked lady, why are you torturing that poor child?' Summoning up a haughtiness I didn't know I possessed, I drew myself up as tall as I could and (struggling to cover myself with my right hand while clasping Samuel against my breast with my left) asked him who *he* was and what he was doing in *our* house?

The supercilious man casually dropped a black duffel on the floor, pulled his flamboyant red-and-gold tie loose, then said that it was his house and he supposed he could come into it whenever he liked.

Fair point, I suppose. It suddenly struck me that my fig-leaf (so to speak) was rooting around at my breasts, trying to suck milk out of my nipples. The lack of milk in the expected place was clearly beginning to bother Samuel, and his cries redoubled in intensity; I held him away from my body, from my resolutely unmaternal breasts, and he began to cry even harder. As embarrassing moments go, this one was probably the most memorable of my life. There was that time with my ex Theo when the next-door neighbour called the police because he heard . . . no, no, this one takes the biscuit.

After a few mortifying seconds, the horrible man (Paul, I suppose I should call him) remarked, over the din of Samuel's screams, that he didn't know Tom was hosting a colony of naturists, but that I should feel completely free to pursue my interests in his house in future.

I threw him a withering gaze (although there wasn't any marked withering on his part, I have to say). 'Please turn your back,' I told him, coldly. 'I'll put on some clothes and then I can deal with this poor child.'

'Well, all right then,' he said with equal coolness, 'but frankly I've seen what there is to see.'

It was starting to feel like something out of a bad farce – or, worse, a porn movie, according to whose script I should suddenly appear, for no clear reason, to be overwhelmed by the need to drop to my knees and – well, you get the point. Obviously I wasn't anything of the sort, although there was a sort of look in his eye which suggested he might be familiar with the script, and ever-so-slightly wondering if the fantasy of a dark moment was about to be realized. Pah. I sort of waved Samuel in front of his face to remind him of the baby's presence, since I have long observed that infants are a reliable passion-killer. It might have been the waving, or it might have been Samuel's hysterical efforts on my behalf, but either way, after a moment or two, Paul silently handed me my pyjamas, which were mixed up with a damp towel on an armchair, and then turned his back. I put the hysterical Samuel down in his bassinet for two seconds, hastily pulled on the pyjamas, then began the long, long business of calming him down.

When, eventually, he had hiccoughed and burped himself into a state of relative calm, I looked up to find that Tom's ghastly friend had vanished. Thank God, I thought to myself, relieved; with any luck he's gone to bed. Or, even better, gone out. To kiss his boat goodnight, or whatever it is rich people like him do. At that very moment, I heard the sound of voices in the kitchen: Q and Tom were back.

Q rushed into the sitting room in a vast clucky panic. 'Samuel – is he OK? Jeanie? How did you get on?' she asked hurriedly, peering down at the moist bundle in my arms.

I conjured up my most confident smile. 'He was – um, ah – fine,' I told her, crossing my fingers tightly behind my back and hoping the heavens would forgive me. 'He slept a bit, cried a bit, you know, the usual stuff, nothing to worry about.'

'Really?' she asked, relief lightening her eyes. 'He was OK?'

'Of course—' I began, but then I stopped because the horrible man suddenly appeared in the hallway. Q and Tom turned in surprise at the sound of his footfall.

'*Paul!*' cried Tom. 'We didn't expect you for hours!'

Paul, who had now changed out of his work clothes and into a pair of jogging pants and a T-shirt, strode forwards and shook hands with Tom and Q. 'I met my deadline early, so I got a head start on the Friday-night traffic leaving Manhattan,' he explained. 'I arrived to find your friend – oh, sister-in-law, I see – tending a peacefully sleeping kid,' he went on calmly. 'Quiet as a mouse.'

Q beamed at me, Tom threw me a look of purest gratitude. Behind their backs Paul looked over at me and grinned a slow, fiendish grin.

No embarrassment at his earlier behaviour, my God! He should clearly have backed out of the room as soon as he saw me in my buck nakedness, then kicked over a few buckets before clunking up the front steps swearing loudly. He should have sworn blind, if asked, that he didn't see a thing. Abject dishonesty was the only honourable course available to him. What an awful man! It made me miss Dave even *more*.

11. Q

Tom and I were on our very best behaviour last night. We avoided the topic of parents entirely, concentrating on less contentious subjects: holidays of the past, for instance, and Samuel's undoubted superiority to all other children. We licked butter from oysters and gorged ourselves on hot plump fries while gazing across the expanse of the Sound, which glittered like a pale opal in the fuchsia lights of the setting sun. We drank cold white Chilean wine, purchased hastily from Sam's Package Store, in plastic water cups until the sea seemed somehow to become a part of my head. We swayed home, warm and together, Tom and Q, a couple again.

'He's a good kid really,' Tom said, picking up on our earlier conversation as we wound our way slowly along the dark driveway. Tall pines reared up all around us, black and still; beneath them, in the red earth, lay pine cones sticky with sap. Before us, at the end of the winding dirt path, surrounded by maples, the house glowed like a giant pearl in the moonlight. 'And he seems so much more alert than he used to be.'

'Did you notice how his eyes swivelled when you came into the room this evening?' I asked proudly.

'Yes. And I really think he heard that gull on the deck this morning!'

After sharing a few more moments of equally dizzying brilliance from Samuel's short life, we fell into contented silence.

Sometimes it is easier to see your infant's perfections when he is not right in front of you.

'*Have* you thought about what you want to do after Crimpson?' I asked suddenly.

'N-no,' Tom replied slowly. 'That is . . . no.'

'What does that mean?'

'It means – it means I can't make any decisions until I know what *you're* going to do, Q.'

I stared at him. 'Come again?'

Tom stopped, and took my hands in his. 'Just what I said. Are you going back to Schuster? Or – not?'

There is such a noise and a jostle in the forest at night; when you stand still it seems as though every leaf, every patch of undergrowth, is bursting with life. There was a rustling some-where behind me, and I turned a little nervously to look; a skunk ambled unhurriedly from between two trees, stopped and gazed at us for a moment, then resumed his course, his white stripe sharply defined in the moonlight. Other, even smaller animals scurried as mere shadows beneath the lowest boughs of the pines. High above, we heard an owl's jubilant call, then the desperate squawk of some little animal. An acre away, a dog clinked his chain, and someone's screen door opened and closed.

'You think I'm *not* going back?' I countered at last.

Tom shrugged. 'I can't see it, quite frankly. You've been losing interest in corporate law for months, if not years. You hate half the people you work with. You can't bear to leave Samuel for twenty-five minutes. Why on earth would you go back?'

'Because – because – they've paid my maternity leave,' I said helplessly. 'Because it's my job. Because I don't know what else I would do.'

Tom half laughed, and put his lips to my hair. 'I'm the one

who's been effectively fired, but you're the one who most needs to quit, Q. Least, that's how it looks to me. When you were on bed rest I was frightened by how quickly you forgot your working life. The moment you walked out of the office it was as if the whole thing slipped straight out of your mind.'

'That's not *quite* true.' I was defensive.

'No, but almost. What do you *want* to do? If you could do anything in the world, I mean? Save gorillas? Teach high school? What?'

We had begun walking along the driveway again, and at this moment we rounded the final corner to see an unknown car parked in the driveway. I had opened my mouth to answer Tom, but as soon as I saw the car I forgot everything: for about three minutes, as I charged breathlessly up to the door, heart thumping, hands shaking, I thought of nothing but our son: was this a doctor? But no, no, of course not; it was only Paul, who had arrived a few hours early from New York. As soon as he walked into the sitting room, he was like a refreshing spirit from another life, his thoughts full of work and gossip, of boats and sailing, of sports drafts and deals and rookies and the new season. Tom's face lit up immediately. 'I'm so glad to see you!' he said happily, and the two of them went out on to the deck.

I fetched a bag of tortilla chips the size of a pillow case for them, then took myself off to bed with Samuel. As I lay in the darkness, I could hear their laughter echoing around the silent, watchful ranks of moonlit pines. (And all too soon, my little son's wails joined them.)

61

12. Jeanie

I have made it clear to Paul that his Harvard-University-*GQ*-spread charms don't work on *me*.

I heard him with Tom outside last night. He was talking about dining with some Supreme Court Judge last month, about going to Washington to meet with White House lawyer-types, about being asked by Bill Gates to advise on some charitable committee ('I said, Bill, sorry, just don't think I have the time . . .'). Tom was clearly impressed. It sounded like humbug to me.

He came inside to fetch some ice just as I was about to go to bed; I was standing by the kitchen sink, filling a glass with water. I stiffened as I caught sight of him. 'Hey, Jeanie,' he said softly, coming up behind me and standing a *little* too close (I felt his breath in the hairs of my neck), 'I'm sorry about earlier. Really. I was a bit – um – surprised when I walked in.'

I moved away, and stared him down. 'You behaved *despicably*,' I told him. (Actually I stumbled a bit, added a syllable, and came out with 'despicabibly', but I think he got the point. Note to self: avoid polysyllabic words in moments of high drama.) 'We have to live in the same house for the next few days, I realize,' I went on, reaching for the tones of an English grande dame, Peggy Ashcroft perhaps, or Maggie Smith as an E. M. Forster Edwardian, 'but I can *assure* you I shall avoid you as much as I possibly can.' We looked at each other for a moment, then I turned on my heel and left the room with the fuck-you poise of one dressed in rustling silks. (It's unfortunate that I was wearing my bunny slippers at the time, but I'm fairly sure my cool demeanour overcame the effect of the pink floppy ears.)

Frankly I think he has an ulterior motive. He clearly imagines a few polite words and a cocked half-smile are enough to win me over, most likely into his bed. He's about to learn that English women are more discerning.

Americans seem to think the British are uptight, but I've yet to meet an English lad half as uptight as these American city types. Work is what defines them. I can't quite tell what they do for kicks, or if they even like having fun. While other Americans are busy pursuing happiness, to these men it seems almost incidental. They're so busy working they've forgotten how to enjoy life.

Take Paul, for example. He's tall and slim, with muscles, but not the muscles of a man who spends his life in the hot oily place under a car. Oh no. Paul has the small, tight, well-defined, perfectly proportioned biceps of a man who attends a sleek white gym in Manhattan. Who sweats discreetly while sliding polished shiny dumbbells up and down a polished shiny rack. I can see him now, wiping three drops of rogue perspiration off his forehead with a fluffy white towel slung casually around his neck. Because he won't want to get his high-thread-count organic cotton T-shirt dirty, will he? Certainly not. He's got a certain standard of personal grooming to maintain. He finishes his circuit then pops into the sauna to open his pores, I expect, and before he heads back to the office he slips a comb of citrus gel through his hair.

This is not the kind of man who'll pull a sickie to take you to the zoo. He probably spends eighteen hours a day at work, gets home at midnight, gives his slumbering wife a chaste kiss, then leaps out of bed at 5 a.m. to face another exciting day of contract negotiations. His idea of living is counting the zeros in his bank account. Meanwhile his wife is probably shagging the doorman and his children are snorting cocaine to get over the unbelievable, ineffable *boredom* of life. This is not the kind of man to appeal to me. And I think I've made that completely clear to him.

Dave, on the other hand, is a different story entirely. 'When d'you want me to come over to America to see you?' he asked me excitedly on the phone.

'You can come out any time you want,' I replied, wondering briefly what Dave would make of this home of rich, elegant whiteness. He's a T-shirts, work-boots and newspapers-on-the-table sort of man. 'But I think you should aim for sometime next month; go for halfway through my trip to split the difference. Limit the amount of time we're apart.'

'Good idea, I'll look into tickets. And you said your sister will help with the cost, right? Bloody marvellous, tell her "thank you" from me. I can't wait to see you, Jeanie. I can't stop thinking about you, to be honest. The bed seems so cold without you.

'I'll feel like a bit of a hypocrite, though, going to Heathrow,' he went on, earnestly. 'Badger's mate Ranger has been telling me all about the environmental impact of air travel. He's, like, an expert; he spent two weeks last year kipping on a runway to demonstrate against Terminal 5. He's seriously *hardcore*. Did you ever think about how many gallons of fuel are used over three-and-a-half thousand miles, Jeanie? And the *injurious* effects of it all go *straight* up into the atmosphere! Still, there's no other way I can get there, I suppose, and I can't wait four bloody months to see you . . .'

I could see him in my mind's eye biting his jagged, worn-down fingernails. 'Dave, I'll have to leave that decision to you,'

I told him, rather impatiently, 'but personally I think politics have to yield to practicality sometimes.' That sounded rather good, so I said it again. 'And anyway, there's bound to be some research you can do out here – you might gain a whole fresh perspective on – on – on the Kyoto Agreement,' I finished, inspirationally.

'True, true . . .' I could tell he was impressed by my argument. 'Well, I'll see what it'll cost, and perhaps I'll ask Ranger to look into the number of gallons an aeroplane really uses on a long-haul flight, then I can make an *informed decision*. Or' – he thought for a moment – 'maybe I'll just say "bugger it" and come over, what do you think?'

I laughed, and told him that sounded like the best plan.

13. Q

'Q, are you awake?'

I pulled the covers over my heard and pretended not to hear.

'Sweetheart, it's eleven o'clock. And it's a beautiful day.' My husband had tiptoed into the room and was peering hopefully into the duvet. 'Paul has a suggestion . . .'

I half opened my eyes. 'What is it?' I growled.

'You don't have to come. I think Jeanie would stay home with you, if you want. So don't feel . . . I mean . . .'

I groaned, clutching my forehead. I had the strangest sensation of having a metal sword lodged inside my brain after the night's terrible screaming. '*What?*'

'Well, Paul has to take a boat to his friend's house this morning, further along the coast. He's going to help him replace some rotten wood in the stringers. His name's Adjile – did you ever meet him? Ex-CEO of G-Metrix dot com? Well, anyway, he's offered to take us all sailing – that is, Adjile's offered to lend Paul a boat for the afternoon so he can get some time on the waves. We could all go. But only if you want, of course.'

I thought about this for a moment. Adjile Olawe . . . 'The baby needs more time outside,' I said at last, throwing back the covers. 'Vitamin D and all that. We should go, it'll be fun. And I'd *love* to try sailing. I don't really know how to do it, but perhaps you can show me?'

Tom's face was transfigured.

I dressed myself quietly – Samuel was miraculously sleeping – and went downstairs to find Paul and Jeanie sitting silent, side by side, in the kitchen. Paul was leaning backwards in a chair, reading the property pages; Jeanie was working her way through a tottering stack of waffles. 'Are you going to come with us today, Jeanie?' I asked.

Jeanie looked up, her face smeared in syrup. She's rather taken with American breakfasts. 'Wha—? Oh, you mean this sailing business,' she said, through a full mouth. 'Well, really' (swallowing hard) 'I suppose I should, but I've always thought boats were just big toys for men with too much money,' she added airily, as if she'd been giving the matter a great deal of thought over the course of a very long life. I stared at her. 'Yes, the consumption of resources and the – er – damage to marine eco-systems from the – um – rudders is positively shocking,' she finished triumphantly. She launched into another waffle.

'Well, we'll all understand it if your political principles prevent you from coming.' Paul had put down his newspaper. 'I wouldn't want you to do anything that makes you *uncomfortable*, Jeanie. I'm sure between us we can help Tom and Q with Samuel, so why don't you just stay here? We'll spend the day sailing on the Atlantic, enjoying the views of the house from the sea (it just won another design award, Q, did you hear?) and you can work on that press release on – what was it you were telling me about? – oh yes, whales' dental cavities, instead.'

Jeanie choked slightly. 'Well, obviously I would under normal circumstances,' she explained carefully, 'but Samuel has been tricky recently, I wouldn't want—'

'No!' returned Paul, banging his hand on the table for emphasis. 'You stay here. Adjile and Lily aren't your kind of people anyway, from what I can tell you'd be shocked by their way of life. They have a personal chef. The desserts are phenomenal, I had this thing with iced chocolate last time that was beyond description. Amazing fish too, fresh caught in the Atlantic. Plus Adjile has a world-class wine cellar, the quality of his champagne beats anything I've had in New York; he sponsors a small family operation in Épernay. All that conspicuous consumption would make you sick, Jeanie, obviously. Much better to stay away. Have lunch by yourself. I think I saw some brown sliced bread in the fridge.'

He went back behind his newspaper. Jeanie put down her waffle carefully, and turned to me. 'Q, love, I think I will come today, in spite of everything, because you look very tired, and I came here to help.' She wiped her sticky mouth on a napkin and smiled virtuously at me. 'And I promise you I will keep all my *deeply held* political ideas to myself today, you don't need to worry. I would *never* embarrass you with your friends.'

I thanked her faintly as I slithered into a chair and helped myself to some breakfast. Paul glanced up over his newspaper, folded down a corner, and looked at her with his head on one side. I wondered what he was going to say, but then, 'You've got some syrup on your face still,' was all he remarked, coolly, and, reaching out, he wiped Jeanie's cheek with a deliberate finger.

14. Jeanie

I love sailing. I am *brilliant* at sailing. Paul told me so.

Dave would probably have been horrified if he'd seen me today, speeding across the Atlantic with a man who wears a gold signet ring on his pinky and designer linen shorts, but Dave wasn't here, and I'm allowed some fantasy time before I settle into life as an Eco-Warrior's spouse, aren't I?

Because it was a fantasy day. I could almost believe I imagined it, except for the sunburn on my shoulders and the fact that the sitting room is still rocking beneath my feet.

Q turned out to be surprisingly amenable to the idea of a trip along the coast followed by a sail ('Don't know what Samuel will make of it but I'm bored to death of sitting in the dark'), so at 11 a.m. we bundled ourselves into Paul's huge olive-green SUV, a boat attached to the back, and drove fifteen miles along the coast to a small peninsula. Just as the road seemed set to end in the Atlantic ocean itself, Paul took a winding, pitted dirt track that led across rocky ground, past clusters of sparse pine trees, to a set of stone gateposts; at the end of a short driveway a huge modern house reared up against the rock, with vast glass windows overlooking the ocean. Adjile (made millions in his dot com start-up, retired at twenty-nine) greeted us at the front of the house dressed in oil-stained clothes with a very charming smudge on his nose and fabulous manners. Mrs Adjile, aka Lily, emerged after a few minutes dressed in similarly stained shorts and a tight ruby-coloured tank-top. 'I'll get on to Ricky about ordering new spinlocks,' she told Adjile briefly, before reaching up to give Paul a big hug. As she turned to us with a warm smile I discovered with a sense of shock that she had *gold eyes* – literally, gold eyes, set beneath high-arched brows. Other than that she was quite normal looking: tanned skin, muscly legs, narrow shoulders and a wide chin – but still, *gold eyes*! Paul, Tom and Adjile vanished off to attend to Paul's boat while Lily offered us lunch on a long hot cedar deck strung across the rocks. We watched the green waves bubbling beneath us while slurping seafood with wholegrain bread and fresh white butter served on ice. Tom and his friends reappeared after an hour or so with the satisfied air of men who have wrestled with machinery and won.

I'm a practical English girl, but I was in serious danger of losing my head. If Una could only see me now, I thought as I flicked out my white damask napkin and sipped at my flute of sparkling rose-coloured wine.

After lunch, Adjile and Lily took us down a steep rocky path, then across the beach to their dock, a long wooden walkway with eight boats bobbing gracefully beside. The air was filled with the noise of their creaking and flexing as the water flopped lazily against the barnacled posts of the dock. The boats were a range of sizes and shapes, and Tom and Paul spent a few minutes exclaiming excitedly over Adjile's new purchase, a 'Tornado catamaran' (which looked nothing like a boat to me, but still). Adjile, Lily and Paul had a quick discussion about which 'craft' Paul should take, finally settling on something called a Flying Dutchman. I was pleased because it was, in my opinion, by far the prettiest, a picture postcard of a sailing boat with a gleaming mahogany deck and bottom and a long, attenuated prow. Adjile unlooped the boat's rope from around a big cotton reel affair while Paul rummaged about in a wooden chest for life-vests. 'Who's coming first?' he asked, when he finally emerged, laden with fluorescent padding.

Tom grinned, bursting with child-like pleasure, and raised his arm. 'Me, me, pick me!'

Paul laughed. 'OK, of course you'll come, Tom, but I can take one more—'

'Go, Q, go,' I said, smiling, 'I'll take Samuel,' and I pushed her gently towards the boat. She smiled back at me. 'If you're sure . . .' she said, with a tiny show of reluctance. 'Of course, I am,' I replied briskly, removing her wriggling bundle from her arms. 'Samuel will be fine with me. Have a wonderful time!'

It seemed suddenly perfect, this golden day in the golden light of the hot wood dock, my tummy full of pink wine and fresh bread and salty fish. Samuel blinked and lifted his head unsteadily as I pulled him towards me, then settled down on my chest with a long sigh. The water began to lap vigorously against the dock as Paul sprang on to the boat. Tom and Q strapped themselves into their life-vests, then Tom helped Q manoeuvre herself gingerly on to the deck to join Paul. After a quick conversation about who should steer ('You wanna go first?' 'No, that's OK, I'll take us home'), Paul settled himself at the stern and took the tiller while Tom started winding and pulling at things energetically; three blinding white sails flew up the masts. They flapped and cracked excitedly in the warm sandy wind; Tom tugged on something blue, and obediently the sails smoothed into an elegant curve. The boat slipped away from the dock in a frothy emerald green trail.

We watched them go, then Lily turned to me with a smile. 'Would you rather come up to the house or wait on the beach for your sister?' she asked, slanting her sparkling golden eyes against the sunshine. 'You're welcome to come inside if you'd like, and we can help you with Samuel, if there's anything we can do for you . . .'

Now, I rather fancied poking about in their fancy architect-designed house, but in the end I decided to wait on the beach. A private beach, of course. Officially, I disapprove of private beaches. Natural phenomena should be for everybody to enjoy. Unofficially – don't tell Badger! – they're rather nice. So I followed Lily back along the dock, down a small flight of uneven stone steps and along the beach to a pair of brightly-striped and padded chaise lounges beneath a pink umbrella. Lily disappeared, then came tripping through the dunes a few minutes later armed with a bowl of warmed pistachios and a glass of something orangey with lots of ice in it and a large slice of mango. It might or might not have had alcohol at the bottom. I sipped at it while Samuel investigated my necklace, and watched the bright white boat slipping simply and easily through the greenish-grey crests of the ocean.

They were out for over an hour, during which time Samuel dozed, pulled my hair, filled his nappy, and generally behaved himself remarkably well. Then, just as he was starting to whimper and root hopefully at my breast, I discovered I could see Tom's shock of dark hair and Q's auburn curls. The boat was getting closer; Tom was bringing them in.

I crunched back along the sand and arrived in time to see Paul helping Q jump over the side of the boat at the end of the dock. She tumbled out laughing; it's years since I've seen her so happy. She took Samuel from me with a broad smile on her face and a little bit of sunny warmth in her skin, freckles popping on her cheeks and arms. 'You had a nice time, I take it?' I asked her, with a grin.

'It was *fantastic* – so much fun. You go out now, Jeanie,' she said breathlessly, nodding back at the boat. Paul was waiting with the sails lowered, holding on to a boat hook thrown on to the dock. 'Yup, it's your turn,' Tom agreed. Like Q, his clothes were drenched. 'We'll take Samuel, have a great time!' he added, brushing the fine sandy grit from his legs.

I looked at them uncertainly. 'But Tom, you can go out again, or at least come with us,' I began, thinking, oh God, me and Paul on our own on the sea, how embarrassing, I barely know him, I've hardly made eye contact since he saw me posed like something out of a Degas painting. What on earth will we find to talk about? 'You love sailing!'

'I've had my "fix" for today,' Tom explained peaceably, watching Samuel nuzzling at Q's breast. 'And Adjile has invited me to come up here any time I want to sail, I think I might take him up on the offer.'

'So it'll be nice for us to have some time to ourselves now,' Q added cheerfully, setting off towards the beach. 'Wait; no that sounds awful, I don't mean—' She stopped and turned around, looking confused. 'Oh God, I'm sorry, Jeanie, if you really want one of us to come of course we will . . .'

'No, no, I just thought you'd want another go,' I explained hastily, picking up Q's abandoned life-jacket from the wood planks. I took a deep breath. Fine, I thought, strapping myself into the slab of purple and lime green, I can do this. I can sail a boat. I can spend an hour with pig-man Paul on my own.

Paul watched me as I approached. 'Just you this time, is it? OK,' he called, coolly. 'I think we can manage. Climb aboard.'

Now that I was actually about to get into the boat, it looked unexpectedly large; I could swear it had grown. For the first time, too, I noticed all the baffling ropes in every hue from cherry to sunflower yellow, not to mention the clamps and hooks and other strange instruments dotting the boat. What on earth did they all do? Was I supposed to know? I investigated the bobbing surface of the deck dubiously, then, holding on to a dock post, reached out a cautious leg.

At that moment the sea seemed to sort of suck the boat down and away. There was a loud 'flub' sound; the boat creaked protestingly, and my leg landed in space. I threw my weight back on to the post, and looked disdainfully at Paul. 'Sorry, sorry, I'm *trying* to hold it,' he said, grinning, the muscles in his forearm flexing. 'Come on, hurry up!'

Holding on even tighter to the post, I reached my leg out again and then, half-closing my eyes, threw myself into the boat. I landed on the deck in an ungainly red heap, limbs sprawling, one foot in a bucket and my face (why, God, why?) smooshed into his lap.

'Well, that's one way to do it,' a voice murmured above me. I felt a wet gloved hand in my armpit, and Paul hoisted me up. 'All right?' he asked, and I nodded, the blood filling my cheeks. 'OK, good,' he said, as if ladies precipitated themselves into his lap on a regular basis. 'Sit over there, on the starboard, that's right, a little further back, ass over the side – perfect,' he explained, releasing the boat hook, and immediately water opened up between us and the dock. 'Now, look up there. Do you see that triangular shaped thing above your head? Hang on to that as we go. I'll do the rest.' His muscular legs were burned dark, the hairs blonde and fine, I noticed, as he arranged himself at the tiller once more.

He pulled on some ropes, the sails rose and swelled and suddenly the boat was moving; I barely had time to make myself comfortable before we began to really pick up the pace. I hung on to the triangular handle nervously, my shoulder tight and strained. A sudden spray filled my nose and my eyes; the boat was thumping across the water now, speeding out to sea in an exhilarating fizz of salt water and wind.

'Ready to come about?' he called after a few minutes, craning forward to make sure I could hear above the noise of the sails. I looked back at him, doubtfully. "We need to turn the boat all the way through the wind, make a ninety degree turn. I'll say "prepare to come about", then you duck right down, keeping your head clear of the boom – this thing – and get over on to the other side of the boat, same position as you're in now, OK? Prepare to come about – *About!*'

I ducked my head down beneath the boom as it swung sharply over, then (as elegantly as I could) scrambled up on to the opposite side of the boat. I'm not quite sure what was happening while I was on the gritty bottom of the boat but suddenly we were setting off in a completely different direction, out towards the open sea (on the first tack we'd been heading towards a cluster of small islands a few miles off shore). Getting comfortable on my new perch, I peered under the taut white sail. There was nothing out there, no boats, no islands, nothing in sight; just sea, sea, sea. The horizon stretched before me, endless blue passing into endless blue.

'It's beautiful out here, isn't it?' he called suddenly to me and, forgetting everything, I nodded, laughing for sheer delight as the water flew through my hair. 'This is my favourite way to spend a weekend, just me, the boat, the sea . . . cheesy, but true,' he explained, leaning towards me. 'I'm a stereotype from a Hemingway novel, I know. But I love the views, the sound of the boat, figuring out how to use the wind. What do you think?'

'I love it too,' I admitted, and he grinned, satisfied.

The water had an extraordinary effect on us. We sailed for another forty minutes, chatting about – I'm not sure really; things we like to do on weekends, countries we want to visit in the future, that sort of thing. The kind of conversation you have with a stranger when you sketch your personality for them, with a little bit of innocent exaggeration and some judicious gaps. Jeanie: fun-loving twenty-four-year-old. Paul: adventurous thirty-year-old. Speeding through the water, watching the wind in the sails, neither of us made the slightest effort to tell the other one anything more.

After a while he asked me if I wanted to take on some of the real work of the boat, keeping the sail taut in the wind, for example, by manipulating one of the cherry-and-white coloured ropes. And then (for ten glorious minutes) he let me take the tiller as well. I don't think I've ever felt so powerful. The boat was quick and responsive in the water, sensitive to the slightest movement. At one point I was distracted by a swift gust of wind and tightened the rope in my hands; for a second I found us up in the air, the sail almost horizontal beneath us, and I wondered for a shocking moment if we were about to go over. Almost by instinct, I let go of the rope and felt the boat lurch back down to the sea. A great rush of water splashed over the boat; I tasted salt on my lips, and pushed the dripping hair out of my eyes. I realized I was laughing, and Paul was laughing up at me too, although with a faintly quizzical expression. 'A bit close that one, Jeanie, not too close, but still –' he yelled over the wind. 'Just pull the sail in enough so it stops flapping, OK? I don't fancy telling Adjile we've capsized the thing, and it's a long swim home.'

He nodded back behind us. I looked over my shoulder; the coast seemed miles away, a thin silver strip already far in the distance. It was, indeed, a long swim home. I shivered.

Paul was watching me. 'It's been about an hour, we should probably go back, I'll take us home, OK?' he said gently, and he came over to me, nudging my damp body aside. Feeling suddenly very conscious of my arms and legs, not to mention my soaked clothes, I surrendered my position and slithered over to my old spot on the side of the boat and grabbed for the triangular hook. We sailed quietly home, watching the grey-green water thump-thump-thumping past us.

Q and Tom were sitting with Adjile and Lily on the beach.

As Paul and I approached we could hear them laughing. Samuel was half lying, half sitting on Q's lap, in a mercifully good mood. I could hear him burbling as he lifted his head like a curious tortoise at the spinning gulls in the blue sky.

Paul steered us towards the dock, lowering the sails to slow down the boat. Adjile had strolled over and was waiting; as we drew level with him he reached over and guided us in. 'Enjoy yourself?' he asked, tying off the hitches, and I nodded. 'It was just – *amazing*,' I said happily, and he and Paul laughed. 'Thanks, Paul,' I said, as he helped me out, 'thanks for showing me what to do. I had such a lovely time.' And then I turned around, biting my lip, embarrassed all over again – I sounded like an awkward English schoolgirl, for God's sake . . . I was also painfully conscious of the imprint of his wet gloved hand on my arm.

'Hey, Jeanie, wait up—' he called softly, as I walked away from him, wringing the water out of my hair. I turned around. He was unfastening his sailing gloves and stripping of his lifevest. 'You're a good sailor,' he went on, grinning. His eyes were glinting in the light of the sea. 'You've got good intuitions, you know?'

'*Have* I?' I started to say, eagerly, then flubbed it, stumbled over the words, and blushed again and again in spite of myself.

All in all (as I explained to Alison, in a hastily-dashed-off email when we arrived back, the words flying out of my fingers), it's a good thing he showed his *true* colours on the way home. Really, a very good thing indeed.

15. Q

'Hey, dude, I'll catch you later,' Paul said, shaking hands with Adjile. His lips touched Lily's cheek. 'Thanks, guys, that was a great day.'

'Always welcome,' Lily replied, laughing, and then she turned towards me, her extraordinary eyes sparkling. 'And it was so nice to meet you and your sister. I'm always *amazed* when I meet sisters who actually get along. My sister and I hated each other when we were children. To be quite honest, I don't think much of her now, either! She's such a catty little thing . . .'

We walked towards Paul's car, her arm linked through mine. 'Have you two always been friends?' she asked curiously. I was acutely conscious of the thin lightness of her body as we walked, her narrow waist, her tiny feet, her lustrous hair gleaming in the sunshine. She seemed almost to fly over the rocks.

I looked towards Jeanie and grinned. 'I think we united against a common enemy as children: Alison, our other sister,' I explained. Alison is hard to explain to new people; I thought for a moment about how to characterize her. 'She's the middle one. Married a minor aristocrat, so now she gets to throw a bit of mud at a wall and call it "art". No one likes to challenge her, of course, so she's become very – smug as an adult. Very superior. But very competitive as well, although she hides that part of herself from everyone but us.'

'Really? So there's a third. How funny,' Lily remarked. 'Isn't she terribly jealous right now?'

Funnily enough, this view of things had never occurred to me. 'I don't think so,' I said though, dismissively. 'Alison has far more important things to do these days. Great Sculpture to complete, for one thing. Of course, her stuff is *terrible*, isn't it, Jeanie?'

'Now you sound more like a sister!' Lily laughed, handing me into the car. 'Sisters see through each other like – like tigers through smoked glass. So I get it now. Alison's the odd one out. Well, I hope to meet her one day. Finish the puzzle. Put all the pieces together.'

'Not likely,' I returned, still trying to exchange glances with Jeanie, who had her back to me and was fiddling with something under her nails. 'Alison came out to see me a few months ago, while I was pregnant, and she made it very clear she'd have better things to do for the next decade than visit again. Jeanie and I don't get on with her terribly well, so we don't really care.'

Tom passed Samuel in to me while Paul helped Jeanie into the front seat. 'I can manage, thank you,' she said, a touch tartly, as he slid his hand beneath her elbow.

Paul shrugged. 'Of course. Whatever,' he returned, coldly brusque.

It was a small moment, but such is the strange chemistry of conversation that it somehow seemed to poison what followed. There was nothing I could put my finger on, but once the final goodbyes had been waved, and our hosts, arms around each other, had receded into the darkness of the starry evening, the good mood receded too. Jeanie, strangely agitated, seemed primed for a fight, and every conversational topic seemed to find her and Paul on different sides. Paul admired a house set high upon the bank; Jeanie thought it far too big. Jeanie liked a song on the

79

radio; Paul called it 'sentimental'. Paul mentioned that he loved to drive; Jeanie hissed about environmental damage. Jeanie sympathized with the travails of a famous popstrel who had recently lost custody of her children; Paul declared her a lunatic. Jeanie said London had the best food in the world; Paul shook his head and asked if she'd ever been to Hong Kong. And so it went on, and on. Jeanie: thrillers; Paul: detective fiction. Jeanie: musicals; Paul: theatre. Soon their arguments were beginning to get personal. 'I can't *think* why you—' 'Oh shut up, Paul, that's plainly *ridiculous* . . .'

By the time we pulled into the driveway, Jeanie was sunk into her seat with her arms tightly crossed around her body, radiating cold fury. Paul was sitting beside her with an air of insolent ease, one hand on the wheel, the other arm lying negligently across the top of her seat, holding forth on the merits of basketball (Jeanie having indicated initially that she preferred tennis). We unpacked ourselves and the baby in silence. Jeanie stalked into the house without unfolding her body, without saying a friendly 'goodbye' or 'thank you' to Paul, without even talking to *me*.

'Nice end to the day,' Tom said ruefully as we stumbled into our room. '*That* was fun. I mean, I'm sorry, Q, but your sister can be really immature sometimes. You can tell she's twenty-four, can't you? *Crazy* behaviour. One minute everything was fine, the next, for no reason at all, she starts scratching at Paul.'

Of course I objected to his characterization ('You were twenty-four yourself not so long ago,' I reminded him) but I took something of his point. 'Do you think they're going to keep this up all weekend?' I asked at last, with a sigh, as we got into bed.

Tom opened his mouth to reply, but his whispered words were drowned out by – what else? – the sound of a very unhappy, very hungry, and very awake small baby.

I'm starting to think there is a great ledger in the sky, and that every moment of pleasure is balanced out by a wail from our miserable son. Oh look, says some awful malignant deity, peering down at us, Tom and Q have managed three minutes of happiness, time to poke a stick in that child's innards to make him scream.

'Are we nearly at twelve weeks yet?' my husband moaned in the cold white grey of 5 a.m.

16. Jeanie

One distinct problem of sleeping in the sitting room is, you can't lie in. I long for my pretty bedroom with its thick mattress and luxurious ensuite – but of course, I've had to give it all up to Paul. I heard Q and Tom and the baby squalling in the kitchen this morning at seven; my head was pounding. After trying to ignore them for twenty minutes, I gave up, and reluctantly presented myself. Ten minutes later, Paul himself emerged, showered, pressed and polished in smart linen trousers with a silky cotton shirt finished with silver cufflinks. Q and Tom suddenly discovered pressing reasons to take the baby outside, which left the two of us glowering at each other over the breakfast table. Looking at his elegant get-up I wished I was armoured in something more than just my pink gingham M&S pyjamas. I'm always underdressed around this man.

He lost no time in getting straight to the point. 'You talk a lot of crap,' he said airily, 'but I like the fact that you have opinions.'

This caused me, briefly, to lose my footing. 'Well, yes,' I said vaguely. 'Of course I do. *Lots* of them, actually.'

This didn't seem to be my strongest point, so I stopped and paid a great deal of attention to my mug, watching the teabag globe swirl a trail of brown through the milk. Paul cut himself a slice of bread, which he covered in a thin, even film of black-currant jam. 'What do you do for a living?' he asked, setting his perfect teeth into the sandwich.

Now let's make this clear: it was a little after 7.30 on a Sunday morning – not a time, you might think, for virtual strangers to start quizzing you on your life and career path. 'I'm going to be a social worker,' I said. 'You know, help people. Think about the needs of others. Devote myself to – um – social well-being.'

'I see. You've just finished training, then?'

'Yes. I have a Master's degree.' Well, almost.

Paul looked interestedly across the table. 'Really? So what kind of social work interests you? What do you specialize in?'

'Family issues,' I blurted, and then felt myself turn four shades of puce. 'That is, I think. Possibly. If I – that is, if I . . .'

'If you?' he prompted.

'It's very complex,' I said seriously. 'Government funding. Limited opportunities. Decline in welfare state. It's not easy to know what you're best at. Course only one year long. And – I'm only twenty-four,' I finished snappishly, detecting a faintly derisive glint in his eyes. 'I don't have to have everything sorted out yet, you know!'

'No, of course not,' Paul returned thoughtfully, collecting crumbs from the plate with his last square of bread. 'So you're done with your course, but you don't actually know what interests you. Perhaps' (tone very polite) 'you'll find out exactly what you want to do while you're here?'

'What's that supposed to mean?'

Paul looked absolutely innocent. 'While you're visiting Q, I mean. Perhaps you'll have some sort of epiphany, a magical moment, and realize your focus. Since I assume . . .' He paused.

'Go on,' I growled at him.

'I assume you're applying for jobs.'

'I applied for one in Cumbria a few weeks ago,' I said a little desperately, and Paul arched his eyebrows.

'Huh. Very interesting. In what town?'

I swallowed. 'Small place, you wouldn't have heard of it.'

'Try me. I know Cumbria quite well as it happens, I have an aunt from Kendal. I spent much of my childhood boating on Lake Windermere, pretending to be in an Arthur Ransome novel. Beautiful part of the country! Has there been much immigration in the area recently? What's the demographic these days?' He sat forwards.

There was that lecture on 'preparing for job interviews' held beneath the flickering lightbulb of Wolsey Hall 103, of course, but I slept my way straight through it. Una and I had hosted a particularly raucous party the night before (the police were called, but then, as Una said, if they *don't* thump the door down the music isn't loud enough). I woke up at one point to hear Professor Simscod talking about 'demographic surveys' for interview research, then slumped under the chair and went back to sleep with my head propped on my ring-binder.

'Cumbria is a – er – rural community,' I asserted now, hopefully. Cumbria is in the Lake District. Cumbria is known for two things, lakes and hills. (*Think of something, think of something . . .*)

And then (it was as if a light had gone on in my head), 'You know, there are some really interesting parallels between Cumbria and Connecticut,' I continued, determinedly wrestling my serpentine adversary. 'That is to say, youth centred in urban areas, older people in the countryside. I think there are fascinating opportunities for research, actually. For an – um – *comparative investigation*. In fact I'm hoping to get more *perspective* on those *compelling* cross-cultural issues by doing some volunteer work here next week.'

Paul looked definitely impressed. 'Really? That's fascinating. Where will you be working?'

There was a small card in a shop window the day Q and Tom and I first went into Sussex. 'Summer Volunteer Wanted, Ten Hours a Week'. 'I'm going to work as a volunteer assistant at the Quiet Lanes Elder Care Home in Sussex,' I announced superbly. 'I'm very much looking forward to it. I'm intrigued to see how geriatric care – um – happens in Connecticut. Cumbria; Connecticut: I think the similarity is more than just beginning with C, you know? I think there's a potential research paper here. I'm going to look after Samuel and help Q in the mornings, then work at the Home in the afternoons, and in the evenings – I've got a political blog to write!'

Paul wiped his mouth carefully, took a last sip of his coffee, and stood up. 'Then you are a very energetic young woman. What's your blog about?'

'Oh, it's an activist thing,' I said airily. 'You wouldn't be interested. Right now I'm writing a piece about ships' fuel. And – um – clouds. Big dark clouds. With rain in them. In fact, I really need to get back to work on it, so if you'll excuse me . . . *thank* you . . .'

I stood up and walked past him out of the kitchen, leaning up against the wall in the hallway once I was out of sight.

Safe. As long as he doesn't ask me for the web address of my blog, that is (if the worst comes to the worst, I'll have to direct him to Badger's www.ecowarriorsunite.blogspot.com, although then he'll probably think I'm insane. Badger's stated goal, in big black type across the banner head, is to 'smash a fist in the ugly face of the Industrial Revolution'. He has several postings on the evil threat to world peace posed by electricity). And as long as he doesn't come back next week and ask why I'm not down at Quiet Lanes, washing old dears.

After wiping my face and splashing water into my eyes, I went outside. 'Are you and Paul on better terms yet?' Q hissed at me anxiously, suddenly appearing from the garden with Samuel strewn over her shoulder. Her sunhat had slipped down rakishly over one eye, as had his; they looked oddly twin. 'We thought we'd leave you two to sort it all out. The sparks were flying last night, my goodness . . .'

I was just beginning to scoff at the idea of sparks (the man is as boring as a drill bit, really) when I heard his voice unexpectedly close behind me. 'I wanted to find you,' he said coolly to Q.

I slipped myself into the hammock on the deck – I don't care if he heard! – armed with a fat, fragrant copy of *Vogue*.

'I wonder if you and Tom could spare me a moment?' Paul went on politely. 'I have a proposition to put to you both.'

Q, looking surprised, explained that Tom had gone on ahead to the beach. 'Let's walk on together and find him, then,' Paul said, gesturing with his hand for my sister to walk on down the steps. 'You see, I've recently heard of a job opportunity that – it's just possible – may interest you *both*.'

When they'd gone, I called Alison to tell her everything. 'He sounds awful,' she agreed energetically (I could hear Geoffrey pulling the cat's tail in the background). 'What an awful man. So snide, so condescending! Why do you think Tom is even *friends* with someone like that?'

17. Q

Paul is mad. I didn't know this until today. Maybe not quite mad, but certainly delusional. Funny how little you know of a person.

Tom is inclined to agree with me but says he's reserving final judgement. 'I've known Paul a long time, Q, from long before he became a superstar lawyer,' he remarked, helping me slip back into my cardigan after nursing Samuel to sleep. We were sitting on the beach at the time, my back pressed against a hot rock fuzzy with dried seaweed, and Samuel's head was lolling back on my arm. 'I've never heard any murmurs about his judgement, you know, from anyone at Prince. Or from people at other firms, for that matter. He's always viewed as the soul of discretion, a man of discrimination, intellect and plain common sense. But this . . . !'

Paul and I had walked along the seashore together to find Tom, Samuel tucked into a baby carrier attached to my chest. The waves were a bright sparkling green; the gulls were wheeling smoothly in the warm air above us, and the sea was dotted with white sailing boats. At first we crunched along the shells in companionable silence.

'I've got an idea: hear me out, OK?' he began. 'A friend of my father's owns a small law practice in Cheasford, a small town just along the coast a few miles from here. Kenton Tyler – that's his name – is looking for someone to take it over so he can retire. He's hoping to find one lawyer – or a couple, ideally – willing to work with him for a few months, get the ropes and the feel of the place, and then when the clients are comfortable with the transition he'll pull out and let the new people take over the practice.'

I frankly gawped. 'You don't mean – you *do* mean – wait, Paul, do you mean *us*, taking over a law practice, here? Tom and me? *Here?*'

Paul glanced down at me. 'Tom told me the other day he was tempted to consider a serious change of career path. He says he can't hack hundred-hour weeks any more. And you know, there's a lot to recommend life up here, Q: cheaper real estate, more square footage, not to mention good, safe state schooling. The usual benefits of suburban life. Didn't you grow up in the countryside? Ah – there's Tom . . .' and we saw him just ahead, skipping stones across the surface of the water. He was bent down, knees almost in the damp sand, with a small pile of rounded rocks collected beside him. As he let the stones fly, with a practised flick of the wrist, there was an expression of intense concentration on his face.

'Hey.' Tom looked up at Paul's voice, then stood up to face us. 'Hey.'

'Walk with us,' Paul suggested, and Tom dropped the stone in his hand. It fell with a soft *tink* on the pile he had amassed. The three of us – four, since Samuel was drooling gently into the front collar of his carrier – set off along the edge of the waves.

Tom listened to Paul's account of the firm, its client base, its advantages and disadvantages, and Kenton's own personality ('Kinda eccentric, but a good old-fashioned lawyer'), then caught my eye behind his back.

'You should go and meet him,' Paul was saying seriously. 'You wouldn't have to make a commitment up front. You could live here, in this house, for as long as you need, and spend a few months with Kenton to get the feel of a rural practice. Of course it would mean resigning from Crimpson . . .'

I recognized the settled patience in Tom's expression. 'Very kind of you to think of us, Paul, thanks. But when Q and I said we were thinking of a change I don't think we meant anything quite as dramatic as *that*,' he explained. 'We were thinking of another pair of firm jobs, or perhaps Q will take some time off for a few years.'

'Another firm job? Get real.' Paul picked up a large rock and threw it overarm, hard, into the sea. There was a pause, then a sharp answering 'plop' in the deeper, cooler part of the sea, fifty yards out from the shore. 'If you take a job at a less prestigious firm you'll work fractionally shorter hours for substantially less interesting work, Tom. And if Q takes time off, she'll effectively quit the field. Law partners don't take kindly to "mommy breaks".'

Again, for a split second, Tom and I exchanged looks.

'Seems to me you haven't fully grasped the reality of your situation,' Paul was saying, picking up another rock and letting it fly off into the sea. The water splashed; a surprised gull leaped into the air. 'Lawyers don't work flexi-time, not in a Wall Street firm! It's time to get real.'

'Paul,' Tom replied, assuming reasonable tones, 'that's obviously true, but Q and I are overqualified for a rural practice. Just because we're parents now doesn't mean we want to spend our days drawing up wills and divorces, you know! There's got to be a job that will let us work flexible hours, but that we'll still find interesting, challenging . . .'

'Name it,' Paul said coolly. 'And as for Kent's job: you think you're overqualified to work here? You think rural practice is boring? OK, if that's what you think: go and meet Kent, I dare you,' he added. 'See what his practice has to offer, then do a cost-benefit analysis. Don't reject the idea out of hand.

'But look, I do have other suggestions,' he went on. 'Justin Van der Bossche at Prince was always a fan of yours, Tom; so if you want to go back to "big firm" law, I'm sure he'd be willing to interview you.'

Tom looked up sharply; I could tell he was flattered. 'Justin? Really?' he asked, surprised, and Paul nodded.

'He was very impressed by the way you handled the Maccabee brothers a few years back. Oh, and in the meantime, I can suggest some consulting work, I have useful connections at DeVelt which might help you span the transition from Crimpson. If you want to resign.'

Tom and Paul walked on along the beach, two tall figures with hands thrust deep in their pockets, while I settled myself down to nurse Samuel, who was beginning to wail. I looked out to sea, thinking about a return to late nights and early mornings, a return to seeing each other on weekends, of packing my overflowing mother-love into a rushed kiss over breakfast toast.

I'm due to go back to Schuster in less than three weeks. Tom's holiday from Crimpson will be over next week.

'Of course he's quite insane,' I offered, when Tom finally came to sit beside me, and Paul had taken himself off to his dock to start working on one of his boats. Tom nodded, gentling our son with tender fingers, as the gulls shrieked and cackled and fluttered in a great white whirlwind at the sound of poor Samuel's wails. 'We can do better than small-town law,' I went on firmly. 'I mean, what kind of a life could we have *here*? The whole idea is simply ridiculous!'

18. Jeanie

Dave phoned first thing this morning to say he's found a cheap flight, and is coming out in five days' time. 'It's a bit sooner than we planned, obviously, but it's a special offer. This week only,' he explained, his voice brimming with excitement. 'Plus Ranger says this airline is investing in researching cleaner fuel options,' he added virtuously. He paused. 'Although, to be honest, I'd have bought the ticket even if they weren't. Bugger the environment. I can't *wait* to see you, Jeanie, I miss you so much. Gotta get my hands on you . . .'

'My boyfriend is flying out to see me,' I told Paul airily. 'This weekend.'

'I'm pleased for you,' he replied calmly, and I flushed.

'He is an environmental warrior,' I went on severely. 'He's very hard core. We'll probably go and demonstrate in Washington against . . .' I frantically rifled the back pages of my mind for something to demonstrate against.

'Air travel?' Paul offered innocently. I scowled.

I was already a little overwrought because I'd had to spend several hours with Paul by myself while Q and Tom went out shopping. Extraordinarily, Paul's office was actually able to do without him for a *whole Monday*. 'Are you sure you can hack it, sitting around here with me doing nothing?' I asked him, once the sound of the car had receded. 'I mean, don't forget the brevity of life!' I went on sarcastically. 'A day sitting lazing in

91

Connecticut is a day you have failed to earn a million dollars on the stock market. Did you think about that?'

Paul looked up at me over his paper. He was sprawled comfortably on the window bench in the kitchen at the time. 'Thanks for worrying about me, but I have an excellent stock portfolio,' he said calmly, sipping at his small white cup of espresso. 'My money will be working hard for me all day. I assume you also have your savings safely invested?'

Of course, I returned coldly, wondering frantically whether I'd ever actually got around to filling in that retirement sheet thingie the bank gave me when I graduated. I mentally cast an eye over my current financial position. One current account, overdrawn to the tune of £562.47 (last time I checked); student loans totalling £16,902; contents of Abbey Savings Account (established for me by my parents when I was born, and regularly rifled since for stereo/bike/shoes/booze cruises): £123.89. I can't honestly say my money is 'working hard' for me today, since it barely exists. I gulped and threw him a discouraging look before leaving the room for the washing machine in the small laundry area just off the kitchen.

'Do you want me to hold the baby while you do that?' He was standing just behind me, I realized, in the door to the laundry room, and was watching me clutch Samuel in one hand while attempting to fold clothes with the other. We've had washing piling up for days now; Q manages to get it all into the machine but then loses the plot when it comes time for the sorting. (I've actually found her in tears over the socks. 'So many of them! And they never match! And half of Samuel's simply evaporate into thin air!' I promised her I'd get on top of it all today, although I'm increasingly inclined to agree with her that the washing machine subsists on a nourishing diet of baby bootees.)

'Of course not, I'm managing perfectly well,' I said, testily, to Paul's outstretched arms. 'You go back to your serious newspaper reading. I wouldn't want to disturb you.' I put Samuel down on the floor on a soft bed of towels and went back to my folding.

Paul sat down on the tiles beside me with a pile of washing in his arms. 'It's fine, I'm happy to do it. I'll start work on this,' he said calmly. 'I'm pretty good at folding. Although . . .' He plucked something out of the tumble of clothes. It was my knickers, of course, and it had to be the pink ones, didn't it, the ones my flatmate Una gave me last year, with the words 'Access All Areas' in white fluff on the front. The ones I wear when everything else is in the basket. I blushed three shades deeper than the undies and snatched them out of his hands. 'I don't think there's enough here to fold,' he said, all innocent bewilderment, and as he was holding on tight to them they sort of *pinged* as I pulled. I turned magenta.

'Get off,' I muttered furiously, scrunching the offending undies into a package roughly the size of a postage stamp.

'Sorry, I apologize,' he said, his expression sweetness itself as he picked up a shapeless grey T-shirt instead. 'How about I do Tom's clothes? That seems safer. You do the rest.'

We sat in silence, folding. There is something indescribably embarrassing about sitting next to a man with your underwear accumulating in small piles between you. He walked around my lacy bras with an excessive carefulness that simply drew my attention to the fact that he was, actually, very conscious of them indeed. Look as much as you want, I told him scornfully with my eyes, because you ain't going to see me *in* this stuff.

'Must be almost lunchtime,' he said with a yawn, when the stuff was organized at last into four separate neat piles – plus a selection of lone baby boots in fifteen hues of blue. 'Why don't we walk into town? We'll pick up sandwiches for everyone, there's a new little gourmet place I've found. And you can show me the place where you'll be working.'

I secretly thanked the heavens that I'd thought to telephone Quiet Lanes Elder Care Home last night – I excused myself when everybody else was eating, correctly anticipating from further experience of Paul that I might need corroborative information. I told the woman who answered I wanted to ask about the position, only it turns out you don't need to do anything so formal as submitting a form, because the job is unpaid and thankless, and basically involves emptying bedpans and singing 'America the Beautiful' and helping with knitting. 'Gee, this is just *wunnerful*,' Mrs Forrest (manager of Quiet Lanes) said, when I explained my background. 'We usually just get sixteen-year-old girls who can't tell a knife from a fork. They do their best, but they keep trying to talk about iPods, y'know? I'll tell the old folks today you might be coming, they're gunna be *psyched* . . .'

I was left with the uncomfortable suspicion that by leaving my name, age and telephone number with the said Mrs Forrest, I had not only applied for but been given the job.

'In fact,' Paul went on cheerfully, 'if you want, we can go in and meet the old folks; I bet they'll be thrilled to see a baby. My grandmother was always transformed at the sight of children. My sister's little boy used to have an extraordinary effect.' We both looked at Samuel, who was just embarking upon one of his fits, purple and thrashing. 'Well, maybe not today,' he conceded after a moment. 'But the walk will do him good at least,' he added. Five minutes later I found myself walking, Samuel dressed and strapped into his buggy, down the driveway, along the road, and into Sussex. Paul achieves an awful lot through sheer force of will.

The sidewalk was narrow; Paul's arm was pressed close to my shoulder. Cars whizzed past us. I was conscious of Paul glancing several times down into my face.

'So tell me more about your boyfriend, Jeanie,' he said, at

last, when Samuel had mercifully slipped back into sleep, his poor tiny face streaked with tears.

'What do you want to know?'

'Are you serious about him?'

'I – yes,' I said. 'I mean, he's very kind, and he loves me, and we have fun together. I know you think I have to have every-thing worked out at twenty-four, but I don't, and for the time being at least, fun and laughter are enough for me.'

Paul laughed. 'Point taken. Actually, fun and laughter sound more than enough, they sound positively good. I didn't have anything like that at your age.'

'Perhaps you were too busy working.'

'Perhaps.'

'So what about you?' I asked suddenly, looking up at him, smiling roguishly. 'Is there anyone special in your life?'

'Yes, there is. She's called Tina. She's a musicians' agent.'

'I see. And why didn't she come with you this weekend?'

'Because she's speaking at a conference in LA.'

'Oh. Is she very important?'

'Very.'

'Is she very beautiful?'

'Very.'

'Oh.' I'd sort of imagined a different reply, something along the lines of 'No, she's not very pretty, just terribly competent.' Now I felt crestfallen, outdone by the absent Tina and her mani-fold talents and charms. She was obviously very glamorous. I sneaked another quick look at him, at his elegant clothes, his handsome face, his heavy brows, his pronounced cheekbones, his long eyelashes. Of course his girlfriend would be stunning. Of course she would be successful. 'Are you going to get mar-ried?' I asked disconsolately.

For the first time since I'd met him, Paul looked confused, even wrong-footed. He coughed. 'Uh – well, you're not the first person to ask me that question, let's put it that way,' he said at last, with a slightly strangled laugh. 'It's – nothing's fixed.'

'I see.' I didn't really. Was the gorgeous Tina less committed to him than he was to her? Or the other way around?

He had paused for a moment, and was standing by a wooden fence overlooking the sea; I retraced my steps, reversing the buggy, and went back to join him. On the beach below, a sun-wizened man was just hauling in a catch of opalescent fish. We watched the bloody, slippery bodies tumbling out of his net on to the wooden deck. 'Actually—' he began, but at that highly interesting moment, a horn beeped loudly behind us, and the car that had just passed stopped, reversed, and metamorphosed into Tom and Q.

'Where are you going?' Q shouted, falling out of the passenger seat in her haste to see Samuel. 'What's going on, is he all right, how has he been doing, is he hungry, why's he wearing new clothes, what happened to his bunny, oh there it is . . .'

Paul and I exchanged amused glances for a fraction of a second – Does she think we can't take care of a child? How silly! – and then I busied myself explaining everything that was needful to Q. She decided she wanted to walk the buggy back to the house, and suggested I take the car home with Tom.

My brother-in-law's face was cold and cross; they'd clearly been arguing. Q was barely looking at him. Paul, after a second's pause, offered to walk home with my sister. There was no room for three-abreast on the pavement so, feeling vaguely cheated, I opened the front door of the car and got in beside Tom.

'What's going on, then?' I asked him, as we pulled off.

He kept his eyes firmly fixed on the narrow bending road.

'Nothing much,' he replied coldly. There was a pause. And then, keeping his eyes straight ahead: 'I love my son, but God, Jeanie, I need a change of scenery,' he blurted. He rubbed a hand over his eyes. 'I don't know how much longer I can take this, to be honest. I have to get out of the damn house, have something else to think about. I mean, what does she think I am? Does she think I can take this – the screaming, the yelling, no sleep – indefinitely? Some days I think I'll just go back to Crimpson . . .'

He stopped himself, biting his lip, then glanced down at me for a second. 'Forget it, Jeanie, this isn't your problem,' he went on, in a tight, hard voice. 'Obviously we'll work something out soon, I mean, she understands, right? She understands I need challenges in my professional life. *Obviously*.'

We drove on in silence. I couldn't quite think what to say.

19. Q

'So you are enjoying motherhood, then, darling?'

Alison's tones were silkily insinuating. In my mind's eye I could see her, sitting at her burnished eighteenth-century desk in the sunny alcove of her expansive study, overlooking a discreet south London garden. A huge oak nods in at the window. The carpet beneath her feet is spotless deep-pile white, the sort that swallows every sound, and as she leans back in her chair, the cable of her old white telephone flexes gently. There are home-made sugar biscuits on a plate of thin bone china at her elbow, a cup of pale tea idling in her hand, and a smile of deep self-satisfaction on her lips.

At this unfortunate moment in the conversation, just as I was summoning up a particularly breezy account of my life and capabilities as a mother, Samuel, resting in my lap, began to cry – loudly. This put me in a tricky position, not least because the phone kept wilfully flinging itself away from my reach. 'He – er – he has his *moments*, of course, but generally he is an – er – easy – um – very easy child . . .'

Alison listened to the yells in silence for a while, then decided to start diagnosing his distress from her lofty perch three-and-a-half-thousand miles away ('I was an unusually attentive mother, I could just *feel* what my children needed. I think it was a gift'). 'He sounds tired,' she asserted, at which point I almost hung up the phone on her because he'd only just woken up.

When she heard this, she switched tack and went down the usual list of causes of babies' crying, which, as I pointed out, in a voice that was testy in spite of my very best efforts, I was perfectly capable of doing myself.

'Well, that is strange,' she conceded at last, sounding unusually unsure of her ground. 'Quite peculiar!' And then (I could hear self-confidence flooding back into her voice): 'In that case, Q, are you sure there's nothing wrong with *him*?'

I spluttered wrathfully in response to this; I did not tell her, of course, that just last night we took Samuel to the hospital, that Tom and I have been worrying for days, weeks now, that something's really wrong with our son. 'Alison, don't be so ridiculous,' I said instead, as forcefully as I could. 'Something wrong – just because a baby cries! Hahahaha! Which one of us is the first-timer here, hmm?'

I won that battle, I suppose, but I put the phone down sweating and disgusted with myself. I don't mind snapping at Alison's heels over clothes, money, Mum, Jeanie – the usual territory of sisterhood, in other words – but I don't want to drag maternity into the mix. There's something particularly horrible about using children as soccer balls, bouncing them backwards and forwards from one side to the other. Still, Alison brings out the worst side of me; she always has.

It was at nine o'clock last night that we heard the first yell from the bedroom. At half-past midnight, Tom strapped Samuel into the car and drove him around winding lanes while Jeanie and I collapsed in the kitchen with a bottle of wine, feeling hellish. At 1.45 a.m. Tom arrived back with – we heard the yells before the car door even opened – a child in a truly frantic state. His face was covered with a sheen of saliva and snot, and he seemed to have developed some sort of rash around his eyes. His legs were drawn tightly up to his chest, and his yell was a horrible monotone.

Tom handed Samuel to me with a grey face. 'We must take him to the Emergency Room, Q,' he said, and his voice was clipped, the tones of a man on the edge. 'It's been five hours now; he cried the *whole* time we were away. I stopped and cuddled him, I put music on, I drove with the windows open, I took him to listen to the sea, I hummed in his ear like a giant frigging bumblebee: nothing helped. We have to take him up to the hospital, Q, this *can't* be normal. Let me just change my shirt. He threw up all over this one, twice.'

I sent Jeanie to bed and stepped out into the cool night air with our poor suffering child. The thought of setting foot in a hospital with Samuel was horrific: tests, needles, wires and IVs; but on the other hand, maybe someone could *help* . . .

We strapped him back into the car seat and drove to the nearest hospital, a brick box building fifteen miles away humming with low-level night-light. The entrance to the Emergency Room yawned like a giant neon mouth atop a dark circular driveway. Tom parked while I ran in and delivered our details to the strained-looking triage nurse through a cacophony of yells. ('He won't stop crying.' 'I can see that'.) The bunch of drunks in the waiting area took one look at us, then moved as a man to the other side of the room.

I stood in the blue-carpeted sea of the waiting room, swaying slowly backwards and forwards, rocking Samuel in my arms – my beautiful, perfect child. The only time I'd ever been in casualty before was when I was thirteen and smashed my finger playing netball at school. I was torn then between the novelty of the experience (an X-ray! Maybe I'd even get a cast!) and the fact that my finger hurt like hell. Plus until my mother arrived I was attended by Mrs Gilbert, the games teacher, who wouldn't stop grousing about the fact that Priscilla, her shaggy golden retriever cross, needed to be let out for a pee.

'What did you do?'

I heard a whisper behind me, and turned to see Tom, clad in a fresh T-shirt, Samuel's change bag slung over his shoulder, staring at me open-mouthed. Following Tom's gaze, I looked down to discover Samuel sleeping quietly at my breast. The hospital's harsh white light showed every blotch on his pale, tired skin, but already we could see that the dark red clouds around his eyes were passing.

'How in God's name did you do that?'

Samuel muttered slightly, stretched, and snuggled more closely into my breast. I blinked dry eyes. 'I've no idea!'

Tom drew me carefully to the hard metal chairs, and we sat together, staring in profound silence at our sleeping son. 'Should we wait to see a doctor or – go home?' I whispered, eventually, while Tom shook his head slowly from side to side. He was shaking.

'I truly thought he'd *never* stop,' he intoned. 'Never, ever, ever. Never.' (The woman next to us glanced at him, drew her jacket fractionally away, and muttered something distastefully about 'getting all types in here'. Since she was garlanded head-to-toe in green toilet paper I thought this not entirely fair.)

Both of us were utterly beyond the point of decision-making. We sat for another half-hour, staring at Samuel, making half-hearted efforts to stand up, failing, stumbling back down – at which point we were called, fortunately enough, to see a sympathetic young doctor perched on a trolley in the corridor. 'No fever, heart rate's good, blood oxygen is good,' he told us, 'and Samuel's not crying now. Colic. Bound to be. But check with your own doctor if you need reassurance.' He waved at us cheerfully before rushing off to deal with a woman who had half a wine glass sticking out of her face.

'Q, gotta do it, gotta call th'doctor in the morning,' Tom pointed out numbly as we dragged ourselves into bed at long, long last, an hour later. 'Describe it all, what's been happening.

Appointment. Arrange appointment for when we go back to the city. Check-up.'

'Tom,' I said, pausing with one leg on the bed, one on the floor, '*Are* we going back to the city after next week? For good, I mean?'

Silence. And then: 'Whaddya saying?'

'Just what I said. Are we really going back?'

'What else?'

'Stay here.'

'*Stay here?*'

'Yes.' There, I'd said it.

'Christ. For how long?'

'I don't know. But I – I was thinking I could call Schuster, put off my return. And then you could call Crimpson, tell them you'll be taking more holiday. Just a few more weeks. Because I . . . need more time. Here.'

This time, a very long silence. 'Q' (chewing his lip) 'I *can't* take more than one more week. And that's a push. No one takes a three-week vacation, not at Crimpson. Not even for a honeymoon. I mean . . .'

'So ask for just one week then,' I interrupted. 'And then . . .'

'And then?'

I didn't reply as I levered myself into bed, just contented myself with a vague 'I don't know' as Tom, in the middle of a thought, collapsed into unconsciousness. All I really know is, I need more time off work, and so does Tom – time to think, time to relax. He needs to learn to unwind. (Well, that's what I'm telling myself. And really, why should I be the only one yelled at?) And I said nothing of this to Alison, either, when she called; nothing about the storms of crying, the hospital, or our lengthening holiday. Alison is one of those people who glide through life unaffected by trauma or crisis, someone who never seems called upon to wrestle big decisions. She couldn't possibly help me. She doesn't need to know.

20. Jeanie

Well he's gone, and apart from the fact that that poor child of my sister's is obviously in the throes of some terribly serious illness, all is well.

'I can't tell you how pleased I am to hear about that volunteer work you'll be doing,' Paul said on Monday night, just as he was heading out of the door. Tom and Q were clustered behind him, thanking him for his hospitality, his extended offer of the house, etc. etc., when he paused and turned to me. 'In the retirement home on Quiet Lanes. It's so great to think that you'll be giving something to this community.'

Tom's mouth had fallen open; Q looked bewildered.

'Didn't you know?' he asked, quivering with apparent surprise. 'Jeanie's going to be helping out with our senior citizens at Quiet Lanes. It's a great place. She has a wonderful idea for a research project, don't you, Jeanie? Well, goodbye then,' he finished, flashing me a smile as big and sparkling as the Koh-i-Noor as he put out his hand. 'It was so nice to meet you! Good luck on the comparative study. And I hope your boyfriend has a wonderful visit.'

Tom stared at the door as it closed behind him. 'What the—?'

'*What* are you going to do, Jeanie?' Q asked in bafflement, and of course I was stuck, wasn't I, with having to agree with the preposterous story.

'I – er – yes, well, nothing's definite, but I've given them a ring, they've suggested I go for an initial visit, so, maybe . . .'

My incoherent wafflings were cut off by Q, who turned to me with an unexpectedly positive face. 'I think that's a *fantastic* idea,' she said firmly. 'You can't spend all day listening to Samuel wail, it's too much for anyone. You need a break from it. And since you haven't got a work visa, volunteer work is a great way to get out of the house.' She smiled. 'I'm so glad, Jeanie. Plus it will be a wonderful opportunity for you to get more experience of caring and welfare, and it'll look good on your CV when you get back.

'And I don't feel so guilty about keeping you in Connecticut, now you have this job,' she added this morning, when she outlined her new plan to keep us all up here for a further week at least. 'If it wasn't for the job I would feel terrible, but it's really wonderful to think you're making a place for yourself here, that you have something to keep you occupied for a few weeks. Actually, we're thinking ourselves about doing something similar. Well, Tom is . . .'

'Bedpans here I come,' I muttered ruefully to myself when the door closed behind her.

Then I began sketching out some questions to be addressed in a comparative study of Cumbria and Connecticut, just *in case* Paul ever appears here again:

1. Compare contributions from government versus contributions from patients' families as percentage of total cost in homes in the two places. [I copied this question from a course paper, and I think it sounds quite impressive.]
2. Compare job descriptions of care managers. How much caring?
3. Compare roles of nursing staff. How much nursing?
4. Compare facilities. Size of televisions, etc.
5. Compare numbers of patients in total, and

6. Number of patients on average in homes across the two regions. [Not sure my maths is up to this, I have to say. I've been thinking wistfully about the years I spent sucking Liquorice Allsorts under the desk instead of paying attention to the dour Mrs Grindley at school.]

Right, time to start digging about on the web, I thought to myself; I could even go to the library, that way if Paul comes to stay – just to be on the safe side – I shall have concrete facts to draw upon airily in conversation. 'Yes,' I shall say brightly, 'I have discovered that only point-four per cent (factoring in the cost of living, taking the rate of inflation into consideration) of geriatric care is administered locally, demographically speaking.' I could even call that lady who runs Quiet Lanes and ask her, maybe she'd fill in a questionnaire!

Alison was very impressed when I phoned her to tell her all about it, although we ended up spending rather a lot of time talking about Samuel and Q. She was really worried when I told her all about the hospital trip, and made me describe in achingly minute detail exactly what the doctor said and how Tom is behaving ('Do you think their marriage will survive?'). But she thinks I'm doing a marvellous job finding a way to set myself apart from other candidates at the interview stage, and even suggested her husband might be able to pull a few strings for me in the government. Really, she's a very handy sister sometimes.

21. Q

'Why are we doing this? Remind me,' I moaned to Tom this morning, unpeeling myself, exhausted, from the bed. 'Because for the life of me, I *cannot* think of a plausible reason.'

'I know it's a little – er – strange,' he returned soothingly, 'but just think of it as meeting a new person. It might be interesting. We can – er – investigate new opportunities. Consider the other side of the question. Assess the practicalities of rural legal practise.'

I could swear I heard him mutter something under his breath about 'stopping the walls from frigging closing in' as he started to get dressed.

Authorized by Tom, Paul phoned the day he left to set up a meeting with the friend of his father's from law school, Kenton Tyler. 'You're not making any kind of a commitment,' he reminded me cheerfully. 'You'll just get a good, honest sense of how small-town law compares to big firm life. You can weigh up the benefits and see how the job might mesh with your changed priorities. And if it's not something that interests you, well, there's no harm done, is there?' I glowered at him.

Over the course of the last couple of days, we've gathered the strangest collection of oddments – baffling fragments – about the old lawyer. 'Old man Tyler?' Marie, the fisherman's wife, said, when we bumped into each other at the farm stand. Her eyes widened. 'He's . . . Let's just say he's a character. A particular –

type – of character.' The lady in the general store gave us a searching look as soon as I mentioned his name, and muttered something about Jose Cuervo. The girl who serves us our gas at the local station giggled, told us her mother knew him, then blushed ferociously. The state trooper's face tightened into blankness. 'Kenton Tyler is connected with half the people in the state, *one* way or *another*,' he said severely, before stalking off down the street.

In spite of my misgivings, though, and my exhaustion, dressing for the meeting was oddly fun. I stripped off my stained T-shirt and Gap shorts and kicked off my grey trainers. Then I slipped myself into an outfit I purchased the week after the baby's birth: a pressed linen skirt, a white cotton shirt, a light blue jacket, all two sizes bigger than my normal size but not – blessedly, not! – maternity wear. I looked at myself in mirror. I looked bigger than normal but, well, not bad. After a good deal of thought, I also donned a pair of heels. Then I brushed my hair, pulling out the worst of the tangles, and twisting what remained into a creditable chignon. I rubbed my grey face with foundation, brightened my eyes with mascara, and – from the depths of my make-up bag – produced some lipstick to give my face some colour. Then I added a pair of earrings, a handbag, instead of a change bag . . . Tom looked me up and down as I entered the kitchen, feeling intensely self-conscious; he raised an eyebrow, but he didn't say a word.

Samuel was restless and distressed before we left. I'm sure he could sense something unusual was happening, and anxiously I tried to calm him. 'Shut up and don't worry,' Jeanie admonished me severely as she wrestled my wailing son out of my arms. 'Of *course* you can leave him with me. I'm sure he's just a bit windy. Now get out!'

I watched her in the side mirror as we pulled out of the driveway, competently hitching Samuel over her shoulder, her hand carefully guarding his still-shaky neck, then settled back against the seat with a sigh. Jeanie is right. I need to switch off my mummy radar – my ma-dar, so to speak – for a few hours.

Our journey to Kenton Tyler's office took us several miles along thickly wooded roads. Clapboard houses flashed past, some old but many new, set on manicured green lots with purplish shrubs lined beneath the windows. Enormous cars sat hot and shining in the sunshine. Children thumped basketballs against asphalt; dogs panted in the cool on the edge of their yards, where clipped grass gave way to thicketed wetlands veined with brooks. Every few miles we glimpsed small lakes glinting through the trees. Dilapidated farm stalls offered tomatoes and cucumbers for sale, and bunches of flowers, wilting gently in the damp warm morning heat.

'There's a good French restaurant a few miles away,' Tom told me, turning left at a small triangle of yellowing grass. 'I drove past it last week; it looked OK, at least. Well, everyone round here raves about it!'

A sign outside a gas station announced that we were entering Cheasford, a small town sprawling around a simple old white church and a thriving general store. Half a mile on, we passed the large wooden general store in the centre of town, turned right, then pulled into a small apron-shaped strip with a pizza joint, a brake specialist and a dry-cleaner's fronting the car park. In the distance, just visible through the large back windows of the restaurant, was the ocean.

In the corner of the strip stood a squat, square, three-floor building with a small weather-beaten sign outside the door and a thin row of hot pink impatiens peering uncomfortably through a heavy carpet of red cedar mulch. The first floor, we learned from the sign, were the offices of Luna Lilly, Reiki Specialist. Julie's Hair Emporium occupied the second (a thick draught of hairspray and singed hair wafted down from her windows as Tom opened the car door). The third floor housed the law offices of Kenton Tyler and Associates, LLC.

'This is it, then,' said Tom bracingly.

The building's painted aluminum door was white and peeling, with a large clear glass panel in the centre. Inside we could see a small, square, anonymous blue hallway, adorned with anonymous plastic flowers in an anonymous glass vase. On the right side of the hallway was another door, on the left a flight of stairs.

There didn't seem to be a buzzer, so Tom knocked. Nothing happened. He knocked again.

The door on the right slowly opened. A face appeared, followed by the body of a short but lugubrious-looking woman in her fifties with suspiciously blond hair restrained by a velvet Alice band. She observed us for a second or two, then opened the front door. 'May I help you?' she asked in honeyed tones, blinking in the daylight. A heady scent of sandalwood swirled around her loose purple cotton robes and silver-fringed shawl.

'Thanks; we're here to see Kenton, the lawyer on the top floor,' Tom explained. 'May we come in?'

The woman rolled her eyes. 'I s'pose I'll have to let you, because he never opens the door. The stupid old FART,' she yelled, suddenly. 'Thinks I'm his fucking SLAVE, he does, fucking moron, drunk old BASTARD.' Luna Lilly jerked her head in the direction of the upper floors. 'He can HEAR ME, I know he's fucking LISTENING TO THIS, pretends he doesn't hear the door, the lazy ASSHOLE!' She was now standing at the bottom of the staircase, holding on to the banister and craning her head up the stairs. 'You hear me, I KNOW you do!' she yelled furiously, shaking her fist, 'and you might as well know this, you old fucker, don't come running to me with a bottle of Kahlúa the next time your ex-wife calls, I'm not doing it again, you bastard, last night was the last time, y'understand? You hear me up there? NEVER AGAIN!'

She turned round, fixed us with a disapproving gaze, then disappeared in a swoosh of purple print and heavy perfume. Somewhere above us, we heard the click of a door opening. '*Is she gone?*' a low voice called.

Tom gave me the kind of look a man gives the woman he's sent, purely by accident, to the guillotine. 'Umm . . .'

'Mr Tyler, is that you? We're friends of Paul's,' I called, setting off up the stairs. 'We're here to talk to you about your practice – Ah! Hello.' I shook hands with a short man with impish blue eyes and a long white ponytail who was hiding, quite unashamedly, behind the third-floor door.

'Hey – good to meet you, come on in,' he said, grinning, pushing a strand of long white hair behind his ear. 'Sorry about that' (with a nod down the stairs) 'we have a sort of – er – love/hate relationship, we're in the hate phase today, it'll pass, but I sorta keep outta her way until it does.' He beckoned us into a small square office thick with stale cigarette smoke. We could virtually see the nicotine curling and expanding, yellowly, in the dark dusty air.

Tom retched. Kenton peered round me to look. 'You all right, young fella?' he asked concernedly; Tom waved his hand vaguely. We stumbled into the middle of the room like children in a fairy tale, our eyes slowly accustoming themselves to the gloom.

The office was lined with about fifteen tottering bookcases from which law books and trial transcripts spilled. Towards the window, on the right side of the room, stood a heavy, over-crowded desk, behind which Kent was now sitting; in the middle of the room stood two red, threadbare velour arm-chairs. Through a door in the middle of the opposite wall we could see a brown metal desk, an orange-cushioned metal office chair and an old computer; this, presumably, was the secretary's office, although there was no secretary anywhere to be seen. A clock ticked loudly by the window. It was twenty minutes slow.

'Sit down, sit down,' Kenton said cheerily, waving at the red chairs. Both were covered in books, ashtrays, yellowing news-papers and – most extraordinary of all – socks. We stared speechlessly at what looked like a month's collection of them, dirty and unmatched, spilling over the arms of the chairs and on to the floor, falling out of every crevice like so many mag-gots.

Tom seemed to have lost all power of speech. I swept the socks casually off the chair on to the floor, lowered myself down and looked expectantly at Kenton.

Comfortably ensconced behind his heavy wooden desk, he was nodding and smiling approvingly at me. Tom subsided into the second armchair.

Kenton picked up a smooshed pack of Marlboros from the table, slid out a cigarette and lit it with a flamboyant *swish* of a match. 'Now then, you two,' he said after a long drag (and a pause for a luxurious exhale), 'I'm meeting you because young Paul suggested I should. I wouldn't normally waste my time on a couple city lawyers, frankly. Still. Why don't you start by goin' through your experience?'

It suddenly struck me, from the attentive look in his eyes, that this was a job interview.

Tom was staring at Kenton with the fascinated look of one confronting a lunatic. I knew what he was thinking. Kenton interviewing *us*? Kenton investigating *our* credentials? Shouldn't he be down on his knees, thanking us for considering taking on this nowheresville practice of his? Us – us! With our degrees from Oxford and Harvard, our years of London and New York City experience . . .

'It's a pretty challenging job, this one, make no mistake,' Kenton was saying judiciously, leaning back in his chair with his fingertips lightly together, cigarette stuck to his lower lip. There was suddenly an enormous snapping sound and the chair pitched backwards, smacking its occupant's head into the window-sill behind the desk. We caught a glimpse of a pair of bony ankles above yellow checked socks as the seat flew into the air. Moments later, Kenton's face reappeared as, with a practised tug on the underside of his desk, he righted himself. 'Must get that fixed,' he explained coolly, reaching around to his seatback and clicking it back into place. Cigarette still glued miraculously to his lip, he tucked a few loose strands of hair back behind his ears with yellowed fingers. 'It may look easy to you, but there are challenges a country lawyer faces that'd make you city types blench. Frankly, I'm not sure you'd be up to it,' he went on severely. 'Do you have your résumés with you?'

Tom made an odd gurgling sound.

'Well, no, we don't,' I explained sweetly. 'Truthfully,' I went on, 'we're not sure if this is a life for us or not. We don't feel ready to apply for your – ah – very interesting position just yet. Perhaps you could describe an average day here at the practice first?'

Kenton nodded. 'Makes a lotta sense, a lotta sense,' he said judiciously. 'Well' (locking his hands behind his head) 'we get some pretty tricky divorce cases, and there're probate problems to be worked through, figuring out how to divide up money between taxes and all the members of a family; some you know about, some you don't – heh heh . . .' He chuckled, and took another long drag on his cigarette.

Tom and I exchanged glances. The odd messy divorce and a trip to probate court once in a while . . . it sounded like a life-time of soul-crunching boredom or an easy way to earn a buck, you could take your pick which way to look at it.

Kenton's face, I suddenly realized, had developed an unexpectedly knowing leer. 'Think it sounds pretty easy, don't you?' he said, leaning forwards towards us. '*I* know what you're thinking, you two! And there's something in it, I suppose; you won't be dealing with multi-million-dollar mergers up here, it's true. But you need something else to practise in these parts, something I don't think – I could be wrong – you two actually have.'

Tom was alert now, sitting upright. I knew what he was thinking, of course. Half of him was frankly disbelieving. The other half was thinking: A hoop I'm being told I cannot jump though! I *must* prove I can jump through that hoop . . .

'What's that, Mr Tyler?' he asked. 'What's that?'

Kenton stuck his cigarette in his mouth and took a long drag. 'D'you know, young man, I don't know if I fancy telling you,' he said slowly, and then, his face splitting into a grin that would not have shamed a Cheshire cat, 'In fact, I've thought about it, and I'm sure I don't!'

22. Jeanie

Dave is coming in two days!

'I'm going to hitch down to Heathrow in the morning to mimimize my carbon footprint,' he told me seriously. 'Ranger's idea. And then I'll hitch up to Connecticut from New York.'

'Dave, I don't think you can hitch in America,' I said faintly. 'Everyone'll think you're a psychotic killer. You'll probably get *arrested*.'

'Then I'll try to persuade a policeman to give me a lift the rest of the way,' he returned cheerfully, and I gulped a bit, because I can't imagine any of the heavyset men with guns and razored hair I've seen around here consenting to chauffeur a loony Englishman.

'Dave, honestly, I think you're more likely to get chucked in jail,' I explained nervously. 'And when you come into the country, for goodness sake, please don't wear your "FUCK AUTHORITY" T-shirt, I just don't think it's a good idea, they have all these cameras in the immigration area . . .'

'Oh, Jeanie, don't be such an old woman,' he said impatiently. 'I think they have something called Freedom of Speech over there, right? Honestly, love,' he went on, 'don't worry about me, I'll be fine. I'm really looking forward to it, they give you free drinks on the plane, right? And you can show me around the area. I've never been to America before, never been out of Europe. Only time I ever travel is when England is playing away!

Ha! Perhaps we can do some trips – if it's all right with you, of course. And if we can lever ourselves out of bed, which I'm not at all sure about. God, Jeanie, every time I think about—'

'I have things to do, Dave, I'm about to start volunteering at a geriatric home,' I cut in, feeling suddenly rather uptight. 'I can't just – I mean, of course I'll show you around, but I do have to help Q. Remember I have responsibilities here.'

'I know, I know. And I can help as well,' he said earnestly. 'I like kids. Funny little scraps. But I really want to enjoy this holiday, Jeanie. I've spent the last three days dealing with my mum, y'know, full time. Poor old sod, she's been very demanding. Yelling the place down, most days. Dad needed a break, so I've been doing it all on my own – apart from Ellen, of course. Thank Christ for her. If she wasn't there to help I don't know *what* I'd have done.'

'Really,' I answered, not rising to the bait.

'Yup. She's such a helpful lass, so – so warm an' understanding.'

'Really,' I repeated. I could hear Dave's irritation grow.

'Mmm. She's been a rock for our family, and she's a pleasant sight at the lunch table n'all. "A good-looking, strapping sort of girl," as dad puts it.'

'Well, isn't that nice. You can all ogle her over the meatloaf.'

'Is there something wrong?' Dave exploded at last.

'Of course not,' I said, feeling tetchy.

'I mean, are you getting your period or something? Because you're being really difficult at the moment.'

'What, because I refuse to ask you what colour Ellen's suspenders are this week?'

'No, because – because – I don't know why, but you just *are*.'

By the time we put the phone down on each other ten minutes later, we were thoroughly out of sorts; we barely said 'goodbye', just sort of harrumphed at each other. It's been a little while since I saw Dave, and it's not surprising we aren't rubbing along as well as we normally do. There's been so much going on in my life these past few weeks. Me here, him there. It's going to take us a while to get back into the swing of things when he arrives. You have to expect a difficult transition.

In spite of that, I'm really looking forward to seeing him. He's promised to stop off at Una's and pick up my favourite red dress, for a start.

23. Q

The young woman was short but lean, her pale yellow hair tucked into an untidy pony-tail. She was dressed in faded jeans and a baggy pink-stripe T-shirt that bore the signs of many meals' cooking. On her feet were a pair of scuffed flip-flops; a pair of large gold hoops dangled from her ears. A scar like a sideways T ran across her nose from one cheek to the other. The nails on her left hand, I noticed, were bitten down to the quick.

It was the Thursday afternoon after our visit to see Kent, and I'd left Samuel with Tom while I went to pick up some food. I saw the yellow-haired woman standing in front of me in the queue at the general store, grabbing on to the wrist of a little boy of about four. His dark brown hair was cut short, and he was wearing a pair of green combats and a Spiderman T-shirt. Sticking out of his pocket was a rough, faded, well-worn scrap of blanket. He was pulling away from her, trying to prise her fingers off his wrist, while she simultaneously hunted with her free hand through an open bag slung over her shoulder. 'I swear I don't know what's happened, Katie, I had more coupons somewhere . . . Paulie, honey, stay *still* . . . !'

The young woman behind the cash desk shrugged. 'Forget it, Emmie. I'll put the milk on the tab this week, OK? You can bring in the coupons next week.' She got out a black notebook from under the cash register, and wrote down the new entry. I knew Katie reasonably well; she was the daughter of the general store's owner, a kind, efficient woman named Liz. Katie was about twenty-four, I guessed; maybe two or three years older than the struggling young mother.

Emmie, blushing, nodded gratefully, produced a few dollar bills to pay for her bread and cans of SpaghettiOs, then ran after Paulie, who had finally broken free and was now attacking the cereal display in the window, which was wobbling precariously. 'Paulie, I swear, if you don't get your ass over here, there'll be no more lollipops this week, *this whole week*, d'you hear me?' she warned furiously, waggling her finger. 'Not one, honey!'

Faced with this serious threat, Paulie shrugged, gave the stack of boxes one more push for luck, then slipped his hand obediently into his mother's. Emmie, bustling back to the cash desk with the boy in tow, suddenly stopped and swore softly. 'I forgot to get soap . . .' she said apologetically, lifting up a small cardboard box from a nearby shelf.

Katie shook her head, laughed, and offered to put the soap on the tab too. In the middle of writing the new item down (and while Emmie was sternly informing Paulie what his gramps would say when he heard about this), Katie looked up with a searching glance.

'You kicked that worthless son-of-a-bitch out yet? For good, I mean?'

Emmie blushed deeper, tightened her lips, then nodded down meaningfully at Paulie, who was now sitting on the floor peeling bits of crackling skin off a large shiny red onion. Katie rolled her eyes. 'Whatever. Did you?'

Emmie nodded shortly. 'Yeah. Yeah I did, as it happens. But . . .' She glanced down at Paulie, then looked carefully around the shop; I hastily dropped my eyes, and pretended to be paying a great deal of attention to a box of plastic sunflower pins being sold to raise money for some local charity. It was none of my business, after all. 'Jeez, Katie, it's, like, a total nightmare. He says he's gonna take Paulie away.' The last words were a miserable whisper. Katie looked shocked. (I saw, because I was peeping between my eyelashes, I couldn't help myself.)

'He does? How come?'

Emmie shrugged. 'You know what he's like,' was all she said, still keeping a careful eye on her son. He was now investigating the fruit display, but, like Emmie, I thought he was listening. There was something quietly alert about him.

Katie rang up the soap, then slipped it and a strawberry lollipop into the top of Emmie's brown bag. 'You don't need to worry,' she remarked evenly, closing the little book and sliding it back under the register. 'He can't beat the crap out of you for three years – oh, shut up, Emmie – then suddenly claim world's best dad award. It just ain't gonna fly. No judge in the state is going to listen to him. I'd forget about it, if I was you. Don't let it bother you.'

Emmie stood, hands on her brown bag. Then she leaned forwards. 'It ain't that simple,' she whispered across the conveyor belt. Paulie had found himself an apple and was taking big, juicy, unnoticed bites. 'I wish it *was*, Katie. But he says stuff. He's starting telling people things. Things that aren't true. And he looks awful good in a suit. He's the one with the proper job, too. I'm worried, Katie, real worried. You know what people think – about me.'

Katie rolled her eyes, looking exasperated; the young mother smiled wearily, then picked up the bag of shopping. 'You know it's true, Katie. And there ain't a damn thing I can do about it.' She turned around and reached for Paulie's hand; dropping his apple, the little boy scampered to join her. As Emmie manoeuvred herself and her son carefully to the door, I caught sight of her face, the scar pinched sharply against her white skin. 'Good-bye,' Katie called after her; we heard the bell on the door jingle sharply as the door banged closed.

Katie moved on to my groceries with a preoccupied face. Tins of tomatoes and packets of fettucini, bags of cookies and pots of yoghurt, all sailed towards her, and were swept through the scanner with rough, unconscious hands. It was only when she'd finished, and was announcing the total, that she looked up at me.

Immediately, her expression sharpened. 'You're that woman from the Dupont house, right?' she asked, sliding her fingers into her jeans pockets. When I nodded, she looked thoughtful. 'Mom told me you people know Kenton Tyler,' she went on abruptly. 'That true?'

'Yes, it is,' I said, briefly wondering how much fodder our household provides for local gossip. *There's three of 'em, and a kid. You should hear the screaming . . .* 'Not very well, though. We just – I – well, my husband's an old friend of Paul Dupont's,' I explained.

Katie took this in, while dropping bricks of tomato purée and quarts of milk on top of the eggs and grapes in the big brown bag. I heard a despairing smoosh as a quart of orange juice landed on a plump juicy peach that had manfully fought loose from its punnet. 'People say Kenton Tyler is the one lawyer round here that ain't too picky about gettin' paid. Is that right?' she asked at last, when everything was packed, standing with my credit card held fast in her hand.

I was in the middle of rearranging the shopping and mourning the peach, whose yellow flesh was now spattering the inside of the bag, but as she spoke I began to see where this was going. 'I – to be quite honest, I can't tell you,' I said feebly. 'I mean, I take it you are talking about – I couldn't help overhearing. The young – er – Emmie, I think was her name . . .'

120

I reached out my hand; Katie was holding my card in a most ferocious grip. 'Emmie's a good girl, and I've known her all her life,' she asserted, a battle-light in her eye. She wasn't giving up the card. 'She's got herself in trouble a few times, I guess, but she's a good mom – the best. That Ryan's an asshole. Everybody knew it, but nobody stepped in when she was stupid enough to get herself hitched to him. Landed her in hospital more than once, not that *she* would tell the cops what happened. It's the old story, y'know?'

I nodded.

'She kept swearing she was gonna leave him, and I guess she's done it this time. But if he's gonna try to get custody of that kid now, well, I'd never say it to her, but there're plenty of folks round here'll be ready to remember the times they've had to sweep her up off the floor down at O'Rourke's. Like *they* ain't had a few too many themselves once in a while!' She snorted. 'She never drinks when Paulie's around, just has to let her hair down once in a while, and when a girl's got bruises the colour of pomegranate all over her chest, why the hell not?

'Now look,' she went on, and I could hear the note of wheedling enter her voice, 'maybe *you* could talk to Mr Tyler, y'know? See if he'd be willing to take on Emmie. Because that girl hasn't a dime.'

This was awful. 'Katie, I can't help you, I have no influence over Mr Tyler, and it's really up to him whom he takes on,' I explained. 'Emmie should certainly go and see him, though, and I can leave you his number. But that's all I can do. Now – could I have my credit card please?'

Katie reluctantly handed it over. 'I guess,' she said dourly. 'But if – if! – you happen to see him, would you do me a favour and mention her name? It's a small thing, just a small thing to ask. We're a community here, we try to help each other . . .'

By the time I got outside, bags propped uncomfortably into my armpits, Emmie had just finished strapping Paulie into his seat and was slipping herself into the front of her battered white car. Hanging baskets of trailing ivy and sweet jasmine were festooned along the roofline of the porch; their rich warm smell came wafting towards me as I walked down the wooden steps in the afternoon sunshine. I watched as Emmie turned around to reply to something Paulie said; he made a funny little gesture in the air, and I could see her laughing in response. She reached over and tweaked his nose, then cupped his cheek tenderly in her hand. He reached both arms forward, and I could even hear the shouted words: 'Cuddle, cuddle, Mommy!'

Impulsively I walked over to the car and tapped on the window. Emmie's pinched face looked startled, but after a moment she rolled it down. A smell of melted boiled sweets and Play-Doh poured out of the interior. 'Yes? Can I help you?'

'Emmie, your friend Katie told me you might want a lawyer,' I said quickly, before I could think. 'This man' – I scribbled Kent's number on to a card of my own, then gave it to her – 'might be able to help you. OK?'

She looked down at the card, then up at me, her brow furrowed. 'I – OK – thanks.'

I nodded perfunctorily, then walked quickly away and started loading my own car; I'd done all I could. By the time I'd finished battering paper bags into the crevices left between the baby buggy and car-seat frame, Emmie and Paulie were gone.

24. Jeanie

Quiet Lanes Elder Care Home is pink – very, very pink. The paint is pink, the doors are pink, the sign that announces 'WELCOME!!!!' is pink. The bed-heads are covered in pink velour. The bedspreads (comforters, they call them here) are a glut of pink roses, and smell strongly of hospital-grade stain remover. In every room dangle pink ruched light-shades, and pink plastic flowers repose in a – yes – pink glass vase in the silent, pink-carpeted entrance hall.

You might suspect that only old people who like pink come to Quiet Lanes, but there is a settled expression on every face that suggests that personal inclination has little to do with becoming an inmate. The old people are clean, and the staff are cheerful enough, but there is an inescapably institutional feel to the place.

'Hello, you must be Jeanie! Gee, we are just so *excited* to have you here,' gushed Mrs Forrest, when I hesitatingly walked into her office. She was an unexpectedly tiny woman of about forty with eyes like a sparrow's, short blond hair and massively strong calf muscles. A scarf of vibrant fuchsia was coiled around her neck. She put her hands up to her face and stared at me with a look of deepest admiration, as if meeting me was pretty much the most exciting thing that had ever happened to her. 'Your experience! Your qualifications! I have, like, a whole *file* of stuff here on you!' she added, waving a (you guessed it) pink envelope file in my face, which appeared to house my one-page CV and a lone faxed letter of reference from college. I wondered what earlier volunteers had proffered.

'Come in, come in; everyone is *crazy* to meet you!' she added, leading the way out of the office and beckoning me energetically towards the day room. I followed awkwardly behind her, down a corridor of badly painted portraits and framed poetry ('Quiet Lanes is the place to be/If you're old and like the sea').

Twenty pairs of eyes looked up as I entered; twenty faces registered a degree of vague interest that Mrs Forrest interpreted as body-shaking delight. 'I *told* you!' she said, laughing deeply as she looked appreciatively around the room. 'Crazy! And here is – Jeanie Boothroyd!' she announced to the assembled company, as if I were a rabbit she had just produced from a silk top hat. She even did a little mime of a drum-roll as she spoke (completing, for me, the likeness between her and the Energizer bunny). Clearly Mrs Forrest is a lady who likes to use her arms.

I smiled awkwardly both then and repeatedly over the course of the next half-hour, as Mrs Forrest introduced me painstakingly to every person in the room ('This is Teddy, he's got Parkinson's, his wife died last year, he has a catheter; this is Sue-Ellen, she's had three husbands, she does fortune-telling, her daughter is a Federal Prosecutor – isn't that *wunnerful*? – and she just had a mastectomy. This is Tim, he does yoga, you must come and watch sometime, we have to take him for a colonoscopy tomorrow. This is . . .').

I was just about to begin a tortuous explanation of how I was unlikely to be able to come ever again (tremendously important obligations requiring my immediate presence elsewhere) when I caught sight of two of the inmates exchanging sly glances behind Mrs Forrest's back. The look said, as clear as day, 'Oh lord, here she goes *again*,' and it gave me pause. The two ladies caught sight of me looking at them and one – the woman called Sue-Ellen, a lady of faded majesty with a bouffant hairstyle – raised her delicately pencilled right eyebrow a millimetre upwards. It was a tiny but unmistakable gesture of camaraderie.

So I allowed myself to be ushered onwards by Mrs Forrest towards the tea-urns, then began to locate lost magazines, slippers and letters, while dodging a million questions. Everybody was very curious about me, it seemed – about who I was, what kind of family I had, what the weather's like in England ('How *do* you tolerate that rain?'), and, most important of all, what I thought of America. I was just about managing to keep them at bay when a cool, questioning southern voice brought me up sharp. 'Did I hear you say you're one of three, my dear?' asked the lady called Sue-Ellen, keeping her foot squarely on a copy of some old lady magazine I was trying to retrieve. I stood up. The foot – encased in an impeccably white plimsole – was down flat and hard. 'That's right,' I said, smiling politely. 'We're the three weird sisters.'

'Hand in hand, hmm?'

'Something like that.'

She slowly moved her foot off the magazine; I picked it up, then returned it to its rightful owner on the other side of the day room, conscious all the time that Sue-Ellen's blue gaze was fixed upon me. When I finally caught her eye, she beckoned me over with a little flick of her forefinger. 'Three English sisters. Sounds less like Macbeth than Jane Austen to me, actually,' she began comfortably, making room for me beside her on the sofa, then patting the open space. Each fingertip was finished with perfect pink polish. 'Tell me, my dear: do y'all compete over beaux?'

I burst out laughing – suddenly we were in *Gone with the Wind* – and, surrendering, I sat down. 'Hardly. My two older sisters are married, and I can't say I fancied either of their husbands.'

'Really? What was wrong with them?'

I shook my head at her. 'Nothing's wrong with them. Just not my type.'

'So what is your type?' Her china-blue eyes were disconcertingly wide.

'My boyfriend is called Dave,' I explained carefully, 'and he is – he is – oh, I don't know. Hard to explain, really. Very friendly. Fun to hang out with.'

'And your sisters' husbands aren't either of those things, I suppose?'

This old woman was quite exasperating! 'I didn't say that,' I returned awkwardly. 'That's not what I meant. But my older sister's husband is too work-obsessed, too ambitious for my taste, and my middle sister's husband is . . . very solid. Dependable. Boring, to be frank.'

'I see. So you like men who can't keep a job and aren't reliable. Do I have that right?' Her wrinkled face was politely bland.

'I wouldn't put it like that! I didn't mean . . . I just – Oh, I'm only twenty-four!' I said, realizing as I spoke that I'd given the same answer to someone else not so long ago. I felt my face flush; Sue-Ellen put her head on one side, looking for all the world like a bright little bird with golden plumage.

'I'm sorry, my dear, I'm just teasin' you,' she remarked after a moment or two, laughing a little as she took my hand in hers. 'I was the youngest of three myself, you see, and we *did* compete over beaux. You should have seen me! I was just dreadful! Whenever one of my sisters brought home a young man, I couldn't stop myself, I just *had* to have him. Or his older

126

brother. Well, you know how it is . . . And I didn't feel bad, because the other two did just the same thing. It's a miracle straight from the Lord that we got married at all – but we all did, you know. In fact, I was married three times.'

'And what happened to your sisters? Did you steal all their husbands away?'

'No, my dear, certainly not,' she replied seriously. 'Once God had joined 'em together, it was a different matter entirely. I wouldn't have dreamed of getting between them. Tilly was married twice, and Grace – that's the oldest – has been married for fifty-five years. So you see, my dear, we were terrible teenagers, but quite respectable once we were grown-up. Although—'

'Can you believe it? Time just *flies* by here!' Mrs Forrester trilled suddenly, dropping her hand on my shoulder, her fuchsia scarf vibrant in the sunshine. She smiled down at me kindly, mouth wide, perfect white teeth sparkling. Sue-Ellen shrugged and allowed me to be steered gently to the door, past the little chattering groups of bridge-players and crocheters, all of whom waved as I passed. I stole a cookie from the kitchen, then let myself out of the building and walked back along the coastal road (the one Paul and I walked along a few days earlier) feeling thoughtful. Quiet Lanes is, in some sense, worse than expected – more claustrophobic, more smelly, and definitely more pink. But the job itself wasn't too bad, I thought to myself, as I let myself back into the house.

It was just a shame (as I explained to Alison, an hour or two later) that it will prevent me from spending time with Dave. I'll be away most afternoons during his visit, helping out at Quiet Lanes. 'I wouldn't worry about that, darling,' Alison replied earnestly across the vast crackling distance between us. 'He'll be delighted to see you engaged in geriatric care, I'm sure. After all, someone placed as he is – the situation with his mother – will be extra-sensitive to the need for *quality* volunteer work in elder homes. Don't you think?'

Which was really an excellent point, one I'm determined to make to Dave himself if he gets uppity about my working when he arrives here tomorrow.

25. Q

This morning Fay called, the partner from Schuster & Marks. I haven't heard from her – or from anyone at work – since Caroline's party.

Her voice on the other end of the cellphone was like an echo from another life, rising thinly, almost inaudibly, through vestigial soup. 'Hello, hello? Where the fuck are you, Q? You sound as if you're on the moon. *Where*? . . . Fuck, you might as well be. What are you doing in . . . None of my business, I suppose. Look, I'm calling because you'll be back from maternity leave in two weeks, and I wanted to bring you up to date on the cases you'll be taking over – we've got, like, zero time to prepare the Mingge Brothers case, and then there's the Castle One Properties merger we agreed you'd take over, and I want to run through the details of Alliance Construction v Gettysfield Industries. So might be easiest if we meet up, you can get right up to speed, are you going to be available any time in the next week?'

I fought a panicky feeling, a charging river of nausea. Actually we *were* thinking of coming to the city in a few days as it happens, I told her, unwillingly. For a quick visit. I'll come into the office on Friday and we can talk then, if you want. I let her think we'd be just chatting about cases, there was no need (I decided) to hint at another subject, so I walked carefully around the holes in my words and jogged determinedly on to the safer ground available to women and colleagues (How's

129

Arlene, when's Chris getting married, what's up with Susan's house – *no!* It didn't! She *didn't!*) At the end of the conversation I hung up the phone, then stared at it.

What have people been saying about me behind my back? The thought of the complicated office politics, of what my colleagues say about women who begin the long slither *down* the greasy pole, made me feel briefly sick. I thought of Caroline's eyes, sharp as green glass, of Michael's supercilious blandness. I thought of the fraught clients, the mind-numbing hum of the air conditioning, the interminable hours of oddly frantic boredom . . . And then I thought of the bigger gossip network, of the two-way flow of news from Crimpson out into the legal community. Now that Tom has asked for an even longer leave, people are bound to be talking . . .

Impossible, impossible to leave Samuel, to hand his small frail body over for someone else to hug and smell and love twelve hours a day, to unclip my bra in the office and spill my breasts into plastic cups and bottles. Impossible. I saw, in a single moment of absolute clarity, the conversation I must have with Fay.

We're going down to the city on Tuesday – in four days' time. And our time there will be busy; apart from my meeting at Schuster, and Tom's at Crimpson, Lucille and Peter are planning to come and see us. We also have lunches pencilled in with our friends Brianna and Mark, and Paul said he wanted to bring us dinner one night.

Jeanie stared at us in bewilderment when we told her about the trip. 'You're leaving me here?' she asked incredulously. '*All alone?*'

I wrinkled my forehead at her. 'No, you'll have Dave,' I replied, surprised, and her mouth hung open.

'But you said you wanted to see more of him . . .' she began accusingly.

'I know, I know,' I returned apologetically, 'but we have to go into work, and we also have an appointment for Samuel at the doctor's. I would suggest you come with us, but there's no room for all five of us in the apartment, not for a full week, and anyway you have your new job, right? You can't skip that. Plus I can't imagine Dave will want to make the trip up and down from New York *four* times in the course of ten days . . .'

She looked briefly as if she was being strangled. 'I see.'

'And look, if you want, you could both come at the end of his trip, he could leave for London straight from New York,' I went on. 'We can squeeze for a night or two in the apartment, I'm sure, and you'll have finished your first stint at the Home by then.'

It's sweet, really, that she's so desperate for Dave and me to get to know each other.

26. Jeanie

"Ello, love,' he said, standing on the doorstep, looking strangely out of place against the Connecticut sky.

I looked round his shoulder into the driveway, fully expecting to see a police car and an armed officer grimly waiting, but there was nothing, just a cardinal hopping in the grass and a few grey squirrels scaling the trees. 'How did you get here?' I asked suspiciously.

He stared at me. 'The heavens opened and put me here. I got in a time machine. How d'you bloody *think* I got here? I flew,' he returned, crossly. 'On the eight a.m. flight, landed at ten-thirty New York time. Then I hitched a ride with some bloke who works in insurance up in Hartford. Nice bloke. Didn't even know that planes contributed to the greenhouse effect. Can you believe it? He does now. I met him on the flight, we had a nice chat, he says he's going to tell his bosses all about it the next time they want him to fly to Tallahassee. Anyway – can I come in, or what?'

I stood back silently to let him come into the house, but he stayed still for a moment, staring at me. I gazed back mutely.

'Aren't you forgetting something?' he asked impatiently.

'Sorry, I . . . ?'

'A bloody kiss, Lady Muck, I've flown round the world to be here with you,' he said, with a catch at the back of his throat, and I flushed, apologized, leaned forwards and brushed my lips against his cheek.

132

He turned his face and our mouths met; his arms went around me, and he pulled me close. I'd forgotten the taste of him.

'Now, isn't that nice – Oh I'm *sorry* to interrupt, but I just wanted to say how pleased we are to have you here,' came Tom's voice from behind me, and he emerged from the sitting room with Samuel clutched and sprawling under one arm. 'Dave, it's so *great* you could come,' he went on cheerfully, rather overdoing it I thought. 'Where are your bags? Christ, is that all you brought? Very impressive. I always seem to end up with a dozen garment bags. Still, it helps if you don't carry suits, doesn't it? Can I help you? Yes, and this is Samuel . . .'

Dave peered uncomfortably into Samuel's face, then took a step backwards as the baby began to howl. 'Don't mind him,' Tom continued cheerfully, 'he does this all the time. Now, how about something to drink? Tea, I presume?'

Q was out shopping, but when she appeared half an hour later she literally threw her arms around his neck. They'd obviously had a conversation up in the privacy of their darkened, muddled bedroom last night about 'making him feel welcome', but Dave looked a bit startled, as well he might, since the last time he saw her she was hissing at him like an overwrought cat about how he was 'taking advantage' of me and was (I think I have the phrase correctly) 'a work-shy, weak-kneed layabout'. Now she effectively laid out a red carpet into the bosom of our family. 'We're so delighted you've come all this way to see us, you must be exhausted, please don't think about us, if you need to go and sleep, just feel free . . .

'And how is your mother?' she went on, pouring him a third cup of sweet tea and producing some chocolate chip cookies from her shopping bag. 'I hear from Alison and my mother that you've been a real rock for her these past few years.' She arranged her features into an expression of sympathy and simultaneous admiration. As well she might; Dave is an exemplary son.

'She's not doing so good,' Dave explained soberly. 'Not good at all. It's no surprise, of course; we've been waiting for this to happen. Alzheimer's – it's a terrible disease.'

'When was she first diagnosed?' Tom enquired, solicitously.

Dave shrugged. 'While I was at uni in Manchester, but she was mostly all right then,' he explained. 'She served up a bloody good Christmas meal that year, just a few weeks after the diagnosis: turkey, fifteen trimmings, homemade Christmas pud, brandy butter, you name it. We all thought: Maybe she'll be the one to beat it, you know? Maybe it won't *get* her. But it was later that night, while we were still cleaning up the dishes, she forgot Dad's name for the first time, started talking about Stan, some bloke she was engaged to before she met Dad, who died of meningitis.' Unused to so much warmth from my family, he was becoming expansive. 'Dad was really upset, because he always suspected she loved Stan best. It was horrible: him in tears; Mam's bewildered face above the turkey carcass . . . Course, it was just the beginning. Dad couldn't handle it, any of it, and neither could m'sister, but thank god mam's cousin Brenda was willing to move in and help. She's been bloody marvellous, don't know what we'd have done without her, and God knows what Dad's been able to pay her. Her step-daughter Ellen's been helping these past few years too, when she can. She works in a home for adults with disabilities and comes to help Brenda with Mam on weekends and at nights. You remember Ellen, don't you Jeanie?'

The first time I saw Ellen I nearly fell off my chair; I'd imagined, from the family description, that she would be a soft-footed, gentle young lady, prompted by an almost spiritual calling to take care of the elderly. She was, in fact, bottle-blonde and twenty, with the kind of plump-cheeked, big-bottomed cuteness reminiscent of a 1960s 'Carry On' film. "Ello, Dave,' she said when she arrived for lunch, kissing him loudly on the cheek, pressing her D-cup boobs into his chest. She chattered merrily throughout the meal, forking great loads of fish and chips into her big, round, lavishly lipsticked mouth with appreciative smacks. God knows what she was saying, I was too busy staring at her cleavage. White shirt open to her nipples, or thereabouts, and tucked into a short navy skirt that bulged over a generously rounded tummy. Every time she sat down or crossed her legs, she exposed the thick tops of a pair of black stockings fastened with pink plastic suspender clips. Dave, exposed to the sight of these undergarments just as he was trying to serve her a cup of tea, was so flummoxed he spilled the hot liquid over the table, which for no reason that I could see required Ellen to peer down her cleavage and say, 'No harm done to these fellas, I'm pleased to say! Eh? Eh!' and nudge Dave furiously with her elbow.

I muttered something ever-so-faintly sarcastic about how Ellen was 'a big-hearted girl', but I don't think Dave heard, he was too busy being smothered in a blanket of warm sympathy by Q and Tom ('Your poor mother . . . So terrible for you . . . What a tragedy . . . If there's anything we can do . . .'). Feeling somewhat upstaged by them, I reached out for Dave's hand and squeezed it sympathetically. He looked up at me for a second, an expression of tenderness softening his face. I drew back my hand. 'I really have got to get to my new job,' I explained. He stared out of the window at the vibrant green of the maples against the peacock blue sky, then turned back to me. 'I understand. What time do you start, then?'

'I should – Well, I mean I think I should probably go now-ish,' I explained. 'I have to do ten hours a week, and – well, we'd arranged that I'd visit today. Such a shame really. But you can sleep a bit, and when I get back we can go down to the beach.'

Dave nodded, and stood up too, picking his huge tatty green rucksack up off the floor. 'Fine. Show me to our room, Jeanie, and I'll get out of your hair,' he said, nodding politely at Tom and Q. I could hear them still clucking enthusiastically behind us ('Anything! Anything at all! Just let us know!') as we walked through the hallway and up the stairs.

Dave, who seemed immune to the opulence of the furnishings in the gorgeous double room I presently introduced him to, settled down with a gusty sigh on the bed, yawned and stretched himself fully out, muddy trainers flaking dirt all over the white counterpane. 'Fantastic, I could do with a kip.' He yawned again. 'It was a long flight, I'm absolutely shattered.' Then he rolled over to face me, stroking the pillow gently with one hand. 'You *really* have to go now, love? Or do you want to . . . well, you know, take a nap with me first? God, I want you, Jeanie, I can't wait much longer . . .'

'Dave, that would be *lovely*,' I replied earnestly, 'but I really *do* have to go. You know how it is, they're all so fond of me. I don't want to keep them . . .'

Dave sighed, rolled back over and popped some tea-tree gum out of a silver foil packet from his jeans pocket. 'All right, Jeanie,' he mouthed, through the hard grey square, 'forget it. I understand. One day this week I'll come with you to the old folks' home, I reckon, but now I'll just have a shower and get clean.' He kicked himself off the bed, opening the door into the dressing room. 'I'll unpack, you go off to your job, I'll keep the bed warm for when you get back.' When I walked in a few steps behind him he was in the middle of rifling through grey T-shirts and underwear; having found what he needed, he stood up, and started to strip off his clothes. In a second he was naked, standing unembarrassed before me, his travel-stained attire in a small heap before him.

Professor Mordaunt has begrudgingly given up my course-

136

work, it seems, because when I walked into the kitchen Q silently handed me an envelope in which I found a certificate telling me I've been awarded a Master's degree by *Kingsbury College* (penned with enough curlicues to satisfy a sovereign). I felt very happy, very relieved and very apprehensive. 'It's time to start applying for jobs,' I said slowly to Q, slipping the certificate back into its envelope, and she laughed.

'You've got to grow up sometime,' she said, scooping up Samuel, smiling with a hint of a challenge in her eye. 'And if you ask me, love, quite honestly it's about time.'

27. Q

'I mighta been a bit hasty.'

Kent Tyler was standing on the front porch, hands plunged in his pockets, a frown creasing his forehead. He was wearing a pressed button-down shirt with his jeans, but there was still something indefinably disreputable about him. 'The other day, I mean.' He passed his hand anxiously over his head, smoothing down his wispy hair, and pulled awkwardly at his ponytail.

'I'm sorry?'

'A bit hasty.' He coughed uncomfortably. 'Y'know, when you visited me. Fancy the firm?'

Tom had come up behind me; I felt his warm hand in the small of my back as he stood over my shoulder. 'Hello, Mr Tyler. What can we do for you?'

As he caught sight of my husband, Kent licked dry lips, then stretched them wide into an oddly misshapen smile. 'I was just stopping by, young fella, to say, y'know, that you passed the test. Congratulations. You did it. When can you start?'

The hand on my back tightened. 'Uh – what?'

Kent did a strange sort of jiggly dance, staring down at his toes, and when he looked up his face had changed expression again. 'The firm. You can have it. Whenever you want. Like, how 'bout next week?'

A gull sailed towards us, then sat down on the porch rail, moving its feet to get comfortable. It refolded its wings, twice, then put its head on one side and watched us with a bright, interested air.

'Mr Tyler, that's very kind of you,' Tom began carefully. 'But I don't think that we . . . I mean, I thought we made it quite clear that—'

'Look, what's the problem?' Kent interjected sharply, grabbing at his ponytail and pulling it hard. 'It's a good firm, you know! Large client base. Good – pretty good – reputation. Offices all paid up for six months. Five months. Four months. Till next week, at least.'

'I'm sure they are, Mr Tyler, but—'

'And you get to live here, in Connecticut!' He gestured broadly around the garden, at the house and down towards the sea. The gull squawked a bit at Kent's carelessly waving arms, left its perch protestingly and settled a few feet further off. 'Lovely views. Big houses, for cheap. State schools. Fresh vegetables. Mmm! And – er – er—'

'Mr Tyler, honestly, it's not that—'

'Did I mention the state schools? Did I mention the real estate?'

'You did, as a matter of fact—'

'I'm telling you' (this with an emphatic bang on the house's wood siding, which caused the gull to fly up with one final, agitated squawk, and sail off into the blue) 'this is the good life, you know? And while running a firm (I'll be honest) is a bit much for one old man, for a young couple it's a *dream*. A dream! You take over my firm, you take on my – er – *position* in the community. You couldn't get this kind of a client base if you was to set up on your own out here. No one would trust you. But if you take over my name, you'll take on the trust. The trust, y'see? Course you might lose one or two of 'em, but mostly they won't bother to shift. Laziness, of course, and unwillingness to change, but it'll stand *you* in good stead.'

He paused, panting a little from the exertion, his faded blue eyes struggling to focus as he looked from one to the other of us. 'Mr Tyler,' I said, taking him by his gnarled brown hand, smiling a smile I hoped was suitably gentle, 'I'm sorry, we're just not really country types, you see? We live in New York. Here . . . I mean, it's very pretty, of course, but just for a holiday; that's all. For now, at least. Maybe, in a few months, things'll be different. I can't say. But we can't make a decision so quickly. We'd need much more time. I'm so sorry . . .'

Kent pulled his hand roughly away, and laughed. 'What ya talkin' about, you're sorry?' he scoffed, thrusting out his chest. 'I was goin' to offer you my firm because young Paul said you was to be trusted, but I've got guys up and down the coast *beggin'* me to let 'em take it on. Offering to pay me big bucks, too.' He slid his fingers together meaningfully. 'I don't *need* you; what, you kiddin' me? I only put you people to the top of the pile 'cause Paul Dupont vouched for you. Otherwise you wouldna got a look in, I'm telling you. Not a chance. Not a *chance*!'

And with that, he walked off down the steps to his old rusty two-tone pick-up, still chuckling loudly. He opened the big heavy door, wincing as he did so.

'Listen!' I felt oddly compelled to continue the conversation and, pulling away from Tom, I walked down the steps after Kent. 'We see the advantages, really we do, Mr Tyler. But if you're a town person, well, you can't just change that overnight, can you? It's something about the space, I suppose.' I smiled pacifically. 'About what you expect to see when you look out of the window – and the noise, too; what you expect to hear. And then there's the job itself. When I compare what you do with what we do now, it's – it's completely different, you know? Not' – I put out my hand in response to something in his face – 'worse, or better; just different. Different kinds of cases, a different spectrum. And different clients.'

I hadn't got it right even now; I was irritated with myself. Kent shrugged again. 'Like I say, it makes no difference to me,' he replied coolly. 'Don't have to explain yourself. *I* don't care.'

'But we – we really enjoyed meeting you!' I added helplessly, still trying to pin something down (I could feel Tom rolling his eyes behind me on the deck). 'And seeing the firm, learning about it. Your beautiful offices. The way you are – part of everything . . .'

Kent shrugged impatiently; placing his foot carefully on the running board, he heaved himself up into his seat and switched on the engine. I stood back as he pulled the door awkwardly closed. 'Seriously, I don't need you. My business is my business,' he added, turning on the radio. Music blared out, twanging guitars and a man's croaky voice filling the hot stillness. 'See ya 'round.' He nodded shortly; I waved slowly as the old truck chugged and spluttered off down the drive.

28. Jeanie

Dave's eyes were full of tears when I came into the bedroom. It was almost dark, and he had not switched on the lamp; he was sitting by the window, waiting for me.

I stared at him; he tried to smile, brushing the tears away with a shaking hand. 'Just got a call from me dad,' he explained in a rough voice. 'Mam's taken a turn for the worse. Happened first thing this morning, just as I took off from Heathrow. Bloody ironic. As if she knew.'

'Oh, Dave, I'm so sorry,' I said immediately, awkwardly kneeling beside him on the floor. 'What's happened?'

'Small stroke, they think. Left side of her face is frozen, and she's not talking. Shit,' he went on, putting his head in his hands, 'it's back into hospital for her again, and you know what *that's* like.'

Of course I did; I went with Dave to visit his mam in hospital three months ago, when a fall and a hip fracture sent her into another sudden decline. The hospital building was about five miles from Dave's house, a huge, squat, hideous block of concrete with endless extension blocks and an overflowing car park. We found Mam in one of those wards you have nightmares about: eight beds of old ladies moaning and sighing and screaming against a backdrop of searing whiteness. 'Nil by mouth' read the large sign above Mam's head, with 'Mrs Tickner' in blue marker pen. You could just see the words 'Mrs Browning' not quite rubbed out underneath.

'Will it be the same place?' I whispered, and Dave nodded.

'Course; it's the only hospital in thirty-five miles,' he said wanly. 'Get 'em in, get 'em out, that's the philosophy of that place. Whether they're ready for it or not. Dead or alive. Well, *you* know; you remember from last time.'

I cast my mind back to that awful afternoon. Mam was lying by herself when we arrived, baffled, confused and dirty; no one had washed her properly since she was admitted two days before (the niceties of hygiene and cosmetics are utterly beyond Dave's dad). We set about her face with some aqueous cream from a big pot by her bedside, cleaned her teeth, and brushed out her matted hair as best we could. Then we changed her nightdress and tried to sit her up a bit higher on the pillows while Dave looked through the charts at the end of her bed. 'Fuck the bastards, they *will* keep upping her dose of sedatives, anything to keep her quiet. They don't give a shit if it's actually *good* for her. Wait until I find that fucking consultant,' he said furiously, and off he went. Soon afterwards I heard him having a furious conversation with a doctor just outside the ward ('Mr Tickner, I understand you have your mother's interests at heart'; 'Yes, I bloody do, unlike you, you stuck-up southern bastard'), which ended reasonably well, from Dave's perspective: they agreed to lower the sedation and try a night of continuous nursing care.

'Don't want to pay for the nurse, do they, they just want to give her some medicine that hushes her up, bloody hospital, bloody National Health, bloody government,' he muttered angrily, all the way home.

I reached now for Dave's shoulder, thinking about poor Mam facing it all on her own without Dave by her side. 'Is there anything I can do?'

Dave bit his lip. 'It's terrible timing,' he said, choking over a strange laugh. 'Me over here, and everything. Still,' he went on, brushing his eyes again, working very hard to grin, 'Dad and m'sister say I should try to enjoy myself out here. First holiday in a decade, y'know. If anything changes – anything serious – they'll give me a ring. And I've only just got here, come halfway round the bloody world, I *can't* go back just yet. Not yet. Jeanie . . . please . . .'

He reached out to me, his hands stretching across the space between us, trying to close the gap, to bring me into his warmth. I knew what he wanted; quite reasonable, when you think about it. But it had been such a long time; and now there was this pressure, I thought, that it should be somehow equal to the occasion. And no matter how hard I tried, it was as if two people were bumping uncomfortably up against each other just when it needed to be – well, transcendent, I suppose; a moment of oneness. I closed my eyes, and felt his weight move above me, his body that seemed both familiar and very, very strange. Try harder, I thought to myself. This is *Dave*. He's suffering. Try harder.

29. Q

'Haven't the women of your family *any* advice?' Tom asked miserably in the cold hours of early morning, when my small family was stretched out in a damp mangled heap on the bed. 'What's the point of having all these sisters? Jeanie knows nothing. And anyway, now Dave's here, she won't be getting out of bed. You won't speak to Alison. Honestly, I'm almost tempted to call my mother . . .'

'Don't you dare,' I muttered furiously, and reluctantly, faced with this threat, I called my own mother today, just after lunch. She's been very busy with her yoga studio recently; I don't think she's had much space to think about me since she left to go back to England when Samuel was a week old. I dialled her number feeling painfully hesitant.

My mother claimed, predictably enough, that all Samuel's problems are caused by my breastfeeding. 'Goodness me, dear, your generation does seem to like making things difficult for itself,' she announced. (I could tell she'd been simply longing for the opportunity to advance her theory.) 'Give the child a bottle of *proper* milk, and I'm sure he'll calm down. And you won't feel so much like a milch-cow.' She finds it impossible to believe that a human being is actually capable of producing enough to feed a child – particularly a son. ('Boys are such *feasters*!' she says, indulgently, never having borne one herself. If she had I'm sure I'd have hated him, though, since he would clearly have enjoyed the biggest portion of pie and the extra bowl of chocolate mousse throughout our childhood. He'd have been able to sleep in on the weekends, he would never have had to tidy his room, and I can see her face now when he brought home a C from school: 'Justin [or whatever] just has *different* skills, dear, he can't be a whiz on the football field *and* a genius in the classroom!')

'Now then, as for the night-time crying,' she went on briskly, 'try leaving the lights off when you feed him. You need to keep the room as dark as possible,' she explained. 'That's *bound* to help.'

'Mother, of course I turn the bloody lights off,' I replied, exasperated. 'What, you think I'm an idiot? I could feed the child by the radiance of a glow-worm, it wouldn't make a damn bit of difference.'

'My dear girl, don't take it out on *me*, dear, I'm just trying to help,' she returned, magnificently. 'And really, I think you just have to accept that babies cry. It's what they do. What were you expecting, dear? That Samuel would articulate his needs in fully formed sentences?'

I slammed down the phone.

Then, at the end of the evening, just as Tom and I discovered we had fallen asleep in front of C-SPAN (I think Tom dropped asleep literally while changing the channels), the phone rang again. When I picked it up, there was a growl on the other end, a low, inarticulate, indefinable mumble of irritation that made my hair stand on end.

Startled into hallucinatory wakefulness, I listened for a second, horror-struck. Just I was just about to grab Tom, the growl metamorphosed into a voice. 'Grrrrrwhat the *hell* – *what the hell* d'ya think ya doing? Huh? What? For Chrissakes?'

I stared at the phone, then cautiously put it back to my ear. 'Hell – hello?

'*You sent Emmie Cormier to me*. What ya think I am, made of money?'

'Oh.' I collapsed back into my chair, hand on my chest, trying to regulate my heartbeat. 'It's you, Mr Tyler. How are you? Now listen, I'm sorry about that, about Emmie I mean. I don't really know her. I bumped into her in the general store, and—'

'Well, *I* know her. Emmie Cormier is a deadbeat, and always has been,' came the uncompromising response. 'Let's not mince words. She's a slut. Look at the way she dresses. Skirts slit to her waist, you can see her—'

'Mr Tyler,' I cut in hastily. 'Listen. As I said, I don't know Emmie personally, I have no investment in this. But it does seem as if her ex is about to try to take custody of her son—'

'Tha's right,' Kent acknowledged unexpectedly. 'He is. Quite right. And a worse low-life you'll never hope to meet.'

'Really? You know him?'

'Yup. Known him since he was in kindergarten. Beat his first wife silly, then when she finally ran off to lose herself in Wyoming, he set about Emmie. Man's an absolute monster. Course, he's got money; works for Joseph Pinkerton, the furniture showroom, over on route one. They say he's the best man in the place. If you was to meet him socially, now, you'd think he was charming. You'd fall for him straight up. "Good morning, how are you, and how are the little ones?" He's a salesman, and it shows. That's how he gets the girls in the first place, o'course – and there're plenty round here that've never seen through him.'

'That's what I heard,' I replied, remembering the details of what Katie told me and the overheard conversation with Emmie.

'Which' (gaining belligerence again) 'is *exactly* why I can't take on her case! It's gonna take serious man-power to defeat

Ryan Cormier, if he's really set his mind on takin' that kid away. You think I've got that kind of time? That kind of money? This ain't the big city, my dear! Think about what it will take! I'd have to face a man on the witness stand who's gonna have half the community swearing he's an angel fresh from the Lord. That his wives have an unfortunate habit of walking slap into walls and twisting their ankles in flowerbeds. I'd have to find that first wife of his in the mountains of Wyoming, for a start (and they say round here she don't want to be found). Then, on top of it all, I'd have to make Emmie Cormier stick to the straight and narrow for as long as it takes, because if she gets herself drunk – or worse – even once, she'll be spotted, and someone'll take a picture on their damn cellphone, and send it straight to his lawyer. That's the thing with the country, my dear: you can't make mistakes. And I can't do that kind of case on my own! Not any more, y'hear?'

I had been faintly protesting for the last five minutes; now, at last, I managed to lever myself into the conversation. 'I'm sorry, Mr Tyler, really I am,' I began placatingly. 'I see that I've put you in a difficult position. But perhaps you could – you could – I mean, if you don't help her, what else can she *do*?'

'Lose her kid,' he replied crossly. 'She can apply for legal aid, o'course. But they're full up to bursting, the system is strained, these days they're turnin' most cases down. If Ryan Cormier's set on takin' that kid, it's gonna be tough; there's plenty of precedent for overturning a custody order if he can just prove he has new information. I'm seeing her Monday night, at Flannigan's Bar, as it happens. Little place in the centre of Sussex. Ten o'clock. I'm going to explain I can't help her. My days of takin' dead-beats chicks *pro bono* is past. And *you*, my dear, you stop butting your nose into business that don't concern you. Y'hear?' The phone clicked.

I looked at it, tapping my fingers slowly on the pile of books

148

on the side table next to the sofa. Samuel was actually sleeping. A rare moment of silence unfolded in the evening; Tom's even slumberous breaths punctuated the discreet purr of the air conditioning. I switched the radio on low, and listened to a lady with a voice like sweet cream caramel talking about how to make sweet cream caramel while wondering – in spite of myself – what I could do to help Emmie.

30. Jeanie

Being with Dave again is a bit like cuddling up with a very familiar blanket. A bit worn around the edges, not particularly handsome, but warm and, well, comforting. I know every part of Dave, every thought in his brain. When I look into his eyes there's nothing dangerous or unexpected lurking inside, just Daveness: a simple, straightforward, companionable, jovial Englishman.

I've heard all the latest episodes in the saga of Badger's on-again, off-again relationship with his bank manager, a neat, tidy, professional woman who is bizarrely attracted to the loafish Badger with his weird shock of hair and multiple pierc-ings, in spite of the existence of a neat, tidy, well-dressed husband. Dave's account of the time he found the bank man-ager – his bank manager too, as it happens – hiding sheepish and half-naked behind the bathroom door made Q choke on her artichoke ('You've got to admit, there's never a better time to ask for an extension on your overdraft').

I've shared my stories too with someone who knows all the characters; I described the unfortunate mess-up at college, and Dave – who used to take courses with Sibelius Mordaunt, before he got kicked out of Kingsbury for non-payment of fees – was pleasingly furious on my behalf. 'Silly old codger, wouldn't last three minutes in the real world,' he declared. 'Sounds like he's lost his marbles, I mean, who could forget *you*?' he added, pulling me towards him. I smiled, and let my hand hang loose in his.

He's been here a couple of days now; days in which Q has been staggeringly polite and Tom staggeringly accommodating. Every time Dave expresses a hint of a wish, they rush to try to find him whatever it is, from Jaffa cakes to 'rough' bath-towels ('These fluffy things! I mean, I'm not complaining, Jeanie, but where's the *friction*?'). And Dave, in his turn, has done his very best to make nice to the baby, peering hopefully into his little bed whenever he's sleeping ('Nothing to do, I'm afraid!') and swearing blind, whenever asked, that no, Samuel's screams do not disturb him at night. He keeps pottering off to the off-licence and coming back with a new six-pack of beer (he's fascinated by local micro-breweries) which he then plies us all with ('Have another? No? Sure? Don't mind if I do . . .')

Then, today, Dave came with me to Quiet Lanes, and entranced everyone with his tales from the frontline of the mighty eco battle. In fact I won a bit of reflected glory from my association with him. The old people had never met anyone like him and were touchingly convinced that he must be a genuine pioneer. They were American enough to find this thrilling, no matter what their own politics on the environment were. 'We need more young men like you in this world,' said Ken, who used to be a fighter pilot, taking Dave's elbow in his hand. 'Sometimes I think young men these days have forgotten *how* to be men,' he went on, and although his palsied hand was shaking, his grey eyes were steady and serious. 'You stand up for what you believe in, son; you keep thinking you can change the world. Might not make a damn difference, but it's the only way to live.' The others nodded their heads in vigorous agreement; I felt curiously proud, although I had a fair idea that Dave was exaggerating his involvement in most of the stories.

Sue-Ellen elected to read his palm ('If I can see through all this dirt, young man. You never hear of soap, perhaps?') and promised him not riches, but a life of independence. 'You're a traveller,' she told him, and Dave grinned.

'Um, yes, but you already knew that,' he said, chuckling. 'Don't need to read my palm for that!'

She was not at all put out. 'I don't mean that you came here on an aeroplane from England,' she said scathingly. 'That's *obvious*. I mean that you'll never settle in one place for long. A restless spirit. You've inherited it from your mother,' she went on, and Dave gave a shout of laughter.

'My mother's lived in a tiny Yorkshire village her whole life,' he said, shaking his head. 'She's no restless spirit, let me tell you. A very normal housewife, in fact.'

Sue-Ellen smiled peacefully at him. 'If she'd lived in another generation your mother's story would have been very different,' she replied, and Dave wrinkled his forehead.

'Eh?'

Sue-Ellen patted his hand gently. 'You're the son of a woman who didn't live the life she wanted,' she said. 'A woman who was never happy. I'm sure you picked that up as a child, children always do.'

Dave furrowed his brow. 'I don't think that's right,' he said, confused, but then he shrugged, and laughed a little defensively. Mrs Forrest was looking on.

'She's quite a woman, our Sue-Ellen, isn't she?' she said, happy and ineffably patronizing. Sue-Ellen looked up at her, folded her fingers neatly in her lap, and said nothing.

Dave, pulling himself together, helped us with lunch; he dashed around with plates, filled cups with cranberry juice, dived under chairs for lost napkins, and was generally very agreeable. 'It's just like Mam's Day Centre in here,' he whispered to me as we flew past each other bearing plates laden with apple pie. 'Old people are basically the same the world over, just want someone to talk to 'em.'

'He's a breath of fresh air,' a quiet old man named Joel told me as he tucked into his dessert. 'Thank you for bringing him to us, my dear.' I smiled proudly.

In fact, as long as we're in public, we're having a lovely time together. Dave and Jeanie: 'You seem like such a team!' But when the light fades, when Q and Tom yawn themselves up to bed, it's a different matter. Then I feel something horrible stirring in my stomach, something cold, gelatinous and a bit twitchy. Something that makes my skin shrink on to my bones. And when Dave slips into bed, slides his hand in my nightshirt, and feels for my breast, my heart sinks, my body freezes. Everything changes.

'Blimey, Jeanie, must be the water around here or something. Never seen you so ill,' Dave said last night, bewildered. 'Can't I make you – better, love?' I pushed his reaching hands aside, and gabbled something incoherent. Everything is fine, I said; I just need to sleep it off. My head is throbbing. I'm very tired. And so I put off explanations for another day . . .

I don't *want* to be different, especially not now, with his poor mother lying ill on the other side of the planet. I want to be the same girlfriend, the Jeanie I've always been; there's so much pain in his eyes these days, I want to take it away, not add to it. But something in my body seems to be pulling me away from him, and no matter how hard I try, I can't stop myself.

31. Q

I was swinging myself out the door at 10 p.m. to go down to Flannigan's Bar when Jeanie appeared in the front hall. 'Where are you off to?' she asked, astounded, I suppose, to catch sight of me dressed to go out. When I explained, a wistful look appeared in her eye. 'A – bar? *Really?* D'you think I could come too?'

Perplexed, I looked at my watch – but something in her eye inspired me to silence. Taking her arm in mine, I pulled her towards me instead. 'Of course,' I said. 'God, we haven't been out for a drink together in years. D'you remember that time we went out with . . . Now what was his name? The funny bloke you swore was "the one". Codger. No, Lodger. Oh, yes! How could I forget? Arty, the Dodger . . .'

We set off arm in arm, through the darkness, down the dirt driveway, then along the narrow footpath bordering the coastal road, and into Sussex. There is not much going on in the town at night, just a few dog-walkers out for a last-minute stroll round the block, some kids waiting listlessly around the gas station and the drone of the occasional passing car. The white clapboard houses, in repose, look untouched by the centuries. After a moment's silence, Jeanie's grip tightened. 'So how did you know that Tom – you know – that he was really the one?' she asked softly.

I grinned, trying to read her face, pale orange in the glare of the street lamps. 'Are you wondering if Dave . . . ?' I began, but she bit her lip and looked down.

'No, I mean, that's not why I'm asking,' she returned hastily. 'Not exactly. I was just wondering.'

I cast my mind back to the early days with Tom. I knew that I loved him, I suppose, almost immediately. Marrying him never seemed like a decision, it was obviously going to happen. I tried to feel out this answer without making her feel bad. 'Well, in my case it all happened rather quickly,' I explained. 'But I think it's different for everyone. Some people take years settling into a relationship.'

She nodded shortly. Her face was deeply preoccupied.

'Do you – enjoy being with Dave?' I tried.

She laughed self-consciously. 'Of course. I mean, he's very funny, and kind, and stuff,' she said. I had the strong sense that there was a 'but' hovering on the edge of her words.

We had come now within sight of the small bar, set in a pur-pose-built block atop a large car park; I felt regretful as we entered the circle of bright floodlight. 'So what are we trying to do here?' she asked. 'With this old man, I mean?'

'We're going to be very strategic,' I explained as we waited for a big truck to park. 'I'm going to try to persuade Emmie Cormier, the young mother, to talk more about her life with her ex. The beatings, the violence. I want to see if she can inspire Kent's sympathy so he'll take her on as a client and help her keep custody of her kid.'

'Why, exactly? I mean, why are we getting involved?'

'Because she can't pay him,' I told my sister quietly, pushing open the door to the busy saloon.

I saw Kent immediately, slumped on a stool at the far end of the bar, staring ruminatively into the depths of a double whisky. Above him a game of baseball blared on a huge TV screen sus-pended on the wall, a wiry pitcher preparing to throw at a batter whose mountainous neck began an inch above his ears. Kent was clearly unconscious of the action – of the batter uncoiling into one swift pump, the sharp crack, the ball flying high, high, high into a forest of outstretched arms. In repose, the old lawyer's face looked older than normal, the lines around his eyes more sharply etched. The corners of his mouth were pulled down, and his cheeks looked grey and papery. I noticed (as I slid on to a stool beside him) that a nerve was twitching repeatedly in his eyelid.

He looked up at me, and then over my shoulder to Jeanie, whose presence he acknowledged with a neutral nod. 'I guess we'll need a booth, then,' he said, stretching out his old limbs awkwardly.

As we were settling into one of the bright red faux-leather booths lining the wall, beneath posters of sports stars and framed match tickets, Emmie herself appeared in the doorway. She looked nervous and high-strung. She was wearing a cropped white top which showed too much bone, and a skinny faded denim skirt from which too-lean, too-straight legs protruded. Her pale blond hair, which needed cutting, was loose about her face. Looking at her, one had the impression of too much *white*.

Emmie's expression, when she caught sight of me, was bewildered. She folded herself into the seat with arms and legs that seemed all angles. She said nothing until after she had ordered herself a beer from the diminutive curly-haired wait-ress, dressed (implausibly) all in green, but when the waitress was gone, she stared me full in the face. 'Who are you?' she asked, her eyes narrowing slightly. 'I saw you at the store the other day, but I don't understand who—'

I opened my mouth to explain, but Kent got there first. 'Pretty much the best friend you'll ever have, so quit the tone, all right?' he interjected belligerently. I blinked; Emmie flushed.

'Mr Tyler, now don't be hasty, I just thought—' she began uncomfortably, but Kent waved his hand impatiently in the air.

'Shut up. *I'll* do the talkin'. This here is Quinn, a young friend of mine, and over here is her sister. From England. That's all you need to know. Let's get on with it. Your story, I mean. Start with the background.'

Jeanie and I exchanged baffled glances. Emmie shrugged, and took a quick slug of her beer.

'I . . .' She paused, and briefly shaded her eyes with her right hand. 'I don't know what you want to know exactly. Ryan – that's my ex – he says he's gonna – he's gonna take Paulie away from me,' she said at last, her voice so low we had to strain to hear her above the noise and another explosion of jubilation on the enormous television monitor above us. 'My little boy.'

'And?' prompted Kent.

'He says Paulie will be better off with him. He says everybody knows it. He says there's no point in fighting it. He says he'll tell everyone I'm an alcoholic, a drug addict, and a . . .'

There was a long pause. Kent, head cocked on one side, watching her, prompted her again. 'A . . . ?'

'A – you know, a whore,' she finished at last, with visible reluctance. 'He has' – she looked down at the table – 'some photos,' she continued stiffly. 'From a few years back. It was a stupid thing, down in a basement, this girl hooked me up with a photographer to earn money. Before I was married, I was kinda desperate. I'd lost . . . my little girl, my first baby, she died of –' Emmie gulped. 'Cot death. Woke up one morning, realized I'd slept through for the first time in months and – there she was. I went crazy for a while after that, missin' Angela so bad, people sayin' it was my fault, I shouldna' got knocked up in the first place. You know how they can be. Well, I went and got myself into real bad credit-card debt.'

I reached out and took her hand almost without thinking; she seemed too young to have been through so much horror. She barely acknowledged my touch. 'I guess I musta told Ryan about the photos.' She smiled a tiny, wan smile. 'Now he's tracked 'em down. He said – he said he'll show the court. He says I'll lose Paulie for good. I don't even know . . .' The misery flooded into her voice. 'I don't even know why he *wants* Paulie, really, except – he wants everything, I guess. And his mother said he should take Paulie away from me, 'cause she's always hated me. She used to say bad stuff about my little Angel. But I won't let it happen, Mr Tyler,' she continued, with sudden and unexpected force, banging her bottle down on the table until the beer fizzed and bubbled in a golden froth all over her hands. 'I won't let him take my son away from me. I'll – I'll tear his heart out first! I'll rip him to *pieces* if he even *touches* my little boy!' Her lip wobbled precariously; a large tear dripped down her cheek.

Kent sshed her disapprovingly, peering theatrically over his shoulder. 'Give it a break, Emmie, OK? Think about how you'll sound in front of a court!' But I found myself imagining how I would feel if someone tried to take Samuel from *my* arms. I'd kill them.

Kent was still looking around, muttering peevishly about 'death threats' and how 'Judges don't take kindly to 'em, young lady' when I leaned over the table.

'Emmie, I've got a baby myself,' I told her softly. 'I think I know – a little bit – how you feel. He's called Samuel. He's a couple of months old.'

'Really? Who's got him now?'

'My husband. You?'

'Grandfather. You nursing, then?' (A quick, evaluative look at my figure.)

'Yes. Did you?'

'Uh-huh. I—'

'OK, OK, ladies,' Kent interrupted irritably, rolling his eyes around in his head. 'Jeez! Let's get back to the point, OK? Keep to the subject. Now look, let me get this straight, Emmie. Are you saying Ryan beat you?'

Emmie became instantly interested in a piece of skin at the base of her thumbnail. 'Uh-huh. Sometimes. When I – when I forgot stuff, y'know. Or – when I was late.' She shoved her thumb oddly upside down in her mouth and started to chew; we could hear the little click of her nail flicking backwards and forwards over her teeth.

'You reported him to the police, right?' pressed Kent.

Self-consciousness flickered in her eyes. 'The nurses begged me to of course, the one time I ended up in the hospital – overnight, I mean. That was the time he broke two ribs, blew out my knee, smashed in my nose, gave me *this*' (pointing at her face). 'I was a *mess*.' She sounded almost, appallingly, proud. 'But I didn't press charges. There was no point. Lieutenant Driscoll was at school with Ryan, they go drinkin' most Friday nights at O'Rourke's. You think I'm gonna tell *him* about it? And Ryan, like he always said to me, *he's* the kind of man people believe. I'm the kind of girl they don't. That's just the way it is.'

She finished off her beer with the air of one who had communicated a deep truth about life. Ryan could go through life taking whatever he wanted, she couldn't; that was all there was to say of the matter.

Jeanie was watching her. 'Did your family ever see the bruises?' she asked suddenly.

Emmie shrugged. She was now picking the foil off her beer bottle. 'My dad saw them all the time, he used to come by and help me with stuff around the house when Ryan was at work,' she answered. 'He got himself killed in a motorbike wreck on route one a year ago,' she added evenly, 'so I guess that won't help us a whole lot. Besides, he got so damn mad at Ryan about the beating he used to get in fist-fights with him all the time. Driscoll was out at our house at least once a month, and usually wrote up the report to make Ryan come out looking good. So I don't think Dad's word would've counted for much in court. If that's what you're asking.'

'And your grandfather?' prompted Jeanie.

'He don't see what he don't want to see,' Emmie explained. 'He likes Ryan, actually, 'cause Ryan gives him a free breakfast every Sunday. The way to Gramps's heart is through his stomach, Ryan knows that. Basically Gramps thinks I should just quit the whole thing and settle down with Ryan again, although he's loyal to his own blood too; he won't stop me from leaving, he just won't help me either.'

We asked a few more questions about the details of her married life with Ryan, and her divorce, which had been handled by a young newly qualified lawyer from Yale, whom she had been put in touch with by legal aid. He had now left the state 'for something big in Chicago, I heard'.

'I gotta get back, Paulie's been wakin' up about this time recently, he hates it when I'm out,' she finished, pulling her skirt down around her skinny hips as she stood up. Then she looked down at us. 'Legal aid ain't gonna help me,' she said, her brown eyes suddenly huge in her thin white face. 'In case you're wondering, I spoke with them already. They said they gotta do the divorce, because of the state, I guess, but custody disputes is different. If you can't help me, I'm gonna lose my son.' Her eyes felt out mine. And then, to Kent, blushing a little: 'You'll call me, right?' He nodded briefly, and raised his bottle to her as she flitted like a restless, awkward little ghost out of the bright bustling bar.

Kent's eyes were fixed on mine. There was a long silence while I debated my move.

'So whaddya think?' he asked suddenly.

I stared. 'You mean about whether she's telling the truth? I think—'

160

Kent clicked his tongue impatiently. 'Of course she's tellin' the truth,' he interrupted. 'Jeez! That's obvious. I'm talkin' about *you*, my dear.'

I glanced down, astonished, as I felt Jeanie's fingers pinching my hand. 'What the—?'

'Q' – Jeanie was laughing – 'you are *such* an idiot!'

'I am?'

'Sweetheart, this is not about you twisting Kent's arm. Haven't you got it yet? This whole thing? *He's* twisting *yours* . . .'

32. Q

We've packed the bags, cleaned the house, spent as much time as we can handle with Dave, and given Jeanie a kiss. Samuel's car seat is ready, complete with the beguiling toys he will certainly ignore for the duration of our trip to the city.

New York
Never doing it again. Never driving four hours with a screaming two-month-old. Never driving with my child again. Never driving *anywhere* ever again.

Tom and I had an endlessly circular conversation over Samuel's yells in the car yesterday about whether to try a nanny rather than daycare. 'You could do with the extra help around the house. You don't cope so well with the crying – what are you going to do when I'm working?' Tom said fretfully, and I lost it, and shouted at him, because he didn't seem to understand he'd just weighed up my motherhood and found it wanting. What I couldn't quite bring myself to say was that, in my mind, a nanny is either a horrible know-it-all Mary Poppins who'll do everything better than me and make our child love *her* best while making *me* feel hideously inadequate, or an organ-thieving axe-wielding murderer who will appear sweet and trustworthy and then kidnap/slaughter/sell Samuel the second our backs are turned. Often, she's both. Tom tried suggesting we hire an au pair, but I can't figure out how an eighteen-year-old is going to cope with a screaming Samuel given that he sends me, a career woman in her late twenties, to the brink of insanity. At least I know *I'm* not going to throw him down the stairs in a fit of pique. (I think I know this.)

This morning, Tom went out for brunch with someone from work, so I was left on my own with Samuel. We went to The Met first, and after examining Ingres's solid beauties we moved upstairs to the flourish and gay chaos of the late Renaissance. It was full of paintings of delighted mothers and fat, giggling children. Samuel goggled owlishly at them for ten minutes, then began to complain. Old ladies and gentlemen, out for their morning constitutional, pulled away and stared reproachfully at us. 'It really isn't a place for children,' I heard one of them murmur discreetly into her guide. Her companion, a dapper little man in a waistcoat with huge rheumy eyes, nodded sadly. I ran downstairs to the medieval galleries, where I felt much more at home. The babies were all long and lean and tortured-looking, and the mothers were wailing.

In the sway of the baby-carrier Samuel eventually dozed off, and I walked down the steps through the sunshine to a small Upper-East-Side trattoria to meet Brianna, a friend and colleague from work. Not one of the people in Caroline's orbit, obviously: Brianna is a paralegal. To someone like Caroline, she's indistinguishable from the copier machine.

It was hot, a grilling sort of day. Tourists swirled around me looking dopey, damp unfolded maps spewing from their unzipped bags, sweaters loose around their waists, calloused feet tripping out of worn flip-flops. Red-faced, red-eyed, hair glistening with sweat, they stumbled blindly towards The Met looking as if they really hoped it might be closed.

Brianna was waiting for me; flicking her gleaming hair over

her shoulder, she tried to enfold me in a huge hug. Samuel rather got in the way. 'So great to see you, Q, I've missed you like *crazy*!' she screamed, jumping up and down like an excited cocker spaniel. Adjusting Samuel's sunhat, I said everything that was needful, then settled with her under an umbrella on the sidewalk and sipped a spritzer while chihuahuas sniffed hopefully at our chair legs.

With some difficulty I'd managed to manoeuvre myself behind the table and into the chair without waking the baby (a complicated dance that at least three other women nearby watched with private smiles of recognition). Apart from the presence of a slumbering child on my chest, the lunch was, therefore, quite like old times: two friends having lunch together.

'I was running out of ideas for take-out,' Brianna began, brightly, referring to the last time we really saw each other – just before Samuel was born. 'It's so great you're out of the house at last, after all those months in bed. You can take a real holiday. He's very good, isn't he?' She peered at his crumpled face. 'But then, babies this age don't really *do* anything, do they? Just eat and sleep. My mother always said you needed maternity leave when they get to be, like, two. This first bit's *easy*! Well, that's what she always said . . .'

She trailed off a bit, which may have been because I was baring my teeth at her. As it happens, I was actually trying to smile, but I'm not sure that's how it came across.

She changed the subject. 'We're so glad you're back. I wish you were staying for longer. Mark was saying just the other day' – she gulped a bit – 'that he was really missing Tom . . .'

Something indefinable had changed in her posture; her shoulders had rounded slightly down. They hadn't slumped, nothing as dramatic as that, but I still knew immediately that something was wrong. She'd been dating Mark, one of Tom's oldest friends, for a year or so now, this in spite of the fact that

Mark's soon-to-be-ex-wife Lara is pregnant with their third child.

I sipped at my water. 'And *how* is Mark?' I asked politely.

'Fine,' she replied. She looked miserable.

'How do you find living together?'

'Really wonderful,' she went on, blinking hard. 'Like, we just get on so well. We both love to – to shop. He's such a foodie. And we go out a lot. Mark says he's making up for lost time. All those years with Lara – and the kids . . .'

We fell silent as the waiter appeared; he fussed with our plates for a moment, officiously rearranging the glasses and the cutlery, then produced our hors d'oeuvres with a flourish: scallops for me, a big plate of garlic bread for her. As if *that* wasn't enough of a clue.

Brianna picked up her bread and ripped it in two. 'Work has been all-consuming – for him, I mean. You probably heard. He just had a big case, it went really well, there's a firm out in LA – Badden and Scutzer – that wants to hire him. He's seriously tempted to accept. Financially, it would make a lot of sense.'

Her long hair had fallen around her face; her nose was just about visible, a little bronzed point peeping delicately through the heavy dark curtain. Rip, rip, rip; she was tearing the bread into smaller and smaller pieces. I squirted my scallops with lemon and began to wolf down my plate – partly because I was starving, partly because I calculated I had six minutes before Samuel woke up. 'How do you feel about living in LA?' I asked through a full mouth.

'It's not – I mean – I have family here, and . . . it will be a big transition for me,' she replied desperately. I watched, fascinated, as the seasoned chunks rained down; her hands were now dripping pale green olive oil. 'I've always lived on the East Coast, and – and I really love the city, y'know? This is my home, I can't quite imagine living anywhere else.

'But LA – people say it's a fantastic place,' she went on feverishly. 'If you have a car, obviously. And I suppose we'll have a villa with oranges in the garden. And peaches. And a swimming pool. So it'll obviously be great. A dream life.'

'What about the children?' I couldn't restrain myself. 'Mark's kids, I mean. How does he plan to see them?'

She had picked up her napkin and began methodically wiping oil from each finger. 'Mark thinks it might be good for them,' she returned, attentively contemplating her right hand. 'He thinks they might find it easier if he's on the other side of the States, actually; he thinks it'll be a clean break. Less messy.' She had now started on her palms. *Scrub, scrub, scrub.*

'And what do *you* think?' I asked, laying my fork and knife down. The waiter walked over and, stiff with disapproval, began to clear our plates. Hers looked like a product of the apocalypse. Mine was picked so clean you could have sutured a wound on it.

'I think . . . I think they're really suffering, if you want my honest opinion,' she said, sitting back with brimming eyes, watching the waiter sweep the table. 'I think Lara's all over the place. I think the kids are bewildered and hurt and angry. Mark needs to stay here and help them work it out – *I* think. But he says I don't know what I'm talking about. He says I don't know the first thing about how to raise a kid. He says I don't really understand what being a parent is like. Of course, he's probably right . . .'

I miss Jeanie, I thought to myself with a little start of surprise, as I walked back to the apartment along the burning sidewalk an hour later. *I miss having my sister around.* My conversation with Brianna had reminded me somehow of her. In a sense I was pleased with the thought; it made me feel terribly sisterly, and it had the added pleasure of reminding me of a lack that would soon be supplied. In just a few days we'll be back in Connecticut, in the spacious coolness of the house, with her. For years (I thought, as Samuel and I picked our way carefully through the steaming traffic) my relationship with Jeanie has been on hold; there's only so much of a friendship you can build with someone over the phone, after all. We've been stuck at the time and date I got on the plane to come to America, caught in a holding-pattern, circling continuously around each other. But these last few weeks, since she touched down, we've been taking stock of each other, of our lives, of who we are now. We've been figuring out the boundaries of our relationship. Now we're ready to start pushing them out.

When I got back to the cool of the apartment, in a burst of enthusiasm I picked up the phone to tell her this. I'm so glad we're having this time together, I said enthusiastically, and I can't wait to come back to the house and be with you. How's Dave?

Fine, she told me. Really wonderful. We get on so well together. I can't wait to see you.

It was only later, when Tom was cuddled up to me sleepily on the sofa, Samuel in the bassinet at my feet, that I thought again of Brianna, on the other side of the city, partying the night away with a man who is using her to forget. And, for that matter, of Emmie Cormier, struggling against all the odds to keep her son by her side. I looked at my son, breathing slowly in and out, and at my husband, and remembered to be glad.

33. Jeanie

On Dave's fifth night here, I slipped into the slithery cotton sheets with a stomach that seemed to have a slab of lead in it. I'd cleaned my teeth so hard they were bleeding. I'd brushed my hair so long the brush itself resembled a small marsupial. My face was red with scrubbing and – for good measure – I'd polished every nail on my feet and my hands with three full coats of 'Parisian Pink'. Eventually, I let myself out of the bathroom and tiptoed across the bedroom floor, listening to Dave's breathing, wondering if he was already asleep.

As soon as my head was on the pillow, Dave's arm came snaking through the covers towards me. 'Give us a hug, love,' he said softly in the darkness.

We hugged uncomfortably. His hand started wandering downwards. I jumped out of bed.

'What the bloody hell's the matter?' he asked angrily, sitting up and staring at me, rumpling his hair in the grey light.

I danced about nervously. 'Um, nothing. Stomach-ache. And a backache. And you – you tickled me,' I enumerated unconvincingly.

'Since when've you been ticklish?' he growled. He watched me in silence for a second or two. 'Ah *shit*,' he said at last, subsiding back against the pillows. 'Stop playing around, Jeanie. You're finishing with me, aren't you?'

His gaze was unwavering, an eye of quiet in the midst of the turmoil.

'Is that right, Jeanie?' he pressed.

He started out strong, but then his voice cracked on my name; he got stuck somewhere on the 'n', stumbled heavily, lost his balance, then failed to lift up the last syllable. Somewhere, because I knew I had to, miserable and desperate, I found a 'yes'.

We stared at each other as the word left my lips, united for a second in a horrified sense of what was lost. Not just a future but a past, a history. It means something as long as it ends in 'happy ever after'. Otherwise it's nothing but a dinner-party story.

I sat down on the very edge of the bed, hands pressed hard between my knees. It was too late – not to mention absolutely cruel – to back down now. 'Dave, I'm just so sorry . . .' I began helplessly. 'I don't know what's happened. It isn't working for me any more, and I don't know why.'

He closed his eyes. 'That's that then.' Then, suddenly, he turned to me, his face set. 'There's someone else.' It wasn't a question.

'Wha—? No, no, of course there isn't—'

'There is.'

'No, Dave, honestly, there isn't.' I felt bewildered.

'Are you sure?'

'Yes, of course. Dave, I haven't even met anyone here in Connecticut except Q and Tom and . . .' I paused, and gulped.

'And?'

'Now, don't get the wrong idea, Dave. There's a friend of Tom's, the man who owns this house, and he came for a week-end, but *he* isn't – I mean, we haven't . . .'

Dave's face was as cold and set as stone. 'What's his name?'

'It doesn't matter.'

'It does to me. What's his name?'

'He's called Paul, but I'm telling you, nothing has happened between us. Nothing *will* happen. He has a girlfriend—'

'I see. You've bothered to work this out, of course.'

'It just came up in conversation. Dave, there's nothing going on between me and Paul, I don't even like him, he doesn't like me, I'm telling you, he's got nothing to do with it – nothing to do, I mean, with *us*.' I was very earnest.

'Are you sure?'

'Yes, I promise you!'

Dave's suspicious look gradually faded; at last, he sighed. 'All right, I'm sorry. I know you tell the truth. I just thought . . . It's funny really. There was me, trying to make you jealous about Ellen – I mean, even Badger said he thought you were trying to break up when you came here. Find a way out. But when you chucked half a dinner service at me I thought he was wrong. I told Badger . . . Christ. And we've had such laughs. I thought we were *strong*, Jeanie! I thought . . .' There was a long pause. '. . . you *loved me*.'

I stared down at the floor and began counting the knots in one board. (*Four, five, six . . .*)

'I don't know why you even bothered to arrange my ticket to America, unless . . . Was it – was it – pity?' His voice was rough as bark. 'Did you just feel sorry for me, Dave the loser, can't afford to pay his own way?'

'Oh, Dave, God, no, it wasn't that,' I said desperately, looking up again at last, wanting to save him something. 'I wanted to see you, of course I did. We've been together for so long, and besides, I really do like you—'

Like – not love. He saw it immediately and groaned, reaching over to the bedside table for some tea-tree gum, which he pressed out of its wrapper and slipped into his mouth. Then he rubbed his arm across his nose. ''Nuff said,' he replied at last through the thick wedge of gum. 'I get it. I'll go back to New York tomorrow, by myself, you don't have to come with me.' He was bitter. 'I'll go back to London, you don't need to see me ever again.'

'Dave, that's not what I want—'

'Well, it's what you'll get.'

I nodded slowly. I wasn't in a position to negotiate. 'I'm so sorry, Dave' (wailing a bit now) 'and you're being really good about this. Much better than I deserve.'

'Don't give me self-pity, Jeanie, I ain't going to deal with it.'

'I'm sorry.'

'Yeah. Well.'

His face was like a window that was abruptly closed, a screen that reflected but gave nothing away. 'I'll sleep on the sofa downstairs,' he said suddenly, standing up and sliding out of the enormous bed in a soft *sooosh* of the sheets. 'Get out of your space.'

'That's OK, I quite understand, thank you, not a problem,' I gabbled with strange formality. I tugged down my T-shirt, uncomfortably feeling the expanse of my legs in the field of his vision as he walked past. But he disappeared out of the room without a backward glance, shutting the door behind him with a sharp, final bang.

I sat on the bed, my knees tucked awkwardly into my shirt, and listened to the sound of the cupboard opening and closing in the corridor, Dave's hasty footsteps on the stairs, the sitting-room door clicking open and slamming closed. The sounds of pulling and shoving and dropping, followed by the blare of the TV. The sounds of Dave walking out of my life. I started to cry.

He must have been watching a film downstairs, because when I finally fell asleep at 4 a.m., I dreamed I was making love to Warren Beatty in the kitchen when poor Dave came in, saw us, and started begging me with loud tears and lamentations to marry him.

34. Q

It's funny what a difference a few months can make. Samuel is only nine weeks old, but already we are the kind of parents who swoop into the pediatrician's office with the weary air of habitués. Our first few visits to see Dr Templeton were exciting adventures, offering exquisite moments that seemed to validate our entry into the mysterious world of parenting. I found myself half watching every secretary, every passer-by, waiting for the usual squeal of delight ('My goodness! A new baby! How old?'). In the waiting room we enjoyed a rather pleasant feeling of entitlement: Tom and I were parents at last, the kind of people who could legitimately pore over leaflets about car seats and vaccines and shake their heads dolefully over the cost of nursery schools. Now all that has passed. We rushed in, sat down and inspected our watches impatiently until the nurse called Samuel's name.

'So what's going on? Samuel sleeping through the night yet?' Dr Templeton asked cheerfully when Samuel was naked on her table. She kneaded his skinny hips with long, probing fingers; he looked surprised for a moment or two, then began to whimper. No he's not, Tom replied, testily; that's why we arranged to see you today. He's not even close to sleeping through the night. And he cries *all the time*.

She shrugged her shoulders, all sympathetic understanding, and checked through her exploding sheaf of notes. He's a breast-fed child I see, she said – hmm. Bottle-fed children often sleep through the night a little bit sooner that those that are breast-fed; formula takes longer to digest; but he's sure to catch up soon. And it's a wonderful thing you're doing for him, she added, turning to me, a wide smile stretching her face. Breast-feeding is the best start you can give your child. So many wonderful health benefits!

'But I'm a little surprised to hear he's not settling down,' she went on, a slight frown creasing the skin between her eyebrows. 'Getting into more of a routine, that sort of thing. How much of the day does he cry, exactly?'

Samuel, as if on cue, switched from whimpering to wailing, arching his body away from the doctor's cool hands. She watched him in a detached fashion for a few moments, writhing on the table; within about a minute he was crying full force.

I couldn't stand it any more. I pushed past her, scooped him up and rocked him gently in my arms. I could feel her watching us.

Samuel continued to scream, a horrible sound – desperate, lost, pained, hopeless. His eyes rolled up in his head, his body became suddenly stiff, his skin flushed purple. 'I'll have to nurse him, it's the only way,' I muttered, frantically trying to get my son's resisting lips to my breast. He opened his mouth, bared his gums and kicked away from me so hard I almost dropped him. *Great*, I thought to myself, *this is looking good. Introducing Quinn Boothroyd, World's Best Mother.*

'Yes, I do see what you mean,' Dr Templeton said, or rather yelled at us, finally, after a few strategic retreats into another office to 'look something up'. 'At this stage I'm inclined to diagnose it as colic: he wasn't crying when he first came in, there's nothing obviously wrong with him, no tender spots, and some babies do keep this sort of thing up for three months, six months, even beyond. But it can't hurt to get another opinion;

there are some obvious possibilities, and we might as well investigate them properly. Reflux, for instance, is a likely candidate. How often does he vomit?'

We discussed Samuel's eating and digesting habits as best we could over the din, establishing finally that (a) it might be reflux and (b) it might not. She's sending us to someone called Dr Ezekial Sykes who apparently specializes in infant gastric disorders and who might be able to tell us more. Or might not.

'Have you tried swings?' Dr Templeton asked us brightly, just before we left. 'Or swaddling? Maybe both at once? With music?' I managed to avoid pressing my fingers into her jugular (barely), although on our way out of the office I did see a leaflet for a 'patented colic-soother' which I stowed in my pocket. Parents across the nation swear by it, apparently, and it has long been a staple in homes in Sweden. 'My child used to cry for hours a day. Then we tried the patented colic-soother and everything changed. Now people tell us our daughter is the happiest baby they've ever seen,' says Birgitta from Stockholm. It's a special bouncy chair that plays soothing sounds of the sea while moving from side to side in a way that is designed to recall the gentle rocking of the womb. Tom tells me I'm being suckered in by advertising, and has prohibited me from buying it.

'Apart from anything, Q, we've got to start thinking more carefully about how we're spending money,' Tom said later, when we were home. He opened his wallet up to me with a comical expression. 'Empty, see? And now you've decided you want us to become small-town lawyers, we just can't afford to waste cash on snake-oil.'

'It's not snake-oil,' I protested faintly. 'And you sent us to Kent first! Besides, I haven't – I mean, I haven't said that we should *commit* . . .'

'Q, I just wanted to meet him. *You're* the one that's got us swept up in some case. But if I'm wrong that you're really committed to Tyler then let's just dismiss the whole idea. Call everything off. We'll call him and say, "Sorry, you got the wrong guys. Find someone else to take over your practice."'

'Oh Tom – think about Emmie!'

'I have been thinking about her,' Tom replied, coolly. 'And frankly, she's not our problem. You barely know her. Look, Kent is clearly sympathetic to her. He'll take her on whether we come on board with the firm or not.' He sat back comfortably on the window seat, peering at the rush outside.

'I don't think so, Tom,' I returned seriously. 'He's pretty hard-bitten. He told me he simply hasn't got the space or energy at this point in his professional life to deal with a woman like her. And I believe him. It's going to take some real digging to find something on her ex-husband to shake his testimony in court. Think about it for a moment.' I came to sit beside Tom on the bench. 'Ryan is polished, good-looking and affluent. Everybody says so. He's cool under pressure, he makes great eye contact, and even Kent has heard stories about him buying up half the toy shop for Paulie. He's going to look great in court. While Emmie is rough, down-at-heel, and let's not forget that bunch of explicit photographs that'll support his claim she's worked as a prostitute.'

'Q' – turning to face me, my husband looked exasperated – 'you do choose strange people to get excited about! I have to ask you this: what is bugging you about this woman? About this case? Because, honestly, at the moment I don't get it.'

Outside, the blue sky was paling in the late afternoon; the moon, almost transparent, was slowly emerging.

'I *know* she's a good mother to that kid,' I said slowly, rubbing a space in the grit on the inside of the window around the outline of the moon. 'Don't ask me how I know, but I know. And that little boy loves her; she's his world. I can't just forget about this case, Tom – or, at least, every time I try to, I think this is the one time the law can make a real difference in a life.'

'Well, Q' (with a sigh) 'I hope you're right, darling. And I hope – God, I hope – *I've* done the right thing.'

Tom resigned from Crimpson, effective this morning. We have known, of course, for weeks, that he wouldn't be able to go back. Crimpson associates don't take vacations, not if they want to stay Crimpson associates. I'm not sure they'd even let him back in the building. But he had nothing to lose, not once the partners told him he wouldn't make partner. At least, that's the way I look at it. Paul has set him up with some consulting work to help bridge the gap until we've decided what to do next, and this will bring in quite enough to cover our expenses. 'Of course you've done the right thing,' I assured him therefore, confidently, nuzzling his neck. 'We don't need to be rolling in money, darling. We just need enough to live, while we decide what we want to do next.'

35. Jeanie

'You might not want to come to New York now – I mean, Paul will be here tomorrow night, he's coming to talk to Tom about work things, and I know you don't think much of him.'

Q sounded as if she was plump in the intersection between baffled, appalled and ecstatic when I explained to her that Dave had already left – that rather than coming down with me to New York for the weekend, as we'd originally planned, he'd gone to the airport to talk himself on to an earlier flight. I was still in a mild state of shock about the whole thing. 'But why did you – but why did he – but I thought that you – Oh, listen, you'll have to tell me all about it later,' Q went on, urgently, 'and I want *all* the details. But in the circumstances it seems a bit pointless to come all this way when, as I said, Paul is coming for dinner.'

'Well,' I began uncertainly, but Q cut in again.

'On the other hand,' she added thoughtfully, 'we could do with you on the car journey back. The trip here was just dreadful. You could help me keep Samuel entertained, so if you don't *mind . . .*'

That settled it. 'Of course I'll come, Q,' I said immediately, realizing suddenly that there was nothing in the whole world I wanted as much as a few days in New York. The sights – the cocktail bars – the shopping; Alison asked me to look for a particular belt in Bloomingdale's, and she's even offered to buy one for me if it's in stock. 'I'll get a train down from New Haven and I'll phone you to let you know what time I arrive,' I explained.

I spent the afternoon working my way through a packet of 'English muffins' (i.e. not cakes) dripping butter over the computer keyboard as I searched databases for jobs in social work (having been passed over for the job in Cumbria; not a surprise). There *are* positions out there, of course; if you fancy spending a hundred-odd hours a week sorting out metamphetamine addicts for £16,000 a year, your options are legion. Of course, with that salary, the only place in London you'll be able to live is a cardboard box under Tower Bridge, and you'll be finding your evening meal in the bins outside Starbucks, but who could be so churlish as to care about that?

But positions that pay well and seem emotionally and intellectually appealing are few and far between. If I'm not careful I'll have to take up my old job at the Firefly Theatre again to keep me going when I get back (I've been working shifts in the front of house there for three years), I thought to myself. They would be thrilled, of course; Marge was at her most seductive the day before I left. 'None of the new staff know a thing about the theatre, darling, we'll miss you dreadfully,' she said fretfully through her pink Sobranie. 'Sergio will have to take over your job, but seriously, sweetie, he's not a patch on you, no organizational skills at all, and he will keep trying to hire his little friends. Half of them don't even speak English, and I just *can't* have them jabbering in the boxes, Val would kill me. Sweetheart, say you'll come back to your old job when you return from America, mmm ? We've got a mad schedule starting in September; I'd love to know you were taking up the reins again. Val was talking about you just the other day, you know, in the most *adulatory* terms!'

It's nice to be wanted, even by Marge, the Firefly's diminutive, fey, narrow-minded front-of-house director and Val, the stomping, sallow-faced general manager. But I stubbornly resisted their blandishments. I haven't spent the last year getting a social work degree to go back to shift work, particularly not at the Firefly (lots of responsibility, no job security, and no chance of advancing as long as Marge is in bed with Val. I only got the job in the first place because Alison knew Marge at university). So I told her no, and consented to be kissed and cried over, and swore blind to myself (when I'd firmly removed Marge's hand from my left breast) that hell would freeze over before I went back.

So I sent off three applications through cyberspace to who-knows-what bored recipients, crossing my fingers as I did so, although I'm not sure if that was to help me *get* the jobs or *not* get them. Then, just as I finished, I received a phone call from my self-obsessed flatmate Una. I wanted to tell her all about Dave but she kept sighing pointedly and asking if I could *possibly* talk more quietly. Aggrieved, I was in the middle of asking her why she'd rung in the first place if she didn't want me to talk when she cut me off mid-sentence to ask if I *really* need my room next month, because her sister is coming to stay and she's promised her my bed. I asked her sarcastically if she'd like me to live in the States permanently, just so her sister could have my room. She actually brightened for a moment and asked if I was serious.

36. Q

My conversation with Fay on Friday went something like this.

Me: Hi, lovely to see you again nice to see the offices everything going well you'll hardly miss me think I need a few more months not ready yet how are you?

Fay: Huh?

Me: Um . . .

Fay: What did you say?

Me: When?

Fay: Just now?

Me: About what?

Fay (taking a deep breath): Q, what did you say two minutes ago when you sat down, please? You spoke so fast I couldn't catch a word of it.

Me: Ah. Yes. Well.

Ten minutes later we more or less understood each other, although there was a glint in her eye that suggested she understood rather more than I necessarily want her to understand right now. We've agreed I'll put together a letter for the partners explaining my request for two more months of leave.

'It won't be on full pay, you know, Q, but I'll see what I can manage. And that's *all* you're asking for, is it? This isn't a preliminary to a resignation, I assume?'

I gulped and dragged a smile on to my face. 'Of course not,'

I said brightly, knowing that if I said it was, the whole game would be over.

Walking out through the building felt strange. After my meeting with Fay I took the flight of steps down to my office, expecting to find everything changed: Fay told me they had to let a couple of summer associates share it last month, but neither of them seemed to have left much imprint of their personalities on the room. In fact, I found things almost as I left them the day I went on bed rest, five months ago. On a pad of fluorescent green Post-it notes I discovered a doodle I suddenly remembered working on, a series of interlocking curls with what looked like a hamster at the bottom (I think it was actually a self-portrait: me at twenty-six weeks pregnant). My screen-saver – an old photograph of our garden back home in Kent – faded in and out, in and out, eerily reminding me of an empty room of my childhood. The plants on the windowsill were unexpectedly thriving: Jayne, a new secretary, stopped by and shyly told me she'd been feeding and watering them. I felt oddly touched, as if someone had been looking after me all this time, and I didn't even know about it. Of course the desk was tidied, the chaos ruthlessly rearranged by some unknown hand, and all the file notes for ongoing cases were sifted, sorted and refiled. It struck me, as I gently pulled the door closed, that the office looked as if it belonged to me, but a *better* me. An organized, hardworking me with a workable filing system, a neat array of highlighter pens, and an excellent supply of Miracle-Gro.

I exchanged cheerful greetings with my colleagues as I walked along the floor and then down in the elevator ('Hey, Q, how ya doing? You look – uh, great!' they enthused, not entirely convincingly). Then, just as I reached the heavy revolving doors – almost safe! – I bumped into Caroline in the hall. Just my luck. She was with a client; he was clad in a formal grey suit, while Caroline was in spotless, pitilessly tailored black. 'What are *you* doing here, Quinn?' she asked sharply.

'I came in to meet Fay,' I explained, smiling politely.

She looked expectant.

'You'll be getting a letter from me asking for extended maternity leave,' I added cheerfully. 'I'd like to take a couple more months.'

'I see.' She almost – but didn't quite – sneered.

No, you don't, I thought to myself, *you don't see anything unless it's directly related to your professional reputation*, but I didn't say anything. Instead, I shook hands with the client. He was someone I'd met before and, remembering that one of his children was disabled, I asked after his health. The man looked slightly surprised, I thought, but he was friendly, and even managed to ask after Samuel. Caroline, who was obviously not listening, was tapping a glossy foot on the great marble floor. I caught sight of her checking her slim silver watch.

'Give me a call the week before you come back, Quinn,' she said abruptly, turning towards the elevator when the client and I had finished speaking. 'We should talk.'

'Of course, Caroline, I'll be happy to.'

She dismissed me with a brief nod as the elevator doors smartly shut them from sight.

I left the building feeling thoughtful. If going to work was just about seeing people and sitting in a quiet office for a few hours every day, I'd be happy to go back. It's the *work* part I'm not so thrilled about: the rush and the fuss, the pointless office politics, the smug clients, and being condescended to by the partners. I hate Caroline's awful superiority. I hate that she's in a position to call the shots. I want (I thought, as I scooped my son lovingly into my arms, when I finally got home) to be in charge of my own life.

37. Jeanie

Just my luck, my train was delayed; I arrived at Tom and Q's flat dripping with sweat, hair starting from my head like wild Medusa serpents, a bare two minutes before Paul swung into the sitting room in a pressed Armani suit, cool and poised as always, with a very expensive bottle of chilled white wine under his arm. He then produced, from a pristine paper bag, an expansive collection of take-out boxes from a place called Jo's Shanghai in China Town: 'Best soup dumplings in the city!'

At first I tried to use Samuel as an excuse to avoid him, but my nephew seemed to have forgotten me and struggled skittishly in my arms. Q worked extremely hard to persuade me that he'd actually been missing me these past four days. 'I think he only really began to get over you yesterday, and then he probably thought he wouldn't see you again, so it was a sort of *coping mechanism* to forget you . . .' she told me anxiously.

Paul, it must be said, was a model of politeness throughout the evening. The food was scrumptious, he wouldn't let anyone pay, he kept our glasses topped up with wine, and he even cleared away most of the mess, pushing a laughing, faintly resisting Q back into her seat. I went into the kitchen to help him. 'Hold open the trash bag for a second, Jeanie, let me get this in – OK, great. And . . .' He cast his eyes quickly around the room. 'I think that's it. So why did you stay in Connecticut by yourself, then?' he asked curiously as we walked back together into the sitting room. 'Why didn't you come down to New York with Q and Tom?'

This was the moment I'd been waiting for. 'I couldn't leave my work at the Home,' I said airily. 'You know how it is. The old people expect me now, I wouldn't want to disappoint them . . .' Paul looked surprised, but then Tom, who was pouring the Scotch, jumped in.

'*And* she was spending time with her boyfriend,' he explained chirpily. 'Nice guy. Name of Dave. Only she dumped him, just when we finally got to liking him . . .' Q kicked him, and he turned to look at her, eyes wide open with surprise. 'Wha—? But didn't you . . .' Q kicked him again. Hard.

I felt myself flush. 'Yes, well. Things didn't go – er, very well,' I said uncomfortably, feeling exposed before Paul's suddenly penetrating gaze. 'We – er – decided it would be better to – um – part,' I said foolishly, sounding like something out of a 1940s radio play. I flushed even deeper. Where did that come from?

Paul looked away. 'I'm sorry. None of my business, of course,' he said politely.

But now an awkward silence fell, and for some reason I felt absolutely compelled to fill it. 'Mmm. It was time to move on,' I suggested, dragging a few more clichés into the mix. 'Er, call it a day, you know. Quit while we were ahead. Give it a rest, finish the deal.' I realized some woman was gabbling pointlessly on, and since I appeared to have control over her mouth, I shut it.

There was another, even more awkward silence. Then, to my complete astonishment, Paul, who was now sitting on the window bench, started talking instead – and, in a quiet, measured voice, he told us all about his break-up with Tina last week, and he wasn't using the language of clichés, he was actually *telling* us, in detail, what really happened. Tina, he explained, was lovely and talented,

184

and clearly a catch, but somehow, to him, brain-deadeningly dull. He'd kept it going for months, he said, hoping they'd click; he'd taken her off for romantic breaks in Paris and Prague until she was half off her head with love for him, but he'd only proved to himself that he couldn't, in fact, care for her. But by this point her mother was making discreet enquiries into the availability of certain high-class hotels on Saturdays in June next year and she (he had it on good authority) had actually tried on a Vera Wang.

As he talked and talked about the nightmarish world he'd found himself in, where a perfectly nice woman was thinking thoughts he himself thought she had a perfect right to think, I couldn't help saying, *I know exactly what you mean*, and *Yes, I felt that way too*. We moved on to the failings of our former partners, the justification for our need to ditch them; then, gingerly stepping over the barrier and coming to sit beside him on the bench, I told him about the time Dave broke off, while we were kissing, to scrawl 'Portsmouth 2, Spurs 1' on the cover of a paperback on the bedside table. And instead of looking shocked or disgusted at the disclosure, he laughed, then told me about the time he saw Tina checking her hair in the mirror at a similarly intimate juncture. An hour later we'd talked ourselves to a standstill – at which point we looked up to discover that Tom and Q were passed out cold on the sofa, snoring slightly. And I swear to God, I don't know how it happened, but suddenly Paul's lips were on mine, and he was kissing me.

Dave's kisses are usually brief and cold, a short match-opener before the real thing begins – hand moves down, underwear comes off, and the whole thing's done in a few short minutes. With Paul, something else happened entirely, a sort of suspension of consciousness. I know we moved out of the sitting room into the hallway, just out of sight of my sister and Tom, and I have a strong mental picture of my top lying, cast off, on the floor, but when or how those things happened, I can't really say. Time passed in a haze. I remember he told me (fingers wound in my hair) that I was beautiful, that he hadn't thought about anyone else, about anything else, since the first moment we met. I remember I told him that he was quite impossible, and I didn't like him at all. But I didn't stop kissing him.

Then Samuel suddenly squawked. We heard Q start off the sofa like a race horse at the sound of a gun.

The woman only sees her child, thank God. Paul and I, laughing foolishly in the darkness of the hallway, righted ourselves hastily, me locating and dragging on the battle-torn top, he fastening his shirt with (I flatter myself) still-shaking fingers, while Q flurried about anxiously in Samuel's basket. The two of us then assumed casual, we-were-just-fetching-this-new-bottle-of-Scotch poses and sauntered into the room. When Samuel was calm, Q sighed thankfully, glanced at Tom (who was still sleeping), then over at Paul and – just perceptibly – above his head at the clock on the wall behind. He immediately took the point. 'I'm so sorry, Q, I must be going now,' he said hastily, spotting his polished wallet on the floor and sliding it into his pocket. 'Say goodnight to Tom for me, OK?' he added, looking down at my brother-in-law's recumbent form. 'And I'll – um – call you,' he added to the air in the middle of the room as he walked out of the door.

Q turned to smile at me, wearily. 'Sorry we fell asleep on you, love, and you must be tired yourself. I hope you didn't mind keeping Paul entertained for us,' she said. I looked at her face closely, trying to see if she was being discreet, but there was nothing knowing in her expression at all.

'No problem, anything I can do to help you both out,' I said with an air of great virtuousness as I padded off to the bathroom through the hall. 'Really, anything at all.'

186

38. Q

We heard from a secretary in the office of Dr Sykes (the gastric specialist) first thing, offering us a cancellation spot for tomorrow afternoon. 'Thank God,' I said to Jeanie fervently, as I put down the phone. 'Maybe he can give us some answers, you know?'

My sister had been grumpy all weekend, grousing about everything from the bread in the local bakery – too many cranberries, apparently – to the thinness of our toilet paper. 'What is this stuff, tracing paper?' she said scathingly on Sunday, appearing in the sitting room with a piece of the stuff suspended disdainfully between thumb and forefinger. 'We got rid of this in Britain in the 1970s!' Tom, who had been getting increasingly irritated with her, said some things at this point that he later regretted. Or at least, I hope he did.

'I don't know how much longer we can keep going. I wish I knew what was wrong with Samuel – if there *is* something wrong, that is,' I continued. 'I can't tell you how much I hope this Dr Sykes can help us. Maybe there's some medicine that will help him, a painkiller, who knows . . .'

Jeanie, dressed in my robe, was bleary-eyed. 'Mmm,' she offered vaguely, clasping her coffee to her chest. She looked shattered, preoccupied, wrapped up in herself.

'I mean, I love Samuel,' I went on, sliding on to a seat beside her, 'but sometimes I think my head is going to explode. All that crying is destroying my brain cells. And sometimes –' I dropped my voice anxiously – 'sometimes I can't help worrying that he isn't developing *normally*. I have a book about child development, and it tells you what a child of his age should be doing. It talks about tracking, you see, which means—'

'Following an object with his eyes; I know.' Jeanie's tone was irritable; she put her fingers tenderly to her forehead. 'I didn't sleep too well last night, Q. Things on my mind . . .'

I ignored this, since *I* was up half the night with a screaming child. 'Actually, he's not tracking well *at all*, Jeanie, to be honest. I've been trying with a red pencil the last few mornings, the way it tells you in a book, skimming it in front of his gaze, and his eyes only follow the object for *twelve*, not *eighteen* inches in an arc. I worry—'

'You got the ruler out, did you?' Jeanie's voice was now frankly acerbic. 'Twelve, not eighteen inches? Christ. You'd better sign the child up for special schooling straight away, Q.'

I stared at her. 'There's no need to be so catty,' I said, wondering what on earth had got into her. 'Is there something wrong?'

She reached over, picked up the pot and poured herself another cup of coffee. 'No, there isn't. I'm sorry, Q, I'm just very tired,' she replied, sighing. 'It's been a really *emotional* few days for me, since I arrived. And you know, Alison says children with colic often experience minor developmental delays, so I think you should just forget about those six measly inches. No point worrying yourself over small things like that.'

For a second, the world seemed to have stopped turning on its axis. 'Alison says – *what*?'

Jeanie choked on her coffee. 'Alison says – I mean, that is to say, she once told me – um – I remember her talking about somebody *else's* child who has colic—'

'Jeanie, have you been talking to Alison about Samuel?'

The expression of guilt on her face was ludicrously obvious. 'No. I mean not really. A bit, I suppose. Now and again. She guessed—'

'Oh my God, you have! You've been talking to Alison. I don't believe it,' I gasped, rigid with fury. 'What have you told her?'

She shrank away from me, her eyes wide and round. 'I didn't mean – I just – I wanted her advice about Samuel, you see, and – and—' She swallowed; her face turned red. 'Christ, Q, you are *such* a prima donna!' She stood up to face me. 'You don't want Alison to know anything! But she just wants to help, you know. She's worried about you, she's on the other side of the world, but you cut her out, you behave as though she's some sort of monster. What, because she has a nice house and she dresses her children in white?'

'Jeanie, I can't even believe you're saying this,' I retorted, puce and apoplectic. 'You know Alison as well as I do – or at least I thought you did. She's not just any old sister, she's – Alison. She's been itching to prove I'm failing for months. I thought we were on the same side. Now it seems you've been going behind my back for – how long?'

'For bloody years!' (We were both panting now.) 'If I want advice, I go to Alison actually, did you know that? I don't go to you, Q, because you just tell me to "grow up". Alison actually listens and tries to help. She gives me practical advice. *You* condescend to me. And you think Alison's superior? Take a fucking look in the mirror, sister dear!

'And you tell everyone – like those rich people we met, Adjile and Lily – that you and I feel the same way about her. "We think her art is terrible. We don't really like her." Did you ever think to ask *me* before you announced my opinion to the world? Of course not! As it happens, Q, I think some of her recent stuff has been bloody good, and I'm not the only one

189

who thinks so. She's had some really good write-ups in the press, not that you'd know anything about it. I think if one of the three of us is going to be remembered fifty years from now, it's going to be *her*.'

'Well, I'm sorry, I didn't realize she had her very own fan club. With you as the president.' The floor seemed to be dropping away under my feet; I was so tired, so utterly bone-shattered, and now *this*!

'Don't belittle me, Q.' Jeanie was mutinous. 'Don't put me down. I'm not an idiot.'

She swooped out of the kitchen in a violent swoosh of pink velvet, robe tie trailing behind her. I stared, baffled, at the space where she had been sitting.

39. Jeanie

'Hello.' His voice was warm and husky. 'Can you meet me at the juice bar over the road?'

I was sitting on the floor in the bathroom, knees hugged to my chest, sobbing in the aftermath of a vast, terrible fight with my sister Q, when the phone began to ring. I waited, expecting her to pick it up, but she didn't; eventually I went and answered it. The apartment was empty.

His voice came pouring like thick honey into my ears. *Will you meet me?* Of course, I murmured, forgetting Q, forgetting the two days of no phone call, forgetting everything. I threw myself into the shower and into some clothes. (Not too many, of course.)

This is too soon, it's too soon after Dave, I shouldn't be doing this: the thought drummed in my brain as I dodged the yellow cabs that dart through the traffic like so many tropical fish, and ran across the road. I saw him waiting for me on a bar stool by the window of the juice bar, and all conscious thoughts evaporated from my mind. One hand was loosely in his trouser pocket, the other was casually, delicately, twirling a straw. He stood up as I came in, a funny little show of old manners, then stooped down to kiss me, swiftly, on the lips.

I sat down on the stool next to him, wishing away the space between us, although he arranged himself so that his knees were touching my hip. Hot as sunburn. 'So?' His voice was low. I had to bend closer to listen.

'So?' I returned, pulling slightly away again, playfully stupid. He put his head on one side, looking quizzical. 'I'll have something – with raspberries, I think,' I went on demurely.

He went to order my drink, appearing a few moments later with a tall pink beaker armed with a swizzle stick topped with a plastic raspberry. 'There, is that what you wanted?' Standing behind me, he murmured the words in my ear; I could feel his hot breath on my skin. Everything prickled. *I don't know you, I don't know you . . .* For a second the thoughts throbbed inside me, but then I looked up into his face, and everything went silent again. I pulled the hair away from my face and drank.

'What did you tell your sister?' he asked.

'I didn't say anything,' I replied, a little consciously. 'She's out.' I investigated his broad, handsome face. 'What are you doing here? Shouldn't you be at work?'

He grinned at me. 'I'm skiving – isn't that what you Brits say? I'm on my way to visit a client uptown, the car kinda found itself on Second Ave, and I couldn't bring myself to sail straight past your apartment building. Driver's waiting over there for me, actually.'

He nodded out of the window. A long black car was parked on the street corner; a man in a black suit with dark glasses was standing beside it, smoking a cigarette while drumming his fingers against the roof. He looked hot and uncomfortable in the morning sun.

'He looks warm,' I said, feeling sorry for him.

'That's New York for you. It's been a terrible summer. Listen, I'm sorry I was out of touch this weekend. When can we have dinner?'

'Well . . .' (sigh) 'We're going back up to your house in Connecticut the day after tomorrow, so . . .'

'Tonight or tomorrow, then,' he replied, musing. 'But tonight is difficult for me, it would have to be late, I've got a midnight deadline for filing papers at the courthouse. I'll have more time tomorrow night . . .' He pulled his organizer out of his pocket and flicked through some screens with the stylus. I can honestly say it's the first time I've ever been out with someone who has to use a BlackBerry to schedule me in.

'It's a shame you're a lawyer,' I said, watching him. 'The hours, I mean. Q complains about them all the time. And Tom too. I don't know how you live like this. So little free time. Were you working all weekend? I mean it's like that film, *The Firm*, isn't it?'

He laughed. 'Not really. And yes, I had a series of meetings with some people from IBM.'

I blushed and twiddled my fingers. 'But you do have to defend all kinds of awful people.'

'What do you mean?' He looked surprised.

I blushed even more deeply. 'Well – murderers and fraudsters, I mean. You have to take on their cases just because they're rich. Isn't it terribly unfair?'

Paul had drawn back from me slightly, but after a moment his face relaxed in a smile and he took my hand. 'Jeanie, you'll have to come with me into the office sometime,' he said, laughing a little. 'You might be surprised. It's not just defending "murderers and fraudsters", as you put it. We even have innocent people.'

'Well, but that's just it, they aren't all innocent, are they? I mean, how do you feel defending someone you know is guilty of raping a woman, and he has the money to hire you, and she doesn't? Or some company has dumped tons of toxic waste into a river, and half the residents glow bright green in the dark, but they can't afford you while the company can? Isn't that terrible?' It wasn't clear to me that this was the best line to take with him, but I was cross, and my mouth just kept on going.

Paul stared at me with an inscrutable expression. 'Is this a settled antipathy to lawyers? Or just the opinion of the moment?' he asked coolly.

It was the BlackBerry that finally did it, I think. It made him seem so unaccountably alien.

'No, I mean – well, I'm just asking . . .'

'And that's what I like about you.' He leaned across the table and suddenly took my hand. 'Listen, Jeanie, sometime we can talk properly about this, I can explain more about what I do. It'll have to be over dinner, though; I can't keep my client waiting any longer. So you'll have to keep imagining me as Satan incarnate for the next twenty-four hours. What do you think: are you willing to eat with the devil tomorrow night?'

He was utterly beautiful, and he was looking back at me with an expression that was frankly desiring. Vague ideas of lawyers and their wrongs evaporated entirely from my mind. I leaned over, and for answer – feeling nervous, a tiny bit shocked at my own daring – I kissed him.

A businessman on the stool on the other side of Paul hastily lifted up his newspaper; at a nearby table, two thin girls with lashings of hair giggled and muttered something spiteful. I vaguely noticed their expressions, and for about a second I felt a tiny part of me that was uneasy in the bottom of my stomach quite acutely, like a pea beneath the mattress. And then it dissolved, or maybe I simply didn't notice it any more. Even in a brightly lit juice bar at 10 o'clock on a Monday morning Paul makes me think of nights on a tropical beach in warm, wet sand. You just wish *you* had a man like this, I telegraphed to the spiteful girls with a small smug smile. He had his hand on the small of my back and was pulling me half off my stool into him, and I had the same hazy feeling of the other night, as if I was losing myself in his body.

He pulled away at last, and rested his forehead against the top of my head. 'This isn't the place,' he whispered into my eyes (I could see his heart thumping through his shirt, the cotton vibrating gently to its rhythm). 'And I really have to go . . .' He reached down and lifted up my chin with delicate, gentle fingers. 'We can't forget about Brett outside in the heat now, can we?' he said, laughing softly. 'I'll call you later today.' I nodded, or maybe I shook my head, I don't quite know, and he kissed me again, then reached down and picked up a brief-case from under the counter. I saw Brett chuck away his cigarette butt as Paul approached, then smartly open the door. Paul got in, and his tall form was immediately lost behind the car's smoky windows. The long black limousine pulled off into the traffic.

I started drinking my weird raspberry drink without really knowing what I was doing. I think I swirled the swizzle stick around a lot, and I clearly spent a great deal of time pleating a napkin. When I eventually glanced up, it was to discover that the newspaper-reading businessman was looking at me as if he was wondering if I offered the same services to all men in suits. The girls at the nearby table looked as if they wanted to strike up a conversation. The little people with white-and-blue hats behind the counter were glowering at me as if I'd besmirched their work environment. I hastily put down the beaker (secret-ing the raspberry swizzle stick in my handbag as I did so, as a small memento), then slid off my stool and left.

I walked slowly to Q's flat. She was back now, and was sit-ting with a newspaper spread out in front of her. 'Just popped out to get – um – some hankies,' I announced, not very con-vincingly, to her poker-straight back.

'We have plenty of Kleenex,' she replied suspiciously. 'Right *there*.' She pointed to a large rainbow-coloured box smack in the middle of the table.

'Well, I needed some pocket ones,' I explained, feeling as guilty as if – well, as if I was having an affair.

My sister looked dour. 'Another secret, Jeanie?' she asked sarcastically, and then she turned round and went back to her newspaper.

40. Q

It took me three attempts to reach Alison. She was out, she explained, preparing for a meeting at the Arts Council to discuss potential funding for a new exhibition of young women sculptors 'seeking to capture the life force'. I was so irritated, so pent up, so desperate to vent my frustration on her, I could hardly sit still for the four hours I was forced, by circumstance, to wait. I remembered a time when we were eight, when she told our mother – something or other, I don't even remember now – but it wasn't true, and I was desperate to accuse her. It felt just like that.

'What the hell have you and Jeanie been talking about?' I began furiously when she eventually picked up my call. There was an astonished pause.

'I'm sorry?'

'I know you've been talking about me. I know she's been telling you all about Samuel. About his colic.'

'Is that so terrible?' Alison's tone was mild as milk toast. 'She's very worried about you, darling. And so am I. We talk about you, and I talk with Mother. We wonder how best to help you. Would you rather we didn't?'

'You know, Alison' – I was almost breathless, choking with rage, but struggling to force my thoughts into coherence – 'you know I find your intervention *very* difficult to take.'

'Yes, I do know that, darling.' There was a long pause;

through the faint sound of her quickened breathing I could hear that damn clock of hers in the background. It's an heirloom, a wedding present from Sir Evelyn Farquhar, granddaddy and patriarch of the Farquhar family, and its resonant tick, marching on inexorably through the centuries, reminded me of everything I find so frustrating about my sister and her new life.

'You don't understand the first thing about me, Alison, but you use everything you *do* know to get one over on me,' I continued wrathfully. 'You would just love to know that I'm a disastrous mother, wouldn't you? Q may have a career, you can say to all your friends, but she's simply terrible at bringing up a baby. It doesn't come naturally to her, somehow.'

'Oh, *don't* be ridiculous—'

'And the idea that you've conscripted Jeanie in this endeavour makes me just furious.'

'You've made your feelings about *that* perfectly clear. Q is angry with Alison. Here we are again. I thought we were making progress during your pregnancy, but obviously not.' *Tick, tick, tick*: Granddaddy Farquhar marched on.

'No. And we won't be making any progress as long as you try to undermine me.' I matched her tone, feeling triumphant.

There was a long silence; Alison was clearly debating her next move. When it came, though, it wasn't what I expected at all.

'Geoffrey had colic,' she blurted out, and at that moment the clock struck loudly in the background, a deep sonorous bass that for a second dominated everything. *Bong, bong, bong . . .* the tones were rich and golden, the clock's voice filling her room, my ear, with confident noise. It was eight o'clock in London. Even as I took in the meaning of her words I found myself wondering where her husband was.

'He had colic? Really?' It is a sign of how poor our relationship has become that I didn't quite believe her.

'Really.'

'I – *When*?'

'From about five weeks to four months, or thereabouts,' she went on jerkily. 'I'm not making this up, Q, so you needn't sound so suspicious! It was the worst experience of my life. By far. I thought I was going to go mad. I'm not sure why I didn't. Maybe – maybe in a sense I did, looking back. One night I was so desperate to sleep I – I almost threw him out of the window. It was about five o'clock in the morning, he'd been screaming for the best part of forty-eight hours, I hadn't slept for two months, and I was right on the edge. *Right* on the edge. It was only the feel of the night air on my skin, when I actually opened the window, that stopped me.'

I took this in. 'You never said anything,' I said at last.

'No.' *Tick, tick, tick.* She laughed mirthlessly. 'Like you, I suppose.'

I tried to think what to say. 'Alison, I—'

'I mean, how could I even *think* about hurting my son?' she cut in; to my utter astonishment, tears flooded her voice. I don't think I've heard her cry in twenty years. 'Every time I look at him, even now, Q, I think about what I almost did. I remember how detached I'd become, how I – almost hated him. I suppose at least,' she half laughed, half gasped, 'I know the worst part of myself now. The bottom; the blackest part. I couldn't explain it all to Gregory, you see, he's not—' She stopped herself. 'I mean, he's a wonderful father in lots of ways, but he couldn't bear it when the baby cried. He said he had too much to do at work, he just couldn't bear it. He wanted me to make it all go away, make the crying stop. But I couldn't, I couldn't!

'Sometimes he'd send his mother over, but *she's* one of those people who thinks you should just give babies to a nursemaid until it's time to pack them off to boarding school. She's from a very different generation to us, or maybe it's the class thing, I don't know. Anyway, every time she came to the house she positively *reeked* disapproval. She told me I was smothering him, that boys need to learn to stand alone; one day, she even said *that* was why he was crying. I didn't believe her, but I – I couldn't fail, do you see, Q? I couldn't fail. I had to prove my way, the loving way, would work. And then when Geoffrey kept crying, on and on and on, no matter what I did, I got so angry . . .

'So you see, Q' (with a strange, hollow bitterness) 'you don't need to worry that I'm judging you. Really, it's not like that at all. I – I meant it when I said I wanted to – to – help.'

'Alison' – the words come slowly, dragged out unwillingly – 'I don't think you're the first mother to be tempted in – in that way.'

She laughed shortly. 'No, maybe not. But I almost did it, Q. I actually got as far as the window.'

I thought back suddenly to a night, a few weeks ago, when Samuel was screaming and screaming in my ear, when the noise was like a blade stabbing and slashing through my brain, when every nerve inside me was flayed and raw and red – when the only thing I wanted was to be asleep, unconscious, beyond sensation. And in that moment I had a flash of a thought, clear as a church bell in fog: if I killed him, I could sleep. Horrified immediately, I buried the appalling thought as deep as I could. I put it in a box, and I shut the lid, and I locked it tight, and then I put it inside another, bigger, stronger box, and I dug and dug through the deepest layers of my consciousness, and when I got to the very bottom of everything I put it there, and I covered it up again, and I hoped it would never emerge. I didn't actually take my son to the window, but . . .

'Alison, I've had Tom by my side, particularly these last few difficult weeks,' I said softly. 'Whereas you and Gregory . . .'

'He's never been able to do "the baby thing", as he calls it,' she remarked. 'He would actually leave the room when the crying began, or go upstairs to the spare bedroom if it started during the night. And the only thing that calmed the baby was breastfeeding, so there was nothing he could *do* anyway. There wasn't any point in him suffering, you see, since he couldn't really help anyway. I was – everything to Geoffrey. Well, *you* know.'

'The law doesn't police thought,' I returned, gently. 'You didn't *do* anything, Alison.'

'Oh, darling!' (her voice as bright and hard as a diamond, through tears); 'Would that make *you* feel any better?'

Tom came home ten minutes later to find me lying on the floor, the phone still gripped in my hand, talking earnestly. Samuel was, for a blessed moment, clasped quietly to my breast. 'Who?' he mouthed at me, curiously, and the expression on his face when I whispered back, 'Alison', was a sight to behold.

41. Jeanie

'I want to take you to my favourite place tonight,' he explained on the phone. 'It's in the Village. I'll pick you up outside the apartment building at seven. We'll have cocktails first, then we'll go for dinner.'

And then, I thought to myself. And then . . .

No sleep for me last night, I was too busy staring at the ceiling thinking about what Paul looks like and feels like and smells like, trying to remember if he has a mole under his neck or if it is just behind his ear, if his eyes are grey-green or grey-blue, if he uses aftershave, and for the life of me I couldn't quite conjure up the sound of his voice in my mind's ear. I am looking forward to getting the answers to these questions properly cleared up tonight. And I have a few more lines of enquiry to pursue.

I spent yesterday choosing/washing/ironing a delectable outfit. I've told Q I'm seeing an old friend from school – I happen to have a friend who's moved out to Brooklyn – although quite why this necessitates borrowing her Versace heels is somewhat unclear. She's not particularly sharp at the moment, though. 'Oh God, if someone can get some use out of these things, I'm pleased,' she said, inspecting the lovely black spiky things as if they were purchased in another lifetime.

'Alison and I have . . . reached an understanding,' she told me quietly last night, after dinner. 'There are some things we find we've shared, I can't quite explain, but I don't want you to worry that you've made things *worse*.' I wasn't quite sure what to make of this (what on earth did Alison tell her?), but at least I seem to be out of trouble. I apologized for being so horrible, feeling very contrite, then Q asked me seriously how my comparative study of Cumbria and Connecticut was coming along. This was tricky, because I haven't given it a second thought since Cumbria rejected my job application. So I suggested I was 'narrowing my focus' and planning a study of Connecticut's geriatric care instead. She insisted on asking me for details, which was quite wearing, although I think I got away with it by diverting her with stories about the people at Quiet Lanes.

I'm not ready to open up to Q about Paul just yet. I want him to be my secret. As soon as I tell her 'I'm seeing Paul' I know what will happen: 'You're not at all like his last girlfriend,' or 'You *are* a bit like his last girlfriend,' or 'Tom, do you remember that time with Paul when we . . . ?' or 'Tom, when we had Paul over for dinner three years ago, didn't he . . .' She'll want to tell me about him. For the time being, I want to find out about him all by myself.

Hair: up. Neckline: down. Hemline: fluttery. Nails: blush. Lips: red. Undies: tiny (almost invisible, in fact. I debated the 'Access all Areas' pair for comedy value, then decided uproarious laughter is not actually what I want to produce if we reach the underwear stage).

Q's in-laws are coming for lunch, and this afternoon they're taking Samuel to the doctor's. Which will keep them delightfully out of the way. I think I will go shopping. A new pair of stockings, perhaps?

42. Q

Lucille was the first in through the door at a little after noon. Hello *and where's my darling grandson*? she called, charging in like a predator in search of its prey, all feline grace, thrusting elbows and pointed archness. She plucked Samuel out of my arms and cuddled him to her bony bosom with what I imagine she thought was grandmotherly fondness; he, of course, immediately began to yell.

'There, there, oh, oh, little one, what's da matter den, cutie-pie?' she crooned to him through pursed pearly pink lips. Samuel, no doubt appalled by the overpowering scent of Chanel, screamed, did a double back-flip, and nearly fell out of her arms.

'Now then, for God's sake, Lucille, be careful,' Peter chided her, and I saw her thin painted cheeks flush faintly. 'You were never any good with them when they were that size.' He had settled himself down on the sofa, legs crossed, hands locked behind his head. Peter is an international authority on minimally invasive coronary artery bypasses. His knowledge of the emotional workings of the heart is quite a bit less developed than Samuel's.

Oh no. It came upon me suddenly, almost without warning. I felt sorry for her.

'It's not your fault, Lucille,' I said kindly. 'He's a bit – um – fractious these days. Even Jeanie's finding him tricky at the moment,' I assured her, and I saw anger flash across her face a second too late. *Even* Jeanie. She drew herself up tall.

'Yes, well, if *I*, his *grandmother*, had had the opportunity to spend as much time with him as your *sister* has, I'm sure he'd be perfectly used to me by now,' she retorted frostily, and subsided like the Boston debutante she once was into our brown leather armchair.

'Anyone for some food?' Tom said helpfully into the silence that followed, and he vanished off into the kitchen and re-appeared with a dish of vegetables, a plate of cheese, and some pâté on toast. Lucille attempted a carrot while Peter wolfed the minced pork with carnal delight.

'So you're doing some consulting?' he began, eyes watchful as Tom launched into a description of his new freelance work. Tom was halfway through when Peter cut in impatiently. 'Seriously, you need to think about the long term, Tom. I mean it's one thing to fuck around for a few months, but what about your retirement funds? And what, are you on your *wife's* health insurance now? I mean, c'*mon* . . .'

Tom was determinedly keeping his face expressionless. 'Thanks for the advice. We've got our insurance needs all straightened out, actually. But that's enough about me. Let's talk about you,' he went on generously, although I heard a dangerous tightness in his voice.

Peter allowed himself the faintest, smuggest smile, and looked over at Lucille, who was smiling slightly too as she smoothed her olive skirt of its lone hair's-breadth wrinkle. 'Yeah, well, things are going very well. My article on stented angioplasties was, as you may have heard, nominated for . . .' I switched off; I've heard some version of this speech about seventy-five times, and it always ends with the words 'Nobel prize' and 'possibly next year' hovering in the background. I pretended Samuel's nappy needed changing in the other room, and excused myself.

I assumed that Peter's litany of marvellous success would still be ongoing when I returned. Somehow, though, in my absence, the conversation had moved from Peter's account of his own brilliance back to Tom's failings. I stood outside the sitting room door, electrified by the sound of raised voices, Samuel tight in my arms. We looked nervously at each other.

'I didn't *get my wife pregnant*, Dad, what the hell kind of language is that? It was a joint decision, we're a team, for God's sake!' Tom was shouting. 'And shut the fuck up about the firm – what, you think I'd still be working at Crimpson if it wasn't for Samuel? Even if that's true – which it isn't – it's a trade I'd make again in a heartbeat. And as for our decision to start a family, that was ours, nothing to do with you. So butt the hell out of our lives . . .'

He paused for air. I wanted to run into the room and hug him, but something stopped me.

'How can I "butt out of your life", as you so charmingly put it, when you're *fucking it up*?' yelled Peter, and then came the loud bang of his hand meeting a table. '*When* are you going to move back to New York? A holiday's one thing. But this!'

'Not yet,' Tom replied, his tones now pointed and icy. 'We're not coming back yet. In fact, I'm not sure if we'll ever move back here. Q has got us involved in this case—'

'What are you talking about? "Involved"? What do you mean? What case?"

'It's just something local to the area.'

'The Long Island pipeline case?' Peter sounded hopeful for a moment. 'There's a lot of money at stake in that. Look, I'm not saying it's *impossible* to find good work in Connecticut—'

'That's not what I'm talking about, Dad. It's much more small scale: a young woman's custody battle, actually.'

'Do you mean that young Hollywood actress – what's her name – the one living in Fairfield County?' It was Lucille's turn to sound hopeful. 'Isn't she fighting with some young drug addict over her twins?'

'No, Mom.' Tom sounded torn between frustration and laughter now. 'Really, it's nothing like that. We've agreed to help a small-town lawyer with a very simple domestic case, out of good will. Although' – I could visualize his expression – 'we are using the opportunity to sort of *feel out* what small-town law might be like. As a life, I mean.'

'Feel it out? Why would you need to *feel it out*?' Peter howled. 'You don't need to feel it with a ten-foot pole, young man! You've got a whole damn city here of opportunities to feel out first, and if that isn't enough for you, there's Washington, DC just a few hours away. And I can help you there, Tom,' he went on. (The cajoling was starting now.) 'A couple of boys from the club have offered to introduce you to some real important people. There's a whole new career out there for you, Tom. You just have to grasp it.'

'And you would make such a wonderful politician, Tom, you're so polished, so articulate. And just think: you could serve the interests of the people. It's truly a noble calling! Surely a little self-sacrifice is called for . . .' Lucille's voice, as she picked up the argument, was like chocolate: smooth, sweet and nearly irresistible.

There was a pause. Samuel, tucked under my chin, muttered something. 'What's your daddy going to say now?' I whispered to him, holding him a little bit away as I spoke. His head wobbled backwards as he tried to look into my eyes.

'That's kind of you, Mom,' Tom replied at last, quietly. 'I appreciate it. Really, I do. We are obviously at a crossroads, as you guys have remarked many times. I don't quite know what we're going to do next. But I can't see myself becoming a politician. Maybe one day in the future – when my kids have grown up – who knows? But I want to *watch* them grow up first. Q and I are seriously considering taking over a firm that happens to be needing new partners, in a town in Cheasford, Connecticut. For a while we weren't sure about it, but I'm really starting to see the advantages. The more I think about it, the more I think this is a real opportunity for us! The firm has a large client base and an *excellent* reputation.'

I couldn't see him, so I don't know if he crossed his fingers. Just in case, I did it for him.

'It would be a very different life for us, obviously. We would be able to buy a big house, send Samuel to state school—'

'*State school!*'

'And, most appealing of all,' Tom continued remorselessly on, 'Q and I could arrange our working life around our family. We could work together, or we could take it in turns to staff the office. Either way, we could develop a more – a more *organic* professional life, instead of the old grind of nine-to-five – or, more realistically, seven-to-one-the-next-morning.'

'In other words, you're going to ruin yourself.' Peter's voice was like barbed wire.

Tom laughed; Samuel, hearing him, turned his head curiously towards the sound of his voice. 'Well, if I am, you'll have to go ahead and let me do it,' he said simply, and suddenly the door opened, and my husband ushered me inside. 'Don't wait any longer, Q,' he said grinning, taking Samuel tenderly from my arms. 'No need for you to be out there in the dark.'

I walked cautiously back in to see Peter and Lucille grabbing jackets – or rather, Lucille nervously grabbing the jackets while Peter stood, cold and furious, in the middle of the room. 'We are leaving,' he announced.

Tom nodded cheerfully. 'Won't stay for lunch, then? Oh dear.'

Peter walked past without even glancing at me or at Samuel. 'Call me when you have come to your senses,' he intoned as he swept from the room.

43. Jeanie

I took the subway down to 42nd Street while Q, Tom, and Samuel entertained the in-laws then went to visit their baby specialist person. ('Will you be all right by yourself? Will you find something to do all that time?' 'Oh, I think I can manage.')

Once I got out of the station I walked, feeling the sun on my face and a deep happiness inside. This is me, Jeanie Boothroyd, in New York; this is me, Jeanie Boothroyd, about to be wined and dined by a ridiculously eligible American who for some reason is obsessed with me. This is me, Jeanie Boothroyd, in a rather nice pair of shoes, with a brand-new bag from a shop on Fifth Avenue. This is me, Jeanie Boothroyd, living a dream. I smiled as I walked, and swung my arms, and felt the breeze lifting my hair. I wondered what Una would think of me now. How could I ever have lived with her?

Crowds of people swirled around me. Ragged, tired-looking homeless people loped side-by-side with businessmen in linen suits. Women in tailored jackets and elegant pencil skirts darted in and out of the throng in sensible trainers. Ladies with tiny poodles inched along in heels, and tourists struggled with subway maps and hot pretzels. This is New York; I'm a part of this, I thought proudly. I'm so glad I came.

So many appealing-looking restaurants; so many interesting boutiques: I stared in fascination at the sheer, extraordinary variety of New York. I passed flower shops, paper shops, pipe shops, shoe shops, wine shops, electronics shops and toy shops; shops selling postcards, shops selling suitcases, shops selling organic coffee in hundreds of tight gold packets lined up against the wall. Chocolatiers nestled beside corner shops, artisanal bakers beside donut vendors. I love this, I love this, I love this, I whispered to myself, feeling the blood sort of *zing* in my veins.

I must (I thought to myself suddenly, with a start of contrition) pick up something nice for Q, a treat of some sort, she's been so weary of late. So I stopped off at a little hushed, discreet patisserie and bought three cakes, one lime, one lemon, one with milk chocolate layers. They cost a shocking amount, but as the woman wrapped them up in a gold box, topped with stiff ribbon, I felt pleased at the thought of Q's face. She loves sweet things. I pushed the door open and manoeuvred myself back into the street, armed with my elegant box of bullion.

Only then, suddenly, I stopped. On the other side of the road, ahead, just visible through the press of people walking towards me, was Paul. I blinked, half convinced for a second I must be hallucinating; perhaps I was thinking so intensely of his face I'd conjured it up in mid-air . . . But no; it was him. And with him was Lily.

Lily of the gold eyes. I thought, for a second, I could actually see the light reflecting off their extraordinary depths, but I can't have done, because she was looking up at him; looking in his face with an expression of intense, passionate love. She was smiling, touching his face so tenderly, that I caught my breath; he was smiling down at her too, as if she was all the world to him, and even through the noise of the traffic, the footsteps of a thousand people, I heard him laugh at something she said. I ducked into the entryway of a pharmacy, feeling suddenly sick, headachy in the bright white light of the sunshine, and watched. It *couldn't* be . . .

As they drew level with me, on the other side of the road, I saw Paul reach out his hand and snake it around her waist. Then gently – oh so gently – it slid down, down, until it was cupped firmly around her bottom. He tugged her towards him. For a second they both stopped, still against the stream of people, suspended, body touching body. The traffic screeched to a halt for a red light; I could see the two of them quite clearly in the space between a bus and a car. Lily drew playfully away from his grasp and then (I saw it all) came back towards him, and leaned into his chest; she slipped her hand inside his jacket and pulled him into her body. He didn't resist; instead he leaned down and said something to her, serious for a second, and she nodded.

After what seemed like an eternity, she removed her hand from inside his jacket – in spite of myself I could imagine her fingers, hot on his skin – and they moved on, still intimately close. At that moment the light must have turned, because the traffic started up again. Seconds later, they were lost to my sight.

I stayed still for about five minutes in the pharmacy entry-way, my hand pressed to my throat, barely able to see through the sunshine that seemed suddenly oppressive. I literally thought I was going to be sick, and it was only when a disapproving-looking security guard came towards me that I fled, stumbling and knocking over a basket of beach balls. Fraught, I stared down at the green and pink and orange balls rolling in every direction, tumbling towards startled pedestrians, even rolling out into the street – cars honked, there were shouts of anger – and I ran off, in the opposite direction from Paul and Lily, away from the pharmacy, away from the guard, feeling the tears on my cheeks.

Paul and Lily, Paul and Lily. But she is married to *Adjile*, to kindly Adjile, and Paul is planning to meet me this evening, we're seeing each other now, how could he? How *could* he?

Suddenly I felt like the stupidest person alive. I've been so proud of myself all this time: I imagined I was in a relationship with Paul Dupont. Paul Dupont! How idiotic: we've shared a few kisses, no more. And he knows I'm in the city for just another day, then a month or two more in the States, and after that I'll be gone. Of course I'm just a bit of fun for him. What was I thinking?

I cast my mind back to all those things he said – about how I was the most beautiful woman he'd ever met, about how he couldn't think of anyone else – and I realized (reality came sharply into focus) that I'd made one of the oldest mistakes: I thought my holiday romance was *real*. I'm no better than some middle-aged woman kicking her heels up in Spain, a back-packed teenager falling in love with a long-haired stranger in Budapest. What was I thinking?

Lily is his lover. Had he been with her all along? I felt confused, dazed. Perhaps that day we saw each other in Connecticut – I rifled feverishly through my memory, trying to recall a moment of particular intimacy – they began an affair. Perhaps *she's* the real reason he split up with Tina. Or perhaps Tina was only ever a cover for his feelings for Lily; perhaps they've been together for months, years. Perhaps he has flirtations on the side. I wonder if he tells her about them, his dates and dinners and kisses with stray, random women?

In fact, maybe *that* was what he and Lily were talking about just now, I thought suddenly, starting to walk again, and it was as if the volume had been switched on in the little tableau I'd just watched. 'I'm having dinner with Jeanie tonight,' Paul said to Lily, putting his arm around her; and she pulled away from him, briefly upset. 'With Jeanie? Q's sister? What, are you *seri-ous*?' And then she thought for a moment, and came back towards him. 'I don't mind you having dinner with her, but you won't take it any further, will you?' she asked. 'Of course not.

212

It's all about us, Lily,' Paul replied. 'It's all about us.' It seemed a terribly plausible fantasy.

I'd been walking for half an hour at least when I looked up and realized I was utterly lost; I'd been stumbling and crying without paying the slightest attention to where I was going. The nearest sign said '27th Street'. There was a coffee shop on the other side of the street, so after a moment's hesitation I crossed over, and ordered myself a bucket of latte.

It was only as I got up to leave that I remembered the patisserie box, dropped and lost somewhere in the streets of New York.

44. Q

Sussex, CT

Such joy to be in Paul's lovely house again, Tom, Jeanie, Samuel and I. We've spent the last few days on the beach, the evenings on the deck, enjoying the view of the sun fading into pastels over the tops of the trees with freshly caught fish for dinner, accompanied by fiery wild rocket from the garden and glasses of chilled white wine.

Only Jeanie seems sad and low, even though I've told her she's forgiven for talking to Alison. 'I know,' she replied gruffly. 'I mean, it's not that I – well, all right.' I watched her carelessly splash out another large glass of wine.

Dr Ezekial Sykes's assessment of Samuel, the day before we left New York, was unenlightening. 'Not an obvious case of reflux,' he remarked, thoughtfully. 'It doesn't sound as if his crying is linked closely to feeds.' He then went through a long checklist of possible gastro-intestinal causes of severe infant crying, none of which, he remarked judiciously, appeared to apply to Samuel. In the end, he simply lifted his shoulders. 'I don't know why he is crying so hard. I'm sorry. I don't think it's serious. I'm sure he will grow out of it.' The door closed softly behind him.

I called Alison as soon as we got home to tell her all about it; she was sympathetic and unsurprised. 'Of course there was nothing, and of course he'll grow out of it,' she said. 'I'm glad you've had him properly checked out, but I think you'll just have to wait. And learn that you can be a good mother and still leave him sometimes, darling, so you can get rest and a change of scenery. The mistake *I* made was to think no one else could look after my baby.

'Is Jeanie being helpful?' she went on, and I explained that she seemed strangely low-spirited.

'Do you think it's about Dave?' she enquired, and I gasped, because I hadn't even thought of this.

'You don't think she's regretting breaking up with him, do you?' I asked, and she clicked her tongue.

'I wouldn't have thought so, but this is Jeanie we're talking about. She's always had a penchant for . . .' She stopped herself awkwardly.

'Losers,' I finished ruefully.

The first morning after our arrival in Connecticut, we called Kent. 'If you'll take me on as an associate – on a temporary basis – I'm in,' Tom explained. 'Q's still technically a Schuster employee, so she'll have to be involved on an informal basis. And I'm not committing long term yet, OK? This is just a try-out, so to speak, for us and for you.'

If we were expecting a joyous response, we were to be disappointed. There was a brief silence. Then: 'Come to court with me tomorrow,' Kent replied. 'I'll introduce you to Judge Ackerman and the other lawyers. You gotta get it over some time,' he added gloomily, with the air of one guiding a couple of sheep through a huge ravine. 'Might as well be now.'

And so, on Friday morning, I left Samuel with Jeanie after breakfast, then Tom and I set off for Middleford, a town a little over fifteen miles north of here, on the banks of the Connecticut River. It has the faintly seedy air characteristic of half-abandoned New England ports. A large highway separates the downtown

215

area from the river, and only a few businesses front directly on to the broad water, which therefore seems strangely incidental to the business of the place. There is one small park with a few wooden benches tucked around a bridge, but it is part flooded and liberally strewn with rubbish, occupied only by occasional flurries of muddy pigeons. The main street cuts a long, wide swath through undistinguished Victorian buildings, which are now occupied by a motley collection of cheap restaurants and regional clothing stores. Pansies burned paper-thin by the summer sun flutter along the sidewalk in cracked stone urns.

The court building, which sits on a quiet side street, is red-brick, with six white Doric columns and a grandly sweeping staircase leading out of the spacious round front hall. We met Kent on the other side of security at a few minutes before nine o'clock. Pausing to whisper something to Brenda, one of the security guards, that brought a blush to her cheeks, he led us to the elevator and into the third-floor courtroom.

There was a cheery hum of conversation in the panelled room when we entered, a hum that was perceptibly checked by our entrance. Four lawyers, clustered together in the central aisle, looked over at us and frankly stared.

Kent raised his hand in mock salute. 'Mick, Sue, Freda – oh, and Charlie, didn't see ya hiding there – how're y'all doing?'

'Morning, Kent,' said one of the women, her eyes keen and appraising. She looked about forty-five, and her expression was redoubtable, Margaret Thatcher-like in its formal intensity. Her blond hair was short and curled close to her head; her suit was a serviceable navy, without much style to it. She wore a simple gold necklace and tired-looking low-heeled shoes over ugly brown tights. 'Heard you're trying out a coupla city lawyers for your practice, is that these two over here?' She looked us over, her right eyebrow twitching upwards.

Kent grinned back at her, and shooed us towards the front of the court. 'Sure are, Sue,' he said with a chuckle. 'Fancy Wall Street lawyers, no less. Want to try out life in the backwoods, I guess. Mick, heard your son made the honour roll at school this month, he's a kid to be proud of, eh? Mick's kid is a smart one, you oughta meet him,' he explained. I had the bright idea of asking which college Mick's son was hoping to attend.

The ice was broken – or at least the surface of the ice was chipped, and soon we were chatting as best we could with the band of lawyers about family matters and then – in lower tones – local politics (''Course he's corrupt, but at least you know where you are with him,' Freda told us of one rising politician, with a broad wink) until the clerk announced, in deep bass tones: 'All rise for the Honourable Alan Ackerman!'

The lawyers flew back to their seats and stood respectfully while a sprightly-looking man in his sixties strode along the bench. Judge Ackerman had bright eyes and a paternal-looking fuzzy grey beard, although (Kent whispered to us, beneath the rustling cover of fifteen people settling back into their seats), 'He's a pretty tough one, much harder than Judge Field. *He* looks like an Old Testament prophet, but he'll give any defendant a break if you can only get 'em to cry.')

The business of the court proceeded briskly, Judge Ackerman listening to the array of driving offences, tenant–landlord disputes and divorce cases with an appearance of undivided attention. Which was impressive, because there was something almost inescapably soporific about the proceedings. Both Tom and I struggled to swallow yawns that threatened to split wide our faces. The expanse of carpet covering the floor muffled the sounds of human activity (chairs moving, people walking) like a thick, deep blanket of snow. The loud hum of the air conditioning focused our thoughts to a single monotone that became, as the minutes passed into an hour, and then into a second hour, and then a third, a trance-like state.

Finally, though, it was Kent's turn at the lectern – case no. 1124 – to ask the judge to consider community service instead of incarceration for his client.

Jay Axelrod, a hopeless-looking young white man in his early twenties, had been found with a glassine of heroin in his jeans pocket when he was pulled over for a driving offence six months previously. Once the prosecutor, a fresh-faced young man in glasses, had finished outlining the case, Kent detailed Axelrod's life with considerable emotion and pathos, lingering over physical abuse from a biological uncle and stints in three separate foster homes. Judge Ackerman listened to Kent's plausible story of neglect and mistreatment with narrowed eyes. In the midst of a particularly harrowing account of how, as a child, the client had been torn from the care of the foster mother he loved in the middle of the night, when the woman was found to be a drug-user herself, the Judge cut in abruptly: 'Yes, yes, counsellor, very tragic, I'm sure. And he never saw her again, and his life was blighted. But let's be practical here, please. Perhaps you'll be so good as to tell me, Mr Tyler, what evidence you have that this young man will *benefit* from the Community Service Labor Program? What reason do I have to think that your client is a candidate for a rehabilitative approach? You have known me many years, counsellor; I have long been concerned about the need for a punitive response on the part of the state judiciary in such matters. So tread carefully, Mr Tyler, tread carefully . . .'

Kent bowed his white head deferentially, locking his hands together in an almost prayer-like gesture. 'We have indeed known each other many years, Judge,' he said, sombrely, 'and you know that I only take on clients I have *confidence* in.' He paused, allowing his words to settle into the faint buzz of the courtroom which, in response, fell into almost complete silence. Kent held the stillness, then flashed a cheerful grin around the courtroom. 'Of course, we can *all* make mistakes, your honour; I am guilty of plenty, you know!' His colleagues – even the prosecutor – laughed appreciatively; the Judge concealed a small smile. 'But it is a man's ability to stand at a crossroads and say: *Now* is the time to change, *now* is the time to forge a new path, that marks him apart from the entrenched villain,' Kent went on, bringing in all the theatrical flourish at his disposal, including a few bangs with his hand on the lectern for additional emphasis. It was a sterling performance.

'Mr Axelrod here has been dealt a terrible hand by fate, but he *does* want to make something of his life. He has a lovely young girlfriend, a child on the way, and a new job as a painter's apprentice,' Kent continued, adroitly turning Mr Axelrod's fractured life into a narrative of partial redemption. 'Today, Judge, he stands in this courtroom at the crossroads of his life. Today he looks at the different roads opening up before him. He has said to me, Judge, that both are rocky; yet one has the promise of fine scenery unfolding in the distance! Your honour, I believe that we, that the state, must allow him to set off on the *right* path today, that we must help him stay clear of the wrong one. And that, your honour, is why I ask for a rehabilitative approach in place of incarceration.' His words rang in the air. Even Mr Axelrod was sitting up a bit higher at the end of Kent's stirring speech, his mouth half open.

Judge Ackerman, who seemed entirely used to Kent's style, looked as if he was resisting its theatrical sway – 'Mr Tyler, I shall nominate you for a Golden Globe one of these days' – but he promptly ruled in his client's favour. Mr Axelrod punched the air delightedly and kissed his heavily pregnant girlfriend loudly on the lips; Kent sat down with a self-satisfied smile. The prosecutor yawned and turned to his next case.

'If *you'd* come in and defended Axelrod, you'd have been home-towned,' Kent told us afterwards, tightening his ponytail over a cup of greasy coffee in the court's small, ill-stocked dining room. 'Meaning you'd have lost. No question about it. Ackerman's no friend to the "drug court" programme, not his politics at all. But he'll work with us, you see,' he explained, '"us" being the local lawyers, that is. He knows us and he trusts us. If you think your client is truly beyond help, you make a bland case and the Judge picks up the cues. He knows you think there's no point in trying to rehabilitate, the client's a hopeless case. But if you crank out something really over-blown, he knows you mean it, and nine times out of ten he'll rule your way. But if a lawyer comes from out of town, the Judge doesn't know if he or she understands the score, see? He doesn't trust the lawyer to flag the truth for him, make the whole case clear. So he'll almost certainly rule against them. It's just the way things work,' he added, seeing the expression on our faces. 'In a rural criminal court, anyway. You'll have to get in good with Ackerman if you're gonna make a success of the practice.'

The door opened and Judge Ackerman himself appeared in the dining room; Kent, grinning, hailed him over, then introduced us.

The Judge had his hands thrust in his pockets. 'My, my, my, if I'd had a dollar for every city lawyer who fancied a new life overlooking the water,' he remarked, rocking back on his heels with a rolling laugh. 'Beautiful place, slow pace of life, that's what you think, eh? Ha ha! Still, maybe you two'll be differ-ent . . . Ha ha ha . . . Kent tells me you have potential, although Kent – well, you haven't been firing on all cylinders recently, have you, ha ha ha! Still, if you two are here next month, I'm hosting a small dinner for the local lawyers, I'll tell Betty my secretary to send you an invitation. *If* you're still here, that is . . .'

He went off, crowing to himself, to bury his head in a large piece of apple pie and cream on the other side of the room. Kent was visibly irritated. 'Acts damn high and mighty sometimes, but we were the ones who got him elected,' he muttered in a furious undertone. 'We decided who it should be, we told him to run; that's the way it's always worked round here. Us lawyers got together, we sorted the whole thing out for him. What, he thinks he can tell me how to run *my* practice now?' He glowered blackly at the unconscious Judge across the room. 'I may have to remind him about that before too long . . .'

The door opened a second time, and the lawyer named Mick strolled in to make himself a cup of coffee from the machine. He slopped in the milk, hesitated for a fraction of a second, then came over and slid out the fourth chair at our table. He took a sip of his coffee, watching us reflectively over the rim. 'Bumped into McColley the other day,' he said at last, casually. 'Al McColley, from Sussex. Representing Ryan Cormier. You're representing the wife, right?'

The three of us immediately organized our features into the appropriate expression of pleasant disinterest. 'Yeah, nice girl,' Kent said, noncommunicatively. He paused a moment. '*Very* nice girl. And a damn good mother,' he added.

Mick raised his eyebrows over his cup of coffee, then charitably took the bait. 'You think so, huh? That's not what McColley says, but you'd expect that, I guess. He's an honest man, though; not the kind to make stuff up. He says he's got big-time, tight-as-can-be evidence Emmie Cormier is a real neglectful mother. I kinda took it seriously, coming from him. Then I saw Ryan a few days later at the Fisherman, that new bar across from the Lobster Pot, crowing all about it to his buddies, saying if his – ah – glamour photos of her don't win the case, he's got other evidence that will.'

Kent's face was smooth as the sand on the ocean floor. ''Course he is, he's claiming all sorts of dumb stuff, that Ryan,' he said neutrally. 'McColley's just spouting what Ryan says. I wonder which one of his half-assed claims he was talking about this time, though . . .' He kept the question mark out of his voice, but left the sentence hanging.

Mick clearly knew he was being played; for a moment or two he watched a heavy-set cleaner mopping the table beside us with slow, deliberate swipes. Then he turned back. 'Kent, I've never known you take a case you didn't believe in,' he said seriously. 'McColley wasn't specific, of course, but I think it had something to do with the first child's death. Something that came up in the autopsy. I suggest you put in an application to the local registrar to get a copy of the death certificate,' he added, draining his cup at last and standing up. 'Ryan was talking about the whole thing pretty publicly at the Fisherman, so I'm not breaking any confidences here.'

Kent slowly put out his hand and grasped Mick's. Then he leaned back and inspected the table top. 'Word is,' he remarked, 'that old man who died of pancreatic cancer three months back, Chuck Monro, never got around to signing the divorce papers from his first wife down in Florida. Anyone trying to sort out the Monro estate might want to check out all the S. Monros living in Tallahassee.'

Mick stared at Kent, who continued his careful investigation of the melamine surface beneath his teacup. After a moment, Mick placed his free hand briefly on Kent's shoulder, squeezed it, and left.

'That's one of the reasons I never miss court,' Kent said to us in a low voice as the door banged closed, looking up with suddenly sharp eyes. 'The gossip. Amazing what turns up. Right then, I'll stop off at the registrar's office on the way home, get a copy of the death certificate. God knows what Ryan's talking about, but we gotta be prepared . . .'

*

'He sounds dodgy to me,' my mother said, suspiciously, of Kent when I described our morning's experiences; 'very *American*, don't you think?' as if the two were synonymous. 'All this stuff about playing the court, about corrupt local politicians – it sounds highly dubious to me. Things aren't like that in England, I can promise you that,' she added proudly in ringing tones (although just the other day she was telling me about how her local MP has been forced to resign for taking 'cash for questions' in the Houses of Parliament. This entire event seemed to have slipped her mind, although I didn't fail to point it out). 'Well, anyway, this Kent chap – I bet he's trying to reel you in,' she went on. 'He says he's got to get out of his firm sharpish – have you ever wondered why? What the real reason is? I bet he's got some disasters hidden in the woodwork, I bet the business is going to hell in a handbasket, he's going to leave you with no end of problems, Q. Still, it's your business, I suppose; you never listen to me . . .'

I relayed this conversation to Tom, expecting a burst of hilarity ('Ridiculous as ever, your mother'), but instead he shrugged. 'Frankly, she may have something,' he said. 'I've been wondering exactly the same thing. Why does he want to get out so fast? Wouldn't be at all surprised if Kent has the odd skeleton in his cupboard. Not much we can do about it, I suppose, just wait for it to rattle.'

45. Jeanie

I would go home now, if I could, away from the entire continent that houses Paul, but my sister is relying on me and, given that she's paid for my flight out here, I can't really leave. Particularly not now she's started working again (well, sort of). But living in Paul's house is a torment. I've had to take his graduation photo off the desk in my bedroom, wrap it in a tea-towel and hide it in the bedroom cupboard. Even so I'm acutely conscious of it. I'm constantly fighting the temptation to go and unwrap it. I could hide it somewhere else in the house, of course, out of my own reach, but I'm worried Q and Tom might find it, and I can't think how I would explain a photograph in a dish towel. I would look completely mad.

But he's in my thoughts constantly, it's a pain I can't get away from. And I also miss Dave. He wasn't perfect, but he was my friend; we've been together a year. I keep wanting to pick the phone up to tell him something, and I'm so sad to remember I can't. I tried to tell Q about this; she was irritable and impatient. 'For goodness sake, Jeanie, make up your mind!' she said, shaking her head. 'First you want him, then you don't, then you do. Honestly . . .' Alison, to my intense frustration, said almost the exact same thing on the phone.

I dialled Paul's number two hours before he was due to collect me last Tuesday evening. 'Paul, I'm not coming,' I said abruptly, before the sound of his voice could put me off my stride. There was a pause.

'I'm sorry,' he said at last, politely. 'Are you ill?'

'No, no, it's not that. I'm not coming tonight, Paul, because I know *everything*. I saw you this afternoon. And I'm not saying what you're doing is evil, maybe some people could put up with it, if I was more sophisticated about these things perhaps I could too, but I'm not, and I can't,' I gabbled, wishing even at this late stage that I could manage coherence in front of him. If only I could sound like the kind of women I'm sure he normally goes out with, women who are brought up to speak in full sentences in the midst of the apocalypse! 'I can't, and that's final. I can't, and I'm sorry but I don't want to see you again,' I finished miserably, tripping over the words, feeling like a six-year-old, hating myself and hating him all at the same time.

'I see,' he said slowly. 'Or rather, I don't. Perhaps you'd like to take me through it again? I seem to be extraordinarily dense.'

Righteous indignation and sick disgust were mixed in with a physical longing for him that, like a wave, threatened to engulf everything else. Somehow, though, I stuck to my guns. 'Let's just say I saw you at lunchtime,' I said meaningfully. 'On the street. I went to this patisserie and – and I saw you, Paul. I saw what you were *doing*, and who you were *with*.'

'I see.' I could hear the guilt in his voice. 'I see. Look, Jeanie, I'm not saying it's the best thing I've ever done, but there are – extenuating circumstances,' he went on carefully. 'If you'll have dinner with me this evening, I think I can explain them to you.'

'Do you deny that you're – screwing her?'

'Screwing her? Well, I wouldn't put it quite like that, although . . .'

'How would you put it?'

'I'm – I'm – OK, I am sort of screwing her. It's true. That's

225

the starkest possible account of what I'm doing, I suppose. But—'

'You people!' I exploded, furiously, hearing the ridiculousness of this claim. 'My God! You're "sort of" screwing her? Either you are, or you aren't! There's no room for "sort of" here. What, are you going to start questioning the meaning of "is" now?'

'You mean Clinton? A lot of people misunderstood that argument, actually—'

'Well, I'm one of them!' I said furiously, panting for breath. 'Don't patronize me, Paul. Words mean something. They just *do*. Let me tell you something, and we'll see if you misunderstand it: *you disgust me*. I think your behaviour is repulsive. You should be ashamed of yourself. I want nothing to do with you.'

'Indeed, Jeanie, there's no room for misunderstanding there,' he replied. The phone, pressed against my ear, seemed to turn cold.

'I'm sorry I ever met you,' I went on, because I couldn't help myself. 'I wish I'd never seen you. I wish you'd never even touched me.'

'Let me assure you, the feeling is entirely mutual,' he returned, angrily. 'You *are* an opinionated little minx, aren't you? I see now that I should never have interrupted your happy little relationship with the delightful Dave,' (his voice dripping scorn). 'Tom told me all about him. Clearly, he was perfect for you, rank trainers and all. Now that you've come to appreciate his sterling qualities, you can achieve a full reconciliation. I wish you both joy, Jeanie,' he continued abruptly. 'I'm sure you'll be very happy together.' There was a click, and suddenly I realized I was holding a silent phone in my hand.

I sat for half an hour this morning on the edge of the bed with a mirror in my hand, waiting for my face to look normal, but try as I might the tears *would* come, my cheeks *would* turn mottled and spotted and red. I mopped my eyes again and again, I thought about raindrops and kittens and copper kettles and all the rest of it, but I still looked like someone from a Shakespearian tragedy in the final act.

'Jeanie? Jeanie, where are you?' my sister called, and eventually I had to go downstairs and plead allergies. I siphoned down a cup of coffee and discovered myself dreaming of brandy or vodka, or at the very least a bottomless box of red wine.

46. Q

'Q, are you ready? Come on! We're late,' Tom yelled upstairs to me at 9 o'clock this morning. When I arrived in the kitchen a few minutes later, a little breathless, Samuel tucked under my arm, he was busy stuffing Kent's old files into his briefcase. 'I'm up to F,' he announced proudly. He brandished a memory stick. 'Everything from *there* is on *here* – well, the basics that is, and the major facts. I figure we can get a secretary to input the smaller details later.'

'Very impressive,' I said, laughing, and he grinned in response.

'What do you think the Crimpson partners would think of me now? No, actually, don't answer that . . .'

Tom has moved into high gear this past week, working to familiarize himself with Kent's business, its history and its full range of clients. He seems to be enjoying the challenge enormously, although I'm not sure Kent is, he has a faintly haunted look in his eye ('D'ya have to keep making such a mess? That file – no, leave it where it is, young man, it doesn't need to – Oh my god, what ya *doin*'?'). When we arrived at his office to join him and drive on to Emmie's, he eyed the memory stick with grave suspicion. 'That itty-bitty thing? Looks like a stick o' gum. You'll lose it, and the entire practice will fall apart, but it won't be my problem, I guess.'

On the way to Emmie's house, the three of us crammed in the

front seat of his battered two-tone truck, Kent explained what he'd just found out. Producing a crumpled document from his breast pocket, he passed it sideways to me. 'That first child, Angela, didn't die of cot death at all. Mick was quite right.'

A horrible fear that had been collecting on the edge of my consciousness since our conversation with Mick now clutched at my throat. 'You're not saying that – that – she—'

Kent threw me a curious look. '*If* you'll just let me finish! It wasn't cot death. According to the death certificate, she died of something called "Reye's Syndrome". You ever heard of that?'

I shook my head, deeply, intensely relieved. But Tom cut in: '*I* have.' I turned my head to look at him.

'Really?'

'Dad's a surgeon; I've been around medical research all my life. And I thought about becoming a pre-med for a while. I did a placement with one of Dad's friends, Ian Whittaker, at Johns Hopkins, and he was finishing up a report on the causes of infant mortality at the time. I know the basics. Sudden Infant Death Syndrome means the baby's death can't be explained after all causes have been ruled out through autopsy, death scene investigation and review of the medical history. Reye's is a neurological illness.'

'You wouldn't happen to know what the symptoms of this syndrome *are*, would you?' Kent asked hopefully.

Tom shook his head. 'No. But I can find out.' He unclipped his cellphone and dialled. 'Hello, Ian? It's Tom here, Peter's kid,' we heard him say, and then: 'Can you give me a quick summary on the presentation of Reye's? I have a professional reason for asking . . .'

The conversation was as brief as men's conversations usually are, a simple fact-finding affair sandwiched between bare slivers of politeness. After a moment or two Tom snapped his phone shut. 'OK. According to Ian the classic symptoms of Reye's are vomiting, fever, severe drowsiness and, in its most dangerous form, seizures. Pretty serious, in other words.'

'*Christ!* The kind of thing no mother should have ignored,' Kent groaned; and then, as Tom agreed: 'She *did* say she was awful tired around then, remember, Q? Maybe she just wasn't thinking straight.'

'Ian says any child suffering from Reye's would – or at least, *should* – have been in hospital for treatment and monitoring in the days, maybe even weeks, before she died,' Tom continued. 'He says he's never even heard of a kid with Reye's dying at home. Bottom line is: Angela should have been in medical care, and Emmie should have seen she was dangerously ill.'

'Which is presumably what Ryan's lawyer found out,' Kent remarked. 'He's going to say she's a careless mom who let her first kid die. As the icing on the cake of all the *other* claims, it's likely to fly with a judge – particularly if McColley hints (which I would, if I was bringing the case) that she was on drugs or drink when the kid was sick.'

The truck banged along a pitted dirt path in the middle of some open fields, past a disused stone quarry, and finally into the driveway of a modern wood bungalow set at the bottom of a low hill. Ducks and geese and a few rangy cats scuttered about the yard; a car sat rusting under a tarp. The windows were dark, the blinds closed; the house had a strange, shut-up feel that was faintly threatening.

'The state medical examiner must have required a full statement of the scene of death,' Tom mused as Kent switched off the car. 'Emmie's baby died at home; a detective must have been called, and he would have taken evidence from Emmie and her family about what happened in the week before the child died. If we can get our hands on the medical examiner's form, Kent, it might help us establish what state Emmie was in at the time of Angela's death.'

'True,' Kent agreed. 'Good point. We'll get on to that later. For now, though, let's get the story straight from the horse's mouth.'

We fell out of the truck, legs bent nearly double. Kent watched us, putative concern written on his face ('Are y'all right? Know you city types are used to limousines'), then leaned past us into the truck's passenger side and removed something from the glove compartment. The something was long, hard, bigger than a man's hand, and wrapped in brown paper. 'Lawyer can never be too careful hereabouts,' he murmured, gesturing to the packet as he slipped it into his jeans' back pocket. 'Never know when you might need this.' Tom and I exchanged glances.

Kent led the way to the green front door and pushed the buzzer.

A dog immediately barked fiercely inside, a dog that sounded as if lawyers were his favourite treat and he hadn't had any for a few long, hungry days. We heard the sound of someone approaching, then a dog's scampering feet coming closer, closer. Kent reached behind him, extracted the brown paper parcel and began to unwrap it, his face watchful. Tom moved me sharply behind him as the door opened; the dog's face and slavering jaws were suddenly visible behind the screen, sharp teeth pulling away from huge black gums. The dog charged out—

'Here you go, buddy,' Kent said, producing from the long paper package – a dog biscuit. A long, bone-shaped, entirely inoffensive, pink dog biscuit. The dog, a curious mix of many breeds, nosed Kent's hand, accepted the biscuit thankfully and slumped down on the doorstep with it, head resting comfortably on Kent's left shoe. Kent grinned back at us. 'What the hell ya doin' over *there*?' he called innocently, gesturing to us to follow him. 'Don't tell me ya scared of this old boy!' He stepped over the animal's recumbent body and into the house.

231

An old man was hovering in the shadowy depths of the hall-way, dressed in blue jeans, grubby white trainers, and a stained blue checked shirt. As we stepped inside, he grunted, then let the door slam behind us and preceded us down the hall into a sitting room that – on brief inspection – bore more resemblance to a garage than a place of family gathering. Pieces of car and generator were strewn around the chairs and tables; oil cans reposed on blackened pieces of newspaper, and a large toolbox was spilling wrenches on to the carpet in front of the television.

'Emmie! EMMIE! Mr Tyler's arrived – get your ass in here!' the old man yelled, picking up a piece of what looked like an exhaust pipe from the coffee table. With a brief nod, he vanished through the hall and into the yard.

Emmie greeted us with limited enthusiasm. 'What can I do for you?' she asked wearily, appearing in the dark hallway with a tea-towel looped round her neck. 'You'll have to make it quick, I've got to get a stew done for the church supper tonight and then I've got to get Paulie ready for a visit to his friend's house.'

We followed her into the kitchen. A neatly swept butcher's block stood in the middle of the room; wood counters were scrubbed clean. There was a vase of wild flowers, not particularly fresh, but still pretty, by the sink, and a few framed photographs of Paulie on the wall. Emmie produced a slab of beef from the fridge and a meat tenderizer, then a bag of carrots, a sack of potatoes and six onions from a cupboard. 'You can help me with the vegetables,' she said flatly, dumping the lot on the counter.

I immediately set about the potatoes while Kent and Tom harassed some onions and carrots and Emmie pounded the beef into submission. 'So what is it' (*bang, bang*) 'you want to' (*bang, bang*) 'talk about?' she asked.

232

Kent watched the meat tenderizer cautiously. 'Well, see here, Emmie, something's sorta come up,' he began carefully.

'What's that, then?' *Bang. Bang*.

'Well, you see, my dear' (*bang, bang*) 'it's – it's a bit of a tricky subject actually – it's about – well' (*bang, bang, bang, bang*) 'maybe you should put down the . . .' (*Bang, bang, bang*.) Kent threw me a piteous look.

'Emmie, it's about baby Angela, actually,' I cut in. 'About her death,' I went on, into the crashing silence that followed.

'Angela didn't die of cot death.' I said the words slowly, very slowly, watching to see the effect of my words. 'According to the certificate, she died of Reye's Syndrome.'

Emmie's face was white. 'What do *you* know about it?' she said, her voice low. 'What are you talking about?'

'Mr Tyler has a copy of the death certificate. He – er – thought he should take a look. And see' – I gave her the document – 'cause of death: "Reye's Syndrome". Now, did you ever hear of that?'

Emmie collapsed into a chair at the table, a pile of bones and thin cotton and straggling hair with a meat tenderizer in one hand and her baby daughter's death certificate clutched tight in the other.

'Have you ever heard of it before?' Kent pressed. Emmie shook her head; her lips formed the shape of a 'no'.

'From what we've been able to find out,' Kent went on, more gently, 'it's a – real bad illness that makes you sick, and gives you a fever, and – ah – do you wanna explain?' he asked hopefully, turning to Tom.

Tom came and sat beside Emmie. 'Reye's Syndrome is a very serious disease. No one knows exactly what causes it,' he explained, 'but it's got something to do with disturbances in the chemical levels in a child's blood. It leads to swelling of the organs: liver, kidneys, even the brain. Symptoms include fever, vomiting, drowsiness and even seizures.'

'Emmie, was Angela ill in the weeks before she died? Did she have any of those symptoms?' Kent asked.

Emmie stared at us all, one after the other, something wild appearing in her eye. 'I – I—' She gulped. 'Angela had a cold, a real bad cold, starting a few weeks before she died; then it sort of got better, the cold part I mean, although she seemed – not herself, you know? I had the doctor up here almost every day, I kept telling him she wasn't right, he kept telling me I was being silly . . . was it my fault, then? *Was it my fault?*'

Kent caught our eye; he had seen the thing we saw, I knew it immediately. His body had stiffened, just as mine had, just as Tom's had, at something in Emmie's words. 'You had the *doctor* out here? Which doctor was that?'

Emmie brushed his words aside. 'Dr Reid. He's our family doctor. Was it *my fault?*'

'Emmie, listen to me,' Kent said urgently. 'How often did you have your doctor out here? What did you tell him when he came? What did he say to you about Angela? *Think.*'

But Emmie had her head down on the table now, her forehead cradled in her fingers. 'It was my fault. They were right, I should have explained better. I should have made him understand,' she groaned, lost in an agony of grief. 'It's just like they said, just like they said . . .'

I went and put my arms around her. 'That's not what we're saying at all. You were *right*, Emmie; you got it right. *He* got it wrong.'

Kent got out his pad and leaky blue pen. 'Tell us what happened, Emmie, day by day, from the time your baby got sick to the night she died. I know it won't be pleasant, but it's gotta be done.'

Angela, Emmie explained, had caught a cold from a neighbour's kid, and was for a week a very miserable two-and-a-half-month-old baby. The family doctor, who lived nearby, came out to see Angela on several occasions and, when she seemed to be in real discomfort, 'He told me to give her some aspirin, just a bit of aspirin to take the edge off the pain, and then a few other things – some kinda lotion in a bowl of water, and this plastic thing to squeeze out her nose.'

However, as the symptoms of the cold got better, Angela seemed, oddly, to get *worse*. She became, in Emmie's memory, lethargic, lying still in her bed, staring blankly ahead, slipping in and out of sleep. Emmie eventually suggested taking her daughter to hospital, but the doctor insisted she was over-reacting.

'Dr Reid said I should just learn to "enjoy" my baby, he said I was being silly, an over-anxious mom,' she told us, tears spilling down her face. 'He said young moms "can't read their kids". He said most women are happy if their babies lie quiet, he said I didn't appreciate what I had. Then the day before Angela died she was real sick, she threw up everything I fed her in the afternoon. I was so frightened! So I called him out again; that time he said my milk musta been bad. I believed him,' she went on, turning to face us, horror vivid on her face. 'I believed him. That's why I bottle-fed Paulie, y'know; I was so frightened my milk poisoned Angela. Was he wrong?'

I could see Kent carefully writing this down in his book, heavily underscoring some words, his pen spluttering with the force: *Angela vomits* day before death; Reid blames milk; *Reid dismisses Emmie's concerns*.

'Emmie, who told you that Angela died of cot death?' Tom asked.

'Dr Reid,' she replied, her eyes half closed. 'Dr Reid. He called me a few weeks after the death, said he had the results of the autopsy, wanted to tell me as soon as possible so we could get on with the funeral. I was crazy the whole time, thinking of my baby in that cold place, all alone, without me. Dr Reid said he wanted to put an end to it all, get her decently buried. That was when he said it was cot death.'

'Are you sure about that? He definitely used the phrase "cot death"?'

'Uh-huh. I wrote it down. He said there was nothing anybody could have done. Said I shouldn't blame myself. And I asked him – I said, what about the cold and the sickness, and he said, "Babies don't die of colds or an upset stomach, it was just a coincidence." So I learned the words, "cot death", so I could say it to the kids in town. And Dr Reid was so kind: he helped me with the funeral. Dad was crazy, Gramps locked himself in the shed, it was the doctor who helped me arrange everything. He even gave me money for a dinner in the church hall afterwards.'

Reid gives Emmie money for funeral expenses, Kent wrote in his looping script; and then, discreetly, *??* by the side. 'Emmie,' he said, looking up briefly; 'did you ever *see* the death certificate? Did you get a copy?'

Emmie shook her head. 'Dr Reid picked up the certificate and gave it to the funeral director,' she explained. 'He said he wanted to save me the trip.' We sat in silence listening to the slow sound of Kent's pen moving across the paper.

'Did you never hear from the medical examiner's office? Did nobody call you to explain what had happened, to offer to help you?' I asked. 'That would be typical state practice.'

Emmie thought. 'I . . . you know, maybe someone *did* call,' she said finally. 'It was all such a mess, I didn't really know what was going on, I was half outta my mind, you know? But I – I think Gramps took a phone call from someone, said she wanted to get me some counselling – counselling!' She laughed shortly. 'Why would I talk to some stranger about my Angel? What could they possibly tell me? So I never called her back,' she finished fiercely. 'I don't need people poking their noses into

236

my life, I had my family to take care of me, my neighbours, Dr Reid ...' Her voice tailed off, consciousness registering painfully on her face.

'You're saying it was *his* fault.' She half stood, her hands strangling the table.

'Yes, dear, that's exactly what we're saying, but for God's sake don't go after him with that meat tenderizer,' said Kent firmly, closing his notebook and stuffing it into his pocket. 'Do you understand me, young lady? We'll follow this up, we'll go talk to Reid, find out what the hell he has to say for himself. But if you start threatening him, you'll get yourself into trouble and you'll lose Paulie for good. It's one thing to menace an abusive ex, it's another to go waving a gun at the local doctor. You do that and McColley will have your head for sure. You stay out of this like a good girl, and we may be able to get you compensation from Reid *and* keep Paulie safe at home. No promises, but I'm feeling better about this than I have in weeks.'

He nodded at her, shortly, then gestured to us to stand up. 'What ya doin' these next few days?' he said, a grin creasing his thin, rough face. 'Somethin' tells me we've got a house call of our own to make. Boy, I'm glad we won't have to go to Wyoming to sort this one out ...'

47 Jeanie

I was walking past Mrs Forrest's office at Quiet Lanes this morning, cheerily swinging a bag of new knitting wool for Sue-Ellen and a magazine about aeroplanes for Ken, when the unmistakable sound of a sob brought me up short. I stopped for a second in the hallway, irresolute, hoping I'd imagined it – but there, it came again: a deep, snuffly, miserable sob. Bright, chirpy Mrs Forrest was crying.

I knocked gently on the office door, and walked in; Mrs Forrest was sitting by the window, holding a letter. 'Oh, Jeanie, it's you. I mean – hiya!' she said, in a ghastly imitation of her usual cheer. Her fuchsia scarf was trailing forlornly over the back of her chair; without it she looked unexpectedly drab. A large cup of tea sat beside her on the windowsill, a filmy skin of cooled milk floating horribly on the top. 'How lovely, gee, everyone's gonna be thrilled you're here,' she went on, struggling to manage a toothy smile, but her hands remained dropped in her lap, motionless. Something was seriously wrong.

'Mrs Forrest, is there anything I can – er – do?' I asked hesitantly, hovering awkwardly on the edge of the room, and then, in response to something in her face, I walked in, closing the door carefully behind me. 'Have you had bad news?'

'Oh, my heavens, Jeanie, how did you guess?' Mrs Forrest looked genuinely astounded.

'I – um – you've had a letter,' I pointed out tactfully. She looked down at the document, then up at me again, tragically.

'You are quite right, Jeanie. It seems I may not be able to keep Quiet Lanes,' she added, now dropping the pretence, the sentence ending in an open wail. 'Oh, Jeanie, I don't think I can bear it. This is my life, Jeanie. My life!'

Mrs Forrest may not be the cleverest woman I've ever met, but the place runs with the peaceful hum of organized inevitability. And the more time I've spent here, the more I've come to recognize the little Home manager's affection for her patients. 'Why on earth will you have to leave?' I asked now.

Mrs Forrest adjusted her wire glasses with trembling fingers, glanced at the letter again with an expression of utter hopelessness, then permitted herself another small sob. 'I've known for a while, Jeanie, that I'm not up to the job of care manager, not – well, not in these days. Once upon a time it was just a question of – of caring, you see. Caring for old people. But now there's all this technology. And – *management*.' Her voice, as she uttered the dread word, dropped to a spectral whisper. 'I can't do it, and they know I can't – the managers of the SeniorOne group of care homes, that is, who own this place. The letter – it says I have six weeks to – to implement – something or other, but really it's just a way for them to get rid of me. I know it!' She ended with a howl; tears began to stream down her face and plop on to her shirt. Wordlessly, I handed her a tissue from a pink floral box on the desk. She blew her nose, loudly.

'But, Jeanie, this isn't your problem!' The wobbly smile appeared again, a flash of brilliant white. 'You go join the residents. I know Sue-Ellen and Joel and Ken are just *longing* to see you,' she added. 'If I have to go – *when* I have to go away from Quiet Lanes, the one thing I'll always be pleased about is hiring *you*,' she remarked tragically. 'You have just shaken us all up in the most wunnerful way, and I—'

'Mrs Forrest, can I read the letter?' I interrupted briskly, cutting through her tremulous praise, and when she nervously held out the paper, I plucked it from her hands, sat down on the edge of the desk and read the epistle through carefully from beginning to end.

It was from someone called Andrew, a vice-president of the SeniorOne Elder Care Group. (A great deal of money had clearly been spent producing a spangly logo which adorned the top third of the cream-coloured page.) Andrew's first paragraph was fairly straightforward (Hello, how are you, the once-yearly inspection of the cooking facilities will be at such-and-such a time). The part that clearly had the little Home manager in a tizzy was a section entitled 'New Mandates' in the middle of paragraph two:

We have become persuaded, after several focus groups [Andrew remarked], *that collaborative enterprise is the most effective tool to promote elder-care excellence. We are therefore enclosing a leaflet which encourages health-care providers to learn to work together through active problem-solving and decision-making. Our goals in response to this new initiative are three-fold:*

1. *socializing health-care providers in collaborative work, in mutual experiences of shared problem-solving and focused decision-making, thereby enabling greater patient benefits;*
2. *creating and enabling mutual understanding of, and respect for, multi-disciplinary contributions; and*
3. *producing, enhancing and developing the necessary abilities for successful and institution-changing collaborative practice.*

*We expect that all care home managers will implement
this new strategy, and plan an inspection in three weeks
to evaluate its progress. All managers must construct a
detailed twenty-page report (FAO Lina Shwartz) on
their implementation strategy by next Wednesday, and a
further twenty pages in advance of the inspection to
indicate goal achievement success rates (numbered one,
two, three).*

Mrs Forrest watched me read this nonsense with eyes like
deep pools. 'You see,' she said at last, miserably, when I put
down the letter, one more tear spilling over. 'I can't do that.
They *know* I can't do that. Jeanie, I don't even know' (again,
that low, horrified whisper) '*what it means*!'

I started to laugh – I just couldn't help it. But it was a mistake, of course; looking deeply offended, the little care home
manager drew herself up to her fullest height. 'I cannot see why
you think this is funny, Jeanie,' she said, sounding deeply hurt.
'I may not be the best manager in the world, but I try my best,
and—'

'No, no,' I interrupted, putting out my hand apologetically;
'it's not funny, I mean, it *is*, but you are *not*. Look, Mrs Forrest,
I've just finished a Master's degree in Social Work. I've
ploughed through whole textbooks full of government initia-
tives and strategies for geriatric excellence, and all the rest of it.
I understand this.' I waggled the letter at her.

Mrs Forrest looked at me as if I had just plopped down in
her garden in a spaceship, fully equipped with antennae and
three arms. '*You do?*'

I grinned at her. 'How much responsibility are you willing to
give me, Mrs Forrest?' I asked, and she gasped.

'Responsibility? Do you mean—?'

'If you want, I will' (tapping the letter) '"construct a detailed twenty-page report on our implementation strategy". It'll take me about fifteen minutes, I reckon. I've got some essays on my computer, I'll just cut and paste stuff into a new document, add a few more syllables and bullet points, and you can sign the thing.'

'But – how can you do that? I don't even understand what they want me to do!' She was wringing her hands now, twisting them up to her face; I was delighted to see them engaged in more normal activities.

'This? All it means is, they want us to learn to work together,' I said, grinning, 'which we don't need to learn, because we do it already. Look, we'll have a few tea parties and a couple of games of pass the parcel, I'll describe them as "entertainment events designed to facilitate greater collaborative understanding of mutual shared aims", Andrew will be delighted, and you'll keep your job.'

Mrs Forrest flung her arms right around me. 'Jeanie, I think the Lord sent you to me,' she said seriously, snuffling like a bunny into my T-shirt.

When I walked into the dayroom a quarter of an hour later, I was almost immediately barraged by questions about 'how that in'eresting young man of yours is doing'. He's very well, I said; he's gone back to London. I don't know when I'll see him again. Ken kept trying to push me, but Sue-Ellen weighed in majestically. 'We will leave you in peace,' she commanded, and Ken raised his eyebrows, took his magazine, and submitted with a very good grace. But several of the other old people seemed keen to take up the challenge so, without looking at me, Sue-Ellen began to tell a very long story about her first husband, who apparently made his money diving for lost ships and recovering their treasure. She showed us a locket she was wearing that went down in 1587 off the coast of Sicily, and described the tea-set she had given her daughter that still has salt deposits deep in its glaze. By the time she'd finished, everyone had stopped thinking about Dave, and even I was so enthralled by her narrative of danger and gold and lost ruby necklaces I lost track of time, then suddenly realized I'd stayed more than the requisite two hours. 'See, Jeanie? I'm telling you; time just *flies* at Quiet Lanes,' said Mrs Forrest, who now seemed almost restored to her twinkly self; her fingers fluttered as she spread her hands gleefully wide.

I was just about to walk out of the door when I felt a soft touch on my shoulder; I wasn't surprised to see Sue-Ellen. 'Honey, we need to talk,' she murmured in my ear, and a little reluctantly I followed her through the French doors on to the patio. Carefully tended pots of ivy and bright red, richly fragrant flowers lined the weed-free concrete; Sue-Ellen settled herself on a bench and crossed her ankles.

Her English counterpart would probably sport tweed two-pieces from Jaeger and burgundy leather court shoes. Sue-Ellen, being American, wears pressed trousers and T-shirts with bright white trainers instead.

'I'm worried about you, Jeanie,' she began abruptly. 'You're going around with a face like a camel from Cairo; you're obviously in some kind of trouble. Is it about that young man you brought here?'

I nodded slowly.

'I'm not surprised. He's here, there, everywhere, zigzaggin' all over, reminded me of a rabbit. There's someone else, I think?'

Again I nodded, more bewildered this time. How did she . . . ? 'And on top of that, you don't know what to do with yourself. You're just treadin' water, I think. Life passes you by so fast, Jeanie! Figure out what you want, and get on with living. Now, one other important piece of advice,' she continued – I leaned forwards, head spinning, wondering what on earth would come next – 'good sex is worth fighting for! You make sure you get plenty of it. That's my strategy. Worst thing about Quiet Lanes, I'll tell you, is having Mrs Forrest walking the corridors when you're tryin' to get it on . . .' I choked and tried neither to laugh nor to think about exactly who Sue-Ellen is tryin' to get it on with (although since the options are limited, it's hard).

'Where did you learn to tell fortunes?' I asked her suddenly; and she laughed.

'Ah, my dear, that was from husband number two,' she explained, rocking gently backwards and forwards in her seat. '*His* aunt was a Romany, you see, a genuine Romany. We visited her in Bucharest in the second year of our marriage. She was – quite a woman; she taught us the basics. Philip, my husband, was real good, he'd obviously inherited the gift, but I . . . well, Aunt Sofia said I had potential,' she remarked modestly. 'She lived in a small house with another old lady, the two of them were known for miles around. I remember sitting with them in their front room, a tiny little dark box, the air filled with heady perfume and walls hung with bright woven scarves. We learned the craft by lamplight. There's no sceptic alive could've come out of such a place untouched,' she added softly. 'You could *feel* the force of the future in their presence.'

'You've never told my future,' I said, and I reached out my hand with a smile. 'You told Dave's, but you didn't tell mine.' I held it steady before her. 'Why don't *you* tell me what's going to happen in my life, Sue-Ellen? Really, it'll make everything so much simpler!'

Sue-Ellen's faded blue eyes were sympathetic beneath her towering sweep of golden hair. 'Oh no, my dear,' she said, gently. 'No, no, no. That's just what I'm talking about. *You* have to work your future out for yourself.'

I felt oddly embarrassed, but still I kept my hand outstretched. 'Oh, come on, Sue-Ellen,' I said, managing a confident chuckle. 'If I cross your palm with silver, I'm sure you'll spin me a good story. That's all it is anyway, this fortune-telling business. It's not as if I was going to – you know, *believe you*, or anything.'

Sue-Ellen stirred a little beside me, and brushed some soft yellow pollen off her trousers. 'Really? Well, if you say so. Listen, my dear: some people need a little push in life. And you are one of them. There are no short-cuts,' she added, seriously. 'Whatever it is you believe in, you've got to work out your future, Jeanie, before it's your past.'

I sat still on the bench for a moment, thinking of an email I received from Una the other day telling me I have to leave the flat: 'Lolly says that now you're not a student any more, I'll have to start paying council tax, so sorry about that. Just can't afford to keep you, haha! And anyway, Lolly wants to move in with me next month, so we'd probably have asked you to sod off anyway. Lolly's amazing, you'd really like him. He's using your room right now to stash his record collection. And Dukey's sleeping there sometimes too, I said I was sure you wouldn't mind.' I haven't got a clue who Dukey is. (Frankly I'm a bit hazy on Lolly's identity as well.)

'I know I have to decide what I'm doing, where I'm going, but it's hard!' I said into the warm breeze, only half conscious of Sue-Ellen's compact little body beside me. 'I'm fond of Dave, and I miss him, but we aren't right for each other. Paul Dupont is . . . not the man I thought he was. I was totally wrong about him. I want to be a social worker – I think. I need a new flat, but I don't have the money. I have to go home to London, but I have to stay here to help Q. I'm *trying* to decide what to do with myself but it's not easy, you know. It's not easy being twenty-four.'

'No, honey, it isn't. Quite honestly, it's not easy being seventy-four either,' said Sue-Ellen beside me.

48. Q

Tom is up to 'S'.

   He's looking like a different man these days, although so is Kent; the old man develops a pained, long-suffering expression whenever he sees my husband; his shoulders sag, his mouth rounds down, and I've caught him sneaking surreptitious drags from a silver hip flask he thinks we haven't noticed under his desk. Tom, meanwhile, has a new spring in his step, and whenever you ask him what he's thinking about, he mentions the travails of some local mechanic or postmaster or veterinarian he's never actually met. 'I think we can get the shed removed,' he told me suddenly, over dinner one night; 'I think I've figured it out!' I hadn't a clue what he was talking about, but Tom was so pleased with himself he got up early and went into the office to talk through his discoveries with Kent.

   Dr Reid's practice has been serving the residents of a small town called Branton for some thirty-five years. 'Most people round here won't hear a word against either of the partners, Phil Reid or Craig Warwick,' Kent told us as we drove there through a dull haze one Friday morning. 'They're well known for getting up in the middle of the night, travelling to the remotest corners of the state, doing whatever it takes to help their patients. This is going to be an unpopular case, I'll tell you. Shouldn't be surprised if I lose clients over it. If *you* lose clients over it, that is . . .'

As we entered, a woman in her fifties looked up at us from behind a wooden desk. Her greying hair was twisted into a bun on top of her head, her ample form was clothed in a simple cotton dress, and a pair of steel spectacles were propped on her nose – spectacles which she immediately lifted from her face and dropped on to the desk as she caught sight of Kent. 'Mr Tyler!' she exclaimed, a hint of red in her cheeks. 'What brings you here?'

Tom and I hung back discreetly near the circle of listless patients while Kent went over to the doctors' secretary. He leaned over the table and cupped his face in his hands about six inches from her nose. 'Elizabeth Summers, it sure is lovely to see you again,' he said; we could just hear his voice, low and caressing, as he smiled at her. 'Tell me, how are those puppies you picked up a week or two back from the Mansons?'

She smiled happily. 'Oh, they're *wonderful*, Mr Tyler, I got two of them, you probably heard; they're beautiful dogs, wonderful proportions . . .'

'And you'll be winning gold rosettes with them all over the state before the year is up, I'll bet,' Kent murmured. 'Never knew anyone like it, you could take a cur from the street and have him looking like a champion in a few months, Elizabeth.'

'Oh goodness, I don't know about that,' she said, her face flushing with pleasure, looking down at the desk and idly playing with a small net purse that lay on top of the appointments' ledger. 'You can't say a thing like that, it's all to do with breeding you know . . .'

'Well now, listen here, Elizabeth, I need to ask a quick question of the doctor, Reid that is, about one of his patients. I wonder if you could get me five minutes?' he asked.

Her brow furrowed a bit, and she dropped her voice even lower. 'I don't know about that, we're running behind today, Fridays are always terrible. Dr Reid had to go up to the hospital

247

in the morning, we've been forty minutes slow ever since, people are waiting . . .' She nodded over to the group of patients, her eyes widening curiously as she caught sight of us.

Kent leaned over and said something quietly in her ear. Her face flushed bright scarlet. 'Well, well – all right then,' I heard her say at last, reluctantly. 'If you promise you'll keep it to five minutes, I suppose it's all right, just this once. And I'll . . .' He twisted his ear towards her mouth to catch her words, and she whispered something inside we couldn't quite hear, although I could swear it involved leaving a door unlocked at half past ten on Sunday night.

At that moment a little red buzzer on the desk flashed and sounded. Elizabeth glanced over at the patients anxiously, then jerked her head in the direction of a door. 'Go on then,' she said in a hushed whisper; 'but hurry up, or there's going to be a riot in here.'

Kent stood up immediately. 'Come on,' he called shortly to us, over his shoulder, and Elizabeth watched, bewildered, as we filed past her in Kent's wake. 'Who – why – who are they—' we heard her quacking, faintly, as we threaded our way along a corridor.

Kent rapped smartly on the doctor's door, and we filed into his consulting rooms.

A well-preserved man of about fifty in shirt-sleeves was sitting at his desk, hunting and pecking on an elderly-looking computer. He turned to look at us over half-moon glasses, and his brow furrowed.

'Unless my medical skills have completely deserted me, you are not an eighty-year-old lady with a broken thumb,' he said calmly.

Kent grinned and sat down, while we crowded in through the door behind him. 'True enough. How're doing, Phil? These are two – ah – new associates of mine. We want to talk to you about Emmie Cormier. Won't take a minute.'

Dr Reid sighed gently. 'Elizabeth is losing her grip, I fear,' he said. 'And I've long known she has a – partiality – for you, you old reprobate. Well, well, since you're here; what is it you want to know? Bearing in mind,' he went on, as Kent began to speak, his hand raised in warning, 'I cannot break doctor–patient confidentiality. And I will not.'

Kent nodded. 'I won't ask you to. Got a letter here, authorizing you to talk to us. I just want to know, on behalf of my client, why you told Emmie her first baby died of cot death, not Reye's Syndrome.'

Dr Reid, after examining the handwritten note for a moment, put his head on one side, and considered Kent's face. 'Excuse me?' he said coolly.

'Simple enough question,' Kent went on briskly. 'She says you told her Angela's death was diagnosed as SIDS, but the death certificate says Reye's Syndrome. Can you explain that?'

Dr Reid stared first at Kent, then at us. 'I wish I had more seating for you,' he said to us gently, 'but I'm afraid I'm not used to entertaining *parties* in my office.' The edge in his voice was just palpable. He looked back at Kent. 'My dear Mr Tyler, I'm not entirely sure what you're getting at. Of course I told Miss Cormier that the child's death was attributed to Reye's Syndrome in the autopsy. I explained the cause of death fully to her – what on earth are you suggesting? But it didn't mean anything to her, she barely remembered her own name at the time, let alone complicated medical terminology. I suppose she has simply internalized "cot death", it's quicker and easier, something most people have heard of. I am not in the business of deceiving my patients,' he finished, drawing himself up, his expression politely aggrieved.

Kent had got out his dog-eared notebook again and was scribbling away. He looked up now at his adversary, unabashed. 'I see. It was her mistake, then. And what about all those trips out to the house in the days before the baby died?' he went on. 'Did you suspect Reye's Syndrome then? Why didn't you get the kid admitted to hospital?'

Dr Reid put his head on one side and contemplated Kent rather as a blackbird examines a worm that's not worth the trouble of pulling from the earth. 'My dear man, I only saw the child once, when she first got sick with a cold,' he said, with a hint of exasperation. 'There was no reason whatsoever to suspect Reye's Syndrome at the time. She had a touch of nasal congestion; it was a minor respiratory illness. The next time I saw the baby, she was dead. Reye's Syndrome sets in in the *aftermath* of a respiratory infection; when I saw her that one time, the disease had not taken hold. The young mother was all over the place, she obviously didn't notice that an entirely new condition developed after our meeting. She was too young and inexperienced to spot the signs. To be fair, it can be hard sometimes. But what on earth makes you think I went there more often?'

'The fact that that's what Emmie Cormier told us herself,' I interjected. I held Dr Reid's gaze.

The doctor had an expression of mild surprise on his face. 'Did she really, Mrs – er—? Well, I can only say her memory is failing her, then. And if she wants to release to you copies of her daughter's medical notes, you will see that I'm right. Or you can ask the medical examiner for his report – it will contain full details of the circumstances surrounding the death. I went to the Cormier house to see the child once, and once only. Of course people in grief remember strange things, I'm not saying she's deliberately making up claims, of course . . .' He lifted his shoulders gently, as if to say, *I'm* not the person making wild accusations.

'Yes, well,' said Kent, clicking his pen closed, 'Miss Cormier will certainly want us to see copies of those notes. And the medical examiner's report as well. You'll be hearing from us again soon,' he went on, '*very soon*, Dr Reid. Goodbye.'

'One last thing, doctor,' Tom said suddenly, his hand rested casually on the doorknob. 'Just for our records: do you happen to remember the name of the detective who attended the scene of the baby's death?'

Dr Reid was writing something on a large piece of card, and he did not look up. 'Driscoll, I believe,' he said coolly. 'Goodbye.' We filed back down the corridor and out of the offices. Kent paused to blow a kiss discreetly to Elizabeth on the way out.

'Good thought, that one,' he said judiciously to Tom when we were back in the car. 'Driscoll, eh? Driscoll. Hmmm.'

'Isn't that the detective Emmie said was friends with Ryan?' I asked, and Kent nodded.

'It's a small police force here, there's only a handful of 'em, it had to be Driscoll or – what's his name? – Johnson, but Driscoll is the younger man, and he's known all around as a bit of a push-over. If only we could get our hands on the report he filed . . . Could be tricky, he's unlikely to just hand it over.'

'We should start with the medical examiner's report,' Tom pointed out. 'We're entitled to a copy of that.'

Kent agreed. 'Sure, but ultimately the responsibility for filing that lies with Reid; it'll be just Reid's official version of events. Still, I'll chat with Emmie and see if I can get a copy faxed to my offices today, before the weekend. It's a good place to start.'

When we arrived home, Jeanie delivered Samuel into our arms with a small smile, a rare sight. 'He's been very good, actually,' she told us, stroking his cheek. 'No trouble at all. He barely cried once. Now what would you two like for dinner?' she went on in a bracing tone. 'I was thinking of making a stew. Or perhaps a pie, I could take whatever's left over to Quiet Lanes, show them what English baking tastes like?'

49. Jeanie

I produced the first fifteen pages of polysyllabic nonsense in a mere two hours. I took my computer to Quiet Lanes the next morning, where Mrs Forrest read through the document with an expression of admiring astonishment. 'You know what this all means?' she asked eventually, wildly gesticulating.

'Of course not,' I explained briskly, 'but neither will Andrew. Now, in the meantime, I have an idea: let's think seriously about what you'd *actually* like to do at Quiet Lanes in the next year. We'll put it in the kind of language he wants, and see what we can wrangle for you and the Home.'

So we sat down together, and she sketched out her wish-list. More tea parties ('excellent opportunities for dynamic collaborative interaction'). More visits from outside speakers ('a series of focused interdisciplinary events developing skills in patients and health professionals alike'). And 'I'd – I'd love to be able to take them all for a day by the sea,' Mrs Forrest remarked wistfully, clutching her hands dramatically to her chin. 'Sue-Ellen just loves lobster, and Ken was saying the other day he's been dreaming of fresh oysters. And Joel loves reading on the beach.' This sounded like a very good idea so, after referring back to my course notes, and a few of the essays that Sibelius Mordaunt actually liked, I typed:

An essential component of collaborative enterprise involves challenging health-care professionals to perform in non-conventional settings. This encourages those in care positions to communicate both verbally and nonverbally, thus developing crucial skills across disciplines. Our goal, therefore, is to create, through a series of focused single-day excursion events, opportunities for employed and volunteer health-care professionals to enhance and develop these vital skills in order to heighten patient benefits and enhance institutional excellence. An ocean-oriented event exploiting Connecticut's vibrant natural resources would allow us to target goals one, two, and three from the current collaborative mandate.

'And that means?' Mrs Forrest pondered, after reading this aloud carefully.

'We'd like to go to the seaside, please,' I finished, grinning, and she stared at me with gratifying admiration.

'Does it really?' she asked, turning her head this way and that, as if reading upside down would make the whole thing clearer. And then, with a reluctant sigh, 'Words *are* funny things, Jeanie!'

She bustled off into the day room to start lunch; I sat in her pot-pourried office with my computer and a plate of twinkie cakes editing, moving things around, and then – as a final touch – adding serious-sounding sub-headings in different typefaces. By the time I was finished it was, I must admit, quite impressive. I printed it out on her little workhorse printer, adding a title page and a list of chapter headings (1: Introduction: Implementing Mandate in Quiet Lanes Setting. 2: Socializing Care Workers: An Overview. 3: Collaborative Enterprise Revisited. 4: Business Plan: Projecting Future Goals). I walked into the day room and presented Mrs Forrest with the fat little bundle. She waved her arms around so much I thought she was going to take off.

I was walking out through the front hallway when I became conscious, suddenly, of a presence behind me. I turned to see Sue-Ellen, hovering strangely in her own shadow. There was something more insubstantial about her than normal; her hair was wispier, flatter, not its usual magnificent golden edifice. 'There's something I've been meaning to tell you,' she said softly. 'Don't want you to hear it from one of the others, I guess.' She reached out and adjusted a sea-shell collage on the wall that had slid fractionally to the side; with great attention, she touched it this way and that with her finger, until she had it exactly, perfectly straight. I waited, watching her, wondering.

'My cancer is not – well, it's not curable, Jeanie,' she said at last, standing back to her examine her handiwork. 'Doctor confirmed it a day or two ago.'

I gasped; for a moment I couldn't think quite what to say. The news should not have surprised me – Mrs Forrest had told me about her mastectomy on my very first day – but somehow Sue-Ellen seems like one of those people that death cannot possibly touch. Her finely grooved face looks as if it has aged as much as it will, and now she has a timeless quality to her, a simple, peaceful elegance that has nothing to do with being sixty, or seventy, or ninety.

She did not look up at me now but stayed where she was, rearranging a few poems and a Childe Hassam reprint. 'So I'll be moving out of Quiet Lanes in a few weeks' time,' she went on, her voice quiet and level, her profile impassive. 'I'm gonna go into a hospice in Old Saybrook, unless I get worse before that, of course. Cancer's spreading, so I guess it's just a matter of time.' Unconscious hands stole upwards to her breast. 'But I think I have a few weeks here left to enjoy. I like it here, Jeanie.

I like the folks.' She smiled briefly, without quite catching my eye, turned around, and started to walk away.

'Sue-Ellen!' I called, and she turned hesitantly to face me.

'Yes, honey?'

'Sue-Ellen, I'm so – so very sorry,' I said. My voice, cracked and splintered, didn't sound like mine at all.

She reached up and patted her golden hair. 'Yes, my dear, so am I,' she replied evenly, and walked back into the day room.

50. Q

Samuel has been surprisingly peaceful this morning, so I have been counting his toes in the bath. He's not thrilled with sitting in a big tub all by himself; every time I touched his feet to the water he squealed worriedly, so after giving the matter some thought I stripped off my clothes and got in with him, propping him up on my stomach. Much better, he gave me to understand, waving an experimental leg in the warm soapy water. 'This little piggy . . .' He observed me solemnly, head on one side, as I pulled each tiny digit, then crinkled up his chubby little neck to stop the piggy finding its way home, and giggled.

After lunch, I left him sleeping – a peaceful sleep, one he drifted into contentedly at my breast – and accompanied Tom on his way through the slow-moving Saturday traffic to Kent's office at Cheasford. My shoulder muscles felt unusual, and it took me a while to understand why; ah yes, I realized, with a sensation of shock, I haven't actually had to carry the baby *all morning*.

'Jeanie's being very helpful at the moment, isn't she?' I said brightly to Tom; he's been irascible at times about what he persists in calling her 'adolescent' schedule ('I mean, who the hell sleeps until noon? Seriously?'). He agreed, although – perhaps unsurprisingly – he's starting to find her presence in our home less than agreeable. 'She's OK with Samuel – not great – and her cooking is delicious – when she bothers to do it. But it never seems to cross her mind we're footing all the bills. I mean, does she never think about money? Has she never thought to contribute something? To give us a gift, at least? Would it *hurt* to get us a box of cookies?'

'You looking for *him*?' There was a sharp tap on the car window; it was Luna Lilly jerking her Alice-banded head in the direction of Kent's office. We nodded dubiously. Seeing Luna Lilly outside in the bright car park was a bit like seeing a Transylvanian vampire amongst the purple chrysanthemums in the early autumn sun.

'He won't be down today, not if I'm any judge,' she said, leaning into the car, a trace of triumph in her voice. The smell of sandalwood flooded in around her, hot and heady, laced with an acrid tang of sweat. 'I heard him yesterday afternoon. Singing, dancing. After you left. I called up to him, I said, you'll party on your *own* tonight. Don't you come looking for me, I know what you've been up to with that cleaning assistant.' She nodded sharply in the direction of the dry-cleaner's shop. 'I mean, who needs their goddam socks dry-cleaned? The drunk, cheating, two-timing bastard! I could still hear him when I left for home, yelling and carrying-on. He'll be dead to the world today. Dead, dead, *dead*.'

She was clearly pleased to be the bearer of bad tidings; her small mouth was twisted into an angry smile, her eyes were needle bright. 'Just thought you should know,' she finished righteously, then, pausing only to peer curiously into the back seat of our car, her eyes taking in the baby seat and the mess of stuffed toys, she waddled back to her office. Tom got out and went after her, jangling his keys; I followed behind.

Luna, turning round, laughed shortly, hands on her cello hips. 'You ignoring me? Fine. But you'll see. There's not much help you can give him, he's past it now. And you won't need *those*; he won't have locked his office door, never does.

Anybody can take anything they want from his place, any confidential documents. You can get anything you want out of those big filing cabinets.' ('We'll see about that,' I heard Tom muttering under his breath.) 'Not that *I* ever go snooping, you understand, through people's private affairs, I'm not like that . . .

'But you won't do *him* any good,' she finished, watching us wend our way up the blue-carpeted interior stairs. 'He won't get up for you today unless you're a glass of whisky sour.'

We pushed open the door to Kent's office which was, as Luna had forecast, unlocked. The place reeked of booze, vomit and cigarettes; the curtains were drawn, and it took us a while to make out Kent's form spread-eagled on the floor. The phone lay next to him, cable pulled out of the wall, an empty glass upturned beside it.

'Kent – Kent, wake up,' Tom said hastily, crouching down and taking the lawyer's thin white hand in his. Kent's hair was loose and half covering his face; I kneeled over him and pushed it away from his nose, eyes, and mouth.

'Kent, are you OK?'

He groaned, rolled slowly over on to his face, and said something like 'rrrmmmf'. His rucked-up red shirt exposed his too-thin body, his dry, white-brown mottled skin. 'I've got a bottle of water in my bag.' I rustled through half-a-dozen tissue pouches to find it, and then, trying to push him gently over on to his back, I said, 'Here, Kent, take this, a little water . . .'

His arm shot up, suddenly and unexpectedly, and he pushed the bottle out of my hands. Half of it slopped out on to the carpet; I grabbed it a second before the entire contents was lost, then looked hopelessly at Tom. 'What are we going to do?' I hissed, sitting back on my haunches.

Luna Lilly, we suddenly realized, was standing just behind us, arms akimbo. 'I told you, there's nothing you *can* do,' she said, gleefully. 'He's a low-down dirty drunk, has been for years, there's nothing anyone can do. It was bound to happen, always does, he can't stay off the stuff. He'll sleep it off, then as soon as he can lift a glass to his mouth he'll start on the next bottle. Leave him to it, that's my advice.'

'*Thank* you, but we'll take things from here.' Tom was cool; under his unwavering gaze hers eventually dropped, and a few moments later we heard her heavy footsteps on the stairs.

'What the hell are we going to do now?' I muttered, peering into Kent's face, then pulling back in spite of myself. The stench of last night's alcohol on his breath was almost overpowering.

'Medical examiner's report – on table. Faxed yesterday. Take it.' Kent's voice was creaky, as if he hadn't used it in years; he licked his dry peeling lips with a hint of a greyish tongue.' Leave me alone – you deal with it now.' He lifted a shaking hand to the side of his head and covered his eyes. 'I'm done. I'm out of it. Don't want to . . .' and then something incomprehensible. He licked his lips, and coughed. '*Go.*'

I stared blankly at him. But Tom, I realized, was holding a copy of the medical examiner's report, which he had prised from the lips of the ancient fax machine. He scanned it, then folded it up and put it in his pocket. 'All right Kent, if that's what you want. Let's go, Q,' he said briefly, placing the remnants of the bottle of water within Kent's reach. He fetched a coat from the back of the door and placed it gently over the old man's form, then turned to me. I looked down at the floor.

'We *can't* just leave him here, Tom, he's in a terrible state, he might choke on his own sick or something . . .' I was aghast.

Tom shook his head. 'Unless I'm much mistaken, Ms Lilly will keep an eye out, even if it's just because she wants to come up and crow over him. And look, what's the alternative? We could drag him outside – maybe, then drag him into the car – maybe, then take him home and hose him off, and spend the next week drying him out. I don't think that's what he wants, Q, and frankly it doesn't sound particularly appealing to me either. We've got a child to think of. The best option is simply to leave him here for now.'

'Ya *still here*?' Kent asked blearily, half lifting his head to look at us with rheumy eyes, and then he mumbled something about the fact that he'd 'never wanted 'em here in the first place'. 'But if you're goin' to stick around you might as well make yourselves fuckin' useful,' he went on, switching to loud anger. 'Why do I have to do everythin'? *Fuck off!*'

With one last doubtful look at the old man on the floor, I followed Tom out of the building and into the sunlight. 'Rattle, rattle,' I murmured, and Tom nodded, as we got into the car.

51. Jeanie

When I arrived home from Quiet Lanes Q met me with a letter. It had taken over three weeks to find me; Ann Dougins received it at college and forwarded it on to the flat, where Una would normally have used it to snort lines, but I suppose she was feeling guilty about kicking me out on the street (and possibly about allowing Dukey, whoever – or whatever – he may be, to sleep in my bed). So she actually bothered to send it on, complete with a big 'Love Una' and a lipstick smackeroo on the back.

'Dear Ms Boothroyd,' it began politely and with due political properness:

We recently contacted Professor Humphrey Sibelius Mordaunt at Kingsbury College to ask if he could recommend recent graduates of the Master's in Social Work and Social Policy as applicants for a new programme to be established in the London Borough of Southwark. This government-funded programme, part of a new nationwide Supporting the Third Age initiative, has two major goals: firstly, to provide support for older people (65+) through weekly day centres (which will provide recreation and physical and mental health advice, as well as co-ordinating community interaction and interfaith meetings); and secondly, to provide support for those caring for pension-age citizens in the community through a monthly magazine and twice-monthly morning drop-in. We are seeking well-qualified applicants to manage this exciting new programme for older people in Southwark, and Professor Mordaunt enthusiastically suggested your name and suitability for the position. If you are interested and would like to find out more, please visit us on the web, where you will also find an application form (see 'So you want to apply?', bottom right, third column, red bubble). We hope to hear from you soon.

Of course there was no wireless signal to be found anywhere in the house, so I set off to Sussex on foot, paid my five dollars at an internet café, and logged on to the site. I read the information about the Supporting the Third Age initiative, but the most astounding part for me was the section where Professor Mordaunt 'enthusiastically suggested' me. He *did*? *Why*? It can't have been my stellar B- performance, after all, so clearly something else possessed the man to put my name forward – unless, of course, he still has me mixed up with Cindy or Amy or someone else entirely from the course.

And then I thought about it as I worked my way ruminatively through a bran muffin, and I realized with a sensation of shock that even if Professor Mordaunt suggested me in a drunken haze after cavorting with his secretary one night, I actually want the job – really, truly. I love working with older people; I love Quiet Lanes. It's something I could build a life around. Everyone else on my course in London enjoyed helping children – because there's hope for their future, I suppose, and because children (even the ones who've set their parents' beds on fire with a blowtorch) look sweet and vulnerable, little round faces covered in goo. Me, I like the stories older people tell; I love hearing about Sue-Ellen's husbands and Teddy's lost wife and Ken's raids over northern France in 1944. I like the peaceful order, the familiar routine, the cheery hum of conversation. No one's going to put their fingers in the electric socket or grow up to murder their sister at Quiet Lanes, it's all far more predictable: serve tea, lift people, clean hands, water plants, talk. I'm no Florence Nightingale, but this is a life I love.

So I went to the website and punched in my application details with a fervent sense of purpose. I can help the older people of Southwark, I thought, I can help them get something out of life in the community, and – well, there was nothing about improving the standard of nursing care in the job description, but I can spend the next five years of my life banging my head against the system trying to improve things, can't I? (Thinking vaguely of Dave's poor mam with her matted hair and scurfy legs.) Of course, I may well need to go on the game in order to afford a flat of my own – the salary is approximately £5000 a year less than that of a shelf-stacker at Sainsbury's, as far as I can see – but at last I've found something that will get me out of bed in the morning.

Only then I got to the bit where you press 'send', and I couldn't; it wouldn't accept the application because I was three days past the deadline. 'Please email us by clicking here to learn about future job opportunities in the London Borough of Southwark', invited a cheery pop-up. 'Thank you for your interest in the London Borough of Southwark.' I stared at the screen, feeling my newfound sense of purpose and inspiration ebbing away. A near miss. Good try, but not this time. No, not yet; no, not here.

I clicked here, and up popped a small box for my email address and a second, larger rectangular message box. 'Please tell us your field of work, so that we may send you details of suitable positions as they become available.' And then, because my school motto (patience and humility) was obviously a non-sense, I punched in a message explaining that I want *one* job in particular, the one whose deadline had passed, and suggesting they should consider my application in spite of its lateness. Professor Mordaunt of Kingsbury College recommended me for this position, I went on, confidently. And I *am* amply qualified for the job. Of course it wouldn't let me attach a CV, so instead I typed in everything I could possibly think of that might per-suade them of my suitability – every placement, every bit of work experience, every piece of coursework on 'issues facing our ageing community', and my volunteer work at Quiet Lanes ('a first step towards a comparative study of geriatric care in the States and in South London'). I really want this job, I said at the end. I want to make caring for older people the focus of my career.

I pressed 'send', and held my breath. Everything went blank. There was a pause, in which I stared at the large screen of white and wondered why I forgot to *save* my epistle of self-confidence before sending it off into the vortex. And then: 'Thank you for contacting us, your message has been received': a rush of relief!

I literally ran back to the house along the coastal road, to tell Q all about it – the job, Professor Mordaunt's recommendation, my application. When I'd finished, she nodded approvingly. 'I'll admit I thought it was weird when you said you were going to work at Quiet Lanes,' she admitted. 'Frankly I got the impres-sion Paul maybe manoeuvred you into it. I couldn't think why. But I was obviously wrong,' she continued. 'I hadn't realized you were so committed.'

'Didn't you?' I said innocently. 'Really? How strange!'

'Phone Alison and tell her all about,' she prompted. 'She'll be really pleased. We were talking about you just this morning, actually. She was saying she wondered if you'd really consid-ered all the options in social work. She even said perhaps you needed an interview with a career counsellor. I mean, I know she can be a bit officious, and to the best of my knowledge she's never sat down with a career counsellor in her life, I didn't know she even knew they existed, but I still thought it was a really good point. I told her I could arrange something down in New Haven for you, and she . . .'

Honestly, I liked it better when they didn't talk to each other.

52. Q

Tom is on to his second memory stick, and he has the look of a man possessed. Every time we want to eat a meal we have to wade through a tumbling pile of files on the dining-room table (currently T–U). And books have been arriving in the mail all week from Amazon, with titles like *Running Your Own Private Practice*, *Practical Law*, and *So You Think You Can Cut It in the Real World*?

It's becoming autumn; we're moving into our second season here in Connecticut. And now at last there seems to be a rhythm to our lives, a regular beat of gentle expectation as the leaves begin to flicker with colour and the nights turn cool. The sea in the mornings is like cold glass against my skin.

The woman who sells fish from her white van to locals on Mondays knows my name, and I know hers. I know when fresh lobsters arrive at the Lobster Pot. The general store has begun to stock my preferred brand of nappies in Samuel's size and extra portions of dried sweetened pineapple – Tom's favorite afternoon snack – in the 'serve yourself' bins (new deliveries arrive on Wednesdays). I've finally persuaded the *New York Times* to deliver to our mailbox. I've weeded out the leggy yellow flowers from the rocket in the garden, so we have fresh salad each night for dinner. Tomatoes are ripening in pots along the deck.

Every morning I collect cicadas in cupped hands from the

floor of the bathroom and drop them gently out of the window. I know to avoid bustling wild turkeys on the road by day and soft-footed deer at nights. We watch flaming cardinals in the trees at lunchtime, while at night a raccoon snuffs at the back door and possums hesitantly vacuum up the crumbs of our meal upon the deck. I know to stay clear when the skunk makes his leisurely evening shuffle past the front door as the moon comes up. I hear the creak of wooden floorboards contracting with the fresh cold air in the dead of night, and I am not afraid.

Every afternoon, when Samuel takes his nap, Tom and I make ourselves cups of coffee which we bring on to the deck, and we talk. It's a precious time of peace and quiet. Today, after calling Luna Lilly to check up on Kent again ('Oh, *he's* all right, can you hear him?' she asked scornfully, holding the telephone up so we could listen to his rendition of 'The Star-Spangled Banner'), we discussed Emmie's case. Tom smoothed out the medical examiner's report that we collected from Kent's office, and we pored over it together on the round wicker table.

According to the document, filed at the state medical examiner's office, Angela Cormier was pronounced dead by Dr Philip Reid at 9.07 a.m. on 1 May 2001. There were no signs of violence in the home, and the child's body was not covered by blankets or any other obvious suffocation hazards. She was lying on her side in her crib, and appeared to have been dead for three to four hours when the doctor arrived on the scene.

Dr Philip Reid, the document claimed, had seen the child once in the two weeks prior to death, on 19 April, at which time the child had been suffering from a slight cold but had seemed, in all other respects, healthy. The mother reported that nothing unusual had taken place since the doctor's visit, although she now recalled that the child's cold had appeared to

267

worsen, rather than improve, since the doctor's visit. *Mother was intending to take the child to see Dr Reid on Wednesday morning (2 May) if child not better*, the notes remarked.

The report was filed by Lieutenant Anthony E. Driscoll, his signature a careful flourish along the bottom. Unless we could find a chink in his story, a gap in the narrative, it was going to be hard to prove Emmie's account of the facts.

'We need to talk to him,' Tom said, standing up, 'to Driscoll, as soon as possible. I'll call to make the appointment for Monday.'

'What if Kent's not sober by then?'

'We'll go by ourselves.'

'By *ourselves*?' I returned, disbelievingly. 'Are you serious? Why on earth would Driscoll talk to us? He's never met us before.'

'He's bound to have heard we're working for Kent. Everyone round here has.'

'But – we can't – I mean, I know you're his associate now, but I think Kent would want to be there,' I replied firmly. 'He's always telling us he's the only one who understands how the local system works.'

'Well, you know, I've been thinking about that, Q,' Tom cut in, bending over and propping his arms on the deck railing. A pair of blue jays was screeching in the branches of a reddening maple on the far edge of the garden; we watched the bright flashes of blue darting in and out of the fire-tipped leaves. 'He told us he'd be on the premises; he knew perfectly well we were coming. So why suddenly tumble off the wagon hours before we arrive? I'll tell you what I think: I think we've been set up again, Q. Maybe he didn't do it consciously. But I don't think he can handle the firm any more. He's got veins popping in his cheeks, and as for that silver flask . . . He wants us to take the firm, Q, and let him retire, cuddle up to his bottle

268

and catch sea bass. I think he got us the medical examiner's report yesterday afternoon, and decided he was done.'

The blue jays shrieked and jeered; I could hardly hear myself think. 'Well,' I said at last, 'if you're right, we should make the appointment for Monday. But I still think Kent will be able to come with us,' I continued, standing up as Samuel's sleepy snuffles turned to wails on the monitor. 'It's probably just a weekend thing,' I added. 'He fell off the wagon on a Friday – he's not the first alcoholic to do that, I'm sure. But now he's seen us he's bound to sober up. He'll be a bit embarrassed, he'll drink a pint of water, and by tomorrow, Monday at the latest, he'll be fine.'

Tom cocked an eyebrow. 'I think I'll make that phone call,' he said coolly. 'For Emmie's sake, if nothing else.'

53. Jeanie

With Samuel propped on my knee and a capricious wireless signal, I typed 'geriatrics' into every social-work database I could find today, while Tom and Q were out. I found about seventy-five jobs that require the applicant to manage several hundred octogenarians and a fleet of under-trained volunteers. I found one job that involves running a day centre for geriatrics with mental health problems, but it would require moving to Poole. I applied for it anyway – never been to Poole, maybe it's lovely – but I baulked at the others. Increasingly, it seems, all my eggs are in the basket of Southwark.

Then I took Samuel to Quiet Lanes, which I've been meaning to do ever since Paul suggested it. The fascination of a small child drove everyone 'crazy', as Mrs Forrest inevitably predicted, clutching her hands to her nose, and Samuel was so entranced by the attention he didn't cry once. Passed from hand to hand, from knee to knee, he felt soft faces with a gentle hand, and even laughed when Ken made loud farting noises against his stomach. Sue-Ellen thrilled everyone by doing her palmistry (Samuel will apparently enjoy an extraordinarily long life, vast quantities of cash, and a beautiful wife from India) and Tim gave Samuel a cranial massage that sent him into a peaceful doze. He may really be getting better, just as Alison predicted.

'I'm thinking of working with old people – seniors, I mean,'

I explained to Sue-Ellen in a quiet corner, 'for my career. I've applied for a job back home in London. I think there's a good chance I'll get it.'

'Marvellous idea, darlin'!' she exclaimed. 'It's been wonderful, having you around these last few weeks, someone who comes because they *want* to, not because their school tells 'em they have to.' She patted my hand. 'You volunteered to work with us out of the good of your heart, Jeanie; we appreciate that. You've restored my faith in young people. The others feel the same way. We've had some kids here, you can tell they're just thinking of a grade at the end of a page, we're just a means to an end. Not like you.'

My heart lurched. 'Sue-Ellen,' I began, miserably, and she looked innocently up at me.

'Yes, dear?'

I opened my mouth, and then I closed it again. I couldn't – well, put it this way, I didn't tell her the truth. What would be the point in puncturing her illusion? Instead, I returned the pressure on her hand. 'If I've found my way, it's got a lot to do with you,' I explained, and I was absolutely sincere about that. 'If things are making sense to me now, I think it's because I met you. I mean it. Thank you.'

I arrived in our kitchen at home an hour or so later to find Q murmuring in hushed tones on the telephone, Samuel splayed on her lap. She looked up, and an expression of conscious guilt passed over her face: 'Oh, Jeanie, hello, I didn't realize you were – uh – home,' she said, in the loud tones you use to tell someone on the other end of the phone that the person they're talking about has just walked into the room. Alison, I presumed, or possibly Mum. I scowled.

'Yes. Would you rather I wasn't?' I replied irritably.

'Of course not, Jeanie, don't be silly,' my sister returned coolly. 'But you did say you'd help me give Samuel a bath this morning, I was waiting for you, and then you *completely* disappeared.'

I stomped upstairs. Alison doesn't seem to phone me so much these days, she's opened up a permanent line to my sister instead, so when I saw a message icon on my mobile, which I'd left on the table, I wondered for a dizzying second if it was *him*. I dialled my messages and pressed the phone a little closer to my ear.

But it was Dave. 'We haven't been in touch for a while. Thought you might want to know I got back all right, changed my flights without any difficulty. I've just got back from Ranger and Magsie's; fancied a break. So I went down to their place in Brighton. They're planning a trip to the Netherlands to meet a bloke who's going to teach them about harnessing the power of the wind, and I might go with them for a bit. It's something to do. Just wanted you to know in case – well, in case you tried to reach me.'

I put down the phone feeling faintly sick. Poor rudderless Dave, meandering around the countries of northern Europe, blown by the wind. But there was nothing from Paul.

54. Q

All day Sunday we called Kent's offices; no reply. Finally, at 4 o'clock, we put Samuel in his car seat and drove to Cheasford. The two-tone pick-up was still in the car park, but there was no answer at his door – which was now unexpectedly locked, the chain slid into place. 'Maybe he's – you know,' I said nervously, not quite meeting Tom's eye above Samuel's head; and then, just as I was debating whether to dial 911, we heard a thin, bleary, but unmistakable voice.

'How many times do I have to tell you to leave me in peace? Get the fuck away from me . . .'

Tom shrugged. 'I'm not wasting any more time on this,' he said impatiently. 'He obviously wants us to take charge. And frankly, he's in no condition to take control of Emmie Cormier's case anyway. This has gone on long enough.' After peering through the keyhole and assuring myself that Kent was recumbent on the ground, not dangling from a rafter, I reluctantly followed my husband back down the stairs.

'We're here to see Lieutenant Driscoll,' Tom announced when we arrived on the premises of the small purpose-built block just after lunchtime on Monday. The bald desk clerk was blandly bored.

'Kenton Tyler's associates – yes, yes – I remember. I'll let him know you're here.'

We sat down in the small, empty waiting room. After a few minutes we heard a buzz; the door opened, and the clerk appeared on the other side. 'He'll see you, but as he explained before, he's only got ten minutes to spare, he's *very* busy at the moment,' he told us, managing to achieve an expression of official officiousness as he ushered us into an interior office. Lieutenant Driscoll – who was not more than thirty, with a simple face, sandy hair and eyelashes – was fiddling aimlessly with a pen when we entered; he began hastily typing at his computer, then gestured to two plastic chairs. As I sat down, I noticed a picture of a little girl in a pink tutu facing him on his desk.

'Old man Tyler said he had a coupla city lawyers working with him,' he began. 'You think you can cut it up here, eh?' he added, with a short laugh. 'If lawyering's anything like police work, you don't stand a chance. You need to be *from* a town if you're going to understand it, the *heart* of a town, that is.' He sat back on his chair and looked over at us with a vastly superior expression.

'I'm sure you're right, Lieutenant Driscoll,' Tom answered respectfully. 'We've only been here a few months, but already we can tell that working in a town like this takes real care, real commitment. But we'll try to help Mr Tyler as best we can.'

Driscoll nodded. 'Sure, sure, I get it. Not much you can do for that girl Cormier, though; she's a – harrumph,' he finished lamely, looking over at me.

Tom leaned forwards. 'We know the score,' he said, 'of course we do. Look, we just need to get a few answers, get the story straight, so we don't look like idiots in court, right? Some of this stuff' – he got out his BlackBerry – 'some of this stuff Tyler wants us to get, I'm not kidding you, it's real obvious, you know? Just details. Like, what was the name of the doctor on the scene when her kid died?'

The young policeman visibly, immediately, relaxed. 'Jeez, that *is* obvious! Half the folks in town could tell you that. Between you and me, Kenton Tyler needs to walk outta that practice before he *falls* out of it, or *off* of it, know what I mean?' he added, guffawing. 'It was Reid, Phil Reid.' He leaned back in his chair. 'Phil Reid has been the Cormier family's doctor for years.'

Tom tapped *Philip Reid* into his BlackBerry. 'That's great, thank you, Lieutenant. You're being a tremendous help to us! Now then, the other people in the house were – I'm guessing – the mother, her father and her grandfather, right?'

Driscoll nodded again, fingertips held lightly together. 'Sure. Terrible upset they were,' he added soberly, a quick glance at the tutu girl on his desk.

'We have a baby boy ourselves,' I put in suddenly. 'My husband and I. His name is Samuel. He's just a few months old. Now I'm a mother, this kind of story . . . I feel it very differently, don't you? Before I had kids I didn't quite grasp what the death of a child would mean. But now, just think' – the tears in my eyes were real – 'think what it would be like if you could never hold your angel again, never kiss her good-night . . .'

Lieutenant Driscoll gulped. 'I can't imagine it,' he said gruffly. 'Losing Polly would be . . .' He reached out unconsciously for the photograph.

'The thing we don't understand is how a child can just die, without warning, in the middle of the night,' Tom picked up the thread quickly. 'I don't mind telling you, Lieutenant Driscoll, since we heard the story about the Cormier baby my wife has hardly been able to leave our son's bedside, have you, sweetheart? She's too frightened to part from him in case he vanishes like that, without warning, no symptoms. Just gone in a second.'

Driscoll had put down the photograph and was leaning forwards to face me now. 'I know what you mean, but it wasn't quite like that,' he explained earnestly. 'The kid had been ill for a week at least, maybe longer. The Cormier girl told me at the time, I remember. She kept saying she wished she'd taken her into the hospital.'

'Is that right? That does make me feel better,' I said, turning to Tom with a sigh of relief. 'Do you happen to know what those symptoms were, lieutenant?' I went on earnestly. 'It would really put my mind at rest.'

'She had this cold that got worse and worse, then she was drowsy, out of sorts, acting kinda funny; Emmie said she'd had the doctor—' He stopped himself suddenly. There was a silence. Tom and I kept our eyes off each other.

'Said she'd had the doctor?' Tom prompted.

But Driscoll's face had clouded over. 'Had the doctor out a week or two before she died. Just like I said before.' His body was stiff with suspicion.

'But Dr Reid wasn't able to help her?' I asked politely.

Driscoll drummed his fingers against the long metal desk. 'You'll have to ask Reid what it was they discussed,' he said, and his tone now distinctly surly. 'The way I remember it, when he came out to see the kid, there wasn't a whole lot wrong with it. Emmie should have called him out again when the kid got worse, but she didn't. I submitted a report about all of this to the medical examiner. You'll find the details there.' He stood up abruptly.

Tom made one last attempt. 'I don't suppose we could see your own notes on the death scene, by any chance, lieutenant?' he asked, standing up to face the young police officer. 'The internal police report? Just in case there's something there – some small detail – that might help us?'

'Help you with what?' Driscoll said immediately, fronting up to Tom, and when my husband mentioned something vague about Emmie's court case with Ryan, Driscoll's answer was short. 'Emmie Cormier is a dead-beat, always has been, always will be. Whatever you need you'll find in the medical examiner's report.' He opened the door. 'If Emmie Cormier loses that kid, she'll have no-one but herself to blame. You tell old man Tyler that from me. If he's sober enough to understand you, of course . . .'

55. Jeanie

I've been asked to schedule an interview in Southwark! A formal 'please contact us at your earliest convenience' email accompanied by a second 'Dear Jeanie' message from someone named Sandra arrived this morning. 'Sorry our initial letter got delayed, we received your message though, loud and clear. Can you send us a hard copy for the files?'

Someone in the world may really want me for a job! A real job! I have spent half the morning sketching out plans for 'Third Age' Day Centres. Everyone else offers bingo; I'll suggest t'ai chi and reflexology. I'll ask Mum for advice on yoga for the over-sixties, and perhaps Alison can help with contacts for programmes in sculpture and art. We should offer reduced rates for both carers and volunteers as well, to improve morale. Maybe we can arrange massages. And cookery courses too.

My happy sense of purpose was only briefly checked when Dave phoned me a few hours ago to tell me (sheepishly, with deep embarrassment) that over the weekend he got together with – *Ellen*.

I won't deny that at first I gulped. The thought of them together brought a strange lump to my throat – Dave finding consolation in those plump round arms, Dave burying his head in that generous white bosom – but, as he nervously explained how they'd got together, I found myself making peace with it all. Mam died late Friday night, poor lady, breathing out her last with Dave and the rest of the family arranged by her side. (A tidy death; the best kind.) And Ellen was there, weeping salt tears for the confused old woman, and their hands met in grief, and the rest followed quite naturally.

As Dave told me this I had an intuition, a premonition of another phone call I'll get about six months from now. Dave will ring me to say he and Ellen are engaged, and will I please come and dance at their wedding? It will be a huge floral affair, I'm quite sure, with Ellen in a vast fairy-tale dress of brilliant white with a low-cut bodice of rhinestones and rose petals strewn up the aisle. Dave will look even more tall and gangly than usual in an unfamiliar suit, but his face will be full of love, and Ellen's will be just the same.

'You're not cross with me, are you?' Dave went on anxiously. 'I mean, it was a bit quick and all . . .' His voice tapered off into embarrassed silence. I laughed with the sudden happy consciousness of complete delivery from guilt, then told him I was actually *looking forward* to seeing them together, as a couple. When I get home.

'To be completely honest with you, Dave,' I said (although frankly there was some stuff I missed out here), 'I need to come back, see my friends, get on with my life. It's all right here, but after a while you miss your mates, people you can really trust. And I've got an interview for a social-work job, so things are really coming together,' I went on semi-self-importantly, because *I* needed to have a story to tell him too, I couldn't quite bear to be upstaged by Dave.

'I'm really glad for you, Jeanie.' His voice was sincere. 'And I'm glad you don't mind about me and Ellen. You and me – well, we weren't really right for each other, were we? Whereas Ellen . . . she's suggested I pick up carpentry again, Jeanie, she found this little stool I built as a kid, and – and I'm not sure I'm going to do so much eco stuff from now on, to be honest.

Badger and Ranger are really cross with me about it, but it's just *so nice* to be with Ellen, I don't feel like I have to escape from my life any more . . .'

Then we talked about Una and Lolly – who is, apparently, the enormous basketball player she got her paws on just before I came to America. Apparently he more or less moved into her bedroom that night, and has never moved out. Dukey is his enormous German Shepherd, and since I'm allergic to dogs the whole thing has worked out quite well. 'Would you like me to help you move your stuff, Jeanie?' Dave asked earnestly. 'I think I can get Badger to help, as long as you rent a hybrid van to move across town.' I laughed, and promised I would. As soon as I can find a new flat to move into, of course.

56. Q

'Driscoll was clearly about to tell us that Emmie called Reid out to see Angela more than once, but he stopped himself in time,' Tom remarked after dinner Monday night. He'd just spoken to Paul, who apparently wanted advice on a conflict he's run into with a Brooklyn-based judge. Jeanie was snoozing on the sofa, half listening to music on her iPod. My husband poured two glasses of cognac, a small one for me, a large one for him. 'For some reason, Driscoll's gone along with Reid – he filled in the report just as Reid asked him to do, and he's protecting Reid now.'

Of course we'd checked in on Kent once more after seeing the lieutenant, but he remained virtually insensate, a tumble of thin arms and legs now folded up into one of his velour chairs. 'How are we going to prove anything?' I asked gloomily, resting my head on Tom's shoulder. 'We could try to subpoena Driscoll's notes, I suppose.'

'Good luck,' Tom retorted. 'I don't think we have enough to get a subpoena, all we're going on is Driscoll's half-remembered story about Angela's illness and Emmie's word she called the doctor out. And she has plenty of reason to make up her claim that Reid saw the baby more often than he says. Her word won't count for much, set against the official report of a police officer *and* the word of a trusted local medic.'

High up in the sky a plane cruised by in the darkness, a steady receding drone.

'Q, we need to think of a different way into this,' Tom said at last, sighing for sheer frustration. 'Let's go over it again – what we know, what we don't know.' He walked over to the table and opened his computer.

We talked through the case, through our conversations with Driscoll, Reid, Kent and Emmie, while Tom tapped out notes. Hearing the sound of the clicking keys, Jeanie looked up. 'What are you doing?' she asked curiously, and when we explained, she pulled out her ear-plugs, swung down her legs and came over. 'Ooh, this is just like an Agatha Christie,' she said comfortably, pulling out a chair. She watched the timeline unfold on Tom's screen, her head tilted to one side. Tom pointedly ignored her.

'What are the gaps?' he asked finally, when we'd filled in every detail we could think of. 'I don't just mean about Driscoll and Reid's relationship, I mean about the circumstances surrounding Angela's death. We've got to find something to help us shake Reid's credibility, Q.' His eyes narrowed slightly. 'This is serious. Unless we can call the medical examiner's report into question, Emmie will go into court against Ryan looking criminally negligent. Ryan'll clean up.'

'This Reye's Syndrome, where does it come from?' my sister asked, gazing attentively at the screen. 'I mean, is it a virus? Can anyone get it? Or just kids? I've never even heard of it. It can't be that common, can it?'

Tom and I looked at each other. 'We don't know much about that, actually,' I replied, considering. 'I thought about that when you were talking to Emmie, Tom. You described the symptoms, then you said no one knows exactly what causes it. Is there a suggestion in the research that some children have a genetic predisposition to it, maybe? Is *that* something Reid missed?'

Tom shrugged. 'No harm in asking Ian, I guess.'

He picked up his phone and called his father's colleague; after a brief conversation, he closed the cell again with a frustrated snap. 'Nothing to do with genetics. Nothing at all, or at least that's the current state of research. It's a strange disease: Ian says it's only been identified in the last few decades, and it's not much understood. As happened with Angela, it often follows a fairly minor respiratory illness, and leads to serious chemical imbalances in the body's major organs. But it can be misidentified because the symptoms are sort of nonspecific.' Tom topped up his glass, and then – after a second's hesitation – splashed a drink out for Jeanie. 'It's also unusual; Angela was unlucky. It's become rare since aspirin was contraindicated for children and teenagers a decade or so ago. Apparently there seems to be some causal connection, although no one quite understands . . .'

My last gulp of cognac rose into my nose; I felt it burning up the tubes from the back of my throat into my head as the meaning of Tom's words hit my brain. I inhaled and choked, and choked again. '*Aspirin?*' There seemed to be fire in my eyeballs.

Tom and Jeanie began frantically thumping my back. 'What's wrong, Q?'

I stood up coughing, gasping for air, and knocked over the chair. It fell with a tremendous bang that seemed to shake the house. '*Reid prescribed Angela aspirin!*' I panted, wiping my streaming face and nose on my shirt-sleeve. 'He did, he did!'

'What? He *did*? How do you know?'

'Emmie told us,' I explained, gaining breath. 'I only remember because I was surprised to hear of a child's taking something other than acetomenophine – Tylenol, you know. That's what we were told to use when Samuel had his vaccines, don't you remember, Tom? I remember thinking, maybe different states suggest different painkillers for infants, I meant to ask Alison what parents use in England, and then I forgot all about it. But I know – I just know – that Emmie said Reid told her to give Angela aspirin.'

'My God. I wonder, I wonder,' Tom began slowly. 'I wonder if she still has the box! I wonder if it was on prescription . . .'

'Phone her, phone her!' yelped Jeanie, virtually throwing the phone at me. She was jumping up and down, eyes brightly delighted, 'phone her *right now!*'

'Emmie,' I began nervously when the young mother picked up the phone a few moments later, 'I need to ask you a question, and it's going to sound pretty weird.'

'Oh, it's you.' Emmie's voice was flat. 'I can't talk now, I've got my Bible study group here. Call again when we're done. In about half an hour.' The phone went dead.

I called back in the teeth of howls of frustration from my sister. 'Emmie, I'm sorry to bother you, but I need to ask you a really important question,' I began carefully, before she could speak. 'It's about old medicines you may have in your cupboard, well, one in particular . . .'

I heard her talking to someone else at the other end; it was a few moments before she came on the line again. 'Medicines? Are you collecting for developing countries too?' she asked interestedly; and then she added, 'You're too late. Elizabeth Summers took all that old stuff. At the beginning of the meeting, as a matter of fact. First come, first served, you know? And it's all in a good cause. Listen, like I said, I'll call you when I'm done. Thanks.'

She hung up again and this time, when I redialled, she didn't pick up.

A knot seemed to be tying itself in my intestines. 'Someone called Elizabeth Summers just collected the medicines. Something about needing them for developing countries, apparently,' I explained, and Tom's face paled.

'Elizabeth Summers – Elizabeth Summers . . . wait, Q, wasn't that *Dr Reid's assistant*? The woman Kent was sweet-talking the other day?'

I nodded. 'Tom, do you think—'

'What's going on? What are you talking about? Who on earth is Elizabeth Summers?' Jeanie screeched, but we ignored her.

'I don't know,' Tom said to me slowly. 'It could be coincidence, but maybe … maybe Reid realized we were on to something the other day, in his office. Maybe he remembers the aspirin, maybe he'd hoped no one would ever realize – it's certainly possible. Let's get into the car, right now, and go over to Emmie's house. We'll see if we can catch this Summers woman before she leaves the house with the medicines. There just *might* be time. Jeanie' (touching her awkwardly on the shoulder) 'Um – Jeanie, will you babysit, please?'

Jeanie's face was a comical mask of frustration. 'I *knew* you were going to say that!' she said, exasperatedly, as we flew out of the house.

57. Jeanie

I sat for three hours waiting for Q and Tom to come home. Staring out of the window at the moon rippling across the surface of the Atlantic. Thinking.

I don't need Dave. And I don't need Paul. I don't even think about him. Not much, anyway.

'So when are you going to see your young gentleman next, honey?' Sue-Ellen had asked me in the afternoon at Quiet Lanes, grinning. 'The one you want, I mean. The one who keeps you up at night, thinking about him.' She traced the outline of her own eyes, then pointed at mine, miming heavy lids. I patted her hand gently.

'You don't understand,' I explained. 'He's not right for me. *Really.*'

Sue-Ellen shrugged, then heaved herself carefully out of her chair. 'You know best, honey,' she said with a sigh. 'Of course in my day it was all about men, about getting a husband. Now you can make your own way. I admire you for it. But I still think you're pining for this man, yes I do!' I watched her walk back slowly to her bedroom for a nap. She's less steady on her feet than she was even a week ago.

When I arrived back at the house, I phoned Alison to tell her to stop gossiping with Q about me; it's been getting very irritating. Not surprisingly, she denied she's been doing anything of the sort. 'Really,' she said crossly, 'the two of you seem to take it in turns to get annoyed with me. It's very dysfunctional. Here I am, sitting all by myself in England, wondering how my two sisters are doing on the other side of the world, wishing I could be there helping them, and they – they badger me, one after the other. Really, I don't think it's fair. Now tell me,' she went on, without pausing, '*when* is that handsome American coming back to the house?'

'What – what handsome American?' I stuttered.

'Paul Dupont – isn't that his name? The fabulously rich man who – yes, I Googled him – rowed for Oxford in the Boat Race, dated a rather famous film star for two years, and owns two quite important Gaugin sketches, not to mention an Audubon. And surfaces repeatedly in the *Tribune* and the *Times* as "one of the most brilliant legal minds of his generation". *That* handsome American. Don't worry, I haven't said anything to Q about him,' she whispered. I could hear a purr of self-satisfaction in her voice. I felt as if I'd lost the power to draw breath. 'You underestimate me,' she continued silkily. 'Would I betray you to Q?'

'By which you mean that *you* like being the one in the know,' I returned furiously, finding my voice. 'Or am I underestimating you again, Alison?'

'Almost certainly, dear!' she replied, sounding utterly delighted.

'My love life isn't just a source of amusement for you and Q,' I scolded. 'What, are you living vicariously through me?'

'Jeanie, do you even know what that means?'

Later, much later, while I was waiting in the expectant darkness for my sister and Tom, I reread the article that appeared about me today in the local newspaper. I carefully cut it out, put it in an envelope, and addressed it to my sister. So she thinks I don't know what 'vicarious' means, does she? She doesn't know that I am a 'prominent British researcher'!

British Researcher Compares Senior Care in UK and US

by Julie Van Der Veeze,
Cheasford Times.
A CT exclusive!

Jean Bothroyd, a twenty-eight-year-old researcher from London, has demonstrated what different countries can learn by comparing strategies for senior care.

After an intensive study (and hands-on experience in our own Quiet Lanes Elder Care Home), Boothroyed has identified a series of strategies implemented in certain US centers that, she says, UK-based geriatric care can easily develop. 'I have compared a number of institutions in Connecticut with centers serving a comparable demographic in London. British Senior Care centers are chronically short of cash. Many are underfunded by the NHS, not to mention caught between responsibilities to local social services departments and to fee-paying individuals. But the focus on collaborative decision-making that many US centers now espouse can easily be implemented in UK centers, by adopting and adapting existing support networks and entertainment strategies.'

Joan, who is twenty-six, was full of praise for Quiet Lanes. 'The patients have their own rooms,' she said. 'And the flowers are really pretty.'

I was rather proud of that bit about demographics. I was almost tempted to send a copy to Paul.

58. Q

We sprinted to the car – or rather, Tom sprinted, I puffed ten paces behind, cursing the extra twenty pounds of baby weight I'd gained and somehow clung on to grimly these past months. 'Do you actually remember the way?' I gasped, levering myself into the passenger seat as Tom revved the engine.

'Sure. Of course. Er – maybe,' he finished, less confidently, peering into the darkness.

'Maybe' was right. 'Tom, I think we're heading towards the sea,' I offered at one point, and after much swearing and yelling he finally admitted that I was right as we rounded a sharp bend at the bottom of a road and the ocean reared up in front of us. We turned around and began to criss-cross lower Connecticut, shouting at each other, ripping at maps in our hasty efforts to read them, craning to read faded street signs in the moonlight, and generally making a complete hash of the twenty-minute drive to Emmie's house. I threw us completely off course at one point by swearing that a disused mine we passed was the one near Emmie's house (it wasn't); we finally arrived at Emmie's home a full forty minutes after the last Bible study guest had left.

When Emmie answered the door, and explained that Elizabeth Summers had gone, we both collapsed wearily on to the steps of the deck at the front of her house, shivering and roundly defeated. Emmie stared at us. 'Do you mind telling me what in the world is going on?' she asked, elbows out, fingers splayed across her thin hips.

I explained that we had hoped to find a box of aspirin in her medicine cupboard – a box of aspirin that Dr Reid prescribed for baby Angela. 'I remember you saying that that's what Reid told you to give her for her cold,' I added. 'Maybe you just bought a generic box, but we were wondering if he wrote out a prescription . . .'

'For Angela's aspirin? Yes he did,' she said. 'He did, because then I wouldn't have to pay for it. Prescriptions were covered by my insurance. In those days I had a pretty good policy, through Dad's work. Not like now, these days I got a high deductible, you wouldn't believe—'

'Emmie, did Elizabeth Summers take the aspirin this evening?' Tom cut in abruptly. 'When she came to clear out your cabinet, I mean?'

Emmie regarded him. ''Course not,' she said.

We stared disbelievingly at her; I found I was actually holding my breath. 'She – she didn't?' I asked, with a gasp. 'But you said she was taking old medicines, she claimed she needed them for some charity to aid developing countries . . .'

'Yeah, she did.' And then a strange half-angry expression passed over Emmie's face. '*Jeez*, you may be a mother, but anyone can tell you haven't lost a child. Wait in there.'

She pushed us into the sitting room, then reappeared a few moments later with a large cardboard box, which she gently laid on the sofa. We craned over her shoulder to look at it.

The box was painted pink, and small magazine pictures of animals – teddy bears, rabbits, kittens – were lovingly glued to the sides. The word 'Angela' was carefully picked out in red marker and glitter pen on the top, and a long, broad strip of pink ribbon was wrapped around the whole box. Emmie quickly retied her hair, then sat down on the creaky bed, unfastened the ribbon, and opened the box.

Inside nestled five tiny, slightly stained white babygros ('Sometimes I think they still smell of her'). Beside them reposed a small brown teddy bear, a few pairs of pink newborn socks, and a strange assortment of baby equipment – a blue rubbery aspirator and a swaddling cloth, a half-used tube of barrier cream and three nappies ('That was what was left of the packet when she – passed away'). And then there was a plastic crib mobile and a pink hat, a hand-knitted woollen blanket edged in white, a birth certificate, a sheaf of Xeroxed notes from the hospital on 'Newborn Care', and a Polaroid in a silver frame of a tiny, red, scrunched-up baby with her eyes tight closed. And finally, in the midst of it all, a brown bottle. *Angela Cormier, 23 April 2001. Reid, M.D. Aspirin. One dropper (.8 ml) to be taken twice a day.*

'Is that what you're looking for?' she asked us, passing it over, and we looked down at it, and at each other, and then back at her, momentarily lost for words.

'What, you think I just kept Angela's stuff in some old cabinet, jumbled anyhow?' she chided us. '*My baby's things?*' she went on, stroking the little photographed face with her finger. 'I don't have my little girl any more, I don't have her to hold in my arms, but everything she had, everything she used, everything with her name on it is precious to me,' she murmured. 'I packed it all up, and sometimes, when I feel she's gone so far away from me, I take it all out, and look at it, and I see her name on this bottle, "Angela Cormier", and it makes her seem real to me again, you know? I like to imagine, for just an hour, that she's still alive. I think about what she'd look like now, how she'd come into this room, calling "*Mommy!*", hair all over the place, dirty knees and a torn dress, teddy in her hands, those big eyes smiling up at me. She'd be a pretty girl, don't you think?' She smiled down at the tiny, scrunched-up face that would never become the girl her mother longed so desperately to know.

'Well, anyway,' she went on, after a moment's pause, 'I guess what you're telling me is, you need to take this bottle.' She handed it over with hands that trembled. 'Tell me *why*, please.'

I took the bottle and slipped it into my pocket. 'Emmie, Reid should never have given this to Angela,' I explained. 'He should have known better than to prescribe this for an infant; it's not safe. This bottle is crucial evidence. Apart from anything, it proves he came more than once to see you, because the date on the bottle is the twenty-third of April; the medical examiner's report Driscoll filed claimed Reid came just once, on the nineteenth. We're going to need to file a medical malpractice claim against your doctor. And if we can prove that he sent Elizabeth Summers today to fetch this bottle, well . . .'

Emmie looked bewildered. 'Reid always prescribes aspirin, he says modern medicine has a – a prejudice against it, he says it's good for the blood . . . You're telling me that – *that* made her sick?'

Tom explained what Ian had told him, that aspirin doesn't *cause* Reye's, but that medical research has found a correlation between children treated with aspirin for minor respiratory illnesses and the development of Reye's. That aspirin use has been limited in children and teenagers for the past decade now, for precisely this reason. She listened.

'I had no idea,' she said when he was done, wiping wet cheeks. 'No idea at all. I just did what he told me.'

The small brown bottle would go a long way towards validating Emmie's claim that Reid visited her multiple times in the weeks before Angela's death *and* that he either lied to Driscoll or persuaded him to omit this fact from the form he submitted to the medical examiner's office.

Emmie listened to us describe the seriousness of falsifying a death report. 'You say Driscoll was supposed to fill that form in after talking to me?' she asked. 'Ha! He didn't ask me a damn thing. Reid gave me something when he came that day, something to make me sleep. He said it would dull the pain. When I woke up, Driscoll was gone. I didn't think anything of it – wasn't thinking about anything except Angela – but I guess he and Reid cooked that thing up together while I was out cold. Gramps'll tell you the same thing, for what it's worth.

'But one last thing,' she went on anxiously. 'How is this going to help us with Ryan? How's it going to stop him from taking Paulie away?'

'This goes a long way towards re-establishing your credibility as a good mother,' I explained.

'It'll help us prove you didn't miss the signs that Angela was seriously ill,' Tom added. 'Practically speaking, we'll probably ask the Judge to hold up the decision about custody while we pursue the medical malpractice claim – a successful verdict in *that* suit will help exonerate you in the custody fight.'

'Ryan'll have a job taking Paulie away from you once we've proved medical malpractice against you and, with any luck, procured damages,' I added.

We left her wiping her eyes awkwardly, a little waif of a thing. I watched her in the side mirror, waving to us in the moonlight, as we bumped our way along the drive, then home to Jeanie, who was so agitated to learn what happened she hardly let us get in through the door. 'What happened? Did she have it? Can I see it? Will you get him? How *incredibly* thrilling . . .' And so great was the excitement that she and Tom actually exchanged energetic claps on the back.

59. Jeanie

Yesterday was my last day at Quiet Lanes, and it was Sue-Ellen's as well. She's gone downhill fast these last two weeks, the cancer spreading through her body taking vicious hold. She should probably have moved to the hospice before, but there was no space; so Mrs Forrest struggled to provide for her, in spite of the lack of appropriate facilities, and the other residents did what they could to help.

I came to help clear out her room. I put her few valuables into a small leather monogrammed case – the locket and her wedding ring, which had started to slip too easily off her bony finger – and gave it into the hands of the nurse who had come to take her along the coast to the Old Saybrook hospice. As she was wheeled towards the waiting van, she looked up at me and grinned slyly. 'Someone's coming tonight,' she said suddenly, raking my face with her sharp blue eyes, and I laughed in sheer disbelief. (Not for the first time I wondered if there's something in her 'Romany' training.)

'Now, how can you possibly know that?' I asked, shaking my head at her. 'You've been prying somehow, you naughty old woman!' She laughed back, delightedly.

'Honey, I see it in your face,' she drawled softly. 'He's coming, and no matter what you say, you're just *crazy* to get your hands on him.'

'He's coming, you're quite right, but it's nothing to me,' I corrected her gravely as her wheelchair was hauled carefully up into the van. I walked around so that I could still see her through the sliding door. 'He's not the right man. There's some-one else in his life, and that's the end of it.'

'Honey, it's never the end,' she said, smiling tremulously at me. 'It's never the end. Until it's *really* the end, that is.' I nodded, and didn't speak; I wouldn't for worlds. Instead I waved at her as the door slammed closed, and I kept waving at that neat, erect head, with its perfect wave of golden hair, long after the van had pulled out of the drive.

Paul was, indeed, coming in the evening, although how Sue-Ellen guessed I can't imagine. We had a phone call from him late one night, about a week ago, saying he needed to come up again to 'winterize' his boat (which is one of those verbs that conjures up images precisely opposite to its meaning. I imagine a process involving a snow-blown craft encrusted in icy rime, rigging cracking with icicles. Tom explained it actually means slathering the decks with weather-proofing grease to protect it from the elements).

And so, last night, he arrived just in time for dinner. I was in the middle of finishing the salad dressing when there was an almighty knocking on the front door (presumably just in case I happened to be swanning around buck naked again. You should be so bloody lucky, I thought to myself sourly). When the four of us sat down, the atmosphere was chilly. Would you pass me the salt, he asked, and I crashed it in front of him with an expression designed to convey the words 'You are an evil bastard and in an ideal world I'd pour this straight down your throat.' This continued for half an hour. Then Tom, in what was clearly a desperate effort to get the conversation moving in a more positive direction, asked about life at Paul's company, and he began to talk.

Of course I switched off – but then suddenly, some stray

word, or perhaps it was the tone of his voice, unexpectedly caught my attention.

'You know, this is really why I joined Prince in the first place,' he was explaining, leaning forwards, the light of the low silver chandelier reflecting in his eyes. 'My work with New York non-profits has been incredibly rewarding these past few years. I'm certain that PHMP Pro, in particular, would have collapsed if we hadn't been able to help them. But we managed to restructure the company, purchase supporting industries to help them finance themselves, and this year they've been able to get AIDS medications to people in some of the poorest countries in Africa. Then last month, I thought I'd made a total mess of the Marathon case, but it worked out OK, the tax exemption will stick, they'll be able to stay in business. Their outreach program to deprived inner-city kids is making a real difference in the city.'

Tom began to ask about how he was negotiating the bureaucracy of the New York State Charities Bureau, but I cut in. 'I don't understand,' I said. '*What* have you been doing?'

Paul looked at me. 'I was just talking about my work at Prince,' he said. 'Defending the indefensible, as you would put it. Or, as I like to say, specializing in supporting non-profit organizations and charities of all sizes.'

I stared at him. 'Really?'

Paul leaned slowly back in his chair and put his fingertips together. 'The reason I went to Prince & Cohen in the first place was that they offered me the opportunity to head their non-profit services.' Paul's body was rigid, but I saw his foot twitching under the table like the tip of a black cat's tail. 'I once offered to describe my work to you, but you didn't wait to let me.'

Just as I was beginning to feel a creeping embarrassment, the other, more serious charge I'd directed against him rose into my mind. 'Fine, so I got that wrong, I suppose,' I said bitterly. 'It doesn't really matter, does it? What you do in your professional life, I mean. You're not exactly a paragon of virtue in your *personal* life.'

Paul looked over at me. 'Jeanie,' he said, abruptly standing up, dropping his napkin on the table, then leaning forwards on his hands to face me, 'I want to tell you, here and now, in front of Tom and Q, that I am *not* having an affair with Lily Olawe.'

I gasped; Q gasped; Tom snorted with laughter. 'With Lily? Good God, I should think not! Why would anyone think you were?' he said, gazing disbelievingly from me to Paul and back again.

'I saw him with her,' I said firmly. 'I saw him touching her, holding her. I saw her stroking his chest,' I went on explanatorily. Q furrowed her brow.

'Would you be kind enough, Tom, to tell your sister-in-law what all good lawyers know about the veracity of eyewitness statements?' Paul said suddenly.

Tom raised his eyebrows. 'About –? Uh – OK. There's no proven correlation between the *confidence* of a witness in what he or she saw, and the *accuracy* of the statement.'

'Precisely.' Paul nodded. 'In other words, people don't always see what they think they've seen. And they're notoriously bad at judging whether they're interpreting events correctly. This makes eyewitnesses tough to handle in court. People will swear blind they saw a black man coming out of a window, but what they actually saw was a man in the shade. They're not lying, they truly believe they know what they saw. As a lawyer, you have to trust the jury to see that just because the witness is confident, it doesn't mean they're correct. Or you have to find a way to prove outright that they're wrong.'

I stared. 'OK, well, thank you for this little lecture, Mister Law Professor, but what has it got to do with you and Lily, please?'

'Jeanie, let me take you back to that day – the day you saw me with Lily,' Paul said, moving around the table and folding his arms lightly across his chest. He seemed coolly collected. 'How far apart were we? What stood between you and me?'

'Oh, I see what you're doing, and it won't work – but, fine, all right. You were on the other side of the road. And there was traffic between us. But it stopped.'

'What kind of a day was it?'

'Sunny.'

'And was I on the bright or the shadowy side of the street?'

'The shadowy, but—'

'Thank you. What did you see as we walked down the street?'

'I saw you stroking Lily's bottom,' I said mutinously.

'As we walked down the street?

'No – I mean, at first you were just walking. And then you reached out your hand, and put it round her waist, and then it sort of moved down. And you stopped walking.'

'OK, so I put my hand round her waist, then moved it to her hip. Did you see stroking or touching? Did I move my hand and caress her?'

I thought this through for a moment, remembering the position of their bodies, the bright sunlight, the traffic and confusion, my distress. 'I'm not actually sure,' I said, doubtfully, at last. 'I thought you did – but I could have been wrong about that. But I'm *not* wrong about—'

'So the sun was in your eyes. Thank you. Now what did Lily do at this point?'

'At first she pulled away, and then she came back and slipped her hand inside your jacket.'

'Could you see what her hand was doing?'

'No, not exactly, but—'

'Why not?'

'Well, because it was inside the jacket, obviously—'

'Did I kiss her?'

'No, but—'

'Did I pull her towards me?'

'No, but—'

'So there was no actual sexual contact between us? You didn't see anything happening except a hand placed on a hip, and another hand placed in a jacket?'

'No, but—'

'So what made you think the interaction was sexual? If there was no sexual contact?'

'It depends how you define "sexual", I suppose.'

'Yes, it does, doesn't it? I quite agree,' Paul returned coolly. 'Isn't it possible, Jeanie, that you simply saw two people laughing and enjoying each other's company? Two friends, who've known each other for a long time, who were sharing a joke?'

I tried to argue that there was very little possibility of an 'innocent' explanation when hands were actually inside clothes, but Paul ignored me.

'I'm going to tell you what actually happened, Jeanie,' he went on, coming to stand in front of me. 'Lily and I went out for lunch that day – *with Adjile*. I paid. Adjile and Lily tried to split the bill with me; I told them I wouldn't take a cent, they'd given the four of us that wonderful day on the sea. Straight after our meal, Adjile went off downtown to see a friend, and I walked Lily back to their New York apartment. But the whole way there, Lily kept trying to slip a bill in my pocket. Just before you saw us, I realized she'd managed to stuff it into the back pocket of my trousers, so I tried to slip it back into her skirt pocket when she wasn't looking. It had become a game. She noticed what I was doing, laughed, told me it wasn't going to work, and put the bill into my inside jacket pocket, begging me to accept it this time. I asked her if it really mattered, and she told me it did, that she and Adjile felt – for reasons I won't go into – that the debt was all on their side. So at that moment I said: Fine, Lily; if you feel that way, I'll accept the money. And we walked on. That was it.'

My throat felt very dry.

'Were we flirting a little bit?' he went on thoughtfully. 'Yes, I suppose we were. Would I have acted the same way if you were there, if Adjile had been there? Absolutely. Did I do anything I'm ashamed of, or that I think you have any right to be angry over? No, not at all. I think you saw something innocent and friendly, but turned it into evidence of a treacherous affair. Why? Because you'd already decided I was so lost to morality I would betray one of my best friends, a guy I've known for decades. You thought I – that all lawyers, as far as I can tell – are villains without souls, Jeanie, so you weren't a bit surprised to "discover" that I was also a liar and a cheat.'

Tom and Q were looking reprovingly at me. 'You really think that about us?' Q clucked faintly, and Tom said something angry about the social value of lawyers and the imperative need for a legal system with 'socially acclimated moral underpinnings'. I stared at their three accusing faces.

'Well,' I began desperately, and then looked to Paul hopefully, somehow expecting him to save me. I caught sight of his expression. Ah. No help there, clearly.

'But you said you were screwing her!' I blurted out suddenly. 'You actually admitted it.'

To my astonishment Paul began to laugh ruefully. 'Oh, Jeanie! I couldn't think what you were talking about, so I assumed you'd seen me with Martha Lundquist (a judge who happens to live in Brooklyn Heights) that lunchtime. I was feeling guilty about it, so my mind jumped immediately to our meeting. I am "screwing" her, I'm afraid. I'm trying to get planning permission for a drug rehab facility in her neighbourhood,

300

but I've told her it's going to be an educational institution. She knows the purchaser is a client of mine, she asked to meet with me because she's worried about property prices and I – well, I obfuscated the facts, shall we say.'

Suddenly, I realized we were alone, although I had no idea where Q and Tom had gone, or when they went. Somewhere upstairs I heard a short yell from Samuel, followed by hush, as if a breast or a pacifier had been shoved hastily into his mouth. Outside the wind stirred in the drying autumn leaves, and the cold sea cast glass and shells at the shore.

'Words are—' I stopped and flushed. 'When did you realize I'd got it all – er – wrong?'

'About twelve hours after I put the phone down.'

'Really?' I was aghast. 'Why didn't you try to explain?'

'It had something to do with being told I was repulsive, I think.'

'Oh. Did I say that?'

'Yes.'

'Ah.'

'Jeanie, maybe it was silly, but I'm not used – I'll be honest – to being spoken to like that. And when you launched into your attack, I thought to myself, Who needs this? I certainly don't need some woman who comes snooping after me—'

'I *wasn't* snooping!'

'Well, whatever you want to call it, then: "observing in secret", if you prefer – I don't need that, and I don't need someone who jumps to the worst possible conclusions about me at the drop of a hat. Particularly not when she comes from England, and when visiting her is going to involve ratcheting up serious frequent flyer miles.'

'You were thinking like that? About coming to see me? At that point?' I was astounded.

'I was, until you told me – let me see if I have this right – that

I "disgusted you", that you wished my hands had never touched your body.'

I stared at his hands. I really, really wished, at that moment, that they were on my body.

'Dave's got a new girlfriend, she's called Ellen,' I babbled suddenly. 'She's three times as buxom as me, and four times as pretty, and she is understanding and very loving, and I bet she never, *ever* jumps to conclusions.'

He cocked an eye at me; I saw something flicker across his face. 'And does this bother you? That Dave is with Ellen, I mean?'

'*No.*' I was emphatic. But I couldn't say anything else. My lips were somehow sealed closed. I looked up at him appealingly.

Paul reached out a hand and pulled me up to him. 'Jeanie, you've got to say something. Frankly, I've gone out on a limb here. I've driven three hours to see this English girl who's done nothing but yell at me, who's accused me of every kind of evil. I've come to see her because it turned out I *couldn't* forget her, because it turned out that I – God only knows why – want her in my life. I don't know what that means yet. But I do know I don't want to let her – let you – slip through my fingers. Now tell me what *you* think.'

'It is – possible,' I said haltingly, 'that I . . .'

'That you . . . ?' he prompted, leaning fractionally closer towards me.

'You're going to make me say it, aren't you?'

'Uh-huh.'

'Do I *really* have to say it?'

'Absolutely.'

In a big hurried gasp now: 'That I care about you, and that I'm sorry . . .'

Somewhere in Old Saybrook, Sue-Ellen cheered.

60. Q

Kent was off the wagon for a full three weeks, during which time Tom more or less took over the firm. On one of Kent's better days we shifted him back to his tiny house on the edge of Cheasford; over the course of the next few days, we watched him seesaw in and out of sobriety. For much of the time he was in a pathetic state, and we were frantic with worry about him, not least because the stairs in his house were hellishly narrow. We tried hiding every bottle we could find in the house, but he seemed to have an almost endless stock of concealed spirits in rafters, under beds, in the basement. Tom threatened him with hospitalization repeatedly.

Then, yesterday, we arrived to find a short quiet Asian woman in a pale green pinafore with the words 'Ocean View Cleaners' on her breast pocket standing beside him, helping him dress. There was a pot of green tea on the desk, and periodically – in response to gentle chiding from her – he sipped at it, and from a glass of iced water. His eyes were still bloodshot, but his hair was combed and his face was fresh scrubbed. The windows of the house were open, and the fuggy yellow air was pouring out. Warm autumn sunlight rippled across the floor.

'He stupid old man,' the woman offered disapprovingly, nodding at Kent as he tried to do up his shoelaces. Kent rolled his eyes.

'Whatever, whatever,' he said, but there was a hint of shame in his voice. And then, 'How've you two been getting on, then?' He changed the subject, looking over at us from under his bushy white-black eyebrows. He nodded impatiently at the door to the woman. Giving him a look that clearly said, I'll come and go in my own good time, mister, she moved with measured pace to the stairs.

We'd told him nothing about Emmie's case; there seemed little point, and in fact for most of the three-week stretch, any reference to the business of the firm made him terribly, desperately anxious – which prompted more drinking. Now, therefore, we observed him cautiously. 'Do you really want to know?' I asked at last.

Kent coughed. 'Course I do. Assuming . . .' He paused, and the faintest hint of anxiety flittered through his eyes again; his face greyed. 'Assuming you're taking over the firm now. For good. Right?'

Tom laughed, and eased the old man into a chair. 'Yes, we're taking over the firm, Kent. Don't worry. Q officially resigned from Schuster on Friday. And I, as a matter of fact, have already sat the Connecticut Bar; I saw the opportunity, and took it. Q will do the same this winter. So we just need to come to final terms about the transfer, Kent.'

The old man closed his eyes briefly. 'Right. Good. And – the – er – rent on the offices, I'm just wondering . . .'

'. . . is all paid up.'

'Ah. Glad to hear you're not – ah – falling behind.'

'We're obviously insane, Kent, but, somehow, this life seems to suit us,' I contributed, resting my fingers gently on the rope cable veins on the back of his hand. 'Samuel's happier, I'm happier, Tom's happier. We like it here. We've even started looking at houses. And if things don't seem to be going right a year from now – well, we can always sell the firm ourselves, and move on.'

Kent pulled himself up, looking for a second his old cantankerous self, then thought better of it, and shrugged. 'All right, all right. That works. I can live with that. So, come on then, I can tell you've got something else to tell me: what happened with young Emmie Cormier and that piece o'shit husband of hers?'

So we told him the story, from our meeting with Driscoll to the revelations at Emmie's, and the medical malpractice suit that was now substantially prepared and simply awaiting his signature.

'Pretty good work,' he said when the story was told. He chewed his lip thoughtfully. 'Pretty good work.'

And then, face cracking into a smile as he poured himself a thumping big glass of tea: 'I *knew* you could do it! I just *knew* it! That Judge Ackerman, what does he know? I showed him!' he crowed. 'He was laughing at me, saying I didn't know what was best for my firm. Did you hear him? Said I was losing my touch! Other people said the same thing – what, you think I didn't know that? I heard 'em, in the market, the liquor store, the diner. Over their pancakes. Kenton Tyler's all washed up, they said; he wouldn't know a piece of evidence if it was covered in blood and fingerprints. *I* heard 'em! Well, people won't be able to talk about my judgement after this, no way! We've tied up Phil Reid nice and tight, there's gonna be a lot of press about this. *Everyone's* gonna be talking about me. About us. About – the name's already over the door, ya know – *Kenton Tyler's Associates* . . .'

Epilogue: Q

Samuel has just turned six months old.

Yesterday the first flakes of snow whirled in the bare branches of the maples, and settled for an instant on the black-green needles of the pines. We lit a fire in the vast stone fireplace, and the glorious scent of woodsmoke lingered in the garden all day.

My son will never be a Renaissance cherub, all chubbiness and easy-going smiles, that's clear enough. He is determined, and cautious at the same time; fascinated by details, yet quickly overwhelmed. He can sit and stare at a piece of lint on the floor for hours. Five minutes of TV sends him into a howling melt-down.

But I've stopped asking him to rake small objects with his fist to check his hand-eye co-ordination, I'm too busy fretting he'll shove them all down his throat and choke. I've stopped worrying whether he can see a moving pencil, I'm too busy worrying I can't see *him*, as he nimbly evades my grasp and hares at breakneck speed – legs and hands moving like tiny pistons – across the carpet into the other room.

Things have changed, but perhaps they haven't really; there are just new worries, new things to check for ('Well, that's mothering, dear,' says Alison). Still, I think we're understanding him better now, and he seems to be making better sense of the world. The improvement we'd begun to notice around the time

Kent fell off the wagon continued, and now it's a rare day that begins, and ends, with crying. He loves his daycare, loves tumbling about on the floor with the other children, loves battling for the best toys, and when we pick him up after work (Tom, and I, on alternate days), his face lights up at the sight of us, then he yells at the sudden realization he can't take every single truck home.

Fay, to my surprise, hugged me tight, and wished me well, when I went down to New York to clear out my office on a chill November morning. People were rushing to their offices in fur. 'Think it's a fucking stupid thing to do, of course, but that's just me, you've gotta do what *you* think,' she said cheerfully. 'We'll miss you though, Q, everyone's been saying for months it's not the same around here without you. Keep in touch. I'll be interested to hear how your new firm works out.'

There were no hugs from Caroline, of course. 'Well, Quinn. I can't say I'm surprised,' she said coolly, resting her fingers together behind her desk. I could almost see her erasing me from her inner computer (there's no space in there for ex-associates. It's all taken up with legal intricacies: client names, legal rules, judicial opinions and the people *she* calls 'successes'). Three months from now, she'll barely remember me. Which is fine by me, actually. Three months from now, I'll barely remember her.

Jeanie left us in early October, dragging suitcases and a lot of the sunshine from our home with her. Dressed in an overcoat, because the weather turned black and wet the week she went; her face full of hair; worldly goods dripping from every pocket; laughing at herself because she's in so many ways a typical Boothroyd woman. Disorganized, scatty. Never quite on time. Opinionated as hell. She went home to interview for her job, which she got, then started the following week. She'll worry her local borough councillors into miserable submission over the course of the next five years, I'm sure, and the older people of south London will be better off because of it.

I held Samuel on my hip the day she left and watched her pack, giggling at her manic chaos. Some things never change, I told her fondly, rescuing a toothbrush from under the bed, covered in dust and grit and sand. Oh, I don't know about that, she replied, washing it off in the sink.

Paul flew out to London two weeks after she left, to stay for almost three months, into the New Year. He's taking up a temporary placement to help set up the new British branch of Prince, which has just opened in London, although there's an opportunity for him to stay in England in the longer term if he wants. I don't know whether Paul would have gone to Britain anyway, or whether something about Jeanie's 'go away' a while back convinced Paul that it could become a 'come hither' with a touch of persuasion and the undoubted convenience of a London home (contract signed, rent and six weeks' deposit already paid). But if it was the latter it was brave of him, I think, to go ahead with the plan, and she thinks so, too, 'But also terribly nice of Prince to move into the London market, don't you think, Q? It'll be very easy for me to commute into Southwark, or maybe we'll just live halfway in between . . .' And then she stopped herself, and blushed, and looked as conscious as she did that first night when she came inside from a walk in the garden, and was holding Paul's hand as if she'd never let it go. With dusty twigs and fragments of dry gold leaves clinging to their clothes, their movements were as deliberately careful as if they were holding something delicate and precious in their cupped hands. A new beginning.

Alison, of course, was fascinated to know every detail. 'I take a bit of credit for the whole thing,' she said airily. 'Their relationship, I mean. I played my cards very close to my chest. I knew if I told you everything you'd put your oar in, Q, then

Jeanie would get all defensive and find some loser just to make us cross, and the whole thing would be *ruined*. It was hard for me, obviously, but I just watched, and waited . . .'

'You just didn't want *me* to be the one to get them together!'

'Nonsense!'

'It isn't nonsense, Alison. That's typical of you. If you'd told me what was going on I might have been able to sort out the mess long ago, but oh no—'

'It's just like Mummy always says, you think you're the only person in this family who makes sensible arrangements. Q the career woman, always in charge. I may be a full-time mother but that doesn't mean I'm utterly impractical, Q.'

'I would never say that! I would never think that!'

'Oh really? You don't secretly think that your advice to Jeanie is weightier than mine because you have a conventional job, and I don't?'

'I don't, Alison, honestly!' I said, and we only managed to make peace when I remembered to ask after Serena's croup.

This morning, when I woke up, I was immediately invaded by a sense of strangeness. I sat bolt upright in bed, and looked around me. My husband was lying still, face collapsed into the pillow, arms scissored beside him; warm, heavy, unconscious. My son was lying in his bassinet on the other side of the room, a hint of sprouting hair just visible above the rim of the basket and – I lengthened my spine and craned to see – chest gently heaving his sleeping bag.

I looked at the clock, glowing blue on the wall in the gloom created by the heavy blanket we've put up to help Samuel sleep. Around the edges of the blanket I could see the creeping light of an early morning winter sun, orange pricking through the thick navy woollen threads. It was 7 a.m. Eight hours had passed since we last switched off our light. *Eight whole hours!*

I almost woke Tom up to share this incredible news with

him. But then, just as my hand was about to touch his shoulder, I stopped myself and looked down. Tom smacked his lips gently in his sleep, then settled a little deeper into his warmed cocoon of mattress, sheet and pillow. I smiled at his childlike pose, then lay down again, curving my own body carefully toward his, knees and foreheads gently touching. And as I closed my eyes, and felt his steady hot breath on my face, I enjoyed the tiny miracle of a morning lie-in with the man I love.